I0760315

A TIME FOR TYRANTS

A Forgotten Gods Tale #6

Christian Warren Freed

Cover design by BroseDesignz
Author Photograph by Anicie Freed

Warfighter Books
Holly Springs, North Carolina 27540
https://www.christianwfreed.com

First Edition: August 2023

Library of Congress Cataloging-in-Publication Data
Name: Freed, Christian Warren, 1973- author.
Title: A Time For Tyrants/ Christian Warren Freed
Description: First Edition | Holly Springs, NC: Warfighter Books, 2021. Identifiers: LCCN 2023909981| ISBN 9781957326351 (trade paperback) | ISBN 8781957326368 (Hardcover) | ISBN 9781957326375 (eBook)
Subjects: Military Science Fiction | Space Opera |Space Fantasy

Printed in the United States of America

10 9 8 7 6 5 4 3 2 1

ACCLAIM FOR CHRISTIAN WARREN FREED

DREAMS OF WINTER
A FORGOTTEN GODS TALE #1

'Dreams of Winter is a strong introduction to a new fantasy series that follows slightly in the footsteps of George R.R. Martin in scope.' Entrada Publishing

"Steven Erickson meets George R.R. Martin!"

"THIS IS IT. If you like fantasy and sci-fi, you must read this series."

THE LAZARUS MEN AGENDA

'This sci-fi noir adventure thriller has mystery, suspense, and plenty of action. A page turning, fun ride from the first page to the last'- Entrada Publishing

'Reminiscent of Tom Clancy or Stephen King, where you can envision everything happening in an era that don't yet exist but feels as familiar as the room you're reading in at the time.'

'The author draws us into a world full of conspiracy in which those who have everything want even more because human greed for power is too great.'

HAMMERS IN THE WIND:
BOOK I OF THE NORTHERN CRUSADE

'Freed is without a doubt an amazing storyteller. His execution of writing descriptive and full on battle scenes is second to none, the writers ability in that area is unquestionable. He also drags you into the world he has created with ease and panache. I couldn't put it down.'

'Gripping! Hammers in the Wind is an excellent start to a new fantasy series. Christian Warren Freed has created an exciting storyline with credible characters, and an effectively created fantasy world that just draws you in.'

Law of the Heretic
Immortality Shattered Book I

'If you're looking for a fun and exciting fantasy adventure, spend a few hours in the Free Lands with the Law of the Heretic.'

Where Have All the Elves Gone?

'Sometimes funny and other times a little dark, Where Have The Elves Gone? brings something fresh and new to fantasy mysteries. Whether you want to curl up with a mystery or read more about elves this book has something for everyone. Spend a few hours solving a mystery with a human and a couple of dwarves - you'll be glad you did.'

Other Books by Christian Warren Freed

The Northern Crusade
Hammers in the Wind
Tides of Blood and Steel
A Whisper After Midnight
Empire of Bones
The Madness of Gods and Kings
Even Gods Must Fall

The Histories of Malweir
Armies of the Silver Mage
The Dragon Hunters
Beyond the Edge of Dawn

Forgotten Gods
Dreams of Winter
The Madman on the Rocks
Anguish Once Possessed
Through Darkness Besieged
Under Tattered Banners
A Time for Tyrants
A Good Day For Crows*

Where Have All the Elves Gone?
One of Our Elves is Missing
From Whence It Came*
Tomorrow's Demise: The Extinction Campaign
Tomorrow's Demise: Salvation
Coward's Truth
The Lazarus Men
Repercussions: A Lazarus Men Agenda
Daedalus Unbound: A Lazarus Men Agenda*

A Long Way From Home+

Immortality Shattered
Law of the Heretic
The Bitter War of Always
Land of Wicked Shadows
Storm Upon the Dawn

War Priests of Andrak Saga

The Children of Never

SO, You Want to Write a Book? +

SO, You Wrote a Book. Now What? +

*Forthcoming + Nonfiction

PROLOGUE

Last Year of the War of the Gods, planet Terotis.

Wind swept through Tannus' hair, lending him a disheveled, almost wild appearance as he stared down at the impossible scene. A finality lingered, just beyond the green flecks of his irises. Events were in motion, culminating under the chains of staggering demise since his open defiance against his father. How could he have known such a deed would be the catalyst for all that followed?

The death of dreams.

Future's collapse.

A war between brothers.

Yet hope remained. Tannus struggled to find a way to preserve a fraction of his old life. A modicum of what could have been. Heavy was his heart, for but a handful of his kind earned redemption. He'd instead become judge and executioner for far too many. Halfway across the universe, on a now dead planet named Occanum, the bones of his people were dust beneath the fury of oblivion.

Heartbroken, he looked down upon the last remnant of his family. His uncle, the despot Rengu, was encased in a stasis pod, locked away forever. With him removed, Tannus had paved the way for humanity's escape from servitude.

It was, all things considered, a minor victory.

For now.

"This has been a day long anticipated," Ruma Zzein said, breaking the silence. She stared at Rengu with a unique combination of cruelty and compassion born from a lifetime of abuse.

Tannus nodded. "There is yet much to do. Our war may have ended, but there is one who remains that can destroy all we fought to achieve."

"Amongeratix," Ruma supplied. "The great destroyer will find exacting his revenge more difficult with your uncle removed."

"Oracle, my brother is relentless. His need for excess drives him … Nay, compels him to deeper acts of depravity. Whatever spark of kindness once blessed unto him has grown infected by dark desires. He will not rest until the last of our kind is dead, me included. This is but the first stage in a new game."

Tannus turned to the third member of their party. "Cousin, are you ready?"

Paradise Tear, blonde hair streaked with grime and matted beneath a sheen of sweat, set her jaw as she replied, "I am. Are you certain this will work?"

"It is the only way."

Five little words. Cold and unforgiving.

Her heart quickened; flesh prickled. Paradise, the genetic code for unlocking the seven hundred stasis pods secreted on different planets across the universe, knew she could never fall into Amongeratix's hands. This had to be done, for sealing her away, here at the end of all things, provided the final measure Tannus required to end the war and move forward.

She stepped forward to ascend.

"How will we awaken her when the time comes?" Ruma asked.

Sorrow placed a hand on his Paradise's shoulder. "I have taken care of it. She will return when she is needed. Not a moment before." He held up a metal cylinder. "This key holds her gene wealth. It can access the pods should needs be."

Two humans ran into the chamber. Dread in their eyes as one shouted, "He's coming!"

Sorrow handed Tannus the key. "Go, Brother. End this. I will distract Amongeratix—he must not get his hands on Paradise Tear. Ever."

"I shall never forget this," Paradise whispered.

Sorrow was already moving, the ones he named the Paladin and the Prophet hurrying to catch up.

Palms pressed against the viewing pane, Ruma stared down upon Rengu's sleeping face. Memories twisted her face. "What about him?"

Tannus' silence provided answer enough. Ruma offered a final look of judgment before hurrying to join the handful of women clustered under an arched door leading to the loading docks.

Tannus watched her go, knowing he had chosen wisely. If they managed to escape the final storm, humanity stood a chance for survival and perhaps something more.

The women rounded the bend, leaving him alone with Paradise Tear. “Come, Cousin. Let us end this war for good.”

Shuttles landed by the score. Each bringing families to the place they would call home. Nameless, the golden world promised life in abundance. More than enough to establish a colony and, in infantile stages, was the beginnings of a civilization. Humanity clustered, their fear of their oppressors edging deeper into memory as the effects of the war diminished.

Hundreds came. Then thousands. They brought with them their prejudices, loves, angers and pain. Above all, they brought their hope.

They leaned heavily on the notions of redemption and possibility; realms that were previously inaccessible to them. The chains of slavery shattered, they scattered among the stars, only to coalesce in great numbers on a world of Tannus’ choosing. They were architects, medicine men, builders, thinkers. They were fathers and mothers. Young and old. Those too weak to survive were culled long ago, a sad collateral of war. Their memories now preserved by future generations. They were to know pain. To experience agony spurring creativity and evolution. It was, in Tannus’ estimation, the cost of living.

He watched from afar as the first human colony established itself and began to grow from a string of ramshackle huts to cities of budding grandeur. They named their planet Vau. The meaning was not lost on Tannus, for it meant ‘hope’ in the old tongue. Only when he grew confident collapse was no longer imminent did he return to his secreted shuttle and leave them to their devices. He resigned himself to be their silent warder. A guardian lurking ever on the edge of vision. For darkness ever hungered: Amongeratix remained at large, and his wrath would be the coming of doom should he come to the cradle of this new civilization.

The war of the gods may had ended, but it paved the way for the beginning of a new conflict that would dominate the next three thousand years.

One pitting brother against brother.

ONE

3215 A.G. (After Gods) Erdef City, planet Romalle.

Life on planet Romalle had never been kind and was made worse by the civil war tearing the Conclave apart. While the planet had thus far avoided declaring for either side, divisions arose among the ruling houses and peasantry as external pressures mounted. Neither rich nor poor, Romalle was considered a backwater planet by those in power and, as such, lacked the necessary funding to propel the economy to greater levels. Generations passed, mired in anonymity. Forced to develop trade with nearby star systems, Romalle eked out a baseline existence in a universe where indulgence overwhelmed other worlds.

Tension lingered over Erdef City, the ever-expanding capital. Trust in the Conclave priests and their Inquisitors waned even as heightened Prekhauten Guard patrols reminded many of a militarized police state. Crime soared despite this, bringing the hierarchy to odds with daily life. It had become a desperate time for weary citizens. Many stood on the brink of war with the interminable agony of waiting for the first shots to be fired.

Riles Tenaru pressed against the second story balcony, blending with the stained brick façade, she looked for prey. Young and with keen wit, she earned her way as a pickpocket and snitch. There being little room for pride, she became a creature of the night. Her dark skin was covered in tribal tattoos dating back to ancient rituals of the Impossible Mother. Bone fetishes dangled from the braids in her hair, masked only by the soft leather vest she wore over her tunic. Stretching back a hundred generations, Riles would wear the relics until her last breath.

Merchants and peddlers were closing shops to head home. Picking them off was no difficult task, the skill came in remembering who she victimized in the last month or so. Riles considered herself a professional, though the local guild argued otherwise and refused her membership. Even after more than one guild member discovered empty pockets upon returning home after bumping into her on the cold, lonely streets.

Summer was in full swing and with it the oppressive humidity bathed her in a perpetual sheen of sweat despite the sun having set hours ago. Linen pants flowed over her slender legs, accented by sandals nearly worn through. Riles made do with bare minimums despite almost having accumulated enough to get both her and her mother off world. Dreams were well and fine, but she had nowhere to go and, given the predilections of those travelers she'd eavesdropped upon, the universe was far from accommodating to those of her status—Romalle remained.

Riles spied her mark exiting the tavern across the street. Half a stumble forced him to lean a hand on the grime-stained wall for support. A grin crept across her face, thin lips splitting to display bone white teeth. This was too easy.

He righted himself and hurried down the cobblestone street under the orange glow of gas lights spaced on each city block. Riles pushed off the wall and wormed down the split stairs to the ground. Not one prone to violence, the only weapon she bore was a small metal cylinder which fit in the palm of her hand. Careful to scan her surroundings, Riles set out after her prey.

Lithe as a jungle cat, Riles edged closer. She had done this innumerable times before. Always securing the purse and flitting away before the mark realized they'd been robbed. Her sandals scuffed once, twice before she picked her feet up. She reached out—Riles slipped back to appear nonthreatening as a band of men and women exited one of the small crofter houses for the night.

Cursing her ill-timed luck, Riles ducked down the first alley, attempting to blend in with those few still on the streets. The night gangs would be out soon, and it was far too risky to operate with them prowling. Riles did an about face and hurried back to the main avenue as the sounds of conversation faded. She gained the edge of the street when the shrill whistle froze her blood. Boots clicked over the cobblestones. Hurrying. Running. She poked her head around the corner and her mouth dropped open. There, twisted in a heap of cooling flesh, was her mark. A pool of crimson spreading beneath him.

Shocked, she turned to run but rough hands snatched her by the shoulders. Riles kicked back and was rewarded with a grunt as her assailant fell away, doubled over, clutching his groin. To her horror she saw the glint of a badge. With no other suspects in the vicinity of the body, the authorities would no doubt pin immediate blame on her. She was many things, killer not among them.

Stealing a final look at the corpse, Riles ran.

Ulfric Hargan stared down at the corpse on the table. The body, already cold, lost its color and turned a sickly shade of blue. A twist in his gut provided the subtle reminder this was his least favorite part of the job. Turning from the body, the chief investigator of Erdef City wiped his lower lip and began studying the chart on the wall until the coroner returned.

"Chief Investigator," the female coroner said with a curt bow. "I had not expected you so soon."

He offered a thin smile. "When a Conclave Cardinal is murdered it demands immediate attention, Hilde. This is an unprecedented event for our planet."

"A most serious matter," she agreed. "Has the city board been informed?"

"Not yet," he admitted. "I need more to go on than *he was stabbed.*"

Hilde slipped around him, snatching the chart off the wall. "I am waiting on the toxicology report to come back."

"The Cardinal was a heavy drinker?"

"I never met the man, but I need to know if his drinks were spiked," Hilde answered. "The question remains however, who hated a Cardinal enough to assassinate him in the middle of the street?"

Political and religious statements were rare on Romalle. Those targeted were usually run out of office and driven into exile rather than landing in the city morgue.

Having served for over three decades, Hargan witnessed innumerable events, but none so bold as this. He needed answers, fast. He could already feel the menacing glares of the city board. Unable to provide more than what they already knew, it took little imagination to see them veer away and settling on a target of convenience. Rage seldom bothered with societal parameters.

"Keep working it, Hilde. I need to know everything as soon as you do."

Puffing out her cheeks, Hilde said slowly, "There is one more task required, Ulfric."

He winced. She knew better than to call him by his first name. Visage grim, he knew what she referred to and nodded. "Do it."

Hilde set the chart down and peeled back the sheet until the Cardinal's face was bare.

Hargan sighed, taking in the worry lines crowding the dead man's eyes and brow. Greying eyebrows accented his salt and pepper hair. "That's him. Cardinal Breed."

"You are certain of this? No possibility of error?"

Hargan dropped his shoulders enough to feign submission. "None, Warder. It was Cardinal Leganas Breed. He was stabbed seven times, in the kidneys and under the armpit, striking the heart and penetrating the lung. Whoever did this was well versed in anatomy and either had a score to settle or was looking to make a statement."

"There will be uproar if we do not learn the truth behind this," Warder Eiters remarked. "It could mean our political futures."

Hargan concealed his frown. Used to their petty ministrations, he had never heard any of the city board utter private thoughts of self-preservation.

"A Cardinal of the Conclave is dead, and you worry over your insignificant careers?"

All heads turned at the stern voice, Hargan's included, to face the imposing figure of Inquisitor Gando. Young, bordering on arrogant, he was lightly muscled and sharp-witted. A formidable opponent for any foolish enough to make an enemy of him. He was also, insofar as Hargan understood, a friend of the Cardinal. Personal relations threatened unnecessary complications he could ill afford should higher offices on Vau Prime decide to get involved.

"We meant no offense, Inquisitor, but you must agree this is unprecedented. We can ill afford our city, much less the planet, to devolve into chaos over the slaying of one of the clergy." Kasop, eldest of the three board members, held up his hands.

Rumor had it the man enjoyed visiting illegal gambling parlors deep into the midnight hour when decent folk were fast asleep. His predilections for barely legal boys should have landed him in a cell, not one of the three seats of power. Hargan had people watching him, collecting his movements and debaucheries, for years now, anticipating a final breakdown presenting him the opportunity to eliminate, in his opinion, a sick man.

Inquisitor Gando was unimpressed. His hawk-like gaze swept over the board members, disgust blatant. “I will be undertaking my own investigation into the murder. No offense, Hargan, but matters of the Conclave must be handled appropriately.”

Hargan shrugged. “No problem. I’ll keep running mine in conjunction. One of us is bound to catch the killer.”

“Or killers,” Gando corrected.

Until now Hargan hadn’t considered the possibility. The prospect of dealing with more than one culprit rippled through his mind. If they were bold enough to eliminate the seated Cardinal their audacity might not stop until it rifled through the very halls of power, threatening to topple Romalle.

The board members’ faces languished in the narrow margins of grief and greed. Yet an unspoken opportunity had presented itself. It was the glory of imagination propelling them to greater heights under the altruistic and inglorious visage of the gods. Greed, Hargan knew, was the catalyst of collapse. The ruin of all things. Each board member was sinking within their private thoughts, delusions of grandeur on scales he could little imagine.

“We cannot let this travesty go unpunished,” Kasop said, slamming a fist on the aged wooden table they sat before.

Flinching, Warder Eiters glanced at the third member of their group. “What say you, Damal? I’ve never known your tongue to be guarded. What shall we do with the hunt for our fallen Cardinal’s killer?”

Licking his lips, Damal’s jowls quivered. A large man of excess, he secured his seat at the board through tenacity and the unwavering ignorance of the word no. Hargan knew he was the true power; a dangerous man playing a dangerous game. Damal wanted power and would stop at nothing to continue accumulating it.

“My worry is how the Conclave will see fit for retribution. The clergy stands with impunity across the seven hundred worlds. For one to be slaughtered in our streets, under our very noses is a harbinger of disaster. We must move swiftly. Justice needs be persecuted with unflinching surety."

"I hardly think slaughtered is accurate. Murdered, yes. But not slaughtered like a common feed animal," Eiters countered.

"You mock his death?" Gando bristled.

"Inquisitor, no one is mocking the passing of our noble Cardinal. We were all friends," she replied. Haughtiness laced her tone. "I am merely suggesting my colleague tone down his rhetoric lest it leads to frenzy in the streets."

Kasop added, "Inquisitor, you have all our resources at your disposal, including the Chief Investigator. We hope you bring this sad affair to a swift and necessary conclusion."

Gando nodded. "I shall begin at once. You understand the Conclave must be notified?"

Eiters offered an insincere smile. "Naturally. I trust you will keep us informed as the situation develops."

Hargan watched the ripple of muscles under Gando's tunic as he stiffened. Clearly the Inquisitor was unused to being ordered around.

"Naturally," he said. "I leave you now."

He stalked away without salute or acknowledgement of their status, much to Hargan's approval. The trouble with people in power was so many acquiesced to their demands. Subservient in every regard.

Clearing his throat, Hargan said, "If you will excuse me, I need to catch up to our esteemed Inquisitor. We have much to discuss."

"Do so, Chief Investigator," Eiters said. "The sooner we get to the bottom of this travesty the better."

Hargan swore he caught the hiss of snakes as the door closed.

"Infuriating them will only unite them," Hargan said, lighting his spice cigarillo.

Gando snorted. "I am not cowed by planetary leaders, even ones so persistent as yours, Hargan."

Unable to argue that, Hargan blew out a puff of blissful smoke. "They are dangerous, Gando. Oh, they present themselves as sophisticated and generous, but darkness festers under the surface."

"Why then do they keep getting elected?"

"Why not? People are sheep. They follow the leader, ignoring the difficulties of individual thought or uniqueness. How much easier is it to ignore trouble than to stand up and explore the options for handling a problem? We see it every day. No one speaks up unless forced to. We turn a blind eye to petty crimes. Look away when disaster strikes all while proclaiming pity or mercy for the victims. How many voluntarily step in the way when danger lashes out?"

"All the more reason for the Inquisition."

"Every flock needs a sheepdog."

"What do you want, Hargan? I have much to do."

Despite what Hargan considered a limited personality, he found himself liking the Inquisitor. Perhaps in another life, under better circumstances they might have shared the bond of camaraderie under the blue-tinged rose. It was a simple dream. One Hargan entertained during those rare moments when life left him to his devices. One slowly fading as time plodded on.

"They will expect me to report on your movements."

Gando nodded. "Of course. Proclaiming it in the planet's best interests while attempting to bring me to heel. Fools. I could have them removed on a whim should I so choose."

"Would Vau Prime bother sending assistance?" Hargan asked. "Rumors of the war raging on a hundred worlds ripple through the city. The people are frightened, yet not enough to prompt change. No one, the board most of all, believes the Conclave or Inquisition will send a force capable of locking Romalle down and bringing it to heel."

Gando rubbed the stubble on his jaw. "What fools, I say again. Do they not understand what is at risk?"

"Like I said, they aren't worried about what's not before them. The war may be real, but it's not here."

"What will it take to make them realize they stand upon the precipice? Hargan, there is more than just civil war gripping us."

Another puff of smoke passed Hargan's lips. "What do you mean?"

The Inquisitor leaned close. "Heresy. Word of this Cult of Rengu spreading has reached me. Worlds burn under his foul touch. Already the low continent on Vau Prime lies in ruin after what has been described as a '*cleansing campaign.*'"

"You are worried this cult will develop here?"

"It is my job to watch for heresy. We can ill afford to rest on the laurels of society when all around us devolves to chaos," Gando said. "I shall do what I must to prevent the war from coming here. More so this cult." He paused, choosing his next words carefully. "We may share our differences, Ulfric Hargan, but I have come to like this quiet part of the universe. Liberty is now threatened should the Conclave or the Inquisitor General decide the time has come to bring Romalle under its heel."

It took little imagination to see an army of occupying Prekhauten Guards marching through the streets, black clad Inquisitors at their backs under the discretion of the Conclave. Not only was freedom threatened, the prospect brought with it the promise of individual demise.

"Whatever you need from me is yours," Hargan said.

"Thank you. First, I must track down Cardinal Breed's next of kin."

Hargan's eyebrow arched. "I did not think the clergy were allowed family."

"Antiquated rules," Gando replied. "Leganas Breed may have had no wife or children, but his brother is an Inquisitor. I will inform him."

"Please don't bring the Inquisition down on us. We do not yet know who committed this crime. It could have been an accident. A pickpocket gone wrong," Hargan said, face pale.

Gando clasped him on the shoulder. "I promise nothing, though will do all in my power to keep Romalle free."

Warder Eiters clasped her hands behind her back. "This is the opportunity we have waited for. Can you not understand?"

"I understand many things, your selfish conceit among them. This threatens to undo all we have struggled to create. And for what? By all accounts the Cardinal wasn't even robbed," Kasop balked. "When word spreads—"

"It will be to our advantage," Eiters interrupted. "How long has our society been beset by street gangs and thugs acting like guilds? This is the chance to remove all crime from our streets and set order the way we see fit. Our people are scared to go out after sundown. We now have the catalyst capable of turning the tables on the criminal element and bring order and justice to Romalle."

"Ambitious," Damal replied. A furtive look etched his face. "Where are we to find the necessary policing force to weed out and destroy these rogue elements?"

Her eyes narrowed to slits. "Think me a fool? I've been preparing for this for years. It is time, my friends, to consolidate our power and ensure we remain a force for many years to come."

Kasop shook his head. "It's too dangerous. We are not in a position to upend daily life. After we crush these gangs, others will rise in their stead. Changing the base of power, while the universe is driving itself to its knees, is foolish."

"Only if we fail," Damal drawled. "Perhaps our colleague has the right idea. We stand to turn a hefty profit from this."

"How so?" Kasop demanded.

Damal drummed his pudgy fingers on the table. "By turning our enemies against each other. Let the gangs do our dirty work while we reap the rewards. Once they burn through each other we sweep in with a modest police force and establish total authority. Reciprocation will be minimal."

Kasop's cheeks reddened. "What happens if word spreads that we are behind this mad scheme?"

"We will deal with each accordingly. This is the hour we have long awaited. Do we sit by idle and watch the Inquisition deliver its brand of justice? Or do we seize control of our city and our future for the good of all?" Eiters asked.

They sat in silence, letting the words digest until Kasop cleared his throat. "Where do we begin?"

Back to the wall, drink almost empty, Riles Tenaru scanned the crowd. Paranoia threatened to take over in the days following the murder of Cardinal Breed. It took little imagination to assume every face she stared into knew she bore witness. She'd become a threat, a loose end in need of tying up. Kill her and they had an easy mark to pin the murder on.

Of course what common sense she let through did nothing to prevent the tiny legs of fear from crawling down her spine each time a door slammed or a voice rose in anger. The bitter taste of ale helped somewhat. Never one for drunken escapades, she found the numbing effects preferable to the feeling of being hunted.

Halfway through her second cup, the young pickpocket relaxed as a familiar face entered the bar. Catching his eye, she waved him over.

"Riles, good to see you, but this is peculiar."

"Nemineon, how is your mother?" she asked.

"Well enough I suppose. The old bat is too determined to pass on to the next life. I get the feeling she doesn't want me to inherit much." He sighed. "She will be glad to know you asked. She always did like you … still don't know why."

His grin evoked fond memories for Riles. They'd grown up together, spending countless hours playing, learning, and developing skills that would carry them through life. Terrors of their tribe, being sent off to a boarding home in Erdef City had felt like a crime when the decision came. Little could either realize the importance of that single act: Nemineon rose to become a powerful factor in the merchanting houses while Riles tried her hand at being a budding socialite. Needless to say, her plans fell through. A flip of the coin often meant the difference between success and failure.

"Because I'm the daughter she never had." Riles punched his arm. "And I smell better."

Nemineon winced. "Says you. Riles, you look like you've been sleeping in a refuse pit. When is the last time you got a good night's sleep?"

She flitted her gaze across the near empty bar. "It's been a few days. Nemineon, Since—"

He leaned closer. "Since what, Riles? What is this all about?"

She told him everything.

A tidal wave of emotions poured forth, leaving her naught but detritus in the wreckage upon the shore. When she finished, she leaned back and drained the rest of her ale, motioning for another.

For his part, Nemineon listened without comment until she finished. "Riles, you need to go to the investigators. Tell them what you saw."

She shook her head. "Are you mad? What do you think will happen to me, Nemineon? They'll see a street waif, one from the tribes no less, and use me as the scapegoat while the real killer goes free. You know we have never been treated fairly."

"It doesn't help having bones in your hair," he chided.

Unlike her, Nemineon had chosen to leave the old ways behind. Telling her once that there was little intrinsic value in marring the flesh in ancient tattoos or appearing a savage in civilized climes. She knew he wasn't ashamed of being from the tribes, but neither was he willing to display his heritage. Not after securing a major place in Erdef City.

"We are children of the Impossible Mother," she growled. "I cannot change who I am."

Old arguments threatened to resurface. But Riles let it go, knowing she needed him on her side now more than ever.

"All the more reason to go underground for the moment," he said. "At least until the killer is found. Do you think it was any of the street gangs? Someone seeking to eliminate competition?"

"I don't know. My mind won't stop replaying those critical moments. The web of possibilities stretches far. It could have been mere chance leading me to that point in time, or perhaps it's the beginning of a conspiracy against the tribes."

"How could anyone possibly know you were following a Cardinal that night?" He scoffed. "No, Riles. You stumbled upon a murder and, as a witness, will no doubt have the perpetrators, if they saw you, after you."

"That's just it. I don't know if I was seen or not!"

Riles remembered hearing the siren and the thunder of boots chasing her. Were the investigators after her as a suspect or because she fled before being questioned? Too many variables. Too many chances to fall. She needed an out. A bolt hole to lay low like Nemineon suggested.

"Riles, I need you to think. Did you see anyone in the street that night?"

She opened her mouth. Did she?

The Cardinal exited the bar. Stumbled down the street and around a corner as she slipped to the ground in pursuit. The edges of her vision blurred. The darkness of the unknown mocking her efforts. She heard the grunt. The wet stick of a blade piercing flesh. Then the body in the street. Nothing else.

"No … wait." She frowned. "I can see shadows. Human shaped, stretching across the street. There were two." She kept the shining badge on the man who attempted to snatch her a secret, for now.

Nemineon slapped a hand on the table. "We have a place to start."

"Start what? You don't think I'm going to try and find the killers do you?" She laughed. "That's what the investigators are for."

"Riles, this is our chance to bring the tribes into a good light. Think of it! We bring in the men responsible for murdering a member of the Conclave. Not only will it set us up as heroes, it will show the rest of the world the tribes are not the filth they have long stereotyped."

She lowered her gaze to the table. "I don't think I wish to play this game."

"There might not be much of a choice," he countered. "I don't know how the future will play out, but I do know one thing."

"What's that?"

He made a show of crinkling his face. "You need a bath."

Behemoth, Deep Space.

The clank of chains across the unforgiving deck was cold. A sound he'd grown far too accustomed to through the generations.

"Do you have any idea how long I languished under humanity's cruelty?" He sighed. "I don't imagine you do—centuries. All wasted years thanks to my impetuous brothers. Each and every day I sat within my cell, retreating into my mind where landscapes of torment waited." He snorted. "For what? Rather than accepting my place in the universe they refused me. Shunned me when I needed them most. I became a pariah. Outcast and alone. Is it any wonder I am now the storm across the stars? Bent and determined to bring the universe to its knees." Amongeratix fell silent.

Leaning back in his seat, the giant templed his fingers and studied his still silent captive. He had yet to elicit any reaction; a remarkable feat considering his enjoyment in torture. He felt rage building. No one resisted his assaults for long. He was a monster to some. Nightmare to others. Family included.

"Come now, Cousin. We have not seen each other in so very long. Why hold your tongue now?" He taunted. "Tannus has abandoned you. Betrayed you to a fate reserved to those who are mired in failure. Will you not offer me an embrace after so long?"

Paradise Tear stirred. One eye was swollen shut. The other focused on Amongeratix with abject hatred. She opened her mouth, and he broke into a grin.

Paradise spat on the floor at his feet then lowered her head.

"Ever the charming creature," he snarled. "I shall break you, dear cousin. Before I finish you will tell me the location of every single one of our kind Tannus hid from me. You will become the weapon you were intended to be. A destroyer of lives unlike any the universe has ever seen. All shall bear witness and curse your name deep into the wells of eternity."

Nothing.

The rage built.

"Why continue this pointless charade? How many more worlds must die for you to see the truth? The universe has changed since our time. These pathetic mortals waste our gifts, choosing ignorance over enlightenment. Think of Kharsis. How easily it wilted and died. Will your conscience be able to withstand such onslaught as world after world burns to your touch?"

The slightest glimmer of raw horror crossed her face.

Amongeratix stared at his cousin a moment longer before leaving the chamber. He had seen enough. The first crack in her defenses. A lynchpin to bringing her haughtiness crashing down.

He stalked through the darkened corridors on his way to the bridge and found Algiss Her awaiting. The fallen Blood Witch, now reverently referred to as the Crimson Mistress by her chattering coterie of sycophants, predictably stood with arms folded and an impatient scowl.

"What do you have to report?"

"Keeping her is dangerous," she snapped. "When Tannus learns of this he will stop at nothing to get her back. You put us all at risk with this game of sibling rivalry."

"I know my brother far better than you, witch. By the time he figures out my destination it will be too late."

She glided closer, feet never touching the decking. "Forces are gathering to stop you. The Grand Mistress has formed an alliance even as Tannus rallies loyalist forces to his banner. They will oppose you every step of the way." She hissed. "Rip the information you require from her blood and dump the body in deep space where it belongs. One less problem before the storm breaks."

"Mind your tongue, witch. You serve me on a whim, nothing more. Think you this game is new? Nay. Tannus and I have played this game for millennia. Well before the first founding of your human empire. It was his love for your putrid species that sparked this war. He chose *you* over his kin. I will not make that same mistake." His voice dropped. "We may be allies, for the moment, but do not think I will not hesitate to slay every last one of your sisters, abominations that they are."

Algiss bristled; electric sparks dancing over her crimson robes. She lowered her arms, fists clenched. "I am not chattel to be cast aside when convenience strikes, Lord Amongeratix. My sisters followed me out of a sense of righteousness, knowing your cause was just. Do not seek to minimize our efforts in your war. Too many have already paid the price. If by helping you end this once and for all I will have secured the future for my kind, it shall be worth whatever torments your insidious mind devises. Until then, I expect to be treated like your equal in all matters."

Amongeratix studied his latest ally, yet another paltry human believing they held some mythical special quality setting them apart from the thousands he used up in previous campaigns. He admitted there was a different air surrounding Algiss. The former Blood Witch was deep in Ruma Zzein's inner council, making her a valuable resource to plunder. Keeping her content not only furthered his aggressions but provided a base from which to expand.

"Very well, *Crimson Mistress*, we shall be peers until neither of us requires the other. Pray that day comes later rather than sooner," he conceded. "Have your sisters keep watch on my cousin. She is crafty beyond her years, despite having slept for so long."

She bowed her head, triumph sparkling in her cold eyes. "As you wish. What is our next objective?"

Collapsing into his command throne, Amongeratix shifted his gaze to the sea of beckoning stars. "We make course for Terotis. There is a task I must do before we arrive on Vau Prime."

TWO

3215 A.G. (After Gods), Great Library, Planet Wexanos.

Tolde Breed wiped the juice running down his chin for what felt the thirtieth time since sinking his teeth into the skull sized acha melon. More delicious than any fruit he'd ever tasted, the melon was a personal favorite of Tannus and the yellow robed librarians. He could see why now after tasting it. Understanding the need for endless groves of acha trees that spread across the southern slopes away from the main buildings.

A content sigh escaped his lips, much to the chagrin of Chief Librarian Fistel standing beside him. Together, they stood upon the northern parapet watching the dull blue glow of transport engines flare to life as the craft entered the upper atmosphere enroute to a distant corner of the universe.

"Will they help?" Tolde asked, speculating aloud.

"Difficult to say," Fistel admitted. "They are the descendants of the first people. Those who stepped forth in Lord Tannus' call for aid against the scourge of his brother during the first war. But that was so very long ago. Blood wanes thin in most. They will present his offer to their leaders and a decision shall be made."

"A simple 'I don't know' would have sufficed."

Fistel offered a smile, crooked and stained teeth almost leering. "Perils of the job I'm afraid. Stick around Tannus long enough and you learn to talk in circles." At Tolde's grunt, he asked, "Has your team recovered from the ordeal aboard *Behemoth*?"

The question stung. It had been months since the failed quest to cripple Amongeratix's command ship that resulted also in the loss of Paradise Tear. Tolde confessed regrets in allowing her to accompany them, though it had felt right at the time. Now the enemy had the key to the ultimate weapon: a planet killer of unremitting consequence. And it was his fault.

Tannus decried otherwise, for no mortal could contend with the eternal tide of evil that was his brother. The absolution did little to assuage Tolde's guilt. They were entering the endgame and Tolde did the unthinkable. This failure bit deeper than his own passing the year prior.

He took another bite from the melon as the final glow of the ship's drives passed into clouds. "Well enough, though the desire for revenge runs high. Even among the Blood Witches," he admitted.

The Grand Mistress surprised them all by not admonishing their mistakes upon their return to the Acumensiis Comet. Instead, she pledged continued support, unwavering in her commitment, and permanently assigned Sister Alessandra to his cohort for the duration of the war.

"An added benefit. Tannus was pleased to see the continued allegiance between the Grand Mistress and himself."

"Lord Tannus wishes to see all of you," the Chief Librarian said. "The Prophet has returned."

Prophet.

Paladin.

Two associated titles bound to the fate of the Three and, it seemed, the universe entire. Tolde's adventures brought him in touch with many unique beings, all of whom played some pivotal role or another in coming events. He had vague recollection of the Prophet. An odd woman from Crimeat named Elise.

"I expect he has mentioned nothing of their quest," Tolde said then grimaced. Not even in his past life had he thrived at playing coy.

Fistel ignored his intent. "Nothing I am at liberty to divulge. Come, we must not keep him waiting."

Elisa stared at her reflection in the window. Gaunt, tanned impossibly dark, and a face plagued by lines and creases too advanced for one so young, she had changed much on the Forsaken Path. Nightmares warred with her sanity since her return to reality. Questions flourished under the burden of newfound knowledge.

The gods were not gods at all. Tannus insisted on this from the beginning, but she refused to listen. After all, how could a twelve-foot-tall man weeping fresh blood slaughter her entire village in the blink of an eye and proclaim sadness to her?

She longed for a return to normalcy. But what was normal? Sorrow swept through her village when she was but a child, influencing her life for the decades that followed. They were now linked at the hip, knowing he survived the Forsaken Path and had returned to his secret fortress according to Tannus. He a tightlipped monster and she his weapon. She felt stretched thin, well beyond the breaking point. Chaos swirled in her mind, struggling to assume control and unleash her inner beast.

Elisa stretched a hand forth, placing her palm over the reflection in the vain attempt of comforting herself. Futility was ever the hallmark of human determination. The righteous pillar of foundation threatening to break under each new crisis. She closed her eyes and wished for the warm embrace of her mother, feeling she was not strong enough to face what was coming.

"Paladin, it is time."

The words rippled through her fractured soul. Thoughts of fleeing, abandoning all Tannus and Sorrow sought to achieve through her, danced in her clouded vision.

"Thank you, Chief Librarian. I am coming."

Tannus stood alone in his private study, contemplating the necessity from which his current collection of mortal champions was born from. None possessed inherently remarkable qualities other than a stubborn willingness to stand up to tyranny. No, these men and women were reluctant, almost fearful of the grim future racing toward them. How could they not? Bravery required little thought. He long ago discovered the quality of heroes came in reaction to desperate situations, not the desire to be more than individual limitations demanded. He had seen others of stronger character fall from less pressure. What then made this group so formidable?

Footsteps in the outer hall announced their arrival. Tannus had come to appreciate each of them. They were the shield wall withstanding the charge. An anvil upon which all enemy forces broke. But would they be enough? He had already lamented the loss of the Senior Inquisitor, even while understanding it was a fixed point in time. Had Breed not died, Elisa would never have been forced upon the Forsaken Path and the truth of his origin would remain a barrier preventing the others from coalescing into a formidable group.

Asking others to march into doom's maw did not come easy, even after centuries of commanding armies in the field. Tannus lacked sympathy, for it marred his ability to lead. Seeing friends and compatriots fall without overreaction required a strong conviction. Their faces and names returned to haunt his dreams, but he continued pushing forward. Marching blindly toward what the Blood Witches called Forever Night. The final doom of his people. Would he be the last? Alone at the end of the universe as the last fire burned out, the rage spent? Did he want to find out?

Steeling his resolve, Tannus went to meet his friends.

Heads turned. Baleful looks cast his way as he entered. While some languished under recent losses, others condemned him for the role he played. It was a position he knew far too well. They resented and respected him. Feared and loathed him. Tannus was immune to their emotions, despite empathizing with them. Leaving a life behind in the inglorious pursuit of salvation was no easy feat.

"Thank you all for coming," he began.

His deep voice rolled among the bookcases and empty chairs. Torches cast and deep glow over the room. They were a luxury and reminded him of simpler times where the pressures of the day always waited for tomorrow.

"What's the point of this?" Elisa demanded. Her tone bore a hard yet hollowed tone.

Tannus appraised her. "The war is turning. My spies tell me Amongeratix will soon strike at the very heart of civilization. He will not stop until Vau Prime kneels before him, subjugated and broken. Our only option, now that he has gained command of *Behemoth*, is to consolidate our forces and make the effort too costly to continue."

Tolde winced at the mention of Amongeratix's command ship. "We crippled the ship. It will take a long time to repair the damage. I don't understand why we haven't struck yet. He is weak. Vulnerable."

"That is what he wishes you to believe, Tolde Breed. My brother is devious in every regard. A snake lurking in the weeds. You have all encountered his devices in one form or another. He wants us to believe *Behemoth* is disabled." Tannus held up a hand to prevent protests. "While I believe you created much damage, there is an unnatural darkness in those corridors. Should we return so soon he will slaughter us."

"Even you?" Luma Kai raised an eyebrow. Her memories of the harrowing plight aboard the command ship left her rattled, doubting her skills when she needed them most.

Tannus' smile was soft, almost warm. "No. I do not think we are capable of killing each other, else as one of us would have done so during our long war."

"That's it then. We step back and let him have free reign of the shipping lanes until he arrives on Vau Prime?" Tolde asked. "Tannus, we have been fighting your war for three years. Each victory is paid for in blood yet the losses mount. A look around our shrinking council suggests as much. We cannot sustain this fight for much longer. What will it take to break his spine and end the war?"

"I wish I knew the answers, Tolde. Your interactions with him are extended and, to a degree, more civil than mine," Tannus replied.

Tolde settled into the cushions of his chair, his mind wandering. Had he been played for the fool from the very beginning? When the previous Inquisitor General assigned him to the greatest prison escape in Conclave history had it been by fluke or were other, nefarious elements at work? He longed for answers, answers he wasn't getting.

"The time has come to focus on the now." Tannus swept his predatory gaze across the assembled. "Progress on Mannus Prime is improving daily. Matthias informs me it will soon be defendable from both planetary assault and orbital bombardment. This is a great victory, but it is only the beginning."

Elisa pinched the bridge of her nose, red hair falling over her face. "Let the armies handle their business. You sent me on the gods damned Forsaken Path to retrieve the weapon capable of killing your kind. I say we use it and be done with this sorry affair before more die needlessly."

Ah'muf laid a consoling hand on her shoulder. The desert dweller from An'kuruku had been at her side every step of the way since the battle of the Deeves and planned on following her to the grave. Somewhere along their twisted journey through space and reality a love blossomed, and he was determined to see it through.

"*Grimfurvor* is no trinket to be toyed with, waved around with casual impunity," Tannus scolded. "It shall be used when the moment is right, not a heartbeat sooner. Besides, I surmise your time with Sorrow is not yet reached an end. Ever has the Paladin and Prophet been linked to my brother. He will have need of you soon."

Glowering, Elisa forced thoughts of the Sorrow away. "I see."

"You're sure this weapon can kill Amongeratix?" Tolde asked. He passed a questioning look to Luma Kai, and then young Ragan Sandinsol, the poor soul he'd rescued on Rastarok and failed to convince to stay home.

Sister Alessandra, hands folded within the ends of her robes and hovering inches off the ground, replied, "It was created long ago, in the aftermath of the sundering. The Grand Mistress, Sorrow, and Tannus used arcane magics no longer known to make a weapon of such power."

"So it has been tested?" Luma asked.

Tannus nodded but didn't elaborate. Some demons remained too powerful to summon. "War forces our hands in ways they are not meant to twist. When the time is right, *Grimfurvor* will do what it was created for."

"When does that happen?" Ragan asked.

Eyes fell on the youth, appraising and judging him in equal parts. He learned much during the quest to find Braewynd. The wonton death and chaos forced him to mature faster than his life might otherwise have allowed. Along the way he discovered an integral truth about himself; he was not as weak as everyone perceived. There was iron in his veins, capable of withstanding great pressure.

Tannus smiled. A warm gesture, genuine and approving. "That, young Ragan, is an excellent question. We cannot forward time or choose our assault points. Matters will develop as they must, and we shall play the long game. Amongeratix will slip up and when he does we shall have our moment to strike. To cut the head from the problem, I believe you are prone to say."

Brimming with pride, Ragan sat back. He no longer felt useless among such admirable peers.

Tannus continued. "In the meantime, we must continue developing our forward base of operations on Mannus Prime. The army and navy must be prepared for a large-scale assault, though whether offensive or defensive remains in question."

He turned his attention to the former bounty hunter from Crimeat. "Elisa, I have much work for you to do. Your training begins tomorrow."

"Training? For what?" she blurted out. Her body ached. Her bones were tired.

"You must learn how to wield *Grimfurvor*," Tannus said, his tone flat and matter of fact.

Elisa bolted to her feet. "Me? No. You said it will kill your brother. That's sounds like it belongs to you."

"Alas I cannot," Tannus replied. "You are the Paladin. It must be you."

Glowering, Elisa sank back into her chair. She grappled with doubt and self-loathing until an unexpected gleam twinkled her eyes. Perhaps, if by killing Amongeratix, she earned her future then she needed to embrace her future and become the weapon the universe needed her to be. Quiet resolve filtered through her frame.

"Am all I am meant to be is a weapon? A useful tool to hasten the end?" she asked.

She risked a glance at Ah'muf and quickly looked away, unable to bear the pain in his eyes. Elisa walked through life hurting others with callous disregard. Seeing your family slaughtered tended to do that, she figured. Now, she stood upon the precipice of finality. The endgame at last beginning. The struggle between renewed purpose and self-preservation warred in the depths of her mind and for that she lamented dragging Ah'muf from the comforts of his desert home. Her heart ached, longing for a life she knew would never come for either of them.

"What are the rest of us supposed do while she trains?" Luma Kai asked.

"Wait."

That single word haunted them, for much remained at stake and, even with the victory at Mannus Prime, the enemy continued pushing with grim determination. Planets fell, rumors of the insurrection on Vau Prime continued, inspiring fresh urgency contradictory to Tannus' command.

Tolde cleared his throat. "Wait too long and there will be nothing left. You cannot expect us to sit idle by as the universe tears itself apart. We must act."

"Against whom? We are too few to effect change on Vau Prime, nor do we have the strength to spread our influence deeper into enemy held territory. I do not suggest staying our hand, rather we must find a way to rescue Paradise Tear before my brother kills more worlds."

"The Grand Mistress is working on such," Sister Alessandra said. "Our Order stands ready to assist wherever the hammer needs to fall, though I agree with the humans. Wait too long and all momentum is lost."

"We are left with little choice."

Tannus gestured to the door.

Tolde tossed his jacket on the back of the small couch in his quarters and collapsed to tug his boots off. His mind with robust decades of experience continued resisting the flesh of his new body. His feet were still getting used to wearing boots every day. Rubbing the soles, he closed his eyes and tried clearing his mind. Making peace with Tannus' decision proved difficult. Action was required. They all knew it, but without a target, any deployment amounted to little more than wasted firepower. Frustrated as he was, Tolde reluctantly agreed it was best to wait and unleash upon their foe on their terms.

Not yet midday, he felt a familiar ache settle into his bones. Since merging with this new body, he found odd similarities transferring with him. Aches and pains from battles past, the parts he longed to forget. He frowned at the irony of being younger, stronger, yet rife with the same old problems hounding him.

Tolde felt trapped. An animal in a cage.

Rolling his shoulders to relieve some of the tension, he flexed his hands one finger at a time. He judged this new body to be no more than thirty standard years, already a far cry younger than his other self, so why the phantom pain? Cursing himself for not asking Ruma Zzein when he had the chance, he decided at least one among them might know the answer. Tolde slipped back into his boots to find answers from Sister Alessandra.

His quest ended at his doorway when he stumbled into a yellow robed librarian. Mumbling apologies while trying to disengage, Tolde helped her to her feet. The librarian bowed, the tips of golden hair peeking from under her cowl.

"My apologies, sir. I have been instructed to bring you to Lord Tannus," she said.

They'd just spoken. What had Tannus to say in private other ears couldn't hear? "Did he say what he wanted?"

"No, sir. Only that you are expected immediately."

Tolde followed Tannus through the antechamber to his private sanctum and settled into a far more comfortable chair than the one he'd just left. Bordering on luxurious, the Great Library contained the wealth of empires and a quiet opulence rivaling the greatest humanity had to offer. It was stark contrast to the life Tolde endured. Once an esteemed member of the Inquisition, he had fallen upon hard times, culminating with his death at the hands of a traitor.

Reborn, he stood among those who he called friend, even while seeing the reticence in their eyes—not that he blamed them. What's dead should remain so. Why was he the exception? His rebirth plagued his conscience. This was not his body, not his voice. Had his soul been transferred through some arcane ritual, or had it fled to the body of this man on instinct alone? Tolde knew the Blood Witches played a heavy hand in his rebirth, though none would explain why. He had been reduced to a plaything.

Tannus placed his hands flat on the ancient desk between them. "You are proof of all that is good in this universe, Tolde. It has been a great pleasure getting to know you and I am honored to stand beside you. But alas this is a far graver matter in need of exposing than your comments in council."

Heart thudding, Tolde clasped his hands together in his lap and waited.

"There is no easy way to put this so I shall be blunt: We have received word that your brother is dead. All signs point to murder," Tannus said, his words lingering between them.

Leganas? Tolde blinked. He hadn't thought of his brother in years, not since before the war. His mind struggled to understand. Murdered? Why? A flood of emotions surged, threatening to break free and subsume his conscience with grief. He fought. Oh how he fought to prevent that. Tolde prided himself on calculating logic, never one for rash actions or thoughts. Pursing his lips, he did not know what to say.

“I understand this is a shock to you, though from your expression I take it the two of you were not close.”

Tolde cleared his throat. “He was a good man. A true believer in what we did ... How was he killed?”

“I know nothing else. The message was intercepted from unofficial Inquisition channels.”

Tolde perked up. “I thought they were all being monitored by the Inquisitor General? Wouldn’t this have given our location away?”

“Under normal circumstance, yes. But I have been doing this a long time, Tolde. I have allies buried within the Inquisition who yet remain loyal to the old ways.”

Tolde wanted to wipe the smug look off his face at the admission. “It could be a trap to lure us out. Remove the bulk of the opposition leadership.”

“Assuming Alain Nye knows our identities then yes, I believe he is but a pawn in this,” Tannus admitted after some thought. “He has designs on ruling the universe, but if he has allied himself with my brother he will soon be shown a truth he’d rather ignore. It should be fine to assume the Inquisitor who sent the message is not in the Inquisition’s back pocket.”

Tolde frowned. “We should—"

“There is more,” Tannus interrupted. “What if your brother’s death was not by coincidence? Our foes might not yet realize your connection but there is the possibility your brother poked his head into matters others deemed unwise.”

Reflecting on Leganas’ nature, Tolde found little difficulty believing that. The Breed brothers were renowned for their ability to find trouble. Fond memories brought the ghost of a smile to his face until he realized what he had to do. “When I joined the Inquisition, it was to serve all humanity. To uphold the laws and standards of the Conclave and ensure our continued peace—I must go to Romalle. If nothing is amiss, I will bury my brother. However, should I discover hidden plots of nefarious intent, I will do whatever is in my power to stamp them out.”

“I was about to suggest the same,” Tannus replied. “I do not think you should go alone. Take Sister Alessandra and Ragan with you.”

Tolde started to protest but thought better of it. Ragan had been attached to his hip since Rastarok and the Blood Witch had her orders. He prayed they included keeping him alive. The only one missing was Matthias, but with the former Prekhauten Guard deployed to Mannus Prime in the main war effort there was little chance of recalling him. No matter. Old confidence flowed through him. Tolde had purpose again. Once more he was to become part of the shadows. A covert force to root out and destroy heresy.

"I shall take my leave and depart immediately," Tolde said and rose. "Oh, do you know the name of the Inquisitor on Romalle?"

"Gando, I believe."

Tolde winced.

"Is that a problem?"

Fighting to keep the scowl from his face, Tolde said, "Not if I can help it."

Sorrow's sanctum, planet Inselcor.

Automatons funneled molten lava from the endless streams pouring down from the volcano range surrounding Sorrow's castle to great vats deep within the earth. There it was transformed through a forbidden blend of alchemy and sorcery to create new machines and weapons of war not seen in the universe for generations. With his brothers renewing their open warfare, Sorrow knew the time had come to play his hand and, if possible, end the hostility before it consumed the universe.

Their game stretched back long before the final battle of Occanum. None of the brothers truly got along the way their father once hoped. They were the product of the new generation: one born instead of created. When Tannus stood before their father in court and questioned him for all to hear it was akin to nails being driven through flesh. The old ways, fractured already, threatened to burst. For Tannus' crime, Amongeratix and Sorrow were cast out too.

Old wounds, those deep enough to become engraved upon the foundations of the soul, seldom fade. Sorrow did the only act left to prevent madness and misery from devouring him—he flensed his flesh and became a compassionless creature destined to haunt humanity for all time. Tremors of his deeds rippled through ages until his name transmogrified into a curse. Such stood the price for eternal emptiness.

Sorrow sat in his favorite chair. Weather worn and battered, much like himself, the polished wood comforted him. A mother's embrace. Here he sat during moments of contemplation. A man of private thoughts, Sorrow endured because he must. Because he alone guarded the light from sputtering out and plunging all into the raw darkness of chaos. Burden and privilege he was never meant to bear. Necessity turned him into a pariah beholden to the virtues of a long dead race.

Gods. Bah! Why humanity insisted on clinging to faulty beliefs, turning his people into deities and forsaking the old histories remained his greatest curiosity. Would they still worship if they knew the truth? That his people once enslaved the universe, breaking and bending it to their will without regard for who they devoured? He thought not, yet there was so little free thought left. Almost as if it had been beaten out of them.

Wracked with aches and pains earned on the Forsaken Path, Sorrow sat with his eyes closed. There was no peace, despite his solitude. Surrounding himself with various automatons was to be his method of solace. Of not wasting words on pointless conversations threatening to lead him astray. Instead, it became his prison. The restorative properties of his species healed him, yet his mind reeled from an unbridled assaults upon his psyche. Greatest of his recent regrets was abandoning Elisa and her desert lover on their journey to earn Grimfurvor. They needed him where he could not follow.

Humans. They continually surprised him with their brash decisions and steadfast will. Elisa had no reason to agree to the quest, knowing it might cost her life. An even trade, all things considered since she now possessed the strength to slay him and the rest of his kind. Her iron determination fused with grim resolve, forging her into a weapon capable of bringing the universe to its knees. Oh how planets will tremble in her approach. Sorrow chose wisely.

"I wonder, dear Amongeratix, what the look in your eyes shall be upon seeing this tiny woman, frail in all the ways of her kind, when she comes for your head," he mused with a grin.

The splits on his upper lip threatened to rip open. He couldn't remember the last beating he suffered. The nightmare creatures of the Forsaken Path had been funneled into existence by residual hatreds of his people. They failed to kill him, though not from lack of trying. He barely escaped with his life and, months later, struggled with recovery. Did the Paladin suffer likewise? He prayed not.

Deep bruises welled under the sheen of blood, mottling him in shades of misery. One stage of his journey complete, Sorrow had much yet to accomplish since recent events reached him. Amongeratix had secured his flagship, capturing Paradise Tear in the process. What fool decided sending her was a good idea? Tannus' pet human, the reincarnated Inquisitor, continued growing stronger. Did he know what fate awaited? Most likely not else he would have disappeared among the stars by now. Civil war among the Blood Witches threatened to undo their greatest ally.

Despite all this, humanity banded together, desperate to stamp out the heresy of betrayal and restore order to their universe. Admirable, but damned to failure unless Tannus took a more active role. After all, this was the product of his long game. A finale worthy of their kind.

Thoughts spiraling, Sorrow struck upon an idea. One neither he nor Tannus had been able to enact since the three brothers entrenched themselves. Groaning as he pushed himself up and keyed in a code to open a channel to Tannus.

"Yes, Brother?"

"Always a pleasure, Brother."

"The time for pleasantries has long since faded between us, Sorrow. What do you need?"

Grinding his teeth, Sorrow said, "We are presented with an unprecedented opportunity. I seek your counsel, such as it is."

"Please get to your point. I am busy planning the next phase of the war."

His brother, ever the diligent savior. How noble. "With Amongeratix securing his atrocity he has no doubt decided the time has come to make his move. Antil IV is unguarded. Vulnerable."

Silence met his assumptions. Sorrow held his breath, anticipating what Tannus had to say.

"His hidden base may well be abandoned but I doubt Amongeratix left it unguarded. You should know better, Brother," Tannus chided. "Still, a probe might be worthwhile. I caution against launching an all-out assault, for should his gambit fail, he will no doubt return to that icy fortress and, upon finding it destroyed, act ruthlessly toward the perpetrator."

"I'm not asking you to intervene, Tannus. This was my idea. I shall assume the brunt of his wrath should it come to that." Sorrow said. He frowned, finding concern in his brother's hollow tone.

"I shall think on this. You will have my decision soon."

THREE

3215 A.G. (After Gods), PGN *Solstice*, enroute to Mannus Prime.

Alone in her cabin, Sharlyn August was stunned by the unexpected realization she missed the chaos associated with Blackheart. There was no love lost between them. Indeed, in any other circumstance she'd have placed him in custody for his crimes. Necessity drove their actions, turning foes to allies in the most unexpected ways. Her thoughts strayed to the bonds of comradeship formed on Crimeat. Blackheart cut a dashing figure, but he was obstinate and hiding his past. She'd read his file. Knew he came from wealth and a powerful family. Why abandon that to raid ships and become a villain? Despite their time together, she was no closer to solving the riddle. The quiet confidence in his eyes, accented by what some considered swarthy skin and a sinister mustache entertained her when she closed her eyes.

"Oh for fuck's sake," August groaned. "The last thing any of us need is me pining over a pirate."

Was it possible to love and despise the same person? August devoted her life to the Guard, to the preservation of humanity, leaving little room for romance. Upon making the navy a career, she called the universe home. Never settling down. Her family and life were contained within the grey walls of her ship. Nothing else mattered. Why then did the visage of Vicente Blackheart haunt her when she let her guard down?

She poured herself a drink, praying it was strong enough to center her thoughts, only what Blackheart would think of her current thoughts.

The *Solstice* hurried on, eager to reach her goal and begin the next phase of the operation. The sooner August got the artifact off her ship the better.

Eger City, planet Mannus Prime.

Jelin Quint snarled at the line of men and women standing before him and spat, "What I don't understand is what you pathetic fuckers hope to achieve. Here you are, volunteers marching off into the depths of the universe with a rifle and a death wish." He eyed the young woman a pace away. "You, you ready to take another life in cold blood? Can you look in his eyes as that last breath rattles free?"

"Y … yes, sir."

"I'm a fucking Sergeant, not a sir! I work for a living." He turned to address the rest of the company. "The next one of you bastards makes that mistake will suffer. I promise you that. Do you understand me?"

"Yes, Sergeant!" they shouted.

He returned focus to the woman, a girl really. "Got what it takes to be a killer, eh? I got a year's pay that says you vomit on your boots before you shoot. War ain't pretty. It ain't fun. Your friends will die. Hells, there's a good chance you might die." He scoffed. "The dreams don't leave you neither. Every night you'll see the faces of the fallen. Beckoning you to join them." He met each one of their eyes. "This ain't a game, kiddies. This is life and death. If you aren't sure, if you don't think you can stomach it, I suggest you slip away as soon as my back's turned. Finding out you don't have what it takes on the battlefield is too late."

No one moved.

He swept his glare across the men and women in search of weakness. The war for Mannus Prime may have ended but the scars remained. Loyal Guards secured the enemy positions, thanks in no small part to the timely arrival of Rear Admiral Falchi and his ground forces. Cut off from reinforcements and presented with an assault on two fronts, those Guards loyal to Alain Nye folded, but not after extolling a hefty price. Consolidation and reconstruction efforts were underway. A flood of material and manpower arriving daily. The once peaceful planet was slowly transforming into a major military hub. A fortress of rock and stone spinning through the universe.

This company … no, that wasn't fair was it? They were recruits now, signed up in the aftermath of the Mannus campaign, unmolded lumps waiting to be forged in the crucible of combat and turned into weapons ready to save the universe—gods help them.

Jelin was no stranger to violence. He alone survived his company's final assault on the enemy trenches. One man out of over a hundred. The indignity fueled his hatred. Why had the gods forsaken him, tormenting him with survival as all around him bled and died? He promised if he ever saw a god he'd slice the fucker's throat open.

Clearing his throat, Jelin Quint stared down his company of recruits. "Right. Let's get to making you soldiers: Company, attention!"

One hundred pairs of boots snapped together.

From his window overlooking the training ground, Torgast, recently promoted to General by Admiral Falchi, broke into a grin upon hearing his former aide barking orders to raw recruits. There'd been a time he was positive Sergeant Quint was bound for a prison cell. Devastated emotionally and mentally from the slaughter of his company, Quint walked a thin line for weeks. Assigning him to the second front under Sergeant Major Matthias proved beneficial to Quint's psyche, despite having to fight his own brother at the end.

Repressing a shudder, Torgast knew it was Quint's defeat of his brother that secured the final victory, ending the near year long siege and opening the way for the transformation of Mannus Prime into a proper military hub. Half a year later they were still burying bodies and sending death notifications to waiting families. A thankless task, but one he felt proud to fulfill.

"It is good to hear him regain his purpose."

Torgast turned. "I don't know why I accepted him to my personal staff. Perhaps it was guilt. My orders sent his company to their deaths. I will bear that burden for the rest of my days."

"He is a soldier, Torgast. A professional. Men like Jelin Quint find ways to rise to the occasion. I tend to think the gods put you together," Cardinal Virom commented. "So long as good people like the two of you remain willing to stand in the breach when the hour grows darkest there is hope."

"How can any man believe in the gods after surviving such madness?" He gave a veiled look, crossing his arms. "Cardinal, I fear you misplace your faith."

"You misread my meaning. The gods are gone, or so I believe. Their final war left naught but dust among the stars. Ashes of a better time. Mankind has been on its own since, yet still we cling to the antiquated notion of faith in celestial beings who can show no regard or notice. The faith I have is in the better qualities of humanity. That alone is strong enough to overcome any darkness."

"A Cardinal of the Conclave refuting the gods? No wonder they send you away from Krenz."

They shared a chuckle.

Cardinal Virom rubbed his right temple. "What can I say? I'm a man of many secrets."

"How can you continue wearing the robes without belief?"

"Just because my faith has taken me down different roads doesn't mean the people agree. Ask around and you'll discover an overwhelming belief in the gods, despite all facts to the contrary. It's easier for us to accept the disprovable than delve deeper into the truth. How often have you witnessed a deed, perhaps a sight of natural splendor, and thought the gods were both kind and benevolent to have created such for us. When in fact, there is a rational explanation to be found should you quest but a little. The nature of faith is not confusing. Mankind needs to believe in more than itself. It provides purpose. Sustains us as we develop and expand."

Torgast grew uncomfortable with the conversation's direction. Faith was not a thing to be questioned. Raised in the church, he joined the Guard out of obligation and the desire to serve others. Selflessness was ingrained in him from a young age. For Cardinal Virom, a man he respected and sought out for counsel, to admit what amounted to heresy in the Inquisition's eyes rattled him.

Eyes drawn together in thought, he pondered Virom's words. The question asked surprised him, even as it poured from his mouth. "How do you kill a god?"

Face darkening, the Cardinal's reply was but a whisper, "You stop believing."

"Why are we still here?"

Lieutenant Fies rolled his eyes, tired of being asked the same question day after day. "Because you're not in charge, Haggle. The Admiral says we stay put, so we stay put. Besides, General Torgast is in charge now and I'm not in his inner circle." He grunted. "Anything else, or can I get back to doing what officers do?"

"What do officers do, sir?" Hollis asked, a grin spreading on her face.

Muted laughter spread through the platoon.

Fies pointed a finger and glared. "We do officerly things."

"Paperwork, he means," Sergeant Annalilly barked. "You should see the callouses on his fingertips from typing so much. Oh, and if they had a medal for papercuts our fearless lieutenant would be a general by now. A hero of the Conclave!"

Another roar of laughter had Fies' face darkening. "I can bust you back down, you know."

"Please do. I liked it better when all I had to worry about was picking my next target," she sassed. "Sir."

Muttering under his breath, Fies stalked off. A wise man knew when to quit the battlefield and he had no intention of angering the woman who shared his bed. Their good-natured ribbing was a time-honored tradition now the others expected. His storming off resulted in having to salute far too many soldiers in passing.

Fies had served with some of them since he first made squad sergeant. War forged their bonds tighter. Action on Crimeat, Hawker's Gate Space Station, Kharsis, and Mannus Prime turned what had been a loose collection of soldiers into one of the strongest platoons in the Guard, on either side. There'd been losses along the way. Empty spots where familiar faces lingered ever on the crust of memory. New recruits flowed in. Some lived. Others died. It was the flow of modern warfare. That so many of his original squad remained surprised Fies, for he doubted any would live to see the war's end.

He was surprised to find the sergeant major dressed in suspicious utilities a far cry from his old uniform and the deep space smuggler, Ishis Gul, awaiting him when he retired to his tent. Unlike the rest of the army, those forces who deployed with Falchi chose to remain separate. They were Marines and commando squads; specialty units forged in the crucible of war. Fitting in with the rest of the Guard sat ill with many. He wondered if that feeling of more than line infantry might prove detrimental down the road.

"Lieutenant," Matthias acknowledged.

"Sergeant Major," he replied and set his rifle down on the small field table allotted his rank. He cast a quick look at Gul. "What can I do for you?"

"You can start by calling me Matthias. You know I'm retired."

Fies shrugged. "Old habits. You brought us through some hairy fights a few years ago. A man doesn't forget his debts."

"I was doing my job. Don't read into it, Fies. You are doing the same."

"Blade for blade," Fies countered before changing the subject. "I thought you were heading back to Wexanos?"

Matthias stiffened. His initial goal of returning to Tannus and the inner circle shifted in the campaign's aftermath. Though he'd partnered with Tolde Breed for many years, their journey was now marching down diverging paths. The old ways were sundered as Matthias no longer needed to stand beside his friend, for Tolde had faced death and come out the other side a different man. The situation stank of the arcane and supernatural and it was best for Matthias to remain where he was needed most.

"Matters have changed. I am staying on with Admiral Falchi for the time being. We have won a battle, but the war goes badly on too many fronts to rest now. Mannus Prime is to be our strongest outpost."

"Supplies and volunteers already stream to the orbital hubs," Ishis Gul added. His rasping voice sent shivers down Fies' spine. "My people are doing a great service in this."

Fies clenched his jaw. Carrion eaters flocked to battlefields. Some in the guise of men. His opinion of Gul narrowed. The smuggler assisted their efforts today, leaving tomorrow open for interpretation. It would be best to kill the man now and be done with it, else be found in the morning with a knife in the back, dead from the bitter sting of betrayal.

Choosing to ignore Gul, Fies asked Matthias, "Do we have new orders yet? The troops are growing restless."

Being at the tip of the spear for extended periods left the Guards raw, glad the fighting was finished yet eager for another scrape. Matthias understood the addiction, for he'd suffered from it for many years before age and time conspired against him.

"The Admiral hasn't said anything but there are rumors circulating about an attempt to break the outer defenses of Vau

Prime," Matthias started, lowering his voice. "Hit and run guerilla raids to alleviate the pressure on the insurgency."

"Sounds too risky," Fies countered. Little enough escaped Vau Prime since the Inquisitor General launched his coup. Without any actionable intelligence there was no way to accurately plan a counteroffensive.

"It is, but necessary. We've picked up reports that General Strannan is dead. The Inquisitor General is making his big push to crush what resistance is left. We lose the planet, and we lose the war."

An emptiness filled Fies. Though he'd never met Strannan, the general had been a staple of the Guard for decades. Legendary, his career provided inspiration for generations. Losing him was a serious blow to freedom. "Even with the additional troops on planet we don't have anywhere near enough for a full invasion. Their navy would blow us out of the sky long before any assault shuttles reached the surface." Fies sighed. "I like Admiral Falchi, the man's done right by us for a while now, but he lacks the ships and firepower to crack the blockade."

"Not a crack so much as little wounds. Slices up and down their lines until enough ships are forced to drydock for repairs,"

Face paling, Fies muttered, "I'll take my chances on the ground. Sounds like a suicide mission."

"I'm not disagreeing. Something about being trapped in space on a tin can isn't appealing." Matthias glanced at the smuggler. "No offense, Gul."

"We each have our talents. Yours lies in the dirt with the others."

Fies noticed the conical hat reaching high above Gul's head. Certain it was fashionable wherever Ishis Gul came from, the man presented little better than a fool in the company of soldiers.

Continuing to ignore him, Fies asked Matthias, "What do we do now? We can't just sit here while the war goes on and I'm not comfortable returning to a large army. Not after all we've been through."

"You're asking to get thrown into another assignment?" Matthias questioned. "I was of the mind to request leave for your people. They've been through more than most. You deserve the break."

Fies winced. Odd pressures swirled around his head. His respect for Matthias kept him silent. "Sergeant Major, I appreciate that. I do. I'm sure the platoon would as well but, realistically, what are we going to do with any spare time? Hard drinking, whoring, looking over our shoulders for invisible foes ready to slay us. I know these men and women. They've become family in a short period of time, and I can tell you with certainty any extended period of time off would be the worst decision you could make. We are already sharpened and honed. Setting us aside while the war rages is a waste of a tool and provides the opportunity for mistakes none of us can afford in the coming campaigns."

"It seems I continue underestimating you," Matthias said hiding a smile. "Your people will forever have my gratitude, and my respect. And one day, when this madness is ended and we can go back to our lives I hope we can all sit down over a good meal, better drinks, and laugh about the old times."

"I'd like that."

Tired. The one constant sensation he'd felt since declaring sides in the opening stages of the war. Little did he know how far he'd come, and fall, in the years to follow. Life as a ship's captain was hard. Dealing with crew and family issues, supply and support, not to mention the occasional combat action, all conspired to transform his once dark hair a lighter grey. Lines now wrinkled his face and spots bespeckled his hands. He felt and looked old, unsure when last he managed a full night's sleep.

Ernst Falchi gazed into a reflection staring back hard. He wasn't sure when he became this man and less sure if he approved. War forced necessity's hand and he was but a willing pawn in a game of death. Recent combat action in the upper orbit of Mannus Prime left him rattled. It had been the first true engagement against Prekhauten vessels since the betrayal and ambush of Hawker's Gate two years ago. This time the odds were level and attacked with the prejudices of a man bent on victory.

"Will there be naught but war in our future?" he asked aloud.

Forcing a slow breath through pursed lips, Falchi doused his face with cold water. There comes a time in every officer's life where they forget themselves and lived only for the men and women serving under them—Falchi was beyond that. He fought for the ideals of the Conclave and the promises of Tannus to end the war and restore order.

Nothing else mattered.

Resigned, he slipped into a pair of dress trousers, a button-down shirt, and slid into his heavy uniform jacket replete with ribbons and medals from a dozen campaigns. A palm smoothed out the wrinkles, ensuring the pockets lay flat. Throwing on his shoes, Falchi snatched his dress cap off the bed and hurried to begin his day.

Captain Samuel awaited in the corridor. "Good morning, Admiral."

"When was the last time we had to wear these?"

Suppressing a grin, Samuel replied, "The early days of the war. Your promotion I believe."

"Uh huh. Damned collar is already chafing my neck," Falchi grumbled. "Is the crew ready?"

"With bells on I believe the expression is."

"I'm sure the Marines will enjoy that."

"Delightful souls, sir. One and all."

Falchi grunted. "Is Asom back to his usual self?"

The ground battle on Mannus Prime showed Asom a different side of war, one lacking the intimacy of ship-to-ship action. There, in the fields and forests, he came face to face with nightmares. Marines died under his command and, despite Falchi's best efforts to convince him that was war, Asom took each loss personally. It was the command's hope his return to the *Indomitable* coupled with reintegrating with the shipboard contingent and acquiring new bodies would salve the mental scarring. It had to an extent, but Asom had far to go before the horrors of war faded enough that he didn't wake up screaming every night.

"He's tougher than we give him credit. They all are," Falchi added after seeing the pain in Samuel's eyes.

"Doesn't ease the hurt though. These are still young men and women we are throwing into the grinder. They fight their former friends; on some occasions there have been reports of brother against brother. I don't know much, Admiral, but one thing is clear: The longer this war goes on the less we become."

Falchi placed a fatherly hand on his former First Officer. "No truer words have been spoken, my friend. Would that I could end it in one final stroke, a decisive battle with every available resource to drive Nye to his knees in surrender. Alas, that is not to be. I fear the end game is not yet in sight."

"Rumor has it Admiral Khe-zhehan is planning a sustained raid on Vau Prime," Samuel said slowly.

Face twisting in disgust, Falchi waved him off. "Foolishness. General Kale has no doubt secured the planet from any orbital assault. The only way to take back the capitol is from the ground, and if the rumors of General Strannan's death are true, there seems little hope of that. Khe-zhehan will bleed our fleet until there is nothing left."

Captain Samuel held his tongue, wisely choosing to keep his opinions private. He'd earned his position through years of dedicated service under Falchi and, despite obtaining his own captaincy, was reticent about countering his commanding officer.

"You're hiding something."

Shoulders sagging, Samuel said, "Sir, we need to act sooner rather than later. Every moment we delay we provide the enemy time to dig in and repel our assaults. The victory here was hard fought, but it has already been close to half a year. We lose the advantage."

"I appreciate your concerns and were the circumstances different I might second them," Falchi started. "Look at this from a different angle. Nye and Kale control the central system. Banking, commerce, the Conclave, Inquisition, and Guard are all under his sway. The only true way to end the war is by cutting him off from the rest of the universe.

"Sir—"

"It may seem like we are losing the advantage, but each day sees new ships join our fleet. Thousands of volunteers and disenchanted Guard units trickle in. Our numbers grow. Soon we shall be formidable enough to open multiple fronts, stretch Nye's forces thin, and make the final strike on Vau Prime. Have faith and hold the course, Captain. We can survive this and save the ones we love."

"I hear what you are saying, sir, but my heart remains heavy." He ran the latest troop strength estimates through his head. With those repatriated Guards and the influx of new personnel the army under General Torgast stood over fifty thousand. More than three hundred and seventy ships of the line comprised their armada. Enough for several fleets, though they lacked much of the heavier firepower of the new battleships rolling out from the shipyards. Yet frigates, lancers, destroyers, and carriers filled the skies over Mannus Prime.

Engineers from a hundred systems poured in to construct an orbital ring of defenses and docking stations, one of which the *Indomitable* was now tethered to. The ship was a formidable metal ring of heavy weapons with battalions of Marines that were itching for a brawl. The former manufactory world was slowly transformed into a defensive position rival to any in the universe. Samuel wondered how long before Nye turned his eye and decided Mannus presented too much of a threat.

"As it should. They may be our enemies for this conflict, but they were all brothers and sisters. Compatriots for the greater good. We owe it to ourselves to take that into consideration each time we engage. Because they serve opposite ideals now does not make them bad people," Falchi cautioned.

"Nor does it make it easier."

"War should never be easy. We storm into the midst of unprecedented times. Not since the first human diaspora after the fall of the gods has our kind been challenged so," Falchi said. "You can be certain of one truth, Samuel: from this war there are but two options. Victory or death. Now come, we have duties to attend."

Samuel winced. "Is this necessary, sir? I'm not in the mood for a celebration."

"Comes with the job, Captain. I suggest you put on your best smile and stretch your hand. There are plenty of people to meet."

An undisclosed moon in deep space.

Stalking through the remains of a once proper castle, the god hunter struggled with the complexities of memory. He had awoken from a long slumber, one induced by necessity as he lay dying in the aftermath of the battle of Occanum. Now Akin Brohl rediscovered a universe that did not know or need him. He wasn't sure what he should do next.

Frustrated as fleeting images of mortal combat danced in his mind's eye, Akin went in search of weapons. He vaguely recalled coming to this ancient keep fully armed and in pursuit of … his mind went blank. He'd been robbed of names and faces, but never of his purpose. Akin Brohl existed to kill the gods for their transgressions against the universe. Charged with this holy mission, he was the scourge of a hundred worlds. Immortality trembled at the sound of his coming, for he was the instrument of justice.

Despite this, Akin Brohl was lost. The universe had changed. The gods were gone, naught but a shadow of their former menace. Humanity rose from the ashes, twisting into a unique monster of its own. A fundamental lack of understanding threatened to render him immobile. Nothing made sense to him. Even in the halls of his own making.

Everywhere he strode was filled with the decay of forgetfulness. The keep was long abandoned, left in the haunted haze of yesteryear whereas once it had been filled with life and purpose. Upon the now dust covered thrones he caught fragments of smiling faces wreathed in golden light, a husband and wife. They looked familiar, though he was unable to put a name to either. Gasping at the futility facing him, Akin placed a hand over his heart and leaned against the nearest cobweb covered wall for support as his aged muscles struggled to remember their old strength.

"How long have I sat abandoned in this tomb?" he questioned the vast emptiness.

Vision swimming, darkness crawled around the edges. Akin Brohl was many things, but never a coward. He searched deep within, accessing the wells of his pride and strength, before pushing off the wall and continuing his trek. Urgency whispered in his ear. He knew not what strange universe he had awoken to, only that his purpose was incomplete. That alone offered the promise of continued life.

The deeper into the keep he ventured the more he began remembering scenes of a great battle. Skeletons in rusted armor lay stretched about; hundreds filled the halls and corridors. Many wore the emblem of twin suns collided, one red, the other yellow. Akin paused, for he too wore the same emblem. Were these his soldiers or had he been part of their force? A doomed force by all appearances.

Wandering through kitchens and storerooms, Akin came at last to what he assumed was his private armory. The familiarity of it all haunted him but it wasn't until he strapped on a timeworn set of body armor that realization struck. This was his keep; he was lord and master. Whatever fate befell his people remained hidden, though his heart was heavy with grief.

Akin finished dressing and headed down the main hallway with renewed purpose. He vowed to never rest again until the last god took their last breath, and the universe was forever expunged of their foul taint. To never stop hunting and gain a measure of revenge on all who'd done his kind wrong.

But where to begin?

He knew not what day it was, nor how long he'd been asleep.

Tracing through the keep down to the hangar decks, Akin discovered more evidence of heavy fighting. He feared there would be no intact craft remaining, and if there were, would it be operable? The god hunter stepped over forgotten corpses, inspecting several fliers in passing. One was missing both wings. Another had half the hull blown out.

Then he spied it—the lone craft that was flightworthy. Wedged between a pair of destroyed gun towers overlooking the hangar bay door, sat the sleek craft. Much of the paint was faded, dulled with time, prompting Akin to fear the worst.

Boots echoing with every step, he swept across the hangar, pausing to lay a gloved hand on the tail. Dust swept away in tiny trails where his fingers dragged across the angled hull. The ship, like himself, was pure predator. A weapon of a bygone era designed for lethality.

A trickle of memory dangled before him and Akin snatched it before it faded. This was his ship. One flown across the universe on his epic quest.

Like him, it was a survivor.

Or so he hoped.

Depressing the button behind the access hatch on the side of the cockpit, he stepped back and waited as the door slid open with a groan. Dust billowed and he coughed.

Akin climbed the small ramp and entered the craft. Naught but the slow ravages of time appeared to have harmed the ship, for it was of a sturdy build. The god hunter headed up the pair of steps into the main cockpit and thumped down in the pilot chair. More memories flashed by, teasing him. His hands went to the steering controls. For the first time since awakening, Akin Brohl felt alive.

He clicked a series of switches on whim and was surprised to find many of the displays operable, not the least of which the time chrono inlaid on the dash. His eyes widened as seeing the numbers …

… three thousand years had passed. Three thousand years during which all he knew and love withered and died.

FOUR

3215 A.G. (After gods), low continent, planet Vau Prime.

The remnants of Davith Strannan's war machines were being ground to dust. Their memories forgotten among the ruins of once proud cities and villages. The dead outnumbered the living here, for fire seldom bothered with consent. After Mobus Kale's purged the year prior it was all gone. Those few who survived either fled offworld or disappeared into the mountains, desperate to scratch out a meager existence until time ran out.

In the months following Strannan's assassination the survivors of his army fled their mountain retreat, trekking overland to the ruins of the Zevistya Spaceport on the far side of the continent. The move was ponderous and taxing as they only moved at night to avoid enemy air patrols. They also fled only on foot and left the few small vehicles behind. Lacking the luxury of dignity, they marched with what pride the uniform of the Guard instilled upon them.

Once the spaceport was secured and enough space carved out for storage and billeting, the fractured command structure made valiant efforts to rebuild and regroup. Mistrust clashed with despair. None expected the assassination of the one man who had kept them together—the only man who had been assuring them victory was still within their grasp.

Gedrick Silk ran a hand through the unkempt hair on his scalp, unused to the sensation even after months of personal neglect. He listened as the various lieutenants and captains bickered with the lone colonel on staff. The shapeshifter remained uncomfortable in their presence, for it was akin to watching a family tear itself apart. Gone was the camaraderie of those early days when fervor gripped the insurrection.

Whispers of tragedy striking the cells left in Krenz reached them through couriers and spies who dared crossing between continents. Many were lost, shot down or captured, but enough trickled in to keep the war effort informed. Gedrick considered himself a stranger to human methods of violence despite long years of service to the departed General.

Their relationship was built upon one's desire to find renewed life without his people and one's need for a card up the sleeve. Losing Strannan broke Gedrick's heart. They shared a father-son bond and now that Strannan was dead, Gedrick could no longer avoid the slow crawl toward final extinction.

"You're not listening. What we need is a modest means to slip commando teams back into Krenz and eliminate the enemy's senior leadership," Colonel Apontee repeated.

"Sir, that's already been tried. We had a man inside, close to Nye once. That window of opportunity is closed," Lieutenant Mal growled. Any pretense of respecting rank was absent. Her short temper had been on full display since recovering from wounds suffered during the assassination.

Apontee jabbed a bony finger at Gedrick, "No doubt thanks to the lack of spine displayed by Strannan's pet project!"

Gedrick stiffened but Mal stepped between them before he could act. "Mr. Silk is of the highest caliber, *sir*. If he claims he couldn't reach the Inquisitor General that's the way it was. You got a problem with that I suggest you go yourself. Show the rest of us how it's done."

"That's insubordination, Lieutenant. I'll have your head for that!" Apontee raged. "All of you should be under arrest for dereliction of duty."

His feelings on where responsibility for Strannan's death lie were well documented. The colonel had been away at the time of the assassination and upon returning decided all who were in the General's immediate confidence had conspired to see him dead. Attempts at retaliation met with stiff resistance, however. The army banded together, stymying his efforts to restore order and assume overall command. Ignorant to the whispers concerning his behavior, Apontee continued ostracizing himself through a series of foolish commands resulting in the unnecessary deaths and the potential revealment of their new base of operations.

"Colonel, we've been through this. Too many times," Lieutenant Abernath spoke up from atop a small stack of supply crates in the corner. "Gedrick did what he could and barely escaped with his life. We need resources more than the death of one man."

"One man capable of uniting the universe against him! Think of what the population would say upon discovering the great Alain Nye was murdered. The enemy will devolve into uncontrolled factions, and we would win back our planet and control of the universe," Apontee argued. "What we need now more than ever is strong leadership. Putting the right person in place to handle the assignment will ensure a swift transition back to the norm."

"And you are the man for this job?" Gedrick asked.

"It just so happens I am," Apontee stiffened at hearing a suppressed snicker. "Oh it won't be easy, and it damned sure won't be bloodless, but this is our only chance to catch Nye and burn his house down around him."

"Our losses will be—"

"Acceptable. This is war. We must expect the empty seat at the table. Whatever manpower we lose in the effort will easily be replaced once word goes out that the rule of Conclave has been restored."

"General Strannan never mentioned you assuming command, sir." Abernath didn't care for the direction of the conversation. Too much bluster from Apontee, and the small faction of his supporters scattered throughout the army, threatened to undermine all they sought to achieve.

Apontee's gaze bore holes into the young officer. "What would a junior officer know of such matters? I am the senior ranking man on the ground. This is my army to lead by right of rank."

"We should be in the process of finding transport offworld to link up with the others," Mal argued. "Any further action in Krenz is suicide."

Apontee sneered. "That is not your decision to make."

"We could help evacuate those cells trapped in the city," Abernath suggested.

"Captain Julian and his people have provided invaluable support throughout the campaign," an older field ajor commented from his seat in the middle of the room. The curling ends of his moustache were grey, matching the flint color of his eyes. "They deserve to be rescued."

Apontee trembled at the outright disrespect. In another time they would have all been shot for insubordination. But desperate times required cunning and the dynamic shift in leadership tactics. The war, already on the brink of total collapse, threatened to unravel all he and those similar fought to achieve. The indignity gnawed on his conscience.

"Major Onof, our insurgent cells have failed. If Captain Julian is alive, he is no doubt in hiding, making it next to impossible for us to extract. There is but so much we can accomplish with separate agendas," Apontee said after letting the silence gather. "Strannan is dead, and this army is now mine. I expect each of you to belay orders to subordinate leaders: Begin drilling and preparing for battle immediately. We will take the fight to our foes and reclaim this planet in the name of the Conclave."

"And die trying," Abernath mumbled.

"What's that, soldier?" Apontee demanded.

Red faced, Abernath shook his head. "Nothing, sir."

"You have your orders. Get to work."

Dismissed, the leadership cell went their separate ways.

Gedrick's gaze bore into Apontee's back. Why couldn't the man realize it had all changed? That there was no going back. Whatever the Guard was founded on was lost; twisted and turned to a shell of hatred and enmity against its own kind. Gedrick knew he was the only one with the power to salvage what remained, but the ask was much bigger than his ambition. Could he?

The shapeshifter slipped away. He needed to bring his plan to the others. Perhaps there was yet time to save Strannan's dream.

Or perhaps it was already too late.

Krenz, planet Vau Prime.

"We can't stay here forever. Not with half the city hunting us."

Aliz suppressed a frown. The older woman respected Julian for his opinions and tactical prowess, but he tended to drift into darker realms of thought. Not that she blamed him. Seeing the love of her life murdered left Aliz equally scarred. She'd vowed to never stop fighting until Lorenu Phos was avenged. Alas, nothing she had done in the years since amounted to much more than temporary relief and the disillusionment of standing on the right side of justice.

The thoughts of the countless deaths that have since followed her vow of revenge failed to awaken the empathy she once relied upon. Suffering in silence, she watched the universe tear itself apart. What began with Cardinal Seniorus in a vicious coup devolved to pure slaughter. Entire districts on Krenz were aflame. Refugee trains out of the city and offworld choked the streets. The Inquisitor General had no choice but to declare martial law, lest those perpetrators of masked violence slip through his fingers to join other cells on different worlds. Supplies continued flowing in, but the masses felt the pinch. Hunger and desperation clashed the tighter Nye's grip grew. Soon the city would either break or declare their dissatisfaction with open aggression.

In war, she had come to learn, the innocent died first.

"What choice have we? General Strannan's death has left a power vacuum among the insurrectionists. Those cells we had here are just as deep underground as we are. Forming larger groups is irresponsible and will only result in seeing us all dead. Zoraq's people are our only chance at remaining free and striking back where it matters, Julian."

His gaze softened. Julian was fighting to preserve the Conclave and keep Aliz alive. He feared doing both was impossible. "You continue to impress me," he confessed. "This type of war drains me. Mentally and physically. I don't have much left to give."

"Again, what choice have we? Look around, Julian. These people need a face to rally behind. A name of deeds and principle to throw their support at. Like it or not, you are that man."

His shoulders sagged. "It should be you. Anyone but me."

She laid a hand on his shoulder. "A wise woman once told me we seldom get to choose how our lives play out. That we must do as we are born to do, else the fabric of reality be torn asunder and all we love and know reduced to ash on the crisp morning winds."

"All that alliteration huh?"

She waved him off as he grinned. "All right, maybe not in so many words. My point is Lorenu was a great leader and she showed me a great deal about human nature and how we fit in this great cosmic scheme."

"I would have liked to have met her."

"Probably not. She was compassionate and ruthless at the same time. She'd waste little time in admonishing you right now," Aliz said. The hint of a smile crept into her gaze before fading. "We cannot abandon the fight now, Julian. We must not. To do so is to admit we were never right in the first place. That our cause was built upon fallacy and Nye's vision for our future was what we were always meant to become."

Admitting defeat, the Guardsman forced an exaggerated sigh. "Very well. If we are to remain in the company of this band of villains and criminals we should at least let them know what we've decided. I wouldn't want anyone else dying without knowing the reason why."

"That's the spirit!" Aliz beamed.

"You're both mad. You know this, right?"

Julian winced. "Keeps things interesting."

Strands of dark hair, oiled and matted to Edam Boone's forehead drew attention away from his look of consternation. The former second in command of a vast criminal underground reminded himself Aliz and Julian were not part of his crew. They remained outsiders, along with the hundreds of others brought to safety during the final purge, despite their months together. How he managed to keep from losing his mind during their numerous arguments and disagreements was lost on him.

"While I respect your positions, how could I not? You've brought in enough weapons and people to start a small army, all while taxing my supply system. Did I mention the city is being drowned in dwindling resources, poverty, and paranoia?"

"None of that is our fault, Edam," Aliz said.

"No, but you haven't made it much better either. Have you?"

"We are in unprecedented times. My people are doing all within their power to assist," Julian cut in. "We have the weapons and manpower, as you said, but our options for assaults are constricted thanks to martial law."

True to character, the enemy encircled Krenz in a strangled grip the moment word arrived of Strannan's assassination. Alain Nye and Mobus Kale used that information like a hammer, striking the very heart of the insurrection. Several operatives slipped away in the night, unwilling to fight any longer. An entire cell abandoned their mission and were later found slaughtered. Their bodies were arranged in a manner leaving nothing to the imagination. Panic rippled through the remaining cells. Those who were able fled to the presumptive safety Julian offered, eager to renew the fight and win back their city. Even with the bolstered numbers their chances dwindled daily.

"Have you thought of returning the favor of Davith Strannan in kind?" Edam asked.

"We're not assassins," Aliz said through clenched teeth.

Seeing his mistake, Edam held up his hands. "No offense meant, Aliz. I am suggesting we use the enemy's weapons against him."

"If that were the case we'd have contracted the Vaumagians," Julian remarked. "The assassin guild is already under contract with Nye and they refuse to accommodate a second player."

"Desperate times, I'm afraid." Edam bobbed his head. "I do have a few names on the tip of my tongue should you choose to explore the possibility."

Defiant, Aliz snapped, "Thank you, but we will continue fighting this war the way we know how. If we give in and use the same tactics as the madman attempting to wipe us from existence how are we better?"

"I don't tend to play by the rules. My people operate any way they can, always searching for a way to mitigate and neutralize with the least amount of casualties on our end," Edam said. "This is a new war for us."

"Of which you have yet to commit bodies to the field," Julian countered.

Edam paused. The limits of his hospitality already stretched thing, he absorbed their grief, their feelings of intimate helplessness, and did his best to ignore it. No one survived long in his line of work by feeling sorry. "Therein lies the differences between you and me. My purpose is one of protection. The men and women in this organization look to me to keep them safe. You represent anarchy. A deviation from the normal," he explained. "Please don't misconstrue my meaning here. I have been and will continue to be your ally in this struggle, to an extent, but I will not send my people into harm's way without good reason or the assurance of victory."

"Perhaps there is a compromise," Aliz offered. Her face slipped into the polished politician façade she'd worn for decades. "Edam, we are not asking for combat power, as Captain Julian calls it. What we need is your network's eyes and ears so we can form a better defense and take some of the bluster from our foes. Surely you understand the necessity in that. If we fall, Alain Nye will grind your people to ashes and leave nothing behind." Her voice dropped to a conspiratorial whisper, "Remember, you are all considered the criminal element and have never been accepted by society. Failure to act will be the death knell to all you and Zoraq sought to achieve."

Edam leaned back and crossed his arms over his chest, gaze softening just enough to allow Aliz a glimmer of hope. She knew how he felt; the turmoil raging within. Zoraq Darc was dead. His network bordered on collapse. Much like the Conclave, they were marching to the brink of extinction. An inglorious demise to what should have been an age of enlightenment unprecedented in human history.

"We need your help now more than ever, Edam," Aliz said, lowering her voice. "Can we count on you to see us through this most difficult phase of the war?"

"Tell me first, Aliz, who will step forth from Strannan's impressive shadow to lead?" he asked.

She had no answer.

"He will help," she told Julian once they were alone.

Pacing the small chamber, he clenched his fists. "How can you be so certain? These criminals hold allegiance to naught but their ideals. They've agreed to keep us safe thus far, but what happens when Mobus Kale makes them an irrefusable offer?"

"I don't see him selling us out, if that is what you are insinuating," she admonished. "He's had multiple chances. By all rights we should either be in an Inquisition prison cell or dead. There is honor in Edam Boone."

"He is a career criminal, Aliz. Don't be so foolish as to trust in him."

"Nonsense. If he wanted us out of his hair he would have turned us away long before you brought in the rest of the operating cells," Aliz said. "We may be straining his logistics, but this network isn't hurting by any means. As for danger, there has always been an element of it since their first founding. You forget, Lorenu sent me to deal with this crew long before Nye launched his offensive."

"Can you look me in the eye and honestly say you trust Edam?"

She paused. Trust was a rare commodity, even in the best circumstances. Aliz never wanted to be more than a confidant, a soothing shoulder for Lorenu to rest her head during trying times. How cruel and twisted the irony of life was. Instead of being the comfort, she sought it. Was this how true leaders felt?

"Yes."

Julian tensed, processing the information. The strategic part in him suggested gathering his forces and equipment, including what remained of their raid on the Tatarast Island armory, and fleeing deeper into the city. Perhaps, if lucky enough, he'd find a way to link up with those on the low continent and either escape offworld or regroup and plunge a dagger deep in the enemy's heart. One last ride of glory before the flames of oblivion swept over him.

But alas, what glory was there in vain sacrifice? They would strike hard, killing as many foes as possible before the end came. A flash. The sizzle of cauterized flesh as his body fell beneath the onslaught of those he once called friends. No, his death served little purpose—not yet at least.

"Very well. Let us hope he goes for your suggestion. We need all the help we can get."

Alain Nye felt old as he watched smoke rising from a dozen explosions. The beacons of light lining Redemption Boulevard were dimmed in response. Telecasts and news briefs urged calm, proclaiming the insurgency was winding down per his orders. Yet public executions were becoming the norm, the bodies often left hanging from flagpoles on taller buildings to deter further aggressions. Thus far it hadn't worked. Ambushes and attacks rose, suggesting his regime was losing control. Should enough of the population believe this, the entire planet might be subsumed with rebellion. Not even Kale's iron fist would be enough to break it.

He was pushed to the breaking point despite having the manpower, resources, and reinforcements waiting in the cold dark of space. Anger consumed him, turning his days into acts of aggression from which there was no mercy. Aides and mid-tier functionaries were replaced quicker than it took for him to learn their names. The unfortunate few who displeased him the most were shipped to the frontlines and cast into the maelstrom. A handful were slain by his own hand in front of their peers—a brutal reminder of the price for failure. There was no retreat from the horrors of war. Nor should there be. The future of the universe was at stake and Alain was willing to stop at nothing to achieve his goals.

He turned from the window and glared at those assembled in the former chambers of the Forum. Since declaring the Conclave obsolete, the Inquisition deployed waves of loyalists to every planet to oversee the war effort. Cardinals, Guard officers, and Inquisitors sat before him. Most had the decency to lower their eyes. The rest glowered back. Alain noted their names and vowed retribution when the moment was right.

"Why is this persisting?" he demanded. The vein on his forehead popped, providing an ugly bluish scar rippling beneath his flesh. "General Kale, you have orders to enforce strict martial law. Cardinals, you have been given the task of quelling potential uprisings. My Inquisitors, why are the cells not overflowing with dissidents? Krenz is on the verge of capitulation and none of you are doing one gods damned thing to prevent it. Why? Why are any of you still alive at this moment?"

Mobus Kale cleared his throat. "We are proceeding with the offensive to cleanse the city and planet. The enemy is dug in, forcing us to combine assets."

"Don't give me excuses, General. I appointed you for a reason," Nye warned.

"Let me do what needs doing." Mobus ignored the implied threat. "I'll burn this city to the ground and kill all who oppose me."

Noting the use of 'me' in his response, Nye retorted, "Ever the ambitious one, eh, General? The low continent was one matter, razing Krenz to the ground is fallacy. We lack the manpower and momentum."

"There are over seven million citizens in this city!" a Cardinal shouted.

Mobus sneered. "While bringing the universe to its knees. Let me end this war my way. Burn Krenz and the enemy will fold."

"Or you turn the seven hundred worlds against us," Nye countered. "I will not be the Inquisitor General remembered for his willingness to murder the population. Find another way. Strannan is dead. The Forum is disbanded. The insurrection has lost steam. Root them out and bring me the leaders."

"It requires a concerted effort by all of our offices, Inquisitor General," Cardinal Shri injected, slamming a fist on the table. "Working alone serves no purpose and increases dissent among the people. Strannan is being hailed a hero despite your best efforts to prove he was a traitor."

"There are reports circulating he continues leading the rebellion. Witnesses claim they have seen him," a Guard officer remarked.

"Unsubstantiated!" Nye shouted. "We successfully removed him from operations on the low continent—General Kale, delegate a loyal officer to continue the mission here. I want you to personally assume command of a battalion and deploy south. Wipe out all enemy forces … by any means necessary."

"With pleasure." Mobus Kale saluted and stormed off.

Satisfied he removed the hostility from the chamber, the Inquisitor General turned back to those remaining. "These are my orders: I want every Cardinal and lower clergy in this city on the streets. Meet with the people. Spread our message and sway them to our side. Once Krenz is secure we can refocus on the rest of the universe. When enough planets fall the rest will step into line and this war will at last be ended."

"A task made much easier if you had not dissolved the power of the Forum," Shri spat. "We are made toothless in the face of our flock when they need us most."

"Find a way to make this work or I will find those who can," Nye said. "Am I clear?"

"Crystal." The word spit from clenched jaws. Her slight form trembled, the folds of her crimson robes vibrating with undisguised energy.

Alain Nye held her venomous gaze and she caught the hollow look lingering behind the mad genius responsible for the war. The Conclave, in her opinion, chose poorly by siding with him. Yet what more could they have done? Lorenu Phos was dead, leaving a power vacuum filled by greed. Now Tinnus Har had joined her in the grave, allowing Nye the opportunity to bring the austere organization to its knees. Humbled, embarrassed, and broken, those remaining proved willing participants in the near genocidal campaign the Inquisition waged.

Cardinal Shri offered a curt head bow and followed General Kale out.

Her dismissal signaled the meeting's end. Cardinals and Guards filed out, back to their separate headquarters. The handful of Inquisitors stood in a knot, whispering among themselves. None dared moved. The blue fringes of their rose emblems were almost drowned out by the darkness of their uniforms. Wholly subservient to Nye, they represented the vile core of his corrupt influence. Falling silent at his approach, they snapped to attention. A lethal group salivating to carry out their next assignments.

"You risk pulling us all down with your defiance," Cardinal Arbalas said with a scowl. Her jowls quivered. The representative from planet Comfor had initially aligned with Nye and his power grab, now she saw the truth behind their situation. Each day the remnants of the Conclave lost power, influence, and longevity. Falling further would have the nightmare become inescapable. She was forced to realign her allegiances just to survive.

Cardinal Shri threw up her hands. "What more can I do? We stand on the brink of annihilation! How much more can we stand before it is our heads in the noose? Control is now with regional Inquisitors while our clergy remain behind locked doors."

Seated on plush cushions across the room, Cardinal Porii Daam frowned. The lines on her forehead furrowed, accenting her already worn looks. "Perhaps more of us should have considered this before jumping in with Alain Nye. Was serving alongside Lorenu Phos so bad we betrayed our ideals for a lie?"

"Arguing amongst ourselves is pointless at this stage. Any ideations we once held for our futures are rendered moot by the dissolution of the Forum," Cardinal Amest Hour said. His voice was drawn, almost rasping. "This is the time to remember our divine purpose and return to our flock. Now more than ever is our influence needed."

"Cut the shit, Amest! The gods aren't real. We invented them in the aftermath of the war and decided to keep it from the population. Should this truth get out, we would be equally rounded up and executed. Do not underestimate the masses. They are base and wicked," Arbalas snapped.

"They are our sole purpose for existing," Amest countered. "If more of us remembered that we might not be in this position."

"Tell that to poor Iden Vis or Quo Kalk," Porii Daam snorted. "Or did you conveniently forget the images of them being burned alive for their crimes against the people? These are perilous times. How we act is as important as when. Alain Nye is the most calculating man I've ever encountered. Ruthless and venomous, he has shown his willingness to destroy anyone who crosses him. I would very much like to continue breathing."

Amest gave her a dour look. His lower jaw quivered, teeth grinding. "You suggest we abandon our principles and allow him to ruin the universe?"

"I am suggesting self-perseverance. My stance on the Inquisitor General is well known. I have not reserved it," she jutted her chin out, "and the only way to survive this war is through cunning. We make Nye see us for what he needs, not who we are."

"How is this accomplishable without betraying our charge?" Arbalas questioned as the fabric of all she stood for threatened to tear, irrevocably unraveling until naught remained but the haunting memories of unrealized dreams.

Shri waved off her concerns. "Nye cares little for the common citizens. What he requires to assume total control is the Guard and Conclave working for him. The sooner this war ends the sooner the seven hundred worlds can return to their normal lives."

"Six hundred and ninety-nine," Amest countered. "You forget Kharsis too easily. Should their sacrifice have been for naught?"

"I doubt any knew why they died, or how," Porii Daam said. "Amest, we must take steps to ensure our Order survives this. We are weak and becoming more so each day. Sooner or later we will break and then it will be too late."

"I must think on this. If there is a way forward that both secures our positions *and* allows for the people to thrive, we must find it," he replied. "What of Tinnus Har? Who do you suppose Nye will promote to replace him?"

A twinkle in her dark eyes, Porii Daam faked a yawn. "Who says he is dead?"

FIVE

3215 A.G. (After gods), spaceport Erdef City, planet Romalle.

The shuttle cleared orbital security and proceeded down to the surface. Ragan Sandinsol stared out the viewport with the wide eyes of a child. His life on Rastarok showed him just how backward he'd been raised. His people believed theirs was the premier world in the universe. Oh how wrong they'd been! Compared to what he'd witnessed since leaving, Rastarok was primitive at best. The Abby of the Blood Witches. The Great Library of Wexanos. Now the oceans and forest continents of Romalle. Ragan marveled at all he saw and vowed to spend the rest of his life exploring the universe once this awful war finished.

Watching him from across the hull, Tolde Breed failed to keep the smile from his face. It felt good to see the youth with wonder in his gaze again. How long had it been since he felt similar? Decades at least. A life in service of the Inquisition robbed him of innocence. If, by protecting the boy as much as possible, he ensured at least one other discovered a quality life of meaning and purpose he considered his personal torment worthwhile. Yet for as much as he found himself liking Ragan, he couldn't fathom what purpose the boy had to play.

"Strap yourselves in, we are preparing to land," Luma Kai called from the pilot chair.

Tolde checked his harness and closed his eyes. He hadn't seen his brother in years and, now that he was dead, Tolde struggled with the unfamiliar host of emotions assailing him. The last of his bloodline, avenging Leganas became a necessity. It fell to Tolde to conduct a thorough investigation in conjunction with Romalle's current Inquisitor, and pray he was either unaligned with Nye's view or indifferent else their quest was all in vain.

"Are you certain this will work?" Tolde asked the Blood Witch.

A pencil thin eyebrow raised. "You doubt my magic?"

"Not necessarily, but you have to understand how uneasy this makes me," he admitted.

Alessandra shifted. "The glamour will hold so long as I deem it. To all you meet you will appear in your old form. Those who know you will see the man they know, not your new guise."

Her silence ended the conversation. Tolde, far from satisfied, settled back into his seat and prepared for planetfall. The shuttle touched down without incident. City security and customs officials waited, arms with datapads and paperwork awaiting stamps, citations, and clearances. Officially here on Inquisition business, or so Tolde claimed in his landing requests, the occupants were spared much of the standard procedures other spacefarers suffered.

The customs agent handed the datapad to the next in line and reeled upon seeing a Blood Witch flow down the ramp. Her gossamer robes shimmered in the midmorning sun. Known by reputation, she watched the locals sign themselves for protection with amusement as she passed. Tolde straightened the wrinkles from his jacket and followed.

Face blanched, the customs agent gestured for the waiting security personnel to begin their inspection of the interior.

"Senior Inquisitor Breed of the Office of Heretical Persecution," Tolde announced and waited. His mind raced back to what he knew of the planet and the man he would be forced to work with. He cared little for Romalle's Inquisitor, and it was not a stretch to believe the man's loyalty lied with the Order but chose to trust in his brother's judgment. The last time Tolde and Gando crossed paths ended in debate threatening violence.

Tongue flicking over his lower lip, the agent said, "Ah, yes, sir. We have received word of the Cardinal's passing. A tragedy. My men will be done shortly, and you and your party will be on your way."

"Thank you," Tolde said. Luma Kai and Ragan joined him. "Where can I find the local Inquisitor?"

"He's right here."

Tolde looked over the agent's shoulder and saw a slender man in an Inquisition uniform heading toward them. Sleek and freshly pressed, the Inquisitor was a visible example of what they all should have aspired to. Filled with regret, he steadied his breathing and, desperate to keep his emotions in check, strode forward to meet his counterpart while struggling with how to explain his change of appearance.

"Welcome to Romalle, Senior Inquisitor. Your brother was a … a friend of sorts," Gando greeted while extending his hand.

Any reluctance Tolde felt during their journey from Wexanos lessened, thawed by Gando's demeanor. The expected Prekhauten squad lurking behind the nearest building failed to materialize, but he still wasn't willing to trust the other man, yet. He'd been in enough foul situations where wolves grinned like sheep, their blades tucked behind them in wait.

"Thank you for sending word of my brother," he replied and clasped forearms with Gando. "I would like to see the body if possible."

Gando's gaze fell on the Blood Witch and he swallowed hard. "Are you expecting trouble? Your comrades are unusual to say the least."

"They have stood beside me for many years now. I trust them with my life," Tolde assured then gestured to the others. "Allow me to introduce Sister Alessandra of the Order of the Blood Witches. She has proven invaluable to my charge on many occasions. Next to her is Inquisitor Luma Kai. We have worked together since I joined the Office of Heretical Persecution. No finer companion could I ask for. And this young man is Ragan Sandinsol. Our paths crossed on a mission last year and we could not be parted after. Perhaps a potential Inquisitor if he tries hard enough."

"A pleasure, all of you," Gando's gaze returned to Sister Alessandra. "Welcome to Romalle, though I wish it were under different circumstances. I fear losing our Cardinal invites a plague of trouble I cannot handle without aide."

"Was a request put through with Vau Prime?" Luma asked.

"No. I thought it best to contact Leganas' brother directly," Gando explained. "There are certain matters that should be discussed in private. That and I do not believe this is a matter for the Conclave to become involved in, all things considered."

"Has Romalle not declared for either side in the war?" Sister Alessandra asked. Her voice carried mirth laced with an undertone of violence.

Gando studied her for a moment before answering. "No, Sister. The City Board stands uncommitted on the issue. Thus far we have remained out of the purview of Krenz, but it is a matter of time before our hand is forced. For now, an uneasy peace reigns, though I fear those days are closing. With your brother's murder our opponents are becoming brazen. Soon there will be riots. Open declarations for the war."

"Which side do you stand on?" Tolde was prepared to take his team back to the shuttle and never look back, brother or no.

Gando stiffened. "I have yet to decide. There is merit in both arguments. Thankfully the continued neutrality of Romalle offers me protection. No man should be forced to choose between duty and liberty."

Tolde nodded, slight and imperceptible to all but Alessandra. He caught the flicker of magic fade from her fingertips. "I am satisfied with that answer, for now. We have no desire to be dragged into local socio-political operations and even less for the war."

"Pardon me, Senior Inquisitor, but your name is synonymous with this war," Gando blurted. "You are a legend in our ranks. Many of us have aspired to follow in your footsteps, for they ring with greatness. The only man to face down one of the Three, twice, and live to tell it!"

"Legends are always exaggerated, Gando," Tolde admonished quietly.

Gando's cheeks reddened. "Your deeds are an inspiration to many Inquisitors. It is an honor to have you here, though I wish circumstances were different."

The security team disembarked the shuttle and scurried off, attempting to avoid the scrutiny of the Inquisition. The custom agent that greeted them followed close behind.

"Are tensions high among the populace? That agent didn't seem too eager to be around us," Luma observed, watching them march away.

"More like they don't trust me," Gando replied. "Tensions continue rising. Your brother's death did little to calm nerves. Between the mounting pressure to pick a side in a war that has yet to reach our planet and the growing influence of the criminal movement we are beleaguered on all sides. I do not relish the struggle to come. It is my hope that by solving this murder quickly we can restore a semblance of order and stability to Romalle. Otherwise…"

Implications hanging in the air, Gando gestured toward his transport. "It would be best if we continued this discussion away from prying eyes."

Tolde's eyes narrowed. "Is there the possibility of open assault?"

"My gut tells me no, but with the Cardinal's death anything is possible," Gando replied. "Please, this way."

Riles Tenaru watched the new arrivals drive off toward the city and leaned back into the rusted metal siding. Her thoughts raced upon seeing a Blood Witch. They were the nightmares of legend. Monsters who stole children and did whatever they saw fit in the name of a cause outside the restrictions of humanity. She'd never seen one, nor had anyone she knew. The glowing robes and the way the witch drifted over the ground sent chills rippling through her.

"Did you see that?" she asked, her voice breathless. "A real Blood Witch."

Nemineon stifled a yawn at her side. "I thought they didn't exist." He grunted when her elbow slammed into his ribs.

"Fool. You never take enough seriously. This is big, Nemineon."

"How so? You're still on the run, or did you forget?" he asked. "Sooner or later the authorities will find you. If the killers don't first."

Face twisting, Riles ran a fingertip over her bottom lip. There was something familiar about one of the newcomers. As if she'd seen him before. The image remained blurred, lingering on the edges of recognition and anonymity.

"I know that," she snapped. Her gaze lingered until the vehicle was lost from sight. "I need help and my options are limited."

"I've already told you to go to the investigators and clear your name," Nemineon countered.

"And turn myself in? Are you mad? They have no suspects, at least none they're broadcasting. If I walk into their office now, I'll never see the sun again."

She began pacing. Whispers circulated the underground; rumors of war and the closing jaws of justice sweeping through the city. Riles seldom placed faith in hearsay, leaving it for what it was; boredom. Cancerous, rumors carried the ability to cripple a society. She'd seen it before. The last one of consequence left a swath of destruction throughout the capitol city, including scores dead. Would the same occur over her? Dismissing her thoughts as ridiculous, Riles knew there was no connection, logical or supposed, between the slain Cardinal and herself. Why then the guilt?

"Come on, I have an idea," she said, pausing midstride.

Nemineon saw the fervor shining in her eyes. "Good. It's getting cold. What are we doing?"

"We need to see Lady DeMauve," Riles said.

Choking, Nemineon wheezed, "Are you mad?"

"She's the only one who can help."

Emmest DeMauve was well regarded among the criminal element as well as the common citizenry. It was said, though never to her face, that she dabbled in dark magic or elemental sorcery. Riles didn't care about any of that. DeMauve had her fingers in almost every major action on Romalle since the civil war began. Riles liked to think the older woman was a major reason the planet had thus far avoided committing to either side. If anyone was capable of helping Riles escape her nightmare it was Lady DeMauve.

Nemineon in tow, Riles hurried back to their aircar and, she prayed for the end of her protracted misery. Something was approaching and though she didn't know what, she was shaken to her core.

Hargan threw his mug against the far wall, snarling with empty satisfaction as it dashed into a hundred pieces, dark brown liquid streaking down white paint. Two weeks had passed since Cardinal Breed was struck down in the streets, his streets, and no one in his office made even the slightest progress toward solving the case. No suspects. No clues. Nothing. If not for the decomposing body awaiting cremation, he'd have absolutely nothing to go on.

The board was breathing down his neck and Hargan knew nothing would never change unless a cataclysmic event developed under their watch. Which was precisely what the Cardinal's murder promised. Once word reached Vau Prime and what remained of the Conclave's power structure there would be swift retribution. It took little imagination to view squads of Prekhauten Guards and Inquisitors patrolling Erdef City. Any neutrality would be lost. Romalle would be plunged into the war with no regard for its citizenry.

Unable to reconcile his failure with the fate of the planet, Hargan needed help. The only man he trusted was the one he shouldn't. The Inquisition seldom put the needs of the planet first, choosing to follow doctrine by protecting against heresy or worse. Until recently, Inquisitors held little to no sway over local politics. The war changed that, transforming them from protectors to warders possessing far more power than was prudent. Fear trailed in their wake. The blood red roses tinged in blue becoming symbols of tyranny on a hundred worlds. That Inquisitor Gando remained outwardly neutral and committed to his original purpose was a testament to his character … or the greatest ruse ever pulled. Hargan decided prudence was in his best interests.

So where did that leave him?

In an empty office with far too many subordinates unwilling to enter out of fear they might say the wrong thing and set him off. Not that he blamed them. His outbursts, increasing as the days dragged on, were becoming the tirades of legend. None of his usual techniques panned out. Investigators swept through Erdef City, rounding up the usual suspects and putting pressure on their bosses. Smaller criminal elements sang away, knowing they were never in any danger of retribution. The larger bosses remained untouchable without Inquisitor backup and Gando was loath to get them involved.

Hargan ground his teeth, staring out the window overlooking the city's main avenue. Aircars and pedestrians mixed in an eclectic sea of humanity. All going about their day without concern for his dilemma and what it might mean to the planet. He envied them, if for no other reason than their ingrained indifference.

Frustrated with how life continued defeating him at every turn, he made a decision. "Bowley! Inform Inquisitor

Gando's office I am on my way," he barked, slipping into the weather worn tan jacket he pulled from the back of his chair. "And requisition me new cups. As many as you can."

Stepping into the morning light, Hargan left without waiting for a response. Outside, he popped a cigarillo in the corner of his mouth, once lit he inhaled the soothing smoke deep into his lungs. Gazing up, he took gauge of the small, scattered clouds, and decided to head off on foot. He stuffed his hands in his jacket pockets, lowered his head, and moved with deliberate purpose, trailing smoke.

A few pedestrians nodded or said good morning as he passed. He ignored them. Any other day Hargan would have reveled in the interaction, knowing that rapport had the power to save lives and prevent crimes. Today, he presented himself a man on a mission and more and more streamed aside rather than risk bumping into him or provoking his ire. Sometimes, he privately acknowledged, it paid being law enforcement.

Hargan arrived at the city center and the office of the Inquisition in no time. He took a final drag off the nicstick and tossed the butt into the storm drain.

Neon signs with flashing holographic messages lined the street offering products and services. He noticed with bemusement the largest one proclaimed how good the current City Board was for Erdef City and Romalle. Hargan reserved his doubts and strode into the office. Gando awaited him in the foyer.

"Hargan, to what do I owe the pleasure?" the Inquisitor asked and clasped his hands behind his back.

Thrown by the familiarity of the gesture, Hargan said, "We are going about this all wrong, Gando."

"Go on."

"I've spent incalculable resources on finding the killer and nothing. What we need to know is why the Cardinal was killed."

"You suspect he was poking his nose where it didn't belong?"

"It makes sense. The Conclave has ruled with impunity for generations. Who's to say they are all acting in our best interests?"

Unclasping his hands, Gando rubbed his temples. "Hargan, I respect your experience and though we may be from different circles I believe you are among the best in your field … but to accuse a Cardinal of corruption bears dire implications … There are some lines we do not cross."

Hargan held up a hand. "Now hold on, I'm not accusing anyone of anything. All I'm saying is we would be foolish to ignore the potentiality of it. No one is perfect, Gando. If I've learned one thing during my time wearing this badge, it is we all hold secrets."

"Secrets get people killed." Gando internally debated whether to divulge his to Hargan, but trust demanded more than fleeting encounters and pleasant words.

News of a second Inquisitor, in the company of a Blood Witch no less, should have immediately gone through the City Board rather than Gando's private communications. He walked a delicate balance. The fewer people in his circle the better, for the moment. Increased pressure from the Inquisition to declare Romalle for Alain Nye kept him preoccupied and unable to fully perform his duties. If Nye knew Gando acted without authority it might spark an invasion.

"Perhaps we should start by going directly to the crime bosses," he suggested after catching the glint of suspicion in Hargan's tired eyes.

"Are you mad? I want to solve this case, not wind up in the morgue beside him."

"As you intone, we are at an impasse. Time is running out to discover the killer. The Conclave will not sit idle once they learn one of their flock has been slain," Gando said. "The decision is yours, of course."

Lostan Fidiuos was a name synonymous with answers. He was the shadow between glances. A figment of imagination capable of shifting the balance when matters needed changing. He walked in the gaps between reality and myth. No question was beyond his reach. No answer unfathomable. Officially, he didn't exist. He was a name with no record. City Board members hunted him for years, wasting resources on a person they eventually deemed inconsequential to the direction they chose to take Romalle.

Sauntering into the dust filled front office of an abandoned shop forced to close doors during a recent economic recession, Lostan took the only seat available and waited. Rodents scurried in a knot in the far corner, scrambling over the scraps of one of their own. Bright red frothed on their lips and fangs. Lostan watched them with idle fascination, reminded of the striking similarities they had with humanity. Foul creatures of habit and inherent destruction, they represented the end of everything.

The door clicked open, and a shadow fell over the front of the shop. The setting sun transformed the dull tile a rich gold. Lostan sat at the edge, ever eager to step into the light but more comfortable in shadow. He watched and waited as his guest closed the door, folding his hands before him. Only the scrabble of claws on tile filled the air.

"What is the meaning of this?" his guest demanded. The assumed authority in his tone amused Lostan.

"The universe is changing. We are shifting down dark roads, Damal."

Flustered, the board member growled, "Speak plainly. You requested my presence, not the other way around. By all rights I should have you arrested and brought before the board on calls of treason."

"How is it treason if I declare no fealty to any ruling body? I remain outside of your politics for a reason, Damal," Lostan snorted. "Do not think to cow me with your empty threats. Not when I come bearing gifts."

"What gifts?"

"How the winds change! A moment ago you desired my head, now you yearn for my hidden knowledge," Lostan chided. "Humbling I would suggest, not being able to control every facet beneath you."

Damal ground his teeth. "You wear my patience thin, Lostan. Do not tempt me further. No one will mourn your passing."

Lostan spread his empty hands. "Yet would I truly be dead, or I am more than a single mortal man?" When Damal went to respond, he shook his head. "Nay, do not seek to answer that, you will only confound yourself in the process. No, Damal. There is no need for animosity. I bring you information freely in the hopes you will use it to ensure Romalle's continued neutrality."

"As if I can control that. War inches closer to our system. The Inquisitor General will see the universe burn until he secures his new empire," Damal replied, impatient. "What is this information you believe capable of saving us from destruction? And why should I believe you? Ever you have hidden from the world, playing factions off one another to your devious purpose."

"Devious? Dubious perhaps, but never devious. I don't have a wicked bone, Damal."

"I shall not warn you again. Say what you summoned me to say or I will devote every resource to burning your network down around you." Damal stiffened, hands clenching to fists that trembled in the fading light. The loose flesh of his jowls quivered.

It had been years since he last laid hands on another man, years in which he longed to feel the exhilaration of striking his opponent and hearing the cheers of the crowd as they basked in his victory. Born into a world he didn't belong, Damal slithered into politics thanks to those supporters who recognized his name and the empty promise he made of transforming Romalle into a paradise for everyone. The thought of pummeling Lostan Fidiuos to a bloody pulp heated his blood.

"All information comes with a price, Damal," Lostan said while feigning indifference. Worry filled him and, for once, he was thankful for the shadows.

"Speak your terms, *broker*," Damal demanded.

"I wish an audience with Chief Investigator Hargan."

Damal frowned. "That's it? Not like the man is hidden. Send the request through his offices. Easy as that."

"Nothing is ever that easy. Tell Hargan I have information concerning the death of our beloved Cardinal. News that could potentially unravel the fabric of our society should it go unacted upon."

Damal's mouth dropped open. Underground legends suggested Lostan was right far more than he was wrong. If there was even a chance his words carried meaning, Damal owed it to the people of Erdef City to protect them. He too stood to gain immeasurably once the dust settled. Romalle would finally join the war, sending thousands of sons and daughters to the frontlines in the name of the Inquisitor General. He would at last be able to extend his influence beyond the forgotten constraints of what he deemed an insignificant planet lost among the cosmos.

"I will take your summons to Hargan," Damal said with a curt nod.

"Do not fail me, Damal." Lostan's voice was low, almost a whisper when he added, "Or else."

True to his word, Hargan found Inquisitor Gando waiting at the temple's steps. Dressed in his uniform, Gando cut an imposing figure. A rash of jealousy passed through Hargan. The bitter investigator looked as rundown as he felt. Years of lines, dark spots on his skin, and almost leathered flesh complimented his faded clothes. He was perpetually tired. Drawn in too many directions with little to no way out. He needed to solve this murder, if for no other reason than to sit back and take a deep breath.

"Chief Investigator," Gando acknowledged.

Hargan grunted, tossing the remnants of his nicstick on the street. "Inquisitor. Shall we?"

Gando gestured toward the door as thunder cracked in the distance. "After you."

"Aren't you the gentleman," Hargan muttered, offering a false grin.

Gando shook his head. "Prudence, Hargan. The locals need to see you taking the lead, not an Inquisitor from Vau Prime. I am here for support only."

"Thank you, Gando."

They entered the temple—authority mixed with deference. A scattering of white robed priests turned their heads. Brown robed monks hurried to greet them, lest the senior priests reprimand them.

The stench of incense overpowered Hargan's senses. Two small bowls sat on ivory pedestals flanking the door. One was filled with water, the other blood. The monks bobbed and supplicated for him to leave until Gando stepped forth. A female priest took immediate notice of him and glided forward.

"Who's in charge here? We are on official City Board business," Hargan announced. His words echoed throughout the temple, turning heads, and causing a ripple of murmurs. An elder woman sidled over to them.

"Chief Investigator. Inquisitor. We welcome you to our humble temple. The gods bless you," she said. "I am Priestess Astrid. How may we be of service this evening?"

"I believe you know why we're here, Priestess." Hargan's voice rattled in his throat, making him sound gruffer than intended.

Making a show to reinforce his position, he placed a hand on the handle of his sidearm.

Astrid's eyes narrowed. "There is no cause for violence within these walls. The Conclave is an advocate for peace, as I'm sure you are well aware."

Hargan's gaze remained impassive. "So I've heard, but I have a dead Cardinal and no answers. Can't afford to take risks at this stage."

"You are suggesting one of us is responsible for Cardinal Breed's death?"

"Murder," Hargan corrected, noting her shock. "He was murdered in the streets like a stray dog."

Gasps circulated those in the temple.

The priestess watched him with veiled eyes. Her shock now hidden behind carefully constructed walls. Cursing his directness, Hargan shot a side glance at Gando.

"Priestess, my colleague does not mean to be gruff in this matter, but these are unprecedented times, as I'm sure you will agree," Gando said, stepping forward. "Our offices are working in conjunction to solve this heinous crime and restore a measure of confidence both to the priesthood and Romalle's citizens. It is a delicate balance threatening to cast us all into the confusion of oblivion."

Astrid's eyes went about the temple, scanning those closest. Heads lowered and she stiffened, rising to her full height. "This is not a matter to be discussed openly. Come, to my office, I shall have refreshments brought." She turned and marched off through the temple without waiting to see if they followed.

Hargan's eyebrow rose and he shared a glance with Gando before following. A last glance at the bowl of blood left him chilled. Gods. He'd never understand them.

Gando noted how the Chief Investigator kept his hand firmly on his sidearm but made no move to his own.

Astrid closed the door behind them and gestured to a pair of navy-blue cushioned chairs near a fireplace. Despite it being summer, a small fire crackled. Catching their stares, she flashed a smile. "It is often too cold within these walls for my liking, thus the fire. I am not mad, at least not yet."

"Comforting, Priestess," Hargan lied. "What can you tell of us the Cardinal? Did he have enemies? Anyone wanting to see him eliminated?"

"We are members of the Conclave. We are besieged by enemies. If not, there would be no need for the Inquisition," she replied. Her voice was flat. "Cardinal Breed was a good man. A kind man. He was not the best of us, but what he lacked he more than made up for with his zeal toward treating all with dignity and respect. He was a paragon of virtue far too many of us seem to have forgotten over these past few years."

"The war bothered him that much?" Hargan pressed, certain she was hiding a key element.

"Aren't you? This war is unnatural, forcing us to take sides against friend and family." Astrid hung her head. "It is no secret the Conclave's grasp on humanity is slipping. The power of the Inquisition grows, and we find our backs to the wall, unable to attend our flock while the universe burns."

Hargan scratched his chin. They all had problems. He wasn't learning anything new and suspected Astrid was leading him astray. "Priestess, let the war handle itself. We will deal with it if and when it reaches Romalle. I am more concerned with solving this crime and getting justice for Cardinal Breed. Was he behaving off in the last few weeks? Any change in emotions or how he handled himself? Can you give us anything?"

Pursing her lips, Astrid finally let out a sigh. "Cardinal Breed was one of the finest men I ever met, but he began meeting with less than favorable elements recently. He would often take off on his own despite our insistence for security." She shook her head, tears welling in her eyes. "There is one name you should check out, though I cannot promise results from it."

"Every little bit helps," Gando affirmed.

"Emmest DeMauve."

Hargan's eyes bulged. "She's a quack! What would the Cardinal need from her?"

"You'll have to ask her that, Investigator. Now, if you please, evening worship is set to begin. I would not have your presence scare away what remains of the faithful."

The meeting was over. They had no answers, but at least were given a direction to proceed. Something was better than nothing.

SIX

3215 A.G. (After Gods), Allied Army Headquarters, planet Mannus Prime.

Jelin Quint slowed his breathing. A veteran of many years, he found it amusing that standing before his commanding officer continually inspired a quickened pulse and unhealthy nerves. He smoothed his hand down over his uniform, careful to avoid messing up his ribbons and medals. No matter how many times he'd been forced to wear the dress uniform, Jelin failed to enjoy it. Give him utilities any day.

Dignitaries, visiting planetary officials, and ranking officers came and went with increasing frequency as the planet continued strengthening its war output. Gazing up, Jelin made out thousands of grey hulks skimming above the clouds as the navy grew. Soon, he guessed, they would be able to take the war to the thugs choosing to serve the Inquisitor General.

An orderly popped his head into the foyer and gestured. "Sergeant Quint, the general will see you now."

Jelin blew out the breath choking his lungs and headed inside. He found General Torgast seated behind a desk overflowing with datapads, paper reports, and more. No wonder staff officers were perpetually grumpy. How was anyone expected to go through this much information on a daily basis? Jelin suppressed a knowing grin lest he incurred Torgast's ire and find himself spending the night going through reports.

"Ah, Jelin," Torgast tossed a datapad aside and looked up. His smile was genuine. "I understand you have an urgent matter to discuss?"

Rumors, whispers among the junior officers and noncoms, had already reached his ears but Torgast knew he needed to hear it from Jelin's own mouth as much as the man needed to say it. To his credit, Jelin remained at the position of attention without so much as a flinch.

"Well, sir, it's like this—I don't belong here. You picked me up when I needed it the most, and for that I'll be forever grateful, but I belong back on the line. Office politics and dealing with people isn't in my wheelhouse. I figure since you got that promotion and have more staff than anyone can need you wouldn't miss me if I headed back to an infantry unit."

Impressed with the held eye contact, Torgast sank back into his chair and clasped his hands together. "You think it will be safer out there?"

"No, sir, but its where I can do the most good. I figure this war is just ramping up. I've seen the measure of our enemy and how far our allies will go to secure peace," Jelin said. "If I can be part of that again and do some good it would be wrong of me to hide behind these walls."

"Not to mention you've already been offered a position with the infantry unit who came to our aid," Torgast remarked. "You are an impressive man, Jelin Quint. Would the rest of my command have half the courage you display this war might already be over."

Their time together on Mannus was bittersweet, Torgast often thought over what had transpired in the passing months. Jelin Quint was part of the soul of the army, but he knew the man was stifled in a staff position. "Very well. Permission granted. You've been a boon at my side, Jelin. I won't deny missing you, but we need to be where our heart is most content."

"Thank you, sir. It has been something."

Torgast rose and crossed the room, extending his hand. "It has been my honor serving with you. What you did…"

Jelin accepted his hand. "Was my job, sir. Nothing more."

Studying the sergeant, Torgast dragged his tongue over the back of his teeth. "As you say. Now, unless I can convince you otherwise, you'd best draw gear and report to your new platoon before they start to question your character."

"Yes, sir."

Torgast stopped him as he prepared to leave. "Are you sure this is the unit you want to join?"

Jelin smiled and left.

"Sergeant Annalilly, a word," Fies called over the endless banter gripping his platoon. He slipped back into the tent after spying her rise and head his way.

Orderlies shuffled about, ignoring their commanding officer as he plopped down on the field chair and waited.

Waiting. That's all they seemed to be doing these days.

Not that he minded. The platoon had been at the tip of the spear since the war began, even without knowing it, and they deserved every day off they received. Only the longer a line unit sat idle the rustier they became. Most of the troops were battled hardened veterans. The rookies and weak had been culled through baptism of fire along the way. Those who remained he trusted with his life. They were, in his estimation, the very best the Prekhauten Guard had to offer.

Fies rubbed his eyes. After years in the field, bouncing from planet to planet, waging war in jungles, deep space, and more, he found himself getting too much sleep. They needed a change, and soon. Command continued delaying, either unwilling to commit to another campaign or unable to find one with favorable odds. None of that concerned him. Fies needed a fight. Now.

Annalilly slipped into the tent and saluted, more for the orderlies than respect. "What's up, LT?"

"How is Haggle panning out as squad sergeant?"

Annalilly shifted, understanding it was about to be one of *those* talks. "Well enough, considering we're not doing anything on this rock. Why?"

"Is he capable of leading those troops in battle? Be honest."

A twinkle brightened her eyes. "Are we expecting?"

He shook his head. "No one's told me anything but you never know. There are a lot of restless folks here. It won't be long before we get deployment orders. No, I need to know if Haggle is a Kastor, or even Jers."

Flashes of Kastor, lying dead in the grasslands of Crimeat distracted Annalilly. She'd looked up to the man and had watched him be slain by a fellow Guardsman. His loss perpetuated a rash of promotions, culminating with her taking the platoon sergeant job. Advancing through the ranks was the goal of every noncom, but it always came with a price. Faces and names checkered her past, trailing behind like welcoming ghosts eager to reunite. Annalilly focused on the men and women still with her.

"Haggle is a good man, you know that, but I don't want his first leadership position to be one in combat,"

Annalilly finally said and exhaled. "The trouble is I don't have the right person to replace him."

"How about a lateral transfer to assistant squad leader?" Fies offered.

She placed her hands on her hips, squaring on him. "What do you have in mind?"

"It just so happens Sergeant Quint's official orders have come through. Guess he's had enough of riding a desk. He should be here any moment now."

She wanted to slap the smugness from his face. "What are you playing at?"

The tent flap pushed back and Jelin Quint stepped in. "Sir, Staff Sergeant Quint reporting for duty."

"You are the last person I expected to see after turning us down earlier," Annalilly told him as they marched through the bivouac area. "Finally got the old man to cut you loose?"

Burdened by a ruck sack on his chest and a duffle bag on his back, Jelin huffed. "It wasn't the general. This was all my doing. I'm wasted behind a desk."

"Thought you were done with the whole war thing after, you know."

Rather than taking offense, Jelin said, "I was. Seeing all your friends and comrades die around you is a recurring nightmare threatening to drive me mad, but I can't allow it to hold me back. One day, when this war is finished, I might go find a head doctor and see what he can do, if I make it that far. Until then, I'm here to keep as many of your people alive as possible." He shifted his weight. "Anything else you need to know?"

"Not at the moment. Here is the noncom tent. Grab an empty bunk." She drew the flap back, motioning him inside. "Once you drop your gear, I'll introduce you to the platoon."

Jelin ducked inside and selected an empty bunk close to the door. A scattering of bags and kit lay about. Makeshift laundry lines with a few jackets and trousers hanging ran the width. It was a homecoming—back on the line where he belonged. The smell of soldiers in the field, though this was considered garrison, wafted up to him. This he understood.

Grinning, Jelin shouldered his rifle and returned to Annalilly who waited just outside the tent flap. "Why are you in tents instead of buildings?"

"What? You expecting room service and a fancy hotel?" she fired back. "This is where command put us, and we don't question. We get three hots a day and a dry roof over our heads. And as far as accommodations go, this isn't the worst. Besides, most of us are itching to get back in the fight. I'm assuming that's why you couldn't take it up on staff."

"You got that right. I owe General Torgast my life, in more ways than one, but I'm no commander. I need to be around the troops to feel alive," he admitted. "How long as your unit been on the line?"

"Our unit," she corrected. "You need to start thinking of this as home. The sooner you get that through the sooner these fools will start respecting you. We've been in it since the beginning. Shit, before the beginning. We were the unit on Crimeat who discovered the first rogue Guard elements."

"What did you do to them?" he asked. Much of the early days of the war were deemed classified and, unless you happened across a veteran of the day, went unreported to most of the Guard.

Her expression hardened. "Killed as many as we could and sent the rest off in chains to spend the war in a prison camp."

Before he could reply, she changed the subject with, "Here we are."

The platoon was sprawled out before them in small groups. One squad was in the middle of a briefing while the others were more relaxed. Several Guards slept in the cool grass, hands behind their heads and patrol caps pulled down over their faces to block out the sun. A few cleaned weapons while others sharpened blades or ate a packaged meal. Jelin assumed they all would be more laid back considering no immediate orders were forthcoming. What did they know that he didn't? Or were they that wound up?

"Haggle," Annalilly barked.

Jelin watched a slightly overweight sergeant pop up and head their way. The look on his face suggested he already knew what was about to happen, and Jelin didn't envy him that.

"Sergeant Quint, this is Haggle. Right now he's filling in as squad leader and you'll be taking his position," Annalilly explained. "No hard feelings, Haggle, but I need the right people in the right positions."

To her relief, Haggle extended a hand to Jelin. "You're not hearing me complain. I like these guys but dealing with all their problems, wants, and needs is too much. I'll happily take my place back in the squad. Nice to meet you, Sergeant."

"You too," Jelin gripped his hand, confused by the deference. What was the point of getting promoted if you didn't want the responsibility?

Annalilly frowned. "You're not getting off the hook that easy, Haggle. Jers quitting put us all in a bind. Quint here may be taking over but I need you to back him up. You're assistant squad leader. Help him fit in."

"Roger that." Haggle bobbed his head. "I'll go round up the troops."

They watched him go.

"He's a good man," Annalilly said. "Been with us since the beginning, but he's clinging to a misplaced sense of sentimentality—Jers was his best friend. I think Haggle feels like most of us, slightly lost and rundown. There's only so much a line unit can bend before it breaks. You'll need him to win over the others."

"That bad?"

"You've been around. What Guard unit welcomes a change of leadership without putting the new guy to the test?" she replied. "You'll be fine. I don't have any doubt about that. Settle in, field your squad. Lieutenant has an evening meeting with all squad leaders at dinner chow. Don't be late."

She left him to the hungry stares of his new squad. Jelin Quint didn't know if he was predator or prey.

"You wanted to see me, Sergeant Major?" Fies asked as he entered the office Matthias accommodated in the aftermath of the invasion.

The retired Matthias, still trying to determine what the point of retiring was if he continued to be on the front lines of the war, glowered at him. "Damn it, Fies. How many times do I have to tell you that's not my title anymore?"

"Old habits," the lieutenant taunted with a grin. "Besides, none of us have figured out what to call you, officially."

"Matthias is the name I was given, as I've told you numerous times."

"You know that doesn't feel right," Fies quipped. "Just because you're not in uniform doesn't mean you don't get respect. I didn't want this bar on my collar either, yet here I am."

"A promotion well deserved," Matthias retorted. "Anyway, we can debate the merits of rank and authority all night long. I have something more important to discuss. This comes from the top."

A gnawing sensation crawled through Fies' stomach as he slid into the empty chair. "I'm not going to like this, am I?"

"I'd be concerned if you did … We've received a request from the governess of Dalafar. She is asking for an extraction. It seems her planet has fallen to the Inquisitor General's forces, and they are systematically eliminating those who were in power, and their families. Moscasco is considered influential among the higher ups and could bring weight to our fight. She has been deemed a priority target."

"When did the Guard care about internal politics? This governess shouldn't be our problem."

"She is if she's capable of rallying scores of planets, and their resources, to our side," Matthias said. "Fies, this could be the moment we've been waiting for. Extract her and we open an entire new front. It might shift momentum back to us."

Fies found it odd to think this way after their impossible victory here. He had to remind himself the universe was massive, and the war stretched across hundreds of planets. With the Three in play, seizing any advantage could mean the difference between victory or defeat.

"What do I need to do?"

"Glad to hear you volunteer," Matthias said. "I want you to select twelve people. There will be a shuttle waiting for you in five days. Your mission is to infiltrate Dalafar and rescue the governess without direct engagement. We're not going there for a shooting war. This is off the books and under the table. No unnecessary killing, am I clear?"

"Clear enough, though I don't imagine too many of my people will embrace your attitude. They were hoping for another fight."

Matthias tapped his fingertips on the desk. "That's your problem to adjust. I'm not ordering anyone to avoid confrontation, just tone down the fighting so it doesn't follow you back here."

"I suppose we can do that," Fies admitted, reservation lingering in his tone.

"I know, that's why I chose you. Figure out what you need and draw it from supply. They give you any problems let me know. Anything you need or want for this one is yours."

"It'll be like a birthday present." Fies beamed. "Are we in uniform or no?"

"No."

"Just like our trip to the Gate." Fies prayed this mission turned out better than their ill-fated infiltration on the space station.

"Go and select your team. I'm not going to tell you how to run your platoon, but you know who to pick. You report directly to me."

The shuttle docked with a jarring thud. Sharlyn August stared out the viewscreen at the scarred and battered bulk of her cruiser. Like the rest of her people, the *Solstice* had seen better days. She suspected soldiers on both sides were in desperate need of a break. The human mind could only sustain so much trauma before it shut down. She'd seen it before, walking shells of human beings staring deep into nothing. Others couldn't move, paralyzed by nightmares. The screams and cries of agony rattled her the most, enough that she prayed to never have to endure what these frontline troops faced.

August shook off her fatigue, the hunt for Presha Von and the planet killer artefact left her drained emotionally and physically and she longed for the day her precious *Solstice* was repaired and refit.

The pneumatic hiss of fresh air pumping into the shuttle announced their docking was complete. Hatches unsealed and the artificial light of the newly constructed space station flooded the gloom of the shuttle. August exited first, smoothing out the wrinkles of her uniform as she went.

Rear Admiral Falchi awaited, unusual for any senior officer, with a squad of armored Marines flanking him. Their lowered visors reflected the dull grey paneling while reinforcing the severity of the situation. Each held their charged rifles at the ready.

"Captain August, it is a pleasure seeing you again," Falchi greeted. He peered over her shoulder, eager for a glimpse of the prisoner.

August saluted then paused. All the words she'd once laid out during the anguish filled moments after losing her quarry and the long journey through space suddenly fleeing her. "Admiral, I—"

Falchi held up a hand. "Forget about it. If we were true masters of our fates, she'd never have been allowed to commit those foul deeds now synonymous with her name. There will come a time when she rears her head again and we must be prepared."

Shoulders sagging as the tension left, August admitted, "Sir, I fear Presha Von might never resurface. She seemed broken."

For a senior officer to struggle with the urge to explain failure spoke volumes of her character, prompting Falchi to acknowledge he'd made the right decision when assigning her to the task. The matter dealt with, for the time being, he turned his attention to the troop of Marines deboarding.

"Where is our friendly pirate lord now?" Falchi asked as the door hissed shut after the last Marine stepped through.

"I don't know. He said he'd had enough and was going to find a quiet planet to rethink his life," August answered. "Sir, I think Blackheart is a good man deep inside. His crew kept us alive when we needed them most."

"Not to mention his involvement on Kharsis … Perhaps Blackheart is merely reshuffling his priorities and waiting to see how the dust settles before playing his hand. I doubt we have seen the last of him."

She couldn't decide whether that was good or not. Events over the last few years showed her a universe burdened with rot. Good and evil were inconsistent ideals often blurring into a matter of perspective based on the moment rather than the situation. August's own perceptions had changed since being assigned to hunt Von down.

August wondered if Von was a willing participant in the evil she wrought or a misguided soul looking for validation. The ghosts of Kharsis might argue differently. They never had a chance. She killed them all without regard and continued showing little remorse. Surely such a soul festered with hatred. How else could one justify the murder of millions?

Falchi started walking, leading August to a viewing parlor from where they could see continuing construction efforts and the planet below.

Crews worked around the clock to prepare Mannus Prime's defenses. In the cold of space, nestled in high orbit and surrounded by the wreckage of ruined ships, several space stations and battle forts were either nearing completion or being armed for war. Hundreds of ships choked the sector, friendly forces streaming in from beleaguered battlefronts or seeking to join the cause. Falchi took comfort in knowing millions of citizens were tired of the rampant oppression and were willing to fight for their values. He also knew just as many were flocking to the enemy's cause, providing a delicate edge.

"Where is the planet killer?"

Clearing her throat at his abrupt question, August stared, marveling at how many ships and what kinds were present. "It is secure in one of my weapon lockers."

"The longer that weapon remains unsecure the higher the risk for us all. As soon as we can return it Tannus the better. Then perhaps we can focus on this," Falchi gestured to the growing fleet.

"The last time I saw this many ships was during a cadet tour of the shipyards," she admitted.

"Fascinating, isn't it? I find it a humble reminder of just how small we all are. This war is exposing certain truths, Sharlyn. We are forced to confront who we are versus what we might become. The lies of a generation have corrupted so many in power. Now that Amongeratix is making his move we are sore pressed to respond."

"Lord Tannus was unable to stop him?"

Falchi shook his head. "Amongeratix has regained command of his ship and has razed the manufactories of Terotis. Together with his contingent of rogue Blood Witches he now threatens every star system in the known universe."

She took a deep breath. "What are my orders?"

"No rush to decompress, refit, and relax?"

A hint of crimson flushed her cheeks when his eyebrows arched. "Sir, this war isn't going to end with good troops sitting on a beach."

"No, it's not. Walk with me," he bade and started walking.

They passed a host of maintenance drones, work crews shuffling between shifts, and personnel from numerous ships of the line. August remained impressed with the immensity of what Falchi had cobbled together. Then she spied the massive carrier looming on the sunside of the facility.

"The Admiral is here?" she mused.

Falchi followed her gaze. No matter how often he laid eyes on the *Revengence* his heart thundered. She represented the best they had to offer. A beacon others flocked to. If only he had a hundred more perhaps then the tide of naval engagements might shift the balance of the war.

"She is. In fact, all staff officers and above are expected to attend a formal dinner reception in two nights. It promises to be a grand event."

August winced. Never one for the classic military dog and pony show, she struggled to find an excuse to leave port. "I'll take that assignment if you please, sir."

His thin smile dug creases across his face. "I'm tempted to join you, but alas, being an Admiral has many disadvantages." He laughed. "Very well, Captain. I have an assignment already awaiting you. Lord Tannus has directed the artifact be sent to him on Wexanos. Seeing as how you already have it secure and are familiar with the device the job is yours."

She swallowed. The prospect of standing before one of the vaunted Three made her tremble. Terrible beings of wrath and legend they were, and she was now destined to have audience with one.

"I shall inform the crew," she said, privately thankful to avoid playing dress up with the other officers.

"Very well," Falchi said. "You leave in three days."

Frozen wastes of planet Antil IV.

Akin Brohl stared out across the unending landscape of pristine white. Drifts blew across the plains nestled amidst the backdrop of snow-covered mountains. He felt the chill through the aged hull, laden with the promise of a quick death should he venture forth unprepared. Long had it been since his exposure to natural elements and the god hunter felt the first hints of trepidation emerging. Raw nerves did little to slow his growing bloodlust, for this was the lair of the universe's most notorious monster. The prospect of eliminating Amongeratix for good imbued him with strength and renewed purpose. He couldn't keep the grin from stretching across his face.

Unclipping his safety harness, Akin slipped into the small cargo hold and began fitting his weapons and gear. An assortment of blades slipped into oiled leather pouches. A pair of energy pistols strapped around his waist, spare power packs filling the magazine holders. Draping the sling of a dual barrel projectile rifle over his shoulders, he grabbed the final piece of his assortment. The spear was shining silver and seven feet tall. Impossibly sharpened, the tip had never gone dull or lost luster. He alone knew the secrets of forging. He alone had been gifted with its use. How many godlings fell to it was lost to time. Even he had forgotten.

Satisfied he was prepared, Akin pulled the lined hood over his head, nestled the reflective goggles over his eyes, and set out into a world of snow and ice.

Bitter winds greeted him. Plumes of breath stretched forth, momentarily freezing on the frigid air before falling to the ground. Experienced on a hundred planets, Antil was unlike anything he had seen. Cold penetrated his gear, burrowing deep in his bones. Frowning, he needed to find access to the villain's castle before he froze to death. The clock was already against him.

Akin checked the rangefinder on his wrist and set off at a jog, understanding the dangers of exertion. Any sweat he produced would quickly turn to ice the moment he slowed. Hypothermia threatened swift demise should he fail.

How long he ran he didn't know, though the sun was already dropping behind the distant mountains before he spied the icy walls of Amongeratix's keep. Flexing his trigger finger, Akin hurried to cover behind one of the large cropping of boulders peppering the landscape. He waited but there was no sign of life. Was the monster already dead? The prospect of missing the opportunity to remove his greatest target …

The only true way of knowing whether the beast was within was by closing and finding a way inside. Akin rose, drawing a deep breath. The cold burned his lungs. His body was becoming sluggish.

Temperatures plummeted. There was no way he'd make it back to his ship before nightfall, leaving him with but one option. He readied to sprint across the last hundred meters before spying a single red footprint. Akin knelt before it, scanning the plain for others. The surrounding landscape remained pristine however, prompting him to examine the print further. His heart skipped a beat as he realized what he was staring at.

Much larger than a man, the print was filled with a still liquid red substance. He smiled without testing it. There was but one thing it could be—blood. A new target for him. One he had run across before. A new game about to begin. Ultimately, he cared little for whichever god presented itself to his rifle. They all needed to die, but the opportunity to sack one of the Three meant more.

"I see you, Sorrow, and I am coming."

Snow picked up, driving down with unprecedented force. The winds swirled funnels of powder through the rocks. A tremor deep in the earth forced him to stabilize himself. Akin had seen this reaction before. The planet knew he was here and knew what foul deed he was prepared to commit. Regardless of the righteousness behind it, murder was still murder. And Antil IV was unprepared to witness the death of its master.

Alone save for the musings of what had devolved into a lunatic, the cold confines of the ship mocked all she once stood for. Presha Von struggled with many deeds, perhaps none so much as the death of her father. No, not death. What she'd done was murder. Patricide. She'd never gotten along with him, not from her earliest memories. The disappointment of being born a daughter echoed in his actions, forming the core of who she was and what she would one day become. The travesty of it encircled her like a comforting blanket and refused to let her go lest she gained a measure of confidence capable of escaping the past.

Knees drawn, arms wrapped around them, Presha lowered her head and cried. Not for the loss of her father, but for the death of hope. She knew she would never again find the grace to be accepted. An outcast, the former Lady Von was doomed to wander the universe a monster of unprecedented proportions. There was no forgiveness for her deeds. She understood that, even if there was no way she could have known how grave they might have turned out. Her mother once warned her that no good could come from dealing with the gods for theirs was a vengeful cycle. Presha scoffed at the time, believing she knew best. It was the frailty of all children to think they knew more than their parents. Rather than come to an awakening, Presha barreled into adulthood thinking hers was the way.

"Are you finished lamenting your deeds?" Geres Auk's rumbling voice ground into her head before she could spiral, again.

She sighed. "Leave me, Geres Auk, lest you too fall under the sway of a madwoman synonymous with doom."

He scoffed. "You are a fool—I have been shown the way and it is one filled with glory. You shall see. We are bound for destiny's embrace."

"Fool am I?" She raised her head, glaring behind a veil of tears. "It was I, not you, who killed a planet. My dreams led to the desecration of life. A deed from which I shall never atone. Who is Geres Auk but a steppingstone for others? A puppet the strong use to achieve their goals? Go away. Leave me to my torments, for they serve me well." She lowered her head, unwilling to continue her spat with the savage.

Geres slammed a meaty fist into the nearest wall and bellowed. "Do not mock me, girl. I once swore my services to you, but those times are ending. I have new purpose. A new master to follow. One who will not treat me as a dog for his beck and call. You shall see. Today is filled with promise for I, Geres Auk, am bound for glory!"

"You are a petty creature, Geres. The universe doesn't need you, don't you understand? You are doomed to follow madmen until your breaking."

He scoffed.

Silence settled between them.

Presha listened to the pace of his breathing, the anger in each lungful of air, and wished she had never aligned herself with him. Geres Auk was little more than a brute best suited for bashing in skulls. Where his newfound sense of purpose stemmed from remained a mystery. One she was loathe to explore. The traits she admired when he served Baron Scura now proved little more than a detriment to her escape into anonymity. For the first time in her life, Presha Von wanted nothing more than to disappear.

Fate was not so kind.

Perhaps it would have been better if she'd surrendered to the Prekhauten Guards on Crimeat and been done with it. The prospect of spending her days in a Conclave prison cell awaiting execution didn't seem so bad considering her current course of action. Though neither spoke of it, she knew where she was headed, and it scared her to the core.

"No witty words, Lady Von?" Geres taunted. "Perhaps it is for the best. Lord Amongeratix will have much to say upon our arrival."

SEVEN

3215 A.G. (After Gods) Industrial District, Krenz, planet Vau Prime.

Julian stared down the scope of his rifle, watching the workers shuffling in and out of the warehouse. Intel suggested this was a major weapons storage hub for General Kale's forward deployed troops. More and more had been springing up throughout the city as the insurrection was hunted down and eliminated. Julian's desire to flee to the low continent was in perpetual conflict with his adherence to orders, albeit from a dead man, and left his nerves raw. He'd been in sniper position for most of the day and was ready for the start time.

Working in hand with the remnants of Zoraq Darc's criminal element, Julian identified three major targets that would not only hamper enemy activity in large parts of Krenz but reduce their combat effectiveness to the point Mobus Kale would be forced to send in more reinforcements, drawing them from other parts of the city. It was designed to be a two-pronged assault. Insurgent cells continued operating their adjusted battle plan, frustrating their foes yet losing far too many capable fighters in the process. The gains from the raid on Tatarast Island had gone south with Strannan's remnants, leaving Julian forced to think outside of traditional training.

The enemy held every advantage but one. The tighter their grip on the civilian population became the more it threatened to unleash a fury. Hatred simmered beneath the surface. Innocents were rounded up and sent to prison camps, others executed in the streets as examples of what happened when one defied the Inquisition. Krenz was a powder keg, one Julian would avoid igniting if possible, though that likelihood was all but gone. He wished there were another way.

He believed in the Guard's mission despite numerous setbacks throughout the war. Three years of heavy fighting, desperate retreat actions, and more loss than any one commander should endure left him a shell of a man conflicted on the deepest levels. Part of his psyche screamed for release, to slip away into the night, book transport offworld and fade away. But too many innocent lives were at risk and, should Nye win his war, they all would lose.

Julian never considered himself faithful or righteous. He was a soldier. Sworn to uphold order and maintain peace whenever possible. It was that charge that found him in an overwatch position with his index finger slipping into the trigger well of a sniper rifle. Steadying his breathing, he cleared both eyes and mind as he chose his first target. His thumb slipped the selector to single shot. The electronic crosshairs settled a step in front of the target, tracking his every movement.

"Everyone in place?" Julian whispered into the small headset wrapped around his face. Forced to abandon their helmet communication relays due to jamming and constant surveillance, the insurgent cells adapted to older, often forgotten technologies.

A scattering of confirmations came in.

Julian drew in a final breath and exhaled slowly, squeezing the trigger.

He shifted to the second target without bothering to see the first hit. He fired three more times. Smoke trickled from the barrel as he lowered the rifle and surveyed his work. All four targets were neutralized. Their body signatures already cooling on his thermal imaging scanner. No alarms sounded but he didn't breathe easy yet. Julian watched as strike teams flooded the building. Half were his, the rest belonged to Edam Boone.

Rushing past the dead, the teams infiltrated the warehouse and headed to their designated targets—Julian kept a running clock. Estimated mission time was less than three minutes before enemy forces were alerted and deployed in response. Barely enough time to grab what they needed.

Scanning the streets for telltale signs of incoming enemy forces, Julian questioned the validity of the strategy. It was one they'd been using for over a year and Kale was wise to it. What should have been a hard target was left all but undefended. Why? He had guesses but no concrete evidence. The chief factor, in his opinion, was an overconfidence on the part of the traitor forces in the aftermath of General Strannan's death. They mistakenly believed the dragon would die with the head cut off.

Julian scoffed at their ignorance. This war devolved the Prekhauten battle tactics to a state they had never been in. One of guerilla hit and runs and quick strikes. While Julian's forces relished the idea of abandoning strategies that would have gotten them killed already, Kale's people continued plodding along without imagination. It was a failure of leadership on every level that felt encouraged. Yet another reason to end the war quickly and attempt to return to normal life. Though Julian feared life would never be the same. How could it? Too many atrocities were committed. Too many families and planets shattered.

A flicker of movement three blocks up drew his attention. He spied the matte black hull of an armored personnel carrier. Ugly wires and additional outer armor transformed the sleek lines into a beast. He sighed before keying the headset: "Enemy patrol inbound. Exfil now."

Julian waited as the vehicle rolled closer. Roadside bombs and boobytrapped roads caused hesitancy in the enemy. That fear worked in his favor. No one wanted to die, regardless if they wore a uniform or not. He only hoped the incoming crew decided their lives were more important than dying for a cause.

Snatching the detonator lying beside him, he counted until the vehicle entered the kill zone. Depressing the button, he watched as a string of anti-armor mines exploded. A ball of flame and smoke billowed up between buildings, decorating the sky with the stench of burned flesh and fuel.

His teams were fleeing the warehouse. The first three each led an antigrav sled laden with supplies to the waiting transports ferrying them back to the underground. The last team, and one Julian was most interested in, escorted a handful of ragged individuals out. He breathed a sigh of relief once they were clear.

The mission was a success.

He waited until the last team acknowledged they were clear of the target before collecting his rifle and slipping away into the growing chaos filling the streets. No one bothered looking at him. Violence and armed men were now standard for the people of Krenz.

Julian entered the room to crisp, if slow, applause. Swallowing, he strode with false confidence to the small table occupied by Edam Boone, his supposed torturer Thopos, and Aliz. Only Edam applauded, producing a glower Julian couldn't prevent from showing. If any noticed they were savvy enough to keep it to themselves, though Julian swore he caught the hint of a smile creeping on Aliza's face.

"Welcome back, Captain," Edam said. "You retrieved five of my people. Alive, I might add. My congratulations and thanks."

"Did we pass the test?" Julian asked, slumping into the remaining chair.

The criminals exchanged a private look. "Enough. You've earned your keep, but I would be remiss if I didn't remind you Zoraq once felt similar—look where that ended." He turned to Aliz, "You continue drawing us into a dangerous game."

Pursing her lips, she replied, "Would that it was just a game. I fear we are beyond the point of return. Continued actions in Krenz are producing diminishing returns."

"What are you saying?" Julian stiffened.

She faced him, stern and defiant. "The time has come to shift our focus from denial to escape."

He shook his head. "I gave my word to General Strannan to fight until the last. We cannot abandon our principles for the sake of personal safety."

"No one is suggesting that, Captain."

Edam crossed his arms, leaning back. "The lady has a plan."

"I do. We need to begin helping others evacuate Krenz. The more lives we save reduces Nye's options to make war. Collapse the cells, decentralize command even further and we prevent this city from ruination."

Alarms sounded in his mind. Good soldiers were trained to follow orders, even if they went contrary to individual survival, but to abandon the fight now felt like cowardice. "You're proposing we cease combat operations and turn to evacuation."

"I think she's trying to save your life," Edam interjected. "Not to mention hundreds more. Where do we stand in your grand design, Aliz?"

"Everyone deserves a chance at life, Edam," she said. "I once believed in Zoraq and his intentions. He placed his faith in me in return. If I can help your people I will, but it will take all of us to succeed, and even then hope is limited."

Edam slapped Thopos on the back. "What are we waiting for?"

"I need a drink," the older criminal replied.

"That's the spirit. When do we begin?"

Julian cleared his throat. "Where are we to evacuate these people to? Every system within light years will have declared for Nye. Getting large numbers to neutral planets will prove all but impossible."

"That doesn't mean we shouldn't try," she countered. "This is our one opportunity to turn defeat into victory."

He threw his hands out. "What about the forces on the low continent? We have no way to reach them now that Kale has cut off all communications."

"They must deal with their own problems, Julian. We are no longer bound to their fate."

The finality of her tone settled like a death shroud. Aliz was numb to death but not the desperate plight of those she once counted as friends. Strannan's murder left her rattled. He replaced Lorenu as her pillar to lean on and for three long years she had come to understand the man and think of him as a brother. His absence sent ripples through the insurgency, prompting her to question all they'd set out to accomplish in the aftermath of Nye's betrayal. The sad truth was that the war had turned against them and fleeing the coming storm was their only chance—even that was slim.

Noticing Julian's reticence, Aliz continued, "Julian, they are well armed and present considerable combat power. Surely that will draw Kale's attention from us."

"And get them killed in the process," he countered. "Aliz, we can't abandon all we stand for."

"We're not," she said. "We are shifting focus to enter a new phase of the war."

"We don't even know if there are others still on our side!"

"Seven hundred planets in our sphere. You don't believe they have all turned for Nye, do you? Why else is General Kale fighting so hard to stamp us out if not to prevent us from spreading our message and grow the rebellion across the universe?"

"You paint the false illusion of hope." The admission stole Julian's breath for ever had he been a staunch defender of the voiceless. His efforts saved countless lives over the course of the war without once thinking of what fate befell the rest of the planets under Conclave dominion. That other worlds were throwing off the yokes of servitude to the dying faith seemed foreign. Could it be true? Were matters less dire than his mind conjured?

"What else is there?" Aliz asked, her voice gentle.

Edam was about to respond when the door burst open. The red-faced young man huffing for breath held up a hand for attention. "Speak, lad. What is so important you felt the need to interrupt a private meeting?"

"My apologies, sir, but there is something you need to see," he panted.

Edam's eyebrow arched. "This had better be good." He turned to the others. "Shall we?"

The purge began before dawn.

Shock troops in midnight armor stormed the streets. Each squad had an Inquisitor at their head, branching off to individual targets in the luxury residential district. Those unfortunate to witness their passing were beaten and forced indoors. Anyone protesting was dragged off. Loudspeakers blared the official message on repeat: Stay in your homes. Do not interfere with Inquisition business. It was this day terror swept through the high class. Doors bolted shut. Windows were drawn as the march of heavy boots echoed down pristine halls.

The first door burst inward shortly after their arrival. The troopers wasted no time in sweeping the apartment. Raw screams and threats of defiance met them but to no avail. One by one the Cardinals of Conclave were dragged from their homes, their beds, and their lives. All under the watchful eye of the Inquisition controlled media. A senior spokeswoman stepped before the lone camera crew granted permission to film. Resplendent in her finest uniform, she was both haughty and meek.

"At the behest of the Inquisitor General and those Cardinals yet loyal to the Conclave we have been ordered to round up subversive elements known to have ties to the insurgency. These former clergy and their retainers will be detained for questioning and stand trial for their crimes should they be found guilty. Due process is accorded each based upon their standing. Those deemed innocent will be allowed to find new assignments on other planets to prevent any disciplinary backlash from affecting them or their families."

She fixed the camera with a steeled gaze. "Make no mistake, these are dangerous times we face. The true test of loyalty is yet to begin. The Inquisitor General reminds all of you to remain vigilant. Treason can come from anyone. Heresy threatens to consume us all the longer this war stretches. We ask you to do your part in maintaining peace and helping us restore order and justice to Krenz."

A line of prisoners filed past. Some were bloodied. All were under heavy guard. More than one rifle prodded them along. Inquisitors compared datapads, ensuring they had secured all the prisoners the Inquisitor General summoned. Transports were loaded, their doors slammed shut before racing back to Inquisition headquarters. The sun was barely cresting the high rises by the time the last Inquisitor left the area.

Across Krenz, a series of hit and run assaults meted blind justice on suspected insurgents. The order had been given for the wholesale destruction of every structure thought to house enemy forces, denying them further use while, hopefully, ending many lives in the process. It was a campaign similar to the firebombing in the low continent. The results were more spectacular, for the tightly packed capitol city was ripe for cleansing. Whole areas were cordoned off without warning in the predawn hours. Small caliber artillery and mortar fire turned the landscape a bitter ruin.

Off his leash at last, Mobus Kale had never felt so powerful.

A wave of terror descended upon the citizens of Krenz, who for so long thought the war was far away and on distant shores. Alone in his offices, Inquisitor General Alain Nye watched as the planet came to understand the true meaning of his bid for power. The time for pretending there might be compromise was ended. In its place he intended to rule with an iron fist, ensuring the planet was secure and ready for Amongeratix's arrival.

For too long he had spiraled with indecision. The balance between giving in to his desires and establishing the foundations of a new universal order was delicate at best. Already the constraints of warfare on an unprecedented scale strained the population. He knew they were ready to turn on him, prompting his actions. The time for open rebellion was finished. Once Kale's forces unleashed their havoc and the true cost of the day became known Nye doubted there would be another prominent uprising on Vau Prime. With the central planet secure at last he could direct his armies to wipe the rest of the rabblerousers and rout from existence.

He'd been content to let matters play out naturally, until the loss of the manufactory planet Mannus Prime. The total defeat stole a massive portion of combat power. Over one hundred thousand Guards were either dead or captured. Countless artillery pieces and naval ships were destroyed, and all reports indicated the enemy was building Mannus into an impregnable fortress. Nye needed those troops and equipment for other planets. Fate decreed otherwise. While his opponents had yet to make further moves, Nye knew it was but a matter of time. Any initiative needed to occur now.

Gathering his cloak, he swept out of the office and, a short time later, entered the command and control center. Inquisitors paused to acknowledge him, each brushed off in a display of practiced impatience. The Inquisitor General was the most powerful man in the universe. Deference was expected, but not at the expense of the mission. Nye studied the holographic images on the walls, pausing to take in the delicious scene of so many troublesome cardinals being arrested. His spokeswoman said her part to perfection. The lies flowed effortlessly off her tongue. Only a handful knew none of the clergy would ever be seen again. Those who were not publicly executed would be shipped off to various prison colonies to spend the rest of their days.

He never considered himself a violent man. Ambitious, but not at the expense of a healthy portion of the population. The last three years changed him. Nye's plans reshuffled as assets died or were removed from play, yet he continued ahead with assurance of purpose. Decades of plotting and scheming were coming to fruition, even if skewed in the delivery. He recognized promoting the fanatic Mobus Kale to general of the armies was a bad move, perhaps so to was aligning with Amongeratix. Desperate times made desperate men.

None of his cunning or guile prepared him from the devastation being wrought upon the screens.

"What is that fucking fool doing?" he growled.

Those nearest him stiffened.

When no one answered, he turned his rage upon the staff. "Someone tell me why General Kale is burning half of Krenz to the ground when I ordered him back to the low continent?"

A thin, aged Prekhauten colonel sidled beside him. Wisps of grey hair poked from under his cap. "Inquisitor General, General Kale thought it best to eliminate all potential threats in one fell swoop before rooting out the remain of Strannan's forces. He has assured the Inquisition no more than is necessary shall be destroyed."

"How does he plan to guarantee that?" Nye ground out. "I want that madman to cease his activities at once and report to me."

The colonel cleared his throat but stood his ground. "Sir, it will be impossible to summon him in the midst of this action. General Kale left specific instructions to be followed by all Guard officers."

"I don't recall asking." Nye narrowed his eyes on the man. "Or perhaps you would care to fall under the Inquisition on the grounds of suspected heresy? My master torturer has become quite proficient of late."

Paling, the man offered a clipped nod and hurried to the nearest comms station. Nye rolled his shoulders and refocused on the events gripping his city. Today, he decided, would be a day long remembered by the victors. After all, what other opinion mattered?

Behemoth, deep space.

In her estimation, space had never been colder. As *Behemoth* plunged on through the depths of space, fresh from the devastation of Terotis, Algiss began feeling disillusioned. She'd fallen sway to the lure of Amongeratix. His honeyed tongue whispered to her soul during those long moments of silence aboard the Acumensiis Comet. Far from content with the direction the Grand Mistress was leading the Order, Algiss knew the time had come for change. Alas she proved unable to complete the task when the moment arose. The physical scars were gone, healed through some foul act of magic, but the internal scars remained. She often reached up to touch the eye Ruma

Zzein destroyed, it was a reminder of her failure and the opportunity to rise from those ashes remade.

Her crimson robes swirled around her in tune with the hum of *Behemoth's* great engines. Repair menials toiled endlessly to fix the damage caused by the renegade Inquisitor and his party and, though much had been returned to functionality, there was much left to go. Adding weight to her worry was the empty weapon racks. Any stored energy from thousands of years ago was long since depleted, leaving the battle frigate's weapons all but useless teeth poking through the skin. Massive, but unarmed, the ship was little more than a battering ram. Why then wasn't Amongeratix hurrying to replenish supplies?

After Terotis the ship took a course toward the heart of the universe. He did not tell her his plans, though she guessed they struck for Vau Prime. Cutting the head from the snake was the quickest way to assume command of the billions of trillions of souls contaminating the seven hundred planets. The sooner Amongeratix assumed his rightful place of authority the sooner she might resume her quest for revenge against the woman she once called a sister.

Eyes closed, she sat upon the unforgiving metal bench in her quarters and meditated. Though she had transformed to the Crimson Mistress, Algiss Her remained the same woman she had always been. Stout, steadfast, and determined to a fault. It was that rigidity which forced the schism between Ruma Zzein and herself. One she did not regret. For too long had the sisters of the Blood Witches been languishing beneath tired trains of thought with little or no purpose in the evolving universe. Ruma Zzein clung to old beliefs that no longer applied. Instead of propelling the Order into the future, she kept it mired in the ghosts of the past. The travesty that followed was born from her complacency.

Algiss thought herself practical, despite the gnawing hunger for power ever lingering beneath the skin. She'd set her sights on claiming rulership over the Blood Witches for some centuries, growing more despondent against the Grand Mistress with each passing year. The final straw came when Ruma pledged the Order to help a mortal hunt down and eliminate Amongeratix. Unable to accept servitude to the same mortals who excommunicated so many Sisters from their homes for the assumed sin of being born different, Algiss collected those allies who would become her Crimson Sisterhood. A mere score escaped the Abbey and followed her to the waiting bays of *Behemoth*. Several more died when Paradise Tear and the others assaulted. Their ranks were depleted.

She convinced Amongeratix growing their numbers was paramount to his overall success, for a host of magic users was a powerful weapon. Algiss was surprised when he agreed and allowed those remaining Sisters to take shuttles to nearby planets in search of any woman of reasonable age with the spark of magic. Several had already returned, and those initiates were being indoctrinated under harsh tutelage. Those who failed to meet minimum qualifications were escorted to a forgotten moon, never to be heard from again.

Algiss knew there was no room for error. Should just one of those women find their way back to civilization and warn the local authorities word would reach Ruma Zzein. Eager as she was for revenge, the former Mistress of Arms was not prepared. She needed time, praying the protective blanket of Amongeratix's name kept her safe long enough. The future balanced on an edge. Her greed and aspirations clashed with rationale. The one constant keeping her warm at night was the thought of bringing her former Mistress to her knees and breaking her, mind and soul.

The Crimson Mistress opened her eyes, taking a moment to adjust to the low artificial light before sweeping down the corridor to the training deck. In his benevolence, Amongeratix offered an unused docking bay for the witches. It was a small boon.

She passed several cargo areas packed with pods containing his private army. A host of genetically mutated creatures he called skulldaerth. Their ghastly appearance appalled her. Fortunately, most remained in suspended animation, awaiting their time to descend and reap violence upon the universe in his name. Those few awakened were survivors of the attempt to prevent Braewynd from falling into enemy hands. Algiss had vague knowledge of the operation only because it involved one of the witches. She'd gleaned little else from her new master during their time together, loath as he was to share.

Most intriguing to the Crimson Mistress was the goblin-like creatures scurrying throughout the ship. They spoke a crude language and seldom interacted with the witches, prompting Algiss to question their necessity. Amongeratix insisted they were the best creatures suited for repairing his ship. She didn't question further, vowing to stay away from the sickly ochre-colored creatures as they went about their purpose. Friendless and alone, Algiss focused her attention on training the new recruits for the war to come.

Training halted as she entered the bay. The effects of wild magic were evident on the walls and gouges cut into the decking. The scattering of Crimson Sisters bowed in reverence, which she ignored. She spied the person she sought and floated over to her. Sister Ibrest watched with a stern expression. Known as a severe woman, she had no sense of humor and insisted on perfection. Falling under Algiss' sway was but a foregone conclusion. Her loss to the Blood Witches lacked significance, but Ibrest proved the necessary catalyst required to launch her bid for power.

"Algiss," Ibrest greeted, folding her arms across her chest.

Glowering at the disrespect, Algiss replied, "It would do to show proper deference in front of the recruits, Sister."

"Respect is earned. I followed you on whim—do not make me regret my decision."

Algiss rose a few more inches from the deck. "How many initiates have we recruited?"

"Sixty-seven who passed the initial assessments. Eighteen others were removed."

The matter-of-fact delivery chilled Algiss. Considered heartless by some, she found Ibrest's statement one of unusual callousness. In the weeks following the schism with the Order those Sisters who chose to follow Algiss grew hardened, inured to the niceties of their former lives. A wave of self-righteousness swept through them, consuming each until they became individual entities seeking only to improve their lives by whatever means necessary. She knew there was little time in which to attempt a binding of purpose, for the wickedness of the human heart ever runs deep. Ibrest, she decided, would be the first to openly declare.

"Why is the number so high? Are we not adhering to selection protocols?"

"Protocols? We are stealing women, girls mostly, and reconfiguring their minds against their will. The forbidden ways prove best. Render the subject compliant and we may produce a better creature of magic." Ibrest paused, staring deep into Algiss' reconstructed eye. "This is what you wanted, is it not? Your vision of a terrible future? The only way we can compete against Ruma Zzein is through unmitigated power. Look around you, Algiss. Already several of the initiates have learned the strength of levitation. Soon the first wave will be ready to unleash our vengeance."

"That is for Lord Amongeratix to decide. We head for Vau Prime, where he plans on subjugating the Conclave to his authority," Algiss said slowly. "Focus your energies on preparing the initiates to combat the Inquisition. Ruma Zzein will have to wait until his goals are achieved. Is that clear, Sister?"

Ibrest remained silent but Algiss recognized the desire smoldering deep within that gaze, for it was one she fostered after Amongeratix first came to her with his seductions. In those quiet moments of empty despair she discovered a hidden truth. One inherent in all. Algiss Her craved power. The ability to attain her desires through whatever means necessary, and she was willing to go through any obstacle to achieve it.

Cackles of power danced over her knuckles. Smoke seeped through the flesh. "I asked you a question."

"I've never been afraid of you, Algiss," Ibrest replied, setting her shoulders back. "The only way to get me to bend knee to you is by breaking my spirit but you will not do so. It is not your way. Long have I watched you, always from a distance. You lack foresight and the stomach for open confrontation. Ever have you slunk in shadows, plotting and scheming while our kin swept across the stars at Ruma Zzein's bidding. You are a craven woman, Algiss. One doomed to a short rule."

Bolts of electricity flashed, each driving into the decking with repulsive fury. Algiss swelled with power, noticing several Sisters and initiates backing away. "Do not think to presume my complacency, Ibrest. I shall flense the very flesh from your bones and throw your carcass to the skulldaerth for their amusements."

Endless years of frustration boiled over. The fringe of her robes caught flame. Hatred blazed in her eyes. Algiss felt the embarrassment of her failure against Ruma Zzein collide with her ambitions. She moved to strike, ready to burn all within the bay to ashes.

Ibrest threw up her hands in supplication. "Peace, Crimson Mistress! I implore you. Peace. I shall do your bidding. The initiates will be ready on time."

"Do not fail me again, Ibrest or your torment will be legendary," Algiss warned and spun away, hate eating away underneath the surface.

Paradise Tear wept. Not for herself. She had endured far worse during her existence. No. She wept for what was to come of her sudden captivity. Common sense whispered she never should have joined the quest to disable Behemoth, for her cousin desired her more than anything else. He'd long ago learned the secrets of her genetic code locking away the remaining seven hundred members of their race in statis and, with her in his grasp, lacked only the key to kill them all.

No doubt Tannus was furious, for he alone knew the traumas she experienced during those final days of the war. Lament notwithstanding, Paradise whispered private apologies to her cousin for her impertinence. Her recklessness promised to bring all they'd worked so hard to achieve over the last three millennia crashing to a halt. With the last remnants of their race destroyed, there would be no stopping Amongeratix from devouring the universe and turning it into a garden of horrors. Paradise's heart grew heavy, for she unwittingly played into his hands.

Now she was alone. The others had no doubt reported back to Tannus of their failure and her capture. Her one solace lay in Amongeratix not having the key. Without it he was unable to use her gene sequence to activate the destruct sequence for those in stasis. She knew each time the key was used it required a recharge of her DNA. Still, she knew time was against her. So long as they remained separated, the universe had a chance.

The mighty *Behemoth* was being repaired as it began the ponderous voyage across the stars. Chances of escaping were limited, though she was obligated to try. Knowing her cousin needed her alive went far in her psyche, for she had the advantage. Wiping away her self-pity, Paradise Tear began working out a plan to get her to the shuttle bay and, she hoped, a way back to Tannus.

The door to her chambers hissed open and Amongeratix stormed inside with a squad of his skulldaerth. They watched her with their emotionless visage, conjuring nightmares forgotten. Her stomach roiled. They were Amongeratix's favored tool, ones wielded with the impossible conviction of the righteousness of cause. But for all their menace, Paradise knew the truth. The skulldaerth were little more than mindless imitations of life brought forth from the depths of madness.

"Cousin, to what to do I owe the pleasure this time?" she teased. "Come to wrest more useless information from me?"

"Quaint," he replied and gestured to the imp scurrying from behind him.

The green skinned goblin hurried to her side, unpacking an array of wicked needles and tubes.

She scowled, her glare predatory.

"My minions have never pleased you, cousin," Amongeratix teased back. "They may seem repulsive to you, but they serve their purpose. Were it not for me their kind would have blundered into extinction long ago."

"Better that they had. What are you doing?"

Skulldaerth surrounded her, pinning her to the cold metal table upon which she was already strapped. It appeared Amongeratix was unwilling to take chances. He watched over the scene with mild interest.

Nonplussed by her struggles to break free, the goblin hummed as he connected the syringe to the first vial. Tufts of ugly grey hair sprouted from his ears, revolting Paradise.

"This will be easier if you relax," Amongeratix said. "A little prick and it will all be over."

Her eyes widened with realization. With enough of her blood, he had no need for the key. Goblins were relics of a forgotten age, notorious for their mechanical creativity; Amongeratix would be able to replicate the key and begin his war on the universe in earnest. She strained, desperate to break the bonds as the needle sank into her flesh and entered the vein.

EIGHT

3215 A.G. (After Gods), Erdef City, planet Romalle.

Inquisitor Gando drummed his fingertips on the metal desk as he stared blankly out the window overlooking the heart of Erdef City. A scattering of aircars hurried to and fro, ignorant of the turmoil gripping the planet. Thus far he'd managed to prevent word of Cardinal Breed's murder from reaching Vau Prime, but it was only a matter of time before the information was leaked. Nothing stayed secret on Romalle long. No doubt the Warders were already squabbling over who would present the news to the Cardinal Seniorus and claim their prize.

"Fools. As if the battalion of Guards now patrolling the streets wasn't evidence enough of the changing tides."

He knew all it took was a word and the city would be locked down—in the name of liberty of course. The Inquisition bore a heavy hand when it came to matters of suspected heresy. With the war raging there would be a purge among the leadership, prompting the total subjugation of the planet in the Inquisitor General's favor. Uncertain whether the official stance of Vau Prime was right, Gando struggled to put the pieces together. Breed's assassination threatened to unravel all he sought to accomplish.

His conversation with Ingrid came to mind. The priestess was adamant that Leganas Breed was a man of excess. That lifestyle drew enemies, awakening a host of possible targets seeking retribution for some perceived slight. Yet while she had no qualms about divulging those dark rumors, Ingrid became reticent in discussing deeper matters involving the church. Gando resisted the urge to dig, choosing instead to follow Hargan's lead and back off. The ruse was sufficient enough to calm the nerves of those within the temple, for the time being.

His thoughts were disrupted when a red-faced Hargan entered the office and sank into the chair opposite his desk.

"What news?"

Hargan wiped the sweat from his brow with the back of a hand. "No good to see you? I fear this case is prompting you to slip back into your Inquisitor façade, Gando."

He fixed the detective with a deadpan look. "You do see this uniform, correct?"

"The uniform doesn't make the man." Hargan shrugged. "At any rate, I might have a lead."

"I'm listening."

"I was at the station when I overheard bits of conversation between a few of the patrollers. One I knew was among the first to arrive at the murder scene. He was asking if the other knew anything about a young girl rumored to have committed the crime."

"Do we know who this girl might be?"

Hargan shook his head. "No, and the more he talked the more it sounded as if he had a vested interest in finding her. It was enough to get me out of my chair."

"Will you please get to the point?"

"I was getting to that, but every good story needs a proper build up." Hargan waved his hand around before continuing. "You just don't jump into the deep end and expect everyone to be caught up. Now, I pulled the officer in and, behind closed doors, asked him to explain why he was searching for this girl and what made her a suspect. Though he was quite forthcoming I noted an awkward tone, as if he was keeping an important piece of information from me."

"I didn't know any of your patrollers was on scene fast enough to catch a suspect."

"Neither did I. After checking the records, I determined none of my people were scheduled to be on that street at that time. There is no way he should have been close enough to bear witness."

Gando frowned. "Unless he was in dereliction of duty."

"More like abandoning his post," Hargan countered. "But yes."

"Is it possible he was part of this plot?"

Uncomfortable with the question, Hargan twisted in his seat. "Possible but unlikely. The patrollers are selected only after rigorous examinations. Their loyalty is to the city."

"Every man is corruptible," Gando reminded. "I trust you are having him watched."

"I didn't get to be a detective for my charm."

"Good. What about this girl?"

"I pulled security footage from a nearby shop. They didn't get the murder on file, but they did catch someone scrambling away from a uniformed patroller. Image scanners identified her as a Riles Tenaru. Minor arrest record. Nothing to suggest she was capable of murder." Hargan held up another hand when Gando scoffed. "I know, we're all capable of murder. What I'm saying is we have a name and a place to start and I would like to solve this case before our offworld visitors, if possible."

"So, what are we waiting for?"

Lady Emmest DeMauve was considered uncanny among Romalle's upper class. Entering the prime of her life, she was the widow of a once prominent politician who met with tragedy when his ship exploded on a deep space transit run. Graced with his wealth and standing, Emmest spun her webs throughout society. She knew all that happened and why within the confines of Erdef City yet there were dark rumors about her. Claims of dark magic and convening with the supernatural trailed in her wake. Whispers of unholy relationships with creatures of myth and legend swirled around her. True or not, Emmest DeMauve did little to prevent them. Their value lay in the enhancement of her standing.

A stunning woman of grace and charm, she held court in her mansion on the outskirts of the city. Suitors and information seekers flocked to her gates, often turned away with little or no regard. Emmest built the myths, turning her name into an enigma. She was the most invited guest on Romalle, a debutant of unprecedented proportions. Fashion trends hinged on her whim, prompting some of the more ridiculous statements. Emmest devoured the limelight while maintaining quiet anonymity. No one truly knew what happened behind those sandstone walls, making it the source of much speculation she did not dissuade.

For Riles and Nemineon to seek her out in such brazen fashion spoke volumes to the young woman's plight. Hunted and haunted, Riles was desperate enough to cavort with the one person capable of ruining her. Nemineon warned her not to go, to avoid the woman at all costs. There had to be another way to clear her name and be free of persecution but Riles insisted. Lady DeMauve was her only choice.

They arrived at the end of the impossibly long lane marking the property. Riles half expected to find a decrepit house surrounded by dying trees under the murk of perpetual gloom. Instead, she saw row upon row of blossoming trees and shrubs bearing every color flower imaginable. Birds chirped, darting from bush to bush. Rolling fields of green stretched to either side. There was no gloom. No sense of deep foreboding. Bathed in light, the straight path to the mansion was the most beautiful sight she'd ever witnessed.

"Would you look at that," she uttered, spying the massive building yet two hundred meters away.

Nemineon whistled. "I see it, though I can scarce believe it."

She slapped his arm. "And you said it was a house of the dead. This place is a dream."

"We still don't know what awaits inside. There could rooms filled with corpses for all we know."

"You don't seriously still think she dines on the corpses of missing people, do you?"

"And bathes in tubes of human blood."

"Just tales meant to spook people like us from seeking her out." Riles frowned. "Come on. With luck she will see us."

"She may not be a bloodsucking monster, but I still don't like this. We don't belong here, Riles. Even with the law after you," he protested, again.

"I'd rather take my chances with her than being thrown into a cell and executed for murdering a Cardinal."

Riles headed for the house, her stride purposeful and driven. Reluctant, Nemineon followed her. A small herd of golag's grazed to their right; velvet covered horns curved and graceful. She caught the soothing trickle of an unseen brook as golden sunlight warmed her head. They reached the outer courtyard, replete with a fountain containing the towering statues of two gods with upraised arms reach for each other and found an elderly man awaiting them.

"The mistress is expecting you," he greeted with a curt bow.

He turned, climbing the marble steps to the main door without waiting for their replies. Riles exchanged a wary glance with Nemineon then shrugged, following the man. The doors were ornately carved metal standing twenty feet tall. Why anyone required so much was lost on her. Used to a life barely above squalor, Riles found the enormous mansion overkill.

They were escorted to a waiting room off the main hallway. Light flowed through tall windows. Plants and flowers lined the way on alabaster pedestals. Paintings and sculptures complete the opulence, further sinking Riles' sense of self-worth. Leaving them in the room, the elderly man bowed and was gone.

"Have you ever seen the like?" Nemineon uttered.

"I never knew such a place existed," she seconded. "She must be the wealthiest person in the universe."

"In Erdef City perhaps, and then only the wealthiest woman," a voice said, chuckling from behind.

They turned, Nemineon embarrassingly stuffing his hands in his pockets as he bore witness to the impossible beauty that was Lady Emmest DeMauve. She flowed into the room, dressed in a simple gown of flowers accented with a necklace of purple stones.

"Not what you were expecting?" she asked.

He shook his head, not trusting his voice.

"I am many things and I perpetuate many facets," Emmest explained. "But even I pale in comparison to the many variations of what others have built me up to be. Let me guess. You thought I would devour your flesh and sup upon your bones if you displeased me?"

"Rumors, nothing more, Lady DeMauve," Riles said. She remained guarded, still unsure of how far she could trust the woman.

The lady of the house took in the young woman for the first time and found her wanting in appearance. Yet despite this there was hidden strength deep within. "Emmest, please. I know the rumors. They inspire great amusement."

"Bu … but my lady, why not quash them and let the people know who you truly are?" Nemineon blurted. "Half the people believe you are a monster."

"And I am glad to let them," she replied. "What do you think would happen if the obscurity of my myth dissolved and the world knew the true me?"

"You'd be ruined," Riles concluded.

"Yes, I would be," Emmest confirmed. "I have many enemies born from the callousness of greed. They would pounce upon me and bring my legacy to waste in a day. The trouble with power is others always covet what you have." She sighed. "But come, you did not travel all this way, through forests of demons and the like for me to bandy possible futures. I am Emmest DeMauve, and I welcome you to my home."

Nemineon bowed awkwardly and his efforts earned him a laugh.

"I am Riles Tenaru and this smitten buffoon is Nemineon. Thank you for taking the time to meet with us … Emmest," Riles said, casting a sidelong glare at Nemineon.

"Well met. I understand you are in dire circumstance. What can I do for you?"

Emmest glided across the immaculate flooring and sank into the cushions of a deep blue couch. She watched them with an experienced eye, knowing the best approach to gathering information was by disarming them and making them comfortable enough to speak.

The youths exchanged a look and sat. Nemineon's right leg started bouncing and Riles glanced down at it, realizing her fists were clenched on her lap. Heart pounding, she exhaled a deep breath and blurted, "I think I'm being set up for a murder."

Emmest remained unmoved. "I see. What cause have you to believe the local authorities suspect you of the murder of Cardinal Breed?"

Her eyes widened. "How?"

"Oh, come now. It's the news of the year. Nothing happens on Romalle, or in Erdef City I do not know about. Increased Prekhauten patrols, a nervous edge to much of the population—putting pieces together is easy enough." Emmest laughed.

"But people are found dead every day," Nemineon injected, frowning.

"Indeed, they are, but none with the status of the late Cardinal. Why else would two waifs come to me, with all my fierce and mysterious reputation, if not in the direst of circumstances?" She watched the young woman bristle. "Now tell me, Riles Tenaru, why do they have reason to suspect you?"

Swallowing the lump threatening to choke her, Riles pressed her palms flat on the tops of her thighs. "I planned on robbing him.

He left the local bar and stumbled down the street. The man was an easy mark and no, I didn't know he was a Conclave Cardinal. He was already dead by the time I came upon him."

Patient, Emmest waited for the rest. Experience taught her few were wholly forthcoming. Many held secrets, mistakenly thinking she lacked intelligence on their situations. Others struggled with what to say or how. None of it mattered to her, for her web of spies and informants stretched all the way to the offices of the Warders. When she boasted little occurred on Romalle without her knowing it was no lie.

At last, after struggling with herself, Riles added, "When I discovered who I was trailing I turned to flee. Hands reached for me, and I saw the flash of a badge on the patroller's uniform."

"What happened next?"

Riles swallowed, eyebrows drawn together. "I ran and haven't stopped. Now with the Inquisitor meeting this new group of offworlders, I fear the noose is tightening."

"There are many strands in a web, Riles. Yours is but a minor deviation from the center. I do not say you are not in jeopardy, for those in power ever yearn for more. A game is being played in Erdef City and you have unwittingly become a central player. You were right to come to me."

The first flicker of hope lit her eyes. "Can you help me, Lady DeMauve?"

"That remains to be seen. Many pieces are in motion and even I am not omnipotent," Emmest retorted. "Let me think on it. Tonight you and Nemineon shall be my guests. I will instruct Mayn to provide you rooms, baths, and a change of clothes. I am a woman of reputations, and while many are fabricated, I cannot abide uncleanliness. Until dinner."

They rose and bowed as she gathered her dress and left them. Mayn, the elderly man who had first greeted them, entered a moment later and directed them to a pair of rooms at the far end of the central hallway.

Apprehensions yet gripped her but Riles knew hope for the first time in days. It was all she could ask for.

"How long are we expected to sit here?" Luma Kai scowled at her reflection in the rain-streaked window.

Her arms were folded across her chest, feet shoulder width apart. The ion pistol at her hip seemed obscene with the black trousers and loose tunic she'd chosen for this mission. She chafed from more than being idle. Since leaving the Office of Heretical Persecution in favor of the rebellion, Luma struggled with finding her identity. For so long she'd been a willing servant to lofty ideals, only to have them exposed as lies.

Setting down his datapad on the stone table, Tolde yawned and stretched. "We cannot risk exposing ourselves to planetary leadership. Trust Gando."

She spun, fixing him with a vitric glare. "Trust a man you clearly have issue with? One who might easily sell us out to the Inquisitor General and have his revenge?"

"It wasn't like that."

Across the room, Sister Alessandra had sunk within her robes, seemingly asleep. Nearby, Ragan rummaged through the small kitchenette for something to eat.

"I have placed my faith and trust in you, Tolde, even after your impossible resurrection," Luma said noticing Ragan watching her. "All I ask if you place the same in me. What happened between you and Gando?"

Forcing out a breath, Tolde leaned forward and clasped his hands together. "I was his mentor during his first year in uniform. We were dispatched to a quiet world under the suspicion of a cult uprising. Once there we performed a quick investigation, and I determined the city exceeding compliance with Conclave mandates. I ordered the Prekhautens to make appropriate arrests, choosing to incarcerate the leadership rather than the average man. Gando protested, claiming the depths of heresy knew no bounds. We clashed and I rebuked him in front of the Guards and other Inquisitors. It has been a point of shame for him for decades now."

"You didn't think to tell me this until now?" she fumed. "Tolde, your history with Gando, whatever that might be, threatens to see us in chains!"

He shook his head. "I don't think so. Whatever grudge he harbors remains his alone. If he sought revenge, he would have already struck."

"I don't like this," she insisted. "We are taking too many chances of late. Losing Paradise Tear to that beast Amongeratix was a blow we might not recover from, and this can further unravel all we are seeking to achieve."

"You forget I am at your side, Luma Kai," Sister Alessandra said, her face concealed within the shadows of her hood but she had straightened from her reclined position. "No harm shall befall you on Romalle."

"That doesn't change the fact I must speak with Gando and attempt to resolve the situation before it devolves into something ugly," Tolde admitted.

A chime sounded, causing them to jump; Ragan coughed and answered. The message came fast, and the call ended. He looked at Tolde, "It looks like you might get that chance sooner than you think. We have been requested to meet with Gando at the office of the local law enforcement."

"See," Tolde said, the look he gave her anything but pleased. "Everything works out. You might want to conceal your sidearm. Our arrival was unannounced. The last thing we need is for the local patrollers to decide we pose a threat."

"I'm not going unarmed."

Tucking his own weapon into a hidden holster by his breast, Tolde said, "I'm not asking you to."

Tolde led them outside where they discovered a young patrolman waiting. His eyes darted back and forth, never settling on one for long, but it was to the Blood Witch he himself stared at the longest. He quickly explained he had been dispatched by command to see them safely to a secure meeting location where Inquisitor Gando and Detective Hargan were.

"Where is the transport?" Luma asked.

"It is but a few blocks distant. Aircars are not prevalent here in the city, ma'am. Detective Hargan thought it fine we walk."

"Did he?"

Tolde slipped in front of her, privately sharing her concerns while assessing the potential dangers. "That's fine. Lead on."

The officer offered a botched salute and hurried down the street without comment.

They passed scatterings of pedestrians unconcerned with their oddity. Finally, Tolde's suspicions got the better of him. "Where is everyone?"

"This is how it always is, sir. Erdef City is caught between breaths if you take my meaning. Most of the people are waiting for an open declaration on which side the planet will side with in the war." He turned off the main boulevard, leading them into a wide alley.

"Where are you taking us?" Tolde demanded.

"A shortcut to the building. There is rumor of a protest this morning. The detective thought it bet you arrive through the back door to draw less attention."

His step quickened, arousing Tolde's suspicions further. His right hand slipped inside his jacket and unsnapped the holster. He spied Luma doing the same. They'd gone but a few meters when his instincts were proven right. A shadow flashed across the alley. Birds scattered from a nearby rooftop. The first shot came a moment later. Superheated energy splashed the wall near Tolde's head. He ducked, drew his blaster, and returned fire.

Luma shoved Ragan into a doorway and did the same. Dust puffed from the bricks with each impact. The Inquisitors took what little cover they could find and sought their targets. Several shooters leaned out windows on both sides of the alley. They were high enough and the alley choked enough to present difficult angles. Tolde ducked into a doorway and fired blindly at the nearest window. Return fire intensified. Unless they managed to eliminate one or more of their assailants, they were done for. He took a glancing round to the chest, grunted, and pitched backward. The door burst open, and he was inside.

"Tolde!"

Rolling to his hands and knees, Tolde coughed and felt for the wound. His protective armor worn beneath his tunic prevented the round from what surely would have been a mortal wound. It did little though to prevent pain from spreading across his chest. Vision swimming as he rose, Tolde used the wall for support and took in his surroundings. The door opened to a narrow hallway with a string of doors on either side. At the far end he spied a staircase. Ensuring the front door was closed, He double checked his blaster and headed for the stairs.

Tolde edged around the corner of the second floor, confident shooters were ensconced in rooms on this floor. He stalked his way down the hall, listening for the sounds of blaster fire and was rewarded with two men venting curses. Tolde pressed against the wall a foot from the nearest ajar door and slowed his breathing. He moved, sure and smooth.

He kicked the door open and shot the two shooters in the back. Their bodies flared as the blue-white energy struck, producing brief screams before he fired a second salvo. He rushed to the nearest and snatched the rifle from beneath the corpse. Conscious of innocent civilians trapped in their apartments, Tolde presented a low silhouette and placed the end of the barrel on the windowsill. He settled in behind the scope and sought out his next target.

Half of the second floor on the opposite building erupted in gouts of punishing green flame. Men screamed, roasting alive wherever the flame touched them. Tolde grimaced as he watched the flesh melt from the bones of one man. His last meal lurched up his throat as the power washed across the building façade. He prayed no one else was hurt.

Tolde peered down into the alley and discovered the source of the blast: Tiny trickles of florescent green fled back into Sister Alessandra's fingertips and went dormant. Smoke wafting up the alley, the battle was finished. He decided keeping the rifle was in their best interests and hurried to rejoin his friends.

"Where is our guide?" he asked after checking to see if any of them were injured.

"Gone," Sister Alessandra replied. "He fled the moment it started."

"It appears the city knows we're here," Luma added. "The question is now whether we continue or return to our quarters. Either way presents dangers. Others may well be awaiting us should we go back."

"I have no reason to believe we were summoned," Tolde said after some thought.

"Unless Gando sold us out," Luma countered. "This is an untenable position. We can't stay on the street. The sound of gunfire will draw others."

"We go back." Noticing Ragan's relieved look, Tolde added, "Let's move."

Tensions lowered after discovering the rooms untouched once they returned to their quarters. Tolde leaned the rifle against a wall and unstrapped his body armor. Fresh jets of pain washed over his torso. The others had scrapes and cuts but nothing serious. He disapproved of the flagrant use of magic by the Blood Witch but recognized they might all be dead without it.

Luma moved to help when he groaned, she gasped at how bruised his chest was.

"I'm fine," he said.

"Sure you are, but you're going to sit down and take it easy anyway." Her tone left no room for debate.

Tolde slumped onto the nearest chair and tilted his head back. "We need to post a watch in case our attackers decide to return and finish the job."

"I'm on it," Ragan said, already in the corner of the front window overlooking the city.

Nodding, Tolde looked at Luma, "Send word to Gando and request his presence. We need answers."

"You don't even need to say please," Luma growled.

"I came as soon as I could," Gando said upon entering a short time later. He caught a flicker of movement and turned to see Ragan level a blaster on him. Across the room, the Blood Witch glared. "What happened?"

"We were hoping you could tell us," Tolde said. "Who is Hargan really working for?"

"Hargan? What has he got to do with this?" Gando asked.

He listened in mild shock as they detailed their summons and subsequent ambush in the streets. The complete failure of it suggested to Gando the assassins were amateurs, but there was a far worse implication. Mention of Hargan told him the patrollers were infiltrated and were willing to stop at nothing to keep the true reasoning behind Cardinal Breed's assassination secret.

"Hargan is a good man. I haven't told him everything about you yet," Gando explained. "There is no way he could have known about your presence or why you are here."

"This location is no longer secure," Sister Alessandra said after determining Gando spoke true. "We must leave. It would be a shame if I was forced to unleash the justice of the Order upon Erdef City."

Gando swallowed. The trajectory of his career hadn't let him cross paths with one of the witches until now and for that he was grateful. How Tolde and Luma stood being in her severe presence astounded him. They were creatures of myth, never boon companions for mortals. Standing in the shadow of unlimited power rattled him.

"You will stay with me until I can get to the bottom of this matter," Gando said.

"Good. Then you and I can have a much needed conversation," Tolde said. "And I would like to meet this Hargan. There is more afoot on Romalle than the mere killing of my brother."

Warder Damal dreaded what came next. His meetings with Lostan Fidiuos resulted in the disastrous attempt on Cardinal Breed's brother. The fools. Surely they did not think they had truly landed on Romalle without being noticed? Damal spent decades building a network of spies. The moment Gando requested the Inquisitor's presence, through private channels, he'd been aware of it. Neutralizing them became his priority. Losing a handful of Erdef City's thugs was a minor setback—one he intended on correcting at his earliest convenience. But first came deliberation over the ambush with the rest of the City Board.

The pointlessness of it galled him. Damal had been pushing for Romalle's independence for years. Perhaps this chain of events might finally lead to open proclamation and the first tastes of liberty away from the smothering dotage the Conclave inspired. They would bicker and debate for endless hours and come away with nothing new. Romalle would still remain in Conclave jurisdiction, her people languishing beneath the promise of civil war. How they'd managed to avoid committing to either faction in three years remained a mystery to him, for the duplicitous nature of many of the senior leadership silently begged to drag the planet into the war for less than honorable reasons.

Sighing his frustration, Damal made the short journey to the City Board chambers. He wasn't surprised to find the others already discussing matters.

"How nice of you to join us, Damal. And on such a lovely day." Eiters smiled with anything but niceties.

"This is not a scheduled meeting, Eiters," he snarled. "Perhaps more understanding is required before judging—"

"Enough of this," Kasop interrupted. "What do you know of this shootout in the streets?"

"Why would I know anything?"

Eiters chuckled under her breath. "Damal, your proclivity for information is well known. For an event of this magnitude to occur without your knowledge suggests you think us blind to your ambitions."

"My ambitions have nothing to do with the men who were gunned down this morning, Eiters," he replied, slipping into an open seat. "Each of you has just as much reason to be involved."

"You are suggesting we had something to do with this travesty?" Kasop fumed. "I need not remind you we were elected to preserve peace on Romalle."

"A job we don't seem to be doing very well at," Damal reminded. "Or have you forgotten the callous murder of the Cardinal?"

"Calm down, Damal. We are bound to disagree," Eiters said, her voice turning cold. "Cardinal Breed's assassination is in the hands of Hargan and the Inquisition. Let them worry over implications." Her eyes narrowed. "What do you know?"

"Why would I know anything?" Damal said, playing dumb.

Kasop snorted. "Yes, what know you of it?"

Damal leaned back in his chair and spread his empty hands. "What is there to know? Armed gunmen accosted a small party in an alley and appeared to have paid for it with their lives. I don't see this as anything more than rival gangs. Order Hargan to put more uniforms on the streets."

"There is no evidence supporting your theory," Eiters replied. "Though the notion does have merit. Crime is rising the closer we get to choosing sides in the war. We stand the risk of losing everything. Already the Prekhauten Guard are increasing their presence. How much longer before this Mobus Kale deploys a full division to subdue us?"

"And there is the matter of strangers arriving in the last few days," Kasop added. "Whispers of a Blood Witch being seen are spreading."

"I imagine you wish to blame this on me as well," Damal mused. "No one has seen one of those foul creatures but in fairy tales and nightmares. You know as well as I they do not exist, Kasop. The notion of a comet speeding through space housing a secret order of eternal women wielding fell powers is childish fancy. Nothing more."

"Be that as it may, we face perilous times," Eiters intoned. "There can be no denying the war inches closer to our system. The time is fast approaching and we can no longer sit idle."

"The Inquisitor General is not known for his patience," Kasop added. "His actions grow increasingly less rational the longer the war rages. He will not give us options should he turn his attention on us."

"Would that be so bad?" Eiters asked. "It would secure us from violence."

Damal snorted. "By robbing Romalle of an entire generation to funnel into Kale's war machine. Are you prepared to be remembered as the woman who allowed millions to march to their deaths on planets they've never heard of?"

"What choice is there? We don't have the strength to withstand the Inquisition," Kasop snapped.

"There is another possibility," Damal said, pouncing upon the opportunity. "One that might see bloodshed but will leave Romalle in a defensible and strong position."

The other Warders gave him their full attention, eager and concerned to hear what he had to say. Rising, Damal detailed the framework to declaring independence and establishing a new order without fear of reprisal from Vau Prime. It was the moment he'd been waiting for, one that would either elevate his position or damn him to the masses.

NINE

3215 A.G. (After Gods), Allied Staging Area, planet Mannus Prime.

"You remember what happened the last time we deployed in civilian clothes?" Haggle asked Annalilly as they waited for their transport offworld.

She grunted, though he couldn't tell what that meant. In his experience, Annalilly was a woman prone to grunts and angry glares, making her the perfect infantry soldier. Then she said, "I do, but this time will be different."

"Uh huh. We're going to an enemy held world and expected to steal the ruling governess without being caught."

"We don't choose the assignments, Sergeant."

Haggle rolled his eyes, failing to understand how Annalilly could ignore their failure on Kharsis. "We were lucky to get out alive, and not all of us did."

"We also didn't realize we were at the start of a universal war," she countered. "Look, Haggle, I don't like this anymore than you, but orders are orders. We've endured so much already and have come out the other side. Trust command and see to your people. That's all we can do."

"I still don't like it."

"No one is asking you to."

Across the cargo hold of the confiscated shuttle, Jelin Quint listened to the exchange with piqued curiosity. He was well aware of the contributions to the war this platoon had made and, while it was an honor to serve among them, wondered why they hadn't been pulled off the line for much needed rest and refit. Other units who'd faced far less were already languishing under extended downtime.

"What do you think, Madness?"

He glanced up at Annalilly, wincing at the nickname given him during those fragile days after losing his entire company to an ill-fated charge across the no man's land on Mannus. He wondered how she learned of it. "Does it matter? We're in this now and can't turn back."

Crossing her arms, Annalilly glared at him. "It does matter. You're a noncom in my platoon. I expect you to voice your opinion when asked and follow orders when told. You know how the machine works. The only way we succeed is by working together and having full and open communication. The others look to us for guidance and leadership. Never forget that."

"All right, I don't know what Haggle is talking about but the idea of slipping behind enemy lines without armor or heavy weapons leaves me with reservations. We can't go toe to toe with the enemy like this."

"We're not supposed to," she reminded. "Our orders are clear. Slip in, pull the governess from her watchers and get her back to Mannus Prime without engaging the enemy. This isn't going to be a glamorous mission, Quint."

"No less dangerous though," he said. "And we don't have much time either."

"When do we ever? This is a snatch and run. No time for drinks," Annalilly said with a grunt. "How confident are you with your people?"

He glanced over his shoulder where a scattering of Guards were sleeping, playing cards, or cleaning weapons. They weren't the best, but all were proven survivors with lengthy combat records. Veterans, Jelin knew, were the cornerstone to success. Several of his new squad had been together since the opening shots of the war on Crimeat. They bore hardened attitudes making them distrusting outsiders. Earning their approval began during the final campaign to end the fighting on Mannus Prime but he had yet to prove himself in the field. The others were more malleable, having come from different units. Like it or not, they were all he had to work with and no time in which to get comfortable with.

"Fine I suppose. We trust each other about the same. This mission should help smooth things over," he finally answered. "No one ever bonds with their new squad leader right away."

"Keep them all alive and they'll follow you anywhere." Her pride echoed in her words.

Rubbing the stubble on his chin, Jelin added, “At least we don’t have to worry about linking up with any local guides. I don’t fancy being led into a trap.”

“About that…”

“Strap in. We’re making our final approach to Dalafar,” Fies called from the cockpit.

The shuttle plunged into the upper atmosphere unannounced. Though the planet was firmly in enemy control the Inquisitor General had yet to order a blockade. Fies started down on a forested planet of lightly inhabited continents and vast oceans. Schematics showed numerous metropolises built upon ocean, one being their destination. He hadn’t counted on that, and a sense of foreboding filled him. The last time his team had been stuck in a similar restricted situation had been Hawker’s Gate. He found too many familiarities with this mission. Perhaps Haggle had the right of it.

Pushing thoughts of walking into an ambush aside, he focused on the task at hand. Get the Governess and hightail it offworld before the local Guard element reacted. An idea struck and he pulled up details of the Prekhauten security measures. Several battalions were deployed across Dalafar with company sized elements on each of the major water cities. Unsettled with being under armed, the first spark of a plan formed. He needed to run it by Annalilly first but that would have to wait. The shuttle bucked and shuddered as it broke through the lower cloud cover and decelerated. Grunts and curses issued from the hull; a Guard tradition. Fies shook his head, fondly recalling his own days as a lower ranking sergeant cursing pilots out.

“Landing Control, this is shuttle Jers requesting docking access,” he called after punching in the code for their final approach.

“Shuttle Jers, state your business and transit landing credentials.”

“We are enroute to the Phaedian System. Order status classified. Transmitting now,” Fies said and keyed in the codes provided to Matthias by the rogue smuggler Ishis Gul.

He counted the heartbeats until the response arrived: “Shuttle Jers, you are clear for docking at landing bay 14. Welcome to Dalafar.”

The twelve undercover Guards trooped down the ramp and into the customs area. After presenting orders to the local Guard, Fies led them out of the landing facility and into the city proper. The air stank of saltwater and sea life. After spending time on Mannus Prime and Wexanos the Guards were left with reeling stomachs.

Exiting onto the main thoroughfare, they discovered a world unlike any they'd experienced. Vendors mingled with pedestrians under the constant glow of neon signs. Giant incense burners stationed at major intersections added their aromas to the damp air, producing a foul odor permeating all it touched.

"You take us to the nicest places," Annalilly remarked. The muscles of her bare arms rippled with frustration. Like Quint, she too wanted her armor.

Fies shrugged. "What can I say, I like to spoil you."

"I'm going to throw up," Haggle called to them.

They turned and saw, with mild amusement, the sickened color spreading across his face.

Annalilly gestured to the massive dome overhead. "At least the city is moored well enough to keep from rocking. Imagine being seasick on this monstrosity."

The portly sergeant hurried to the side of the closest building and vomited to a chorus of chuckles and jeers from his squad.

"So much for blending in," Jelin murmured to Annalilly. "There's no way we look like we belong here."

"Leave that to me," Fies jumped in. "I have an idea. Can you use those staff skills and draft up some supply requisition orders?"

Jelin frowned. "I suppose so, but why?"

"We're about to be on an official mission," Fies explained. "I don't like the look of this city. Too many narrow streets. No natural egress points. We'll be pinned down and slaughtered the moment we try to get the Governess."

"What are you talking about?" Annalilly asked. "Did you see the air traffic? There must be hundreds of ships coming and going. Who's going to question the Governess with a private security detail?"

"No one when they see us in Guard armor," Fies said.

She scowled. "You're going to get us killed."

"The fun has to end sometime," he replied. "Let's get off the street and find a terminal. The sooner we're moving the better."

"What about making contact with Moscasco? How are we supposed to do that?" Haggle asked, wiping a string of bile residue from the corner of his mouth.

Fies opened and closed his mouth, eyes narrowing. He'd been focused on infiltrating Dalafar he hadn't given linking up with the Governess any thought.

Annalilly snorted and led the way across the street. Clouds of incense smoke settled on her scalp and shoulders. Uncaring, she stormed through the city, silently daring anyone to halt her. A drawback to displays of confidence is drawing attention. The one thing Fies didn't need and the one thing he couldn't prevent. Several passersby halted to take in Annalilly's fiery presence before shuffling about their business. He was certain there were more he couldn't see. Word of their arrival would reach the wrong ears in no time, forcing him to get his people away from prying eyes as soon as possible.

Already drilled on conduct for the duration of the mission, the squad broke down into small groups of two and three. For any more than a casual observer there was no hiding the fact they were professional soldiers. No matter how hard they tried to blend in, soldiers stood out by their rigidity of stride and purposeful movements. Latent intensity in all they did served as a clarion call, in uniform or not.

It took some time before Annalilly tracked down an administration center and plugged into an empty terminal. She, Fies, and Jelin were alone. The others were ordered to gather at a nearby eatery. Annalilly took a chair by the door while Fies and Jelin drafted their new orders.

"You do know I wasn't really on staff," Jelin warned. "My job was protection, nothing else."

"General Torgast trusts you and I know enough that no one who works on staff is unaware of official documents. Make it look passable. We'll do the rest."

Fies left off what the rest entailed, though Jelin Quint served long enough to recognize the veiled threat of violence from a ranking officer. "How did you make lieutenant? You act more like a grizzled old sergeant major."

"War is boon and bane. Me and Annalilly moved up through the ranks with each major engagement. Pisses her off, but I make sure to bump her up every time I do. She may be fiery, and difficult to control, but she is one of the best soldiers I ever served with," Fies finished with a smile and a lingering stare at her.

Jelin whispered, "You're in love. Does she know?"

"Sergeant Quint, she won't let me forget."

"No, I don't suppose she would."

Junior Inquisitor Alpof stood with the arrogance of man far above his natural station. He watched Governess Moscasco with frightening alacrity, as if eager for signs of betrayal. Alerted to a potential breach of loyalty, he'd been given specific instructions to keep her isolated. His shock blond hair in stark contrast to the sinister black of his uniform, Alpof represented the new breed of Inquisitors. Men and women groomed for their strict obedience and willingness to follow Alain Nye's orders without thought.

At his side, Captain Donab of the Prekhauten Guard was decidedly less intense. He was a career soldier who'd grown disillusioned with the war and the damage being wrought upon his people. Being assigned to Dalafar was supposed to offer a reprieve from the rigors of combat. It turned out to prove far more challenging. A handful of terror attacks on Conclave facilities and offices forced him to dedicate more time, personnel, and resources to rooting out insurgents. Each day a new line creased his weathered face.

"This is unacceptable," Alpof complained. "We are unable to neutralize a minor insurrection with all the firepower and influence the Inquisition brings. Why are you not doing more, Captain?"

Grinding his teeth, Donab crossed his legs, one boot bouncing. "I don't answer to you, Alpof. Remember that. Nor am I in charge of Guard reactions. In case you haven't noticed, I report to the Colonel, not you or the Inquisition."

Rage brightening his eyes, Alpof spun and jabbed a finger. "Careful, Donab, else I bring you up on charges of heresy. How would you like to spend the rest of the war in an Inquisition prison cell?"

"You won't live long enough to find out," Donab retorted in an almost serene voice.

Sputtering, the Inquisitor turned away.

"Gentlemen, I am a busy woman. Is there a reason for this childish display or shall have my security escort you from my offices?"

Governess Adris Moscasco remained nonplussed, having grown used to the bickering fools before her. She wondered if the brash Inquisitor knew he was little better than a puppet for his masters on Vau Prime, or if he cared. The Guard captain was a different story. Older, professional and uncompromising, he was a man of duty, choosing to follow the rule of law instead of the whims of madmen. Why he hadn't turned to the insurrection was a mystery she had yet to solve.

"Governess, need I remind you th—"

"That you are here only because I remain a loyal servant of the Conclave. You have no power her, nor shall you," she interrupted. "Do not forget your place, Alpof."

"Or perhaps you will run back to your masters on Vau Prime requesting she too is subjected to the Inquisition?" Donab mused.

Anger trembling through his slender frame, the Inquisitor stormed from the Governess' office.

Waiting for the door to close, Moscasco leveled her gaze upon the Captain. "Provoking him is dangerous, Donab. You don't know what he is capable of."

"I've seen his kind enough before. They fume and bluster but won't pull the trigger when it comes to it."

Moscasco's gaze remained on the door, imagining the embarrassed Inquisitor had his ear pressed against it in hopes of learning some treasonous secret enabling him to unleash the full power of his badge upon Dalafar.

"He is more dangerous than you give him credit for."

"He needs to be put over a knee," Donab muttered. "Still, our young Inquisitor is proving more trouble than he is worth. He is determined to find heresy and will stop at nothing to prove his worth to the Inquisitor General. Be careful with him."

"Captain Donab, you may not have noticed but he has his sights set on you," Moscasco said. "Does he have legitimate reason to believe there are heretics among us?"

"My people have uncovered nothing significant," Donab explained. "Despite the small number of terror attacks spread throughout the ten cities there is no reason to believe there is any interstellar plot in play. That does not preclude those responsible from seeking to bring the insurrection here. I have ordered increased patrols in each of the major districts. Battalion is following suit across the planet. I am confident we'll find those responsible and put them behind bars where they belong."

"How soon?" she pressed. "Time is against us, Captain."

"There is a natural reluctance among the population. No one wishes to see their friends or loved ones in chains. We have several leads. Some are proving valuable, others dead ends."

"The war has not come to Dalafar yet, Donab. I wish to keep it that way."

He shifted, failing to keep the wince from crossing his face.

"You have more to add?" she asked. Her tone elevated just a bit.

"It is not easy for me to bring up, you understand. The hierarchy is in place for a reason. Perhaps if you used your influence with the Conclave our task might be easier."

Relations with the Conclave had been strained since the death of Lorenu Phos. They once shared private correspondence and Moscasco considered the Cardinal Seniorus a friend. Her death shocked the universe and introduced suspicions to the governess. Official reports from Vau Prime said she passed in her sleep. A ridiculous notion at best, a lie at worst. Years later, the power void in the capitol system plunged the universe into a widening war and left Moscasco in a quandary.

Her loyalty to the Conclave remained firm, yet enough had transpired to give her pause. The messages being sent from Vau Prime didn't match the actions of so many rebelling planets. Moscasco began her own fact-finding operation, deploying eyes to fifty planets either in the act of open sedition or simmering with impotent rage. The results rattled her and the first inklings of abandoning the Conclave arose. Alain Nye and his idealistic grab for power was sure to bring all to ruin if enough good people didn't rise against him.

A practical woman, Moscasco refused to draw her planet into unnecessary conflict. Neither did she see a way out without damning Dalafar. Then word of a massive conflict on distant Mannus Prime reached her and she discovered hope, sending an unofficial envoy to meet in secret with the seditionists. A rescue mission was detailed to escort her off Dalafar and into safer hands. How and when they would arrive remained to be seen. Furthering her danger, the governess needed to play her hand closely. Too many variables remained at large, trust being the greatest.

"Any connections I once had with the Conclave were all but severed years ago," she said. "My influence with Vau Prime is greatly reduced. Even if I were to get through to the Inquisitor General, I doubt he has the manpower to spare. Not with the war spreading the way it has."

"It was worth a try." Donab exhaled, slapping his palms on his thighs, he rose and bowed. "Governess. I will redouble our efforts. Rest assured those responsible will be in custody soon. Dalafar shall be spared the violence of war if it is in my power."

"I have no doubts, Captain. Good day."

Governor's Mansion, Eger City, planet Mannus Prime.

The ballroom was awash with resplendent uniforms of pristine white and navy blue. Rows of campaign ribbons decorated chests, accented by gold stripes and embroidered patterns of rank on the sleeves. Men and women with over a thousand years of military experience combined mingled, danced, and exchanged pleasantries with dignitaries, Conclave officials, and those they had not met before.

Soft music echoed from the ceiling under the soothing glow of lamps and decorative candles. Tables filled with food stretched from door to door. Servants brought drinks and appetizers. Yet for all the pleasantries involved, an undercurrent of concern hovered in a miasmic cloud over the officers and senior noncoms assembled. War was ever on their minds, souring the flavors of the feast.

Sharlyn August ran a finger between her collar and throat, desperate to reduce the choking sensation she forgot the uniform inspired. A half empty glass of golden amber beer filled one hand. It was the same drink she'd been nursing since the ball began. Celebrating their recent string of victories was meant to be a joyous occasion, but all she could think of was her impending departure for a planet not listed on any travel charts—Wexanos.

"Loosen up, Sharlyn. This is meant to be fun."

She turned and snapped to attention as Admiral Falchi sidled his way next to her. The older man held his hands clasped behind his back. He smiled and nodded at those making eye contact. Falchi looked at home among the upper echelons. A warrior and diplomat. She, on the other hand, didn't belong.

"I might if not for the fact I am shipping out tomorrow, sir," she replied. "Is this necessary? Admiral Khe-Zhehan won't notice my absence. She doesn't know who I am."

"You'd be surprised what the Admiral knows, Captain. Never underestimate the senior leadership." He paused. "Ah, look. Here she comes now."

Falchi strode forward to intercept Khe-Zhehan—August was fascinated by the subtle confidence he exuded.

Her heart quickened as the Admiral appraised her. There was weight behind the look. One suggesting intimate knowledge and silent judgment. August started to salute but Khe-Zhehan waved her off.

"Enough of that, Captain August. These events are formal enough without having to salute every two minutes. Instead allow me to shake your hand. Without your efforts a dangerous weapon would still be in play."

Stunned, August took the proffered hand. "Thank you, Admiral, but my mission was far from successful."

"Nonsense," Falchi intervened. "The weapon is secure. Without it there is little Presha Von is capable of that cannot be easily countered."

Cheeks reddening, August accepted the praise in silence.

Khe-Zhehan continued. "I understand you have been given a noble assignment. Do not fail us, August. A great many lives depend upon you."

"I won't fail you, Admiral," August replied.

The Admiral patted her forearm. "I know you won't. Well, Falchi, shall we go finish with the official duties? I'm not as young as I used to be."

"Comes with the rank, or so I'm told."

The jib, while jovial, rang true for himself. Falchi was but a senior captain at the beginning of the war. Three years and numerous engagements, complete with tragedy and loss, aged him far beyond his years. His hair was greying much too fast for his liking and stress lines filled his face and hands, lending him a seasoned appearance.

Khe-Zhehan cast a stern look upon him. "Feeling sure of yourself tonight, aren't you, Ernst?"

He smiled. "One must take what they can get—"

"When they can," she finished.

Laughing, the duo stalked off and left a confused August standing alone.

"I'm not suggesting rebuilding the Conclave here, but something must be done in the event Vau Prime falls," Cardinal Virom said to the small crowd assembled. "We are the strongest beacon for freedom in the universe at the moment. Our victory here cemented the possibility that the old ways won't die when, or if, Nye completes his takeover and reshuffles the balance of power."

"Setting yourself up to be Cardinal Seniorus, Virom?" General Torgast asked.

"Not at all, though I am suggesting we send the word across the universe. Any who adhere to the true rule of law and desire a free universe should be welcome on Mannus Prime. We must not seek to emulate Krenz, but we can establish a haven for all who feel threatened by our foes."

"The infrastructure is not in place for such an endeavor, Cardinal. Nor should this devolve to a military state. Mannus Prime is a staging area for future deployments. Placing any ruling body on the same planet makes us too great of a target for Nye to ignore."

"Every day our strength increases. We are not weak or defenseless, even should half the fleet and army deploy," Falchi said as he took in the motley collection of minor dignitaries and planetary officials.

The old governor was missing, having fled during the height of the final stage of the war and taking a large chunk of the treasury with him. The result plunged Mannus Prime into a recession the planet struggled to escape. Interplanetary trade rose to combat the dearth of supplies and funding. The influx of personnel and equipment to support the growing army did little to help matters, threatening to push the local economy to total collapse. Bringing untold numbers of cardinals, administrators, and senior military leaders in might buoy the system for a while but it was a stopgap measure at best.

"My staff is ready to assist where necessary, but we lack the internal structure to run the planet," Virom admitted. "I need as many loyal officials as possible if there is any chance of solving our problems and completing the transformation to an independent state."

"Surely this is but practical theory," Khe-Zhehan injected. "There has been no official talk of usurping control from Vau Prime."

"Is it?" Virom squared on her. "Three years is a long time, my friends. What was once solid leadership has melted to a mutation of all we once held dear. The Conclave is a ragged shell of what was. Cardinals and clergy are being persecuted for failing to follow Alain Nye's lead. Martial law has been imposed across the stars, rending the Conclave neutral. Those few who have remained loyal to our true purpose are hunted like beasts by the mad general Nye has let loose. We stand upon the brink of elimination. Failure to plan will lead to the extinction of all we hold dear."

"He's not wrong," Torgast said. "With the Conclave gone there are no tenders to the faith. How many trillions will find unrest in that void?"

"The religious implications are seldom considered when matters of violence argue," Virom added. "Without the Conclave there will be a crisis of faith the likes the universe has never seen."

"So, you suggest rebuilding the order here?" Torgast pressed.

"I cannot be responsible for administering faith to seven hundred planets, General," Virom answered. "No, I fear we can never return to the old way of thought. The Conclave has proven inadequate, corrupted on irreparable levels. We must look to a new dawn. A new way of thought that will see the seven hundred planets find their own way forward until a better system can be established."

"This is dangerous talk," Falchi said. "Vau Prime yet stands. Until it falls, we must hold to hope."

They paused as a trio of visiting dignitaries walked by, immersed in their own conversation.

Virom tensed. "We cannot ignore the highest levels of leadership on Vau Prime have been compromised. That being said, I merely suggest having a discussion about contingencies. Ladies and gentlemen, I would like to present to you Minister Standou of Orlei. He and I have known each other for years and I believe he is a worthy man."

"It is my pleasure to meet you all. Your reputations are known throughout the universe," Standou began taking in the others, all military professionals save Virom, "though for different reasons to different people." Dark hair and dusty skin, Standou wore thick mustachios drooping down below his chin.

"What can we help you with, Minister? This is meant to be a celebration, not business discussion," Torgast threw back the rest of his drink and set the glass on the nearest table.

"It is no secret the universal order is crumbling. The Conclave is ruined. Both the Guard and Inquisition are nests of vipers. Where can the people turn in such state? Without alternatives the population has no choice but to submit."

"Which is what we are fighting for," Khe-Zhehan said. She panned over the others, looking deep into her officers' eyes. "Humanity faces its greatest test. Not since the end of the gods has our world been threatened. We stand upon the precipice. You all know where my loyalties lie and, if it were possible, I would blockade Vau Prime and force Nye to submit. But that option is gone. He has encircled the planet with several fleets, drawing in mercenaries and worse to bolster numbers. While our numbers continue to grow, we lack the firepower to clear enough space to land the necessary ground units to liberty the planet."

"There is more you are not aware of, Admiral."

Heads turned as Matthias strode into their midst, silently apologizing for his late arrival.

"Ah, Sergeant Major. I was wondering when you were going to present yourself," she greeted with a crispness he'd almost forgotten.

"Please, just Matthias. There is another side of this war none of you are aware of. One upon which our survival hinges," he explained.

"A military threat?" Torgast asked.

"If only it were," Matthias replied. "I will not speak of much here, for I do not know if the enemy has ears within this room, but I will say this. The Three have been engineering this war from the beginning. Amongeratix has secured his legendary warship and makes for Vau Prime. His brother Tannus believes he has a weapon capable of killing him, but he needs time."

"How come you by this information?" Khe-Zhehan asked.

Falchi cleared his throat. "There are a few of us who have been working with Tannus for several years. We were all sworn to secrecy."

Suspicion hardened her features. "Indeed. Why has Tannus not announced himself to those of us yet loyal?"

"He bides his time," Matthias interjected. "Lord Tannus has assembled a small force and conducts his part to help us win the war. There is yet hope, Admiral."

"Why now?" Virom asked after absorbing this new information. "We have been at war for almost three years. Untold millions have died, including an entire planet. Is Tannus truly on our side or has he individual motivations?"

"He has been involved on deep levels since the first battles of Crimeat. Guards, Inquisitors, and Blood Witches have fought and died on several planets, including Kharsis, in the name of freedom. Tannus wants nothing to do with ruling the universe. He seeks to prevent his brother from putting us all in chains."

"How can you be sure?" Torgast asked. The idea of being beholden to a mythical being rankled him.

"Where do you think your reinforcements came from?" Matthias asked.

Torgast's eyes narrowed. "But they were Guards. Does this Tannus command Guard units now?"

"Certain ones. When General Strannan was forced into exile, he decentralized several units that then ceased to exist. Those who arrived on here for the final campaign have been working with Tannus for the last three years."

Khe-Zhehan focused her gaze on Falchi. "You were part of this?"

"Since the disaster at Hawker's Gate. It was a necessary deception," he replied. "Perhaps this is not the best venue for such discussions."

Minister Standou twisted his lips, pulling on a mustachio. "I don't like this. We cannot hope to succeed without full transparency and communication. Holding anything back leaves the advantages with our enemies."

Matthias stiffened. "I'm sure you can understand Lord Tannus' reluctance to entrust the future to men and women who have shown an eagerness to betray and murder each other. He has endured this scenario for three thousand years since the fall of his people. We have only known it for a handful."

"The gods killed themselves," Virom said. "What troubles me is Tannus has seen fit to abscond numerous members of our society to further his needs without telling the rest of us."

"His needs are ours, Cardinal," Matthias insisted. "We have been on the front lines for too long but continue to be the tip of the spear. Many of our people have died in places the rest of the universe has never heard of. We don't do it for recognition or reward. We know our lives are on the line with each engagement, yet we continue deploying forth so that others won't have to."

"There is more at work here than we know," Khe-Zhehan agreed. "I believe this is a conversation that needs more exposition. Perhaps tomorrow morning?"

Heads bobbed. They agreed to meet in Virom's offices before filing off to different parts of the ball.

The Admiral scratched at the corner of her mouth and beckoned Falchi to her side. She watched with amusement as the younger man swallowed his nerves and attempted to regain composure. "You've been keeping secrets, Ernst," she chided low enough others couldn't hear.

Falchi refused to meet her gaze. "I didn't have a choice."

"Obviously. Tell me straight. Can we trust Tannus to act in our best interest?"

Falchi leveled his most confident gaze on her. "Admiral, he is the only one who does."

TEN

3215 A.G. (After Gods), Zevistya Spaceport, Low Continent, planet Vau Prime.

Bryn Mal was awakened by the incessant tugging on her boot. Still recovering from wounds suffered in the failed defense of General Strannan's life, she groaned and attempted to roll over in the vain hopes of having a bad dream. The tugging continued until she sat up with a growl and a grunt of pain. "This had better be good."

"Quiet, Lieutenant. I need you to come with us."

Squinting, she peered into the dark and the vague features staring back at her. "Silk? What are you playing at?"

"We have a situation. Quickly. Dress and grab your sidearm. I will be waiting outside."

The shapeshifter slipped from her tent, leaving her confused and concerned. Mal slipped into her boots and donned a fresh, well fresh enough, blouse before snatching her blaster and following. Her body ached as the medicine last administered was at the point of wearing off. In another time she would have been on convalescent leave, recuperating on the Guard's credits until docs cleared her back to active duty. Here on the low continent, being alive was her reward.

Unsure what to expect, she found Jash Abernath standing beside Gedrick Silk. A handful of haggard Guards clustered behind them. Suspicions rising, she asked, "What's this about? I'm in no condition to wander around on nightly adventures."

Gedrick blew into his palms and rubbed them together. A chill clung to the air, the perfect accoutrement for the night's work. "I was coming back from the head when I spied Colonel Apontee and a group of soldiers sneaking into the communications shed. Curious, I followed him. What happened next I cannot say, for I did not bear witness, but I saw the soldiers carry two bodies out of the shed and dispose of them behind an empty shed by the runway. They now guard the entrance."

"Wait, you're saying the Colonel ordered the murder of two of our people?" Abernath said. "That doesn't make sense."

"It does if he's going to sell us out to Kale," Mal concluded. "Gedrick, how sure are you of this?"

"I only know what my eyes saw."

"If you're wrong…"

They both bore natural reservations against the upstart colonel. He was intent on taking the war in a new direction but remained secretive as to which way. Mal's suspicions remained hers, but a quick look around suggested the others felt similar. Drawing her weapon, she began walking to the commo shed. The rest fell in behind.

They reached the shed, clinging to the closest wall to avoid being seen. True to Silk's word, a pair of Guards flanked the door, weapons at the ready. Each watched their assigned sectors, clearly on guard. It was enough to confirm Mal's worst fears. She looked up to the roof and was dismayed to see the antenna relay whirling in search of a signal.

"He's calling Kale," she whispered. "We need to move. Now."

Abernath clicked the safety of his rifle. "What do we do? We can't just storm in there. He'll do whatever he came here for before we can get past those guards."

"I have an idea," she said and pulled them close to explain.

The guards stiffened as Mal and another officer approached. Given clear instructions to keep all others out, they shifted closer together and raised their weapons. Mal slowed, portraying a natural confusion.

"That's close enough," one guard said. "Colonel said no one enters."

"Colonel Apontee?" she questioned. "I have an urgent communication for the insurgent cells in Krenz. New orders before we bug out."

They looked at each other, unsure what she was saying. "Don't know nothing about that, ma'am. Orders are orders."

She nodded. "Do you have any idea when he might be finished? I really need to get this out."

"He didn't say. Only that we hold the door. Can't trust anyone these days. There're rumors of enemy spies in our ranks."

Mal hummed. "We're all under strain down here since the general died."

"I'm sure he won't be much longer," the second guard said. "You should be going before he comes out."

Message understood, Mal thanked them and took a step before turning. They were lowering their weapons—it was their last mistake. She and Silk fired once with silenced weapons. The ion rounds struck the guards in the chest, and they crumpled to the ground. She gestured and the rest of their team hurried from their concealed positions to clear the bodies before replacing them. How they accomplished so much undetected left her stunned. Once finished, she led the rest back into the night where they awaited the renegade colonel.

Jash Abernath discovered a measure of strength during the last few weeks. He wasn't sure why he joined the Guard, only that it might help bring him closer to his father. It did, but at the cost of a strained relationship neither figured out how to navigate. They hadn't spoken since, leaving Jash to think the problem was him all along.

He climbed his way to the top of the commo shed one agonizing foothold at a time; he still wasn't convinced the colonel was turning them in. And even if they stopped him from transmitting there was no way to hold him accountable without actionable proof. It would be his word against theirs and that was a fight neither junior lieutenant could win. Regardless of personal feelings, his duty lay with the true Guard and, until he had orders otherwise, that meant the vision of Davith Strannan.

Gaining the roof, Jash slithered to the base of the relay. He wasn't sure what he was looking for or what to do. That part of the plan never actualized. Getting on the roof and knocking out the relay sounded like a good idea when Mal presented it, but now that he was here Jash had no idea what he was doing. He fumbled about in the dark for power cords or a control panel but found nothing.

The sound of Mal's voice told him time was up. A scuffle broke out, followed by the hurried march of several pairs of boots. Frustrated, Jash sat down and did the one thing he could think of. He kicked the relay base as hard as he could.

It didn't budge. He kicked again and again, rewarded at last with a shower of sparks and the cold metallic groan of the relay ripping free from the roof. Leaning back, Jash breathed a sigh of relief. He didn't know if his actions were in time to stop the suspected transition or what might happen when the others stormed the shed, but he'd done his part. Snatching his rifle, Jash slipped over the edge and hurried back to the ground.

The door burst open, followed by Mal, Gedrick and the other Guards. A stunned Colonel Apontee jerked away from the control panel. The young Guard at his side made the fatal mistake of raising his rifle and was shot in the chest for it. Guards swarmed in, dragging the colonel away and placing him in restraints.

"What is the meaning of this?" he demanded, red-faced and spitting with each syllable.

Gedrick checked the transmission logs.

"Anything?" Mal asked.

"No. He was unable to transmit," the shapeshifter confirmed.

Apontee, struggling against his bonds, glared at her. "Lieutenant, you had best explain yourself or I'll have you shot for treason."

She edged closer, the cold tip of her barrel pressing against his chest. "Treason? What were you doing here, Colonel? No external communications are permitted."

"I am ranking officer," he seethed. "Do not question my authority."

"You never had authority. General Strannan kept you from his confidence," she said. "I have reason to believe you were about to sell us out to the enemy. Do you deny this?"

"Nonsense," he said after blinking rapidly. "I am trying to keep us alive."

"By giving us to Mobus Kale?" Gedrick Silk asked.

Apontee snarled. "What would a non-human know of our struggle? Strannan should never have involved you. Perhaps if you had been successful in your assignment this would all be over, and I wouldn't have to make difficult decisions."

Mal stepped between them. "Who were you attempting to contact, Colonel? Where are the guards assigned to this post?"

Stiffening, Apontee fell silent. Frustrated, his captors were left with no admission of guilt, though his actions suggested otherwise. Mal clenched a fist and struggled with the urge to lash out at the man.

"Take him away and make sure he is kept under guard until this is sorted," she ordered. "I don't want him speaking to another soul. Am I understood?"

"Yes ma'am."

She jerked her head. "Get him out of here."

They marched the colonel away, leaving Mal and Gedrick alone; Jash entered once the others were gone.

"What did I miss?" he asked, a boyish grin spreading across his grime smeared face.

"I didn't shoot him, if that's what you're asking," she replied. "What do we do now? Regardless of his intentions, he was the senior ranking man here. Chain of command should go to Apontee."

Gedrick folded his arms, face locked in thought. "We must discover how deep support for him goes. If the core of our force is riddled with dissent, we are undone."

"I don't need a bloodbath on my hands because of one man seeking to save his own neck," she snapped. "How can we determine who remains loyal without causing too great a disturbance? We are in a dangerous position."

Jash snorted. "We've been in one since the war began. The real question is how long before Kale learns of our presence and sets out to eliminate us?"

"Mobus Kale is focused on more pressing matters," Gedrick explained. "The promise of a great darkness is approaching. A time where worlds burn. A time for tyrants and madmen. The age of reason is falling apart. Perhaps it is time to enact the final step of Strannan's plan."

"Abandon Vau Prime and all we have bled and died for?" Mal exclaimed.

"If it means keeping the bulk of our forces alive, yes."

"What about the teams in Krenz?" Jash asked. "We can't abandon them. Not after all they've been through."

"There might not be a choice. The winds of war shift, Jash Abernath. Where it blows next none may guess," Gedrick said.

Outskirts of Krenz, planet Vau Prime.

"Keep moving."

The line of dark figures slipped through the night, avoiding the searching lights. Hearts in their throats, the men and women shuffled closer to the extraction point where a shuttle would escort them offworld and, if all went well, the growing allied encampment on Mannus Prime. Much could go wrong from here to there, but it was a risk they had to take. The alternative was death.

Julian laid a hand on every shoulder, taking headcount. He had a number but not the names to go with it. This presented potential issues should one of Kale's people infiltrate the evacuation. Again, risk versus reward.

After deliberation it was decided the insurgent cells needed to leave Krenz while they could. Already the streets were inundated with fresh Guard battalions, special police units, and new Inquisitors loyal to Alain Nye. Combat operations slowed to a trickle as the noose drew tighter. Edam Boone and his network secured several transports and the race to leave the corrupted central planet was on.

"Thirty," Julian whispered.

Aliz, ever at his side as the tides of war shifted against them, watched as the bobbing figures huddled in the lee of a storage building. The low cloud cover reflected orange lights, creating a haunting glow. She shuddered as she imagined seeing hundreds of black uniforms sweeping in to gun down the insurgents. "How much longer before the shuttle arrives?"

Julian checked his wrist chrono. "They're already late." He paused as she gasped. "Relax, Aliz. We have people watching every avenue of approach, including the sky. If Kale is on to us, we'll know long enough in advance to get these people to safety."

There was no safe place in Krenz. The almost continent sized city had become a hotbed for hatred and division. Violence was the currency of the day.

Aliz began rubbing her index finger and thumb together, counting the moments until the first blinking green and red lights penetrated the orange haze. Downward winds swirled, curling around the scorched hull as the shuttle dropped. She tensed, searching through the haze for sign of incoming missile or rocket fire.

"Come on. Come on," she muttered.

Julian placed a hand upon her shoulder, gently squeezing. “If the enemy had scouts in place we would know.”

“I can’t relax until that ship is in space and clearing the system,” she replied. “Why is taking so long?”

“Because it means so much.”

The shuttle touched down with a groan, the back ramp already opening. A pair of flight crew emerged. They were dressed in dull grey flight suits. The visors on their helmets obscured their faces. Sidearms were strapped under the arms. One, the crew chief, removed his helmet and approached.

“I heard you need a ride,” he said with a little amusement.

Julian clasped his offered hand. “With plenty more to come. Good to see you.”

“You almost didn’t, Captain. We had to dodge a few patrols to make planetside. The sooner your people are aboard the faster we can hightail it out of system. Kale’s locking everything down.”

Julian stepped aside as the selected thirty hurried to the waiting shuttle. “That bad? We’ve been cut off from external comms for a while now.”

“Looks like something pretty big is about to go down,” the crew chief confirmed. “New fleets are gathering around the moon bases. Vau Prime has become a fortress since Mannus fell.”

At least some aspect of the war was going right. Julian took hope in the crew chief’s words, even now knowing any escape from Krenz grew increasingly more dangerous with each flight. Sooner or later their luck would run dry. The risks were necessary. Every fighter he evacuated today was another gun for the army gathering half the universe away.

“Any word from the low continent?”

“Last we heard General Strannan had been killed and his army was retreating to the east … Captain, I have to tell you this doesn’t look good. Between the Inquisition and Kale there are rumors of a dark power heading this way.”

Aliz edged closer to them. “Dark power?”

Sensing the crew chief’s hesitance, Julian said, “She was in the office of the Cardinal Seniorus before the war.”

"Nothing concrete has been said but people are talking about the Three," he said, accepting Julian's judgment. "The last thing we need is the gods getting involved."

The last man boarded. Time up, the crew chief offered his hand a final time. "We'll try to make another run as soon as we can, but like I said, the window is closing. Good luck, Captain. Ma'am."

"How much time do you think we have left?" Aliz asked after returning to Boone's hideout. She swirled the cup of caf, concentrating on the ripples.

Leaning against the wall and doing his best to ignore the dull throb of a pulled muscle in the middle of his back, Julian didn't have answers. He grew weary of seeing his people die, even burdened with the knowledge their sacrifices ensured the lives of countless others continued. He grew tired of fighting. Constantly looking over his shoulder for that fateful round that would deliver him to oblivion. "Not much. Kale appears to have had enough."

At her silence, Julian studied her. This incredible woman who should have broke years ago. Where she found the strength to continue fascinated him. He wondered how he would have handled losing everything, scraping by in one harrowing misadventure after the next only to discover nothing he did mattered. The enemy grew stronger. The insurgency dwindled each day. Yet Aliz stood strong. A final warrior upon the rampart holding her banner high. Was it hope or revenge that inspired her? She hadn't said, and he was afraid to ask.

Lips pursed, Aliz suddenly flung her cup and watched it shatter against the wall. Dark stains trickled down. "When does this end? Is there no sense of fairness in the universe left? How can good people come to this ruin while villains like Nye and Kale gather power and extend their influence? It's not right."

"No. It's not, but that's life. We can't control what happens or to whom. You know this. The only thing we can do is keep fighting for our friends and for those we lost," he soothed. "I know what you're going through. I do, but it doesn't help lashing out blindly. Channel your rage and use it against our enemies."

"Isn't that what we've been doing?" she snapped. "Three years of fighting and dying and we are no better off than at the beginning!"

He wanted to enfold her in his embrace, take away the pain. The woman who had become almost a second mother to him teetered on the edge of madness. Everyone had a breaking point. He feared she was barreling toward hers and he was powerless to stop it.

"I wish I had answers for you, Aliz," he told her, keeping his voice even. "The best we can do is hope the other planets are rebelling against this rising tyranny."

"We don't know that. We don't know anything."

Face contorting with fury, Aliz wanted to lash out. She hadn't felt this negated since the early days of keeping her relationship with Lorenu private. Ever hidden behind the curtain for fear of being used against the Conclave's rising star. That absence from public life continued long after Lorenu was elected Cardinal Seniorus. It was her greatest lament.

"Aliz, you heard the shuttle jockey. Armies are gathering. We are not alone, though it may feel so. Wherever evil rises there is good to combat it. That is the way of things," Julian said. His voice was low and calm, an old trick he learned when first dealing with others. "Vau Prime may be a losing battle but the cause remains strong. Do not give in to your fears. Not now. Not after all you've sacrificed."

Sacrifice. The word stung, knocking down some of her rage. Exhaustion rushed in, filling those now empty places in her resolve. "I'm sorry, Julian. You'll have to forgive an old woman her miseries."

"There's nothing to forgive. I feel the same way."

Wiping a tear from the corner of her eye, Aliz asked, "How do you deal with it?"

"I have people counting on me to remain strong. As long as one other soul falls under my command what choice have I but to stand in front and lead?"

"Have you ever thought of having children?" she asked, unsure where the idea stemmed from. "You'd make a good father."

His smile lacked warmth. "I fear that's something I'm not going to get to experience."

The knock on the door ended their conversation.

General Mobus Kale towered over the kneeling, bound figure. Battered and bleeding, the man was an affront to all Kale strove to build. A cancer of the old ways. Where he once served as a loyal Guard, Kale only saw a broken traitor throwing away his principles to side with those who would serve themselves instead of the greater good. A ring of guards, hand selected for their veracity and devotion, encircled the scene in the remains of the former insurgent safehouse. He insisted on conducting business within as a show of force against other cells operating in this part of the city.

His allegiance to Alain Nye grew strained. Ever did the Inquisitor General, the self-proclaimed ruler of the universe, seek council from dark powers anathema to man. What this Amongeratix offered remained to be seen and the general planned to deal with it when the time came. Until then, Kale intended on running the war as he saw fit. The only way to end a rebellion was to crush it so thoroughly no one dared pick up a rifle ever again.

"Where are the others?"

Head down, drooling spittle and blood, the insurgent no longer strained against his bonds. "Why would I tell a monster like you?"

Scorch marks from countless ion rounds scored the walls. Holes were blown out by rocket propelled grenades, leaving the building on the brink of collapse. Bodies were stacked carelessly against the far wall. Their lifeless eyes watching the scene.

Crouching, Mobus used his metal hand to lift the insurgent's face until they stared one another in the eye. "I like to see the measure of the man I am about to kill. Tell me where the other cells are located, including your command and control, and I will let you die with honor. You have my word."

"Fuck you."

Kale punched the insurgent in the face with his metal arm until nothing remained of his head but a bloody pulp. Uniform sleeve ruined, bits of flesh and bone wedged into the joints, he rose and shouted, "Burn it to the ground. String the bodies from the streetlights. I want everyone to know what happens when they dare resist."

Amongeratix's fortress, planet Antil IV.

Long rifle vibrating in his hands, Akin Brohl stalked the deepest recesses of the fortress. Yet to stumble across the architect of endless suffering and bloodshed, he slew menials and a score of those nightmarish creatures Amongeratix preferred over human fodder. The skulldaerth proved fearsome opponents but nothing capable of fully arousing his lust for battle. Akin had hunted them before and, despite countless centuries trapped in the cold oblivion of sleep, felt no fear. They were little more than obstacles for the god hunter.

Deeper and deeper he went, striking for the heart of the inner sanctum. Step by step, modern technologies of the upper floors disappeared. He hadn't seen a window for some time. Amongeratix was cunning and wily, untrusting of his own lieutenants. Traps were strewn throughout. Numerous doors were sealed, all funneling Akin closer to his goal: Find Amongeratix's lair and finish the task begun three thousand years ago. Even if Amongeratix was gone and killing him might not happen this day, that was fine. He had another target.

The air turned stale. How long it had been since any strode these halls was a mystery. Akin avoided dust covered cobwebs stubbornly clinging to the walls and ceiling. He stepped over the skeletal remains of small animals and an occasional human dead far longer than they ever lived.

He stepped upon the lowest level and stilled.

His target was close.

"I'm coming for you, Bloody Man."

The fortress shifted in response, throwing him off balance as it rocked deep within the bowels of the planet. Akin's pace quickened. Slime covered the walls. A mucus sinew clinging wherever he touched it. The thin glow of light emanating from the end of the hall appeared, mocking him. Akin gripped his rifle tighter, flicking the safety off with his thumb.

He crept through the darkness and pressed against the wall framing the door. Slowing his breath, he let his eyes adjust to the light before slinking his head around the corner.

Sorrow. The giant was rummaging through long forgotten crates, tossing metallic pieces across the workshop. Venting frustrations, he'd amassed a large debris pile as he searched.

The god hunter crouched, one knee touching the dust covered stone floor, and leveled his rifle at the base of Sorrow's neck. The pad of his index finger curled onto the trigger and lightly squeezed.

Sorrow jerked, spinning aside the instant before the round tore through the space where he'd been standing. It exploded on the far wall, sending shrapnel and superheated matter across the shop. Snarling, the Bloody Man caught his assailant preparing for a second shot and charged. Each step caused a rumble of thunder. The quiver of his muscled frame wept blood as he crossed the distance in three strides and swung a mighty fist. The mortal ducked and rolled away as Sorrow's fist smashed through the already crumbling stone wall.

"Who dares assault me!"

He kicked, catching Akin in the side and sending him sprawling down the hall. The rifle clattered away and Sorrow crushed it beneath his heel before turning towards his would be assassin. He watched as Akin crawled away, fear clouding his eyes. Upon Akin in mere heartbeats, Sorrow reached down to throttle the life from the hapless man when recognition flashed. Sorrow tried pulling his hand back but it was too late.

Akin had reached in his waist holster and drew his blaster waiting to fire until Sorrow was upon him. The giant staggered back as Akin emptied the power charge, rewarded by the sizzle of flesh and cries of agony. "Die, monster!"

Black smoke poured from Sorrow's wounds; Akin dropped the empty charge and fumbled for the second pack in his ammo pouches on the belt at his waist. Sorrow recovered and swatted him with a backhand that sent him into the nearest wall with the crunch of breaking bones. Weeping ichor, the giant fled.

On his back, curled in agony, Akin howled as his bones knit and organs healed. The regenerative process, designed to mirror the metabolism and DNA sequence of the gods, worked with blinding speed. Soon he was on all fours, panting and dripping sweat. When at last his vision cleared, Sorrow was long gone. Whatever he'd risked coming to Antil for forgotten.

The god hunter climbed to his feet, staggering the first few steps, and hurried in pursuit. There was only one destination for the twelve-foot-tall monster to head. The airfield. Akin bent to inspect his rifle. The ancient weapon was mangled beyond repair. He felt a pang of regret. The weapon had saved his life more times than he remembered. But he needed to keep moving, there was still time to catch his prey.

Tracing his route back to the surface agonized him, for Akin was forced to slow too many times to avoid springing traps. Sorrow, by all accounts, appeared to have avoided the main routes altogether. No blood trail was evident. Nor were there any footprints to guide him. Had the Bloody Man sheltered in a forgotten chamber in the lower levels in the hopes of his attacker passing him? He wouldn't have been the first to attempt such. Others were foolish enough to try.

Frustrated by being this close, the god hunter ran.

Pain unlike any he'd felt in a thousand years wracked his body. Chemical fires burned deep within his flesh, preventing the healing process from completing. His breath came in ragged gasps. Each step an agony. Sorrow knew the god hunter from days long past. Knew and feared him. Akin Brohl was part of a covert program begun by the Blood Witches. Ruma Zzein's attempt at taking vengeance upon those who'd kept her in chains for centuries. His brother Tannus appealed to her good nature, convincing her to abandon the program, but not before Akin escaped and began doing what he'd been created for. The results were catastrophic, for he was naught but a loose cannon without handler or ally.

Why was he here though? The question gnawed at Sorrow as he fled through abandoned corridors. Cloning chambers comprised many of the lower levels. Laboratories in which Amongeratix perfected his unholy skulldaerth. Sorrow had come to destroy them, but the god hunter's unexpected arrival unraveled his plans. Antil was no longer safe, prompting him to question whether Akin had been compromised and now served his brother. Far from ridiculous, the idea unsettled him.

He needed to contact Tannus—the course of the war hinged upon it.

ELEVEN

3215 A. G. (After Gods), Erdef City, planet Romalle.

Whalen Arbist sat on the comforts of his back porch overlooking his extensive rose gardens with a glass of his favorite wine. Soft music played in the background. The setting sun turned the horizon shades of crimson, marred by the rolling hills and far-reaching orchards of his estates. The villa behind him was a sprawling compound worth more than most of Romalle's citizens made in a lifetime.

Self-important, Whalen was born into wealth. He multiplied it exponentially with weapons deals for the Prekhauten Guard and several smaller factions flying under the Conclave's radar. Unscrupulous when it came to profit, Whalen soon became the richest man in the sector. He wasn't stopping there. Whalen extended his influence to local politics, cultivating deep relationships with the City Board as well as some of the major players on Vau Prime. He was a man who knew how to win and tonight he enjoyed the spoils of those victories.

Eyes closed, Whalen tipped his head back into the soft cushion. He never heard the footsteps approaching from behind. It wasn't until the cold barrel of a hand blaster pressed against his skull that he opened his eyes.

The last thing Whalen Arbist saw was the dying sun.

Jameson Ith considered himself a pioneer. His grandfather arrived on Romalle with a handful of credits and a dream. Two generations earlier the planet was a faint step above uncolonized. One of the newer planets open for settlements, the Conclave was quick to swoop in and claim dominance. Where it went so too went the opportunists. Jameson's grandfather cashed in his credits and jumped on the first transport he could find. Nearly one hundred years later Jameson was the owner of the largest mining corporation on the planet. Rumors, he failed to deny or clarify, suggested he was so rich he bathed in gold.

Housecoat undone and dressed in a short pair of swim trunks, he stalked through his mansion with a drink in one hand. A handful of his favorite mistresses lounged by the pool. Tonight he planned on enjoying them all. Jameson wielded his wealth with callous disregard for those deemed beneath him. He was a man who got what he wanted and let nothing stand in his way. So what if he hadn't earned his name? Jameson stood upon his forefather's legacy, reputation and generational wealth.

Grinning, he refilled his drink and headed back outside. Jameson's mouth dropped open upon seeing the bloodstains on the rockcrete and in the water. His mistresses, four unfortunate souls drawn to his power, lay strewn about the area in mangled poses. His drink slipped from his hand, shattered at his feet. Jameson turned, desperate to call for security before remembering they'd been given the night off so as not to intrude on his proclivities.

Turning, Jameson came face to face with the murderer. The blade flashed in the flickering light and plunged into his heart.

Emmest DeMauve stared at the endless rows of books. In a digital age, she relished collecting old fashioned hardbound copies of her favorite tales. What started as fancy quickly turned to obsession. She boasted the largest collection of traditional books on Romalle and, she suspected, Vau Prime. Only the legendary Conclave vaults were rumored to contain more volumes.

Inspired by her collection, she dabbled in writing, though her brain and fingers seldom worked in concert. A hundred started stories lay in reckless folders in her private office. Her ideas, always rich and enticing when locked within the corners of her mind, failed to convey into words. Rather than succumbing to frustration, she continued the attempt at bringing her innermost fantasies to life.

The hour was late, the sun having set long ago. Emmest enjoyed the quiet tranquility of her library when the world slept. A creature of habit, she sat and thought and wrote until her eyes fluttered shut. Accountable to no one and protected by a nefarious reputation, she did what she could with the time she had left.

Done for the night, she yawned, stretched, and set down her ink pen. Where Emmest found such items remained a mystery to all but her and her supplier. Her fingers cramped from staying curled around the slender object for so long, but it felt good. The bones in her spine cracked as they snapped back into place when she stood. Hours of sitting in one place did wonders for bad posture. Blowing out the candle, she glided from her library and down the hall to her bedroom. The slightest hint of movement caught her eye.

Emmest's gaze narrowed. Few demonstrated the audacity to invade her private sanctum. Perhaps, she surmised, it was a trick of the moonlight, whispering shadows where no belonged. Chalking it up to being tired, she continued as the promise of long sleep on a soft bed enticed her. She laid her hand on the golden handle of her doorknob and pushed down. The door swung open—

A cold rush of air snuck up behind her. Emmest wheeled, all tiredness evaporating. She blocked out the man's efforts to assault her and launched a flurry of blows to his neck and abdomen. The man grunted and fell back. A blade clattered against the floor. She attacked with unrelenting fury. Ribs snapped. Nose broke. Emmest brought her knee to his groin and the man collapsed. Not stopping, the Lady DeMauve continued her assault until the last breath escaped his lips.

Gasping for air, she stepped back and placed her hands over her head. Her hair was a mess. Sweated beaded across her golden flesh. Her vision cleared. The aggression slowed and she began assessing the situation. The possibility of more than one assassin was high, unless the fool lying at her feet was overconfident in his ability. She doubted any of the major guilds backed him, nor did he bear the telltale mask of the Vaumagians.

Approaching footsteps drew her attention. She tensed, only to find Mayn with a long rifle in his hands. Emmest smiled at the elderly man. "No need for that, Mayn. Our friend here will trouble no one else again. See to the perimeter. I want to know if he came alone or if we can expect further surprise."

"Yes, my lady," Mayn said. He looked grumpy at having been disturbed so late in the night. His bandy knees wobbled as he turned and headed for the security center.

Emmest watched him go, fretting over what she would do if she ever lost him. Once she was alone again, she knelt before the corpse and searched for any telltale scars, tattoos, or discernable features.

"I believe I must speak with young Riles Tenaru again," she concluded after her inspection produced no results.

Confident she would find nothing else, Emmest grasped the body by the ankles and began dragging him down to refuse pit for tomorrow's burning. No point in wasting time for the authorities to come. They had their hands full enough with the Cardinal's murder.

"Gentlemen, what an unexpected surprise," Emmest greeted through a false smile.

Gando and Hargan fidgeted under her gaze. They'd come at the insistence of the priestess Astrid but had no idea what to expect. Gando's time on Romalle seldom involved murder cases. The Inquisitor maintained a low profile, adhering to Conclave restrictions and staying in his lane. It was only through Hargan's pleading and the loss of a dear friend he became involved with what was fast becoming a nightmare.

Just yesterday he learned of the ambush of Leganas' brother. Thankfully none of his team was involved, though implications suggested Hargan's department was riddled with spies. Gando did his best to calm a furious Tolde Breed down when the man confronted him, and they resorted to old grievances. Hours of shouting and wild accusations led to a mutual understanding. Gando felt relieved to be free of the burden after so many years, but a new problem arose.

The longer he'd stared at Tolde the more he realized this was not the same man who had once mentored him. The explanation proved ridiculous. How could anyone return from the dead? Gando had witnessed much during his tenure with the Inquisition, but no form of heresy compared to the miracle that had been standing before him. If not for Tolde's recounting of their past, Gando might never have guessed it was the man he once knew.

Deciding it a matter for another time, Gando vowed to get to the bottom of the assassination attempt. He didn't know if it was connected with the Cardinal's death, but he'd be surprised if it wasn't. Evil tended to cluster once the breach was opened.

His day went from confusing to odd when Hargan arrived that morning. They were scheduled to pay Lady DeMauve a surprise visit later in the week in the hopes of discovering what she might know, but the spat of recent murders hurried their timeline. Rumors aplenty swirled around the widower, but one thing was certain. She was a woman with her finger on the pulse of the planet. Hargan bet his badge on her intimate knowledge. Coaxing it out of her remained to be seen.

"Lady DeMauve, I'm Inspector Hargan. This is Inquisitor Gando. Might we have a moment or two of your time?" Hargan asked.

The steel in her eyes lingered just behind the feigned look of shock. "Of course, might I inquire what this is in reference to?"

"Cardinal Leganas Breed," Gando said, his voice stern and authoritative.

Emmest stepped aside and gestured with an open palm. "Please come in. This weather has turned something frightful of late."

Dark clouds loomed on the horizon. Erdef City braced for a storm—Gando hoped it was one just related to the weather that was about to break.

They soon occupied the very same seats where a few days earlier Riles and her reluctant companion sat; Emmest delighted in the irony of it as she asked, "Would either of you care for refreshments? I hate to think you came all the way out to my estate on empty stomachs."

"No thank you. We are fine," Hargan answered. "Lady DeMauve, what can you tell us of a young woman named Riles Tenaru?"

Emmest folded her hands on her lap. A look of mild interest twisting her face as she passed a judgmental glance between them. "What is your interest with her?"

Gando squinted. In another time he might have her hauled away on heresy charges, but she remained too valuable on the street. Not trusting his tongue, the Inquisitor let Hargan take the lead.

"We have an eyewitness account placing her at the scene of the crime moments after it occurred." Hargan had nothing to hide. He knew her reputation, any subterfuge on his part would result in DeMauve pulling away. "She was here, wasn't she?"

"I see why you are the city's lead investigator. Very wise, Hargan. Very wise indeed," Emmest said. "Yes, she came to see me a few days ago. What we talked about remains our business, though I got the impression she isn't the one you are looking for."

"Why would you say that?" Hargan asked.

"You can't possibly suggest she is a suspect. If she were wouldn't it also be safe to assume she had a part to play in the ambush of Leganas' brother yesterday?"

Hargan and Gando shared a look before Hargan said, "Fair enough. I won't embarrass either of us by asking how you knew about that or that Breed's brother was on planet. Riles may not be the killer, but I have good idea she saw who did it."

"That places a target on her back," Emmest mused. "One she would be hard pressed to escape given the current circumstances."

Erdef City was abuzz with what the media dubbed a night of slaughter. Two of the most influential figures with votes on how Romalle would either enter the war or remain neutral were found brutally murdered in their homes. False reports flooded the station as terror rose among the upper class. Hargan suspected this rash of violence began with the murder of Cardinal Breed. Where it went from here was anyone's guess.

"The truth is, Lady DeMauve, we need to find her and pull her from the streets before those responsible get her. She is in grave danger and, after the events from last night, doesn't stand a chance against the wave threatening the city."

Gando's gaze flit to his companion after he spoke. Where had that come from? The wave threatening the city? A handful of assassinations were not worthy of sounding the alarm. Not yet at least. They had no actionable intelligence of a coup attempt nor were there any active heresy cells on Romalle. All they had to go on were three dead bodies and a young girl afraid for her life.

"Unless we find the real suspect her name will be plastered on wanted posters across the city. I won't be able to help her or find the killer if that happens," Hargan pressed. "These are unprecedented times. With the war vote approaching I'm afraid for the future."

"Investigator, I share the same concerns. Would it comfort you to know I may have a way of finding the girl and keeping her safe?"

"You can do that?"

"Perhaps. I met her but briefly, not enough to know her haunts or routines," Emmest admitted. "But as I'm sure you know, I have my ways of discovering the truth of matters."

"If you can get her out of harm's way and free me to do my job I'll be in your debt."

"Careful, Hargan. One does not pledge his debts to a lady like me casually," she said with a predatory grin as he stood. "But if I hear anything I shall inform you at once. Fair?"

"Thank you."

She waved off his gratitude. "Think nothing of it. I took a liking to young Riles. It would hurt my feelings to learn she died because neither of us acted in time." Emmest saw Mayn standing in the doorway and waved her hand. "Good day, gentlemen."

They were in the foyer, against their wishes, when Gando called over his shoulder. "Lady DeMauve, you weren't affected by the assassinations last night, were you?"

She stiffened, just enough for his attuned senses to catch it. "No, Inquisitor. Thank you for asking."

Halfway down the long entrance road, when he was sure they were beyond the range of any listening or surveillance devices, Hargan looked at his friend and said, "She's lying through her teeth, you know."

"That she is, Hargan. We need to head to my offices. It's time I introduced you to someone who can help us solve this case and set matters right."

"Do I want to know?"

Gando shook his head. "I'd rather keep it a surprise."

Alone in the dregs she called a hab, Riles found her thoughts devolving. Nothing worthwhile came from her meeting with Emmest, nor had she or Nemineon turned up any actionable evidence capable of getting her off the hook for the Cardinal's murder. She was trapped. The walls were closing in. Soon she expected to hear the march of angry boots before they kicked her door open and dragged her to a prison cell complete with a mock trial before the public execution.

Did it hurt being hung? How much could one feel after the snapping of the neck? How long before that last breath struggled to escape the crushed throat? What if her neck failed to snap and she hung there for all to see until her slender frame stopped struggling?

Hurried footsteps aroused her worst fears. She cringed, drawing back into the darkest corner of the room and fumbling for the knife that was her lone weapon. The door slid open and a red faced Nemineon barged. He held a crumpled sheet of poster in his left hand, waving it angrily at her.

"Riles, we need to leave the city. Now."

She lowered the knife. "What? Why?"

"They're looking for you. You've been named suspect number one."

Riles bolted to her feet. "How? Only one man knows I was there, and he barely had time to see my face. Where did they get my name from?"

"It doesn't matter. If we don't get you out of the city soon … you know what will happen."

Trembling, Riles rushed into his arms and wept. She didn't know why any of this was happening to her. Nothing made sense. It was a matter of wrong place—wrong time. Couldn't they understand that? But no. Whoever she'd collided with that fateful night latched onto the notion of making her the scapegoat. They wouldn't stop until she was in custody.

"I don't understand any of this," she confessed into his shoulder. "I'm scared, Nemineon."

The poster fell from his hand, drifting face up to rest on the dusty floor. "I know, Riles. I am too." He hugged her back. It was an act he'd longed for but never found the opportunity to enjoy. Now that he had her in his arms he never wanted to let go. She owned his heart, and he lacked the nerve to let her know. He leaned his head against hers and closed his eyes.

"What are we going to do?" she asked, wiping the tears from her face. "I have nowhere to go."

"We go back to the tribes," he offered. "They'll protect us until we can figure out how to convince the investigators you're innocent."

"Or they'll start a war with Erdef City," she replied. "You and I both know all the tribes need is the right excuse to launch a war with the city. I don't want that bloodshed on my conscience. There must be another way."

"We could try going back to Lady DeMauve," he suggested.

"I doubt she'll be so kind to accept our company a second time."

He collapsed onto the mattress she claimed was her bed. Dust billowed out from under him. "That leaves us almost out of options."

"Are you going to stick with me?"

The redirection in the conversation threw him. Nemineon almost blurted he would follow her anywhere, but he caught his tongue in time. "What do you have in mind?"

"There might be one we can trust. One who won't sell us out."

He spread his hands and asked, "Who?"

"Investigator Hargan."

He groaned. "You think the lead investigator has your best interests at heart? Are you mad?"

Perhaps she was. "Come on. We don't have much time."

Word spread through Erdef City. A suspect in the brutal slaying of Cardinal Breed had been identified. Police and security forces busied scouring the city as the population remained locked in panic. The war many feared was at last seeping into the fabric of their society, threatening ruin. Flights offworld were booked. Entire families packed and prepared to leave the city in favor of the far rural countryside dominated by the tribes, deeming the risk worth it. The City Board's attempts to quell the rising fears accomplished little. Official newsvids from the central systems promised the war was proceeding according to plan. The insurgency was on the brink of annihilation. The end at last in sight. Despite this, snippets of truth found their way to Romalle. The promise of bloodshed grew stronger with each passing day.

Combined patrols of Prekhauten Guards and local law enforcement all but placed the city under martial law. Pedestrians were halted, their faces scanned. Traffic control points were established on all major routes in and out of the city. Teams deployed to the larger housing buildings, going door to door as new intelligence became available. Everyone in Erdef City wanted Riles Tenaru.

Tolde watched the news, curious how it failed to mention much about the recent spate of killings.

"This is madness," Ragan said after finishing the last bite of his meal. "How could one girl be responsible for so much uproar?"

"Anything is possible when a weak target is provided for the masses to devour," Tolde said. "This Riles Tenaru is unlikely to be the true perpetrator. It is the thought of a suspect driving the hysteria."

"Allowing the real killer to go to ground," Luma added.

"Perhaps." Tolde felt their mission unraveling. His brother's killer remained at large, and they had no substantial leads, and Nye's loyalist faction knew Tolde's team was planetside and making efforts to eliminate them. He needed to speak with Gando at once. "Where is Sister Alessandra?"

They looked about the suite of rooms Romalle's Inquisitor called home but found no trace of the witch. Tolde frowned at the unsaid implication then looked about the room. He feared they arrived on the brink of a rebellion, but for which side remained unclear.

Unconcerned with the issues now facing Romalle, Alessandra slipped from the main rooms. She needed to contact the Grand Mistress. Alone. No one saw her produce the small communicator device from her robes and activate it.

"Sister Alessandra, is your mission going well?"

Bowing, Alessandra removed her hood. "Grand Mistress, we are no closer to discovering the murderer. I fear time has expired."

"That was ever the possibility when Lord Tannus suggested you deploy to Romalle. But this is not the reason you contacted me."

Alessandra blew out the pensive breath she'd been holding. Wise and powerful, Ruma Zzein represented the best of the Order. "I sense something terrible is approaching, though what I cannot yet discern."

"You are strong beyond your years, Alessandra," Ruma said. "Amongeratix is slowly making his way to Vau Prime. The damages you inflicted on *Behemoth* are being repaired. Soon he will be back to full strength and ready to wage his war on the universe."

Terror awakened in her veins. She was young by Blood Witch standards and knew little of the giant, yet her experiences aboard *Behemoth* showed her an unstoppable monster capable of bringing humanity to its knees, leaving a swath of corpses in his wake. How anyone had the power to end his eternal lust for domination remained a mystery. She thought of the bounty hunter Elisa and her quest to retrieve *Grimfurvor* but failed to see how a small blade could kill a monster mistaken for a god. Nor could she fathom what Tolde's purpose in this grim tale was. The universe felt upended with no way for self-correction.

"We failed."

"Yes and no. Losing Paradise Tear hurt our efforts, but crippling his ship bought much needed time."

"Time? For what? Even Tannus has proclaimed there is nothing in our arsenal capable of withstanding the hatred of that ship."

"There are other elements at work," Ruma said. "Powers rising to stop Amongeratix and prevent Forever Night from damning the universe. All is not lost, nor hopeless, Sister. Keep true to your purpose. Tolde Breed must survive to reach the final battle, which I feel is imminent. The pieces are all in play. Soon we shall be thrust into the center of a millennia old war. We must stay focused."

Frustration boiled over and Alessandra failed to keep the anger from her voice. "I would better serve the Order at your side. Not on this distant rock with no bearing to our efforts."

"If that were true, I would not have allowed you to leave."

The admission stung, sending her into a spiral of conflicting thoughts and emotions. Alessandra was strong but she lacked the foresight to view the plan in entirety. She knew trusting the Grand Mistress was central to discipline and success, but the sensation of being outcast when needed the most refused to dissipate.

"Alessandra, there is more at work on Romalle than you may guess. The death of Leganas Breed is more than mere happenstance. My heart tells me this was calculated. You must discover the killer if we have any chance of winning this war."

"Grand Mistress, who else knows the Inquisitor has been resurrected?"

The silence was answer enough. Her fear took route even as her heart fell. "He knows, doesn't he?"

"It is inescapable at this point. Surely Algiss Her has whispered to her master of the resurrected man. Tolde is in more danger than he knows," Ruma admitted. Long ago, before the fall of the gods she'd divined a prophecy of a resurrected man who would play a pivotal role in bringing down the monster Amongeratix. Centuries sped by and the prophecy was lost to all but her and the Three. The time of fulfillment was upon them.

"I understand," Alessandra said. "I shall do all in power to ensure his survival."

"I expect nothing less," Ruma replied. Her image began fading. "Oh, and Alessandra, take care. I sense you are caught in a trap."

The transmission ended, leaving Sister Alessandra alone with a cold sensation coursing through her.

"Any news?" Tolde asked upon her return.

The Blood Witch, hood returned to conceal her face, swept into the room, taking a moment to look at each. She found courage, and hope. She chose her words carefully then, for to reveal the full truth would undo the fabric of all the Blood Witches had sought to achieve throughout their storied existence. "The Grand Mistress has informed me Amongeratix is moving on Vau Prime, no doubt in concert with the Inquisitor General."

"Can we stop him?" Luma asked. "We've risked our lives for years to stop a tyrant from overthrowing the order of power only to find him at the precipice of success."

"That task falls to others, Luma Kai," Alessandra chided. "The Grand Mistress also believes your brother's death was no coincidence, though she would say no more on the matter. We stand upon a crossroads, my friends. To move forward we must solve the riddle on Romalle."

Tolde stared at her, trying to read anything from her gaze. "Gando is due to arrive at any moment, but there are complicating matters. Last night's murders suggest a greater threat to the planet than we initially suspected. I fear they are on the edge of being overthrown."

"Thus dragging Romalle into the war. Why, we must question. This planet holds no strategic value nor is it populated enough to support our foe with additional forces," she concluded.

Ragan groaned. This adventure was a far cry from what he envisioned when deciding to follow Tolde across the stars. "We're never going to be free from this nightmare, are we?"

"That remains to be seen, young Ragan," Alessandra said softly. "There are many forces at work in the universe, for good and evil. What happens next is unknown but there is always the hope of a brighter tomorrow."

His gaze narrowed, viewing her dubiously.

The door chimed, a matter of courtesy, before sliding open. In walked Gando and a haggard looking man.

Gando waited for the door to close before saying, "This is Investigator Hargan. He is the lead detective here in Erdef City. Hargan, this is Leganas' brother, fellow Inquisitor Luma Kai, Ragan Sandinsol, and Sister Alessandra."

Hargan's focus centered on the Blood Witch. His tongue swelled, filling his mouth as he choked on any clever retort.

Behemoth. Enroute to Vau Prime.

Algiss Her stood in the shadow of her new lord and master as steam and smoke hissed from the shuttle's boarding ramp. She failed to see the significance of the moment, for those boarding were failures. Castaways from another time where their miniscule contributions to the campaign were all but forgotten.

Once proud, Presha Von approached Amongeratix a shell of her former self. Algiss snarled and shifted her gaze to the giant at Presha's side. Everything she'd heard of Geres Auk proved true. He was a brute in human form, barely more than a barbarian from the dark time when humanity struggled in the power vacuum after the battle of Occanum. Heavily muscled with a wide forehead and sunken eyes, he reminded her of those lesser species who had long since burned from existence. He was, in a word, magnificent. She watched amused as the giant clumsily dropped to a knee before Amongeratix.

"My lord! We have come to your side at last," Geres said.

Ignoring him, Amongeratix eyed Presha. "So it seems. Where is the key?"

She refused to meet his withering gaze. "Lost. Our enemies took it. I come to you in failure."

Broken. That was the legacy of Presha Von. Algiss gathered power, tiny bolts dancing over her knuckles in anticipation of removing her stain from *Behemoth*. Failure deserved harsh consequences. Yet Amongeratix did not give her the command.

"This is a disturbing setback, but all is not lost. You will be permitted to live, at my convenience of course, while I ponder your punishment. Perhaps you will be of use to me before the end."

"What of me?" Geres prostrated himself upon the deck. Locks of mangy hair swept from his shoulders.

Amongeratix hummed. "I always have use for those willing to serve. What is your name, human?"

"Geres Auk."

"Come, Geres Auk. Today you begin the rest of your life. Today, you will stand at my side as we bring the war to my enemies."

Geres Auk slid forward and kissed his master's boot; Algiss Her felt her stomach twist.

TWELVE

3215 A.G. (After Gods), planet Dalafar.

"I'm tired of waiting."

Annalilly rolled her eyes. "I heard you the first seven times. This is the game, Quint. We sit. We watch. We wait."

Glowering at the crowds of pedestrians passing by, he said, "Doesn't mean I have to like it. How are we supposed to know friend from foe?"

"Treat everyone as hostile. You'll live longer."

Jelin Quint still hadn't figured his new platoon sergeant out. She presented complications no one person should have. A hard fighter and determined professional, Annalilly represented the best of the Prekhauten Guard in war. Vicious and cruel, she performed every task with the inherent ferocity of one born for battle. That's where her humanity seemed to end. Quint knew she was in love with the lieutenant. How or why remained unknown, but she wore her emotions on her sleeve. There was never any doubt to her intentions, or loyalty. He wished he'd had leaders like this during his formulative years in uniform.

"The whole planet can't be hostile. That doesn't make sense," he said with a frown. "We'd be forced to fight every single person to extract."

"What makes you think we won't? Look, I want to get out of here as much as you. Hiding in plain sight surrounded by enemies isn't my idea of a good time. Orders are orders," she reminded him. "We wait until the governess sends her people."

"They could be any one of this crowd and we'd never know."

She laughed. A harsh, wet sound making him wince. "Quint, you may have missed it, but we don't exactly fit in here. They'll know. Get another cup of caf. It's not like there's anything else to do."

"My back teeth are already floating. If I drink any more, I won't be able to sleep for a week," he grumbled. "This isn't what I signed up for."

"What makes you think this was on the top of my list?" she countered. "Look, trust Haggle to keep the others frosty and do your job."

Glowering at her, Quint focused his attention on the passing crowds. Nothing about the scenario appealed to him. They were exposed, undergunned, and too far from reinforcements. He regretted not staying on Torgast's staff for a moment only before remembering he was a professional soldier and went wherever the mission dictated.

"First time in civvies?" she asked after considering his glum attitude.

"That obvious?"

Annalilly felt a bond begin to form between them and chuckled. "When we hit the Gate, I felt out of place. Like we stuck out. Nothing I did felt right. We're Guards. Trained to assault the breach in full body armor. No sneaking around or covert operations. I wasn't mentally prepared for it, and it damned near got us all killed."

She fell silent, eyes glazed over as old memories threatened. Annalilly presented herself as a hard woman. What else could she be? The universe was run by the powerful. Weakness was synonymous with failure. From the day she entered a recruiting station to now she worked harder than any other soldier in her unit. They deserved. She deserved it more. If it hadn't have been for a night of drunken excitement with Fies she doubted she'd ever change. What began as a tension reliever developed into love. Annalilly mused, she hadn't been ready for that either.

"What I'm trying to say is suck it up. This is our assignment. There's no specialty units. No one to turn to if things go bad. We're it. The twelve of us. Understood?" she fixed him with a steely gaze.

Some of the tension left. A soldier's life became easier with fewer complications. Annalilly ripped away any external problems to lay the situation bare. Quint appreciated the honesty, if not the brutality of her delivery. He gestured for the server to bring another round and yawned.

"What's the deal with you and Fies?" he changed subjects, a wicked glint in his eye.

She jabbed a finger at him but said nothing.

Alleviating the feeling of his back teeth floating from too much to drink, Jelin Quint couldn't shake the feeling of standing out as he prowled through the city. He was bigger than most in the city and wore a natural scowl prompting others to steer clear. Unwilling to believe he always looked mad, Quint spent hours in front of the mirror before accepting the obvious. He considered himself a happy man. Always laughing and cracking jokes to alleviate pressure in tense situations. Those friends who proclaimed him an angry person were all dead. He'd never get the chance to tell them they were right.

Hands stuffed in his pockets, Quint stalked through the crowd at Annalilly's side. Their contact failed to show, and they were heading back to their safehouse. Tomorrow was another day. Another opportunity.

Clothing aside, no one on Dalafar dressed like them, he needed to find a way to blend in without arousing more suspicion. He felt the stares—he was armed only with a blade tucked into his boot and a side arm strapped to his shoulder under the faded jacket he wore. Not enough to stop a mob from doing what his brother's army couldn't.

The café behind them, Quint and Annalilly stepped aside, feigning interest in a merchant's stall, while a Prekhauten patrol sauntered past. Careless, they were sloppy in their arrogance. He wondered if he'd ever been guilty of the same. Probably. There was an air of authority imbued in the uniform. Respect earned from generations of service. Now half the population saw the Guard as occupiers while the others clung to the old beliefs that the Guard were protectors. He snorted. If they only knew the truth.

The patrol passed, oblivious to their presence. Quint exhaled his relief when he caught someone staring at him harder than they should have. To his dismay, he recognized the face.

"We've been made," he said under his breath. "Young female with red hair and a black jacket. Opposite side of the street."

"Are you sure?" Annalilly asked without following his gaze.

"Positive. She hasn't taken her eyes off us since the café."

"Shit. Okay, keep moving like nothing is wrong."

His fingers twitched the way they always did before a fight. "What's the plan?"

Annalilly looked up and down the crowded street. Day shift workers were heading home or to their favorite watering holes. The streets were packed but that wouldn't last long. "Isolate her from the crowd then try and take her alive."

She left the implications should they fail off. They both knew what would happen if the woman escaped to warn whoever her masters were.

"What about contacting the others?" he asked.

"Too risky. Our comms might be tapped," she replied. "Split up at the next intersection. You go left. I'll take right. Let's see if she's after us or if you're imaging things."

He bristled but stayed silent.

Shifting through the masses of laborers and fishermen, Quint cut across the street at a leisurely pace. His movements were calculated, measured to avoid appearing as if he knew he was being watched. Slipping a hand inside his jacket, he unsnapped his holster and thumbed the power button on the blaster's handgrip. He couldn't risk a shootout in the middle of street but needed to be prepared if the tail followed him instead of Annalilly.

Quint slowed his breathing, remembering his training. Isolate the target. Verify intent and eliminate if necessary. He hadn't shot anyone in a long time … he was starting to think he was overdue.

An alley opened up ten meters ahead, Quint headed for it. He knew turning around to verify if the tail followed only exposed him to additional attention, so he quickened his pace. Cans overflowing with trash cluttered the alley beside grime-stained doors. He surmised they were for various eateries and shops. The stench proved far worse than the fishy odor suffocating the city. He stepped in a pile of something he didn't need to investigate, wincing as the squish inspired a new fetid stench.

"Stop right there."

The voice froze him midstride. Quint thought of reaching for his weapon but figured the chances of being gunned down were much higher than him succeeding. He scanned the alley for cover. His luck had run out.

"What seems to be the problem?" he asked without turning.

"Put your hands up and turn around. Slow. No funny business or your head gets sent home in a box."

A dozen scenarios played out in his head. All of them ending with him bleeding out in the alley. Allowing his shoulders to sag, he did as he was instructed. He figured he stood a better chance of escaping once they closed on him. Then it was a matter of brute strength, not blasters.

He started turning when a pair of blaster shots blazed the alley. Smoke and the stench of cauterized flesh drifted to him.

"You can put your hands down."

A woman's voice this time. Confused, and more than a little reluctant, Quint dropped his arms. He couldn't keep the amused look from crossing his face upon seeing the pair of bodies facedown in the alley with the red-haired woman standing over them.

"Should I say thank you?" He gestured to the bodies.

Blaster pointed at his chest, she stood with legs shoulder width apart. "Depends on why you're here."

"See, that is not something I'm at liberty to say."

"Really? Why is that? Seems I got the jump here. There's no way you can pull your gun before I blast—" The woman froze as the cold end of barrel pressed against her head. She saw Quint break into a grin.

"Drop your weapon or you don't have a head for your funeral," Annalilly growled in her ear.

"The Governess has been expecting you but security measures at the compound have been increased since the rash of terrorist bombings. I was sent to make contact and report back to her."

Fies stared at the woman, silently questioning Annalilly's judgment in bringing her to the safehouse. Too late now, he shifted focus to the trio of noncoms clustered around him. They were the brains of the operation, despite him being in overall command. Fies knew the special relationship sergeants had with their chain of command and their subordinates. Small unit leaders were expected to make judgment calls in the field and execute missions with minimal guidance. He couldn't blame Annalilly for her actions, knowing he'd have done the same, but she placed incredible pressure on their mission.

"How does the Governess know about us?" he asked the woman, who'd given the name Tempest. "It was my understanding we were to make contact, not the other way around."

"Governess Moscasco is an influential woman, Lieutenant," Tempest said. "She intercepted a message from a relay station in the Orest Sector. We have been waiting for this for a long time. Those men who were about to murder your man, they worked for the Inquisition. It seems your secret mission isn't as secret as you supposed."

"Shit." Annalilly punched the nearest wall. "We need to bug out while we still can, Fies. We walked into a trap."

Tempest quickly said, "No, you haven't. The Inquisition is looking for any excuse to arrest the Governess and assume control of Dalafar."

"Why?" Quint asked. "This is out of the main space lanes. Dalafar serves no strategic purpose. What makes this so important?"

Smoothing her tunic, Tempest admitted, "Dalafar is not the prize. Governess Moscasco is. Our enemies know that should she defect or fall into your hands her knowledge has the potential to turn the tide of the war."

Fies found logic in that, though one thing yet bothered him. "Why not just arrest her on suspicion of heresy? Why the wait?"

"Inquisitor Alpof is being held up by the local Guard captain. So long as he is in the way the Inquisition will not move forward."

"Doesn't sound like them," Quint snorted.

"Moving against the Guard confirms the people's suspicions and makes potential enemies of the only armed force on Dalafar," Fies remarked. "Sounds like we have an Inquisitor to bring down."

"Our orders are to grab the Governess, not start a civil war," Annalilly fumed.

Fies offered his most charming smile, browning teeth showing between his lips. "When have you known anyone to feel bad for the Inquisition?"

PGN Solstice, high orbit over Mannus Prime.

Captain Sharlyn August stood with her hands clasped behind her back overseeing the final loading of supplies. The *Solstice* was scheduled to depart for Wexanos within the hour. Additional Marines were assigned in the event of unexpected enemy engagements, and Admiral Falchi ensured the magazines were topped off with as much ammunition as she could carry.

The prize August carried could mean the difference between victory and defeat. No one left anything to chance. August and her crew risked their lives running down the renegade Presha Von and securing the artifact capable of murdering entire planets. Von might have escaped, but the artifact fell into her custody. Nothing mattered more than getting it to Tannus. Falchi believed in the mission so much he detailed an escort flight of corvettes just in case.

She had everything necessary to reach Tannus and deliver the weapon. Why then were her nerves so high?

"Captain. I thought I'd find you here."

The tension left her clenched hands at the sound of Falchi approaching from behind. Of all the commanders she'd served under, he provided the best, most unique experience. He was also singularly responsible for sending her into harm's way more times than she could count.

"Admiral," she greeted.

He stopped beside her. "I trust you are ready to depart?"

"The crew is performing the final preflight checks now. We will depart on time," she confirmed.

"What delays have you anticipated?"

"None, in a perfect world. However, given our recent endeavors at Hawker's Gate and Crimeat it is safe to assume the enemy knows we have the artifact and will attempt to disable the *Solstice* and retrieve it. Worst case scenario is a complete destruction of ship and crew."

Falchi raised an eyebrow. "Our foe is cunning, but I doubt we need to take such severe precautions. Word is he is focused on Vau Prime. Still, it is always best to be safe. The escorts I provided should be enough to allow you to escape in the event of an ambush."

"You expect me to leave them behind?"

He exhaled against the weight building in his chest. "The key must get to Tannus. Everything else is of secondary consideration, Sharlyn. We must think beyond ourselves. The fate of the universe is at stake. Should you fail…"

"We won't fail, sir. I have full faith and confidence in my crew to see the mission through," she affirmed.

"Of course they will," he agreed. "The coordinates will see you to the rendezvous point. From there you will be guided in to Wexanos."

"Admiral, we've been over this several times. I know what to do."

Falchi stiffened and offered his hand. "Captain August, fair sailing."

"Aye, sir." She clasped his hand, praying he didn't feel the clamminess. Letting go, she quickly saluted and headed for her command shuttle. No point in delaying any further.

She stalked off, a predator in search of her prey. The greatest mission of her career lay ahead. Whether she was up to it or not remained to be seen.

August sank into her command chair on the main deck as the final combat checks were completed. Once all was in order and the ship secured, she gave the order.

Solstice surged forward, slowly at first as the engines devoured power. Soon she was racing through the stars, enroute to a planet she knew nothing about, carrying a weapon she dreaded being set loose. Every aspect of this mission sat ill with her, yet she wouldn't have it any other way.

Her thoughts briefly turned to the rogue pirate Vicente Blackheart, and she wondered what had become of the captain and crew of the *Shrike*. She had a feeling she'd miss them should the enemy engage. August knew she could contact the pirate when needed, though was loathe to do so. Too much rode on the future for her to submit to basic emotions. Scowling, she watched as Mannus Prime and the orbital defenses and various docking stations faded to blackness and she was once again alone in her world. The *Solstice* soared on with her corvette escort spread around her.

Army Command Headquarters, Eger City, planet Mannus Prime.

Cardinal Virom liked to think he understood the universe. Perhaps it stemmed from his unique insights to the gods and the elevated sense of worth he conveyed to his practitioners. As it were, faith seldom made sense. You either felt it or you didn't. No amount of preaching prevented heresy from spreading, nor did it offer salvation to those in need. Faith, Virom determined, came from within. Therein lie the sadness of the Conclave. Those in the Forum forgot why they were selected to represent their planets. Forgot the sacred charge they were given by assuming the title of Cardinal.

For a time, during the darkest moments of the Prekhauten campaign, he abandoned wearing the crimson robes, thinking they no longer served a purpose. The universe spiraled out of control, the fires of war spreading unchecked. What good came from one man desperately clinging to old beliefs? It wasn't until the war turned that he noticed people in need. They ached to be saved. To return to those beliefs that had seen them through generations. Life became a precious thing once again. Virom dusted off his robes and began administering the faith to those who asked and then those who didn't.

Buoyed with strength, he stalked through the acquired military command center in search of the one man who never stopped believing in him. Soldiers, administrators, civilians, and more filled the complex. Hundreds of potential recruits from scores of planets waited in lines for their entrance physicals and background clearances. Once accepted into service they were shuttled to one of several training bases scattered across the main continent to begin Prekhauten combat training. Many, he knew, wouldn't pass. Those who did would be assimilated into the growing army, ready to deploy.

Virom found his way to General Torgast's offices, smiling and waving at those passersby who recognized him. A secretary came forth to escort the Cardinal into the meeting room. He seemed pleasant enough to Virom despite the swarthy air encircling him. Declining refreshments, he took a chair and waited for the others to file in. Soon he was joined by Torgast, Falchi, and the enigmatic and determined Khe-Zhehan. He still hadn't figured her out.

"Thank you all for coming on short notice," Torgast began. As regional commander, he was responsible for executing the coalition's intent. The others agreed to his authority, checking their egos and pride for the betterment of all concerned. "Admiral Falchi, please."

"The *Solstice* departed at dawn. With luck she will deliver the artifact to Tannus in a day."

"Still not going to reveal Tannus' location?" Khe-Zhehan asked with a knowing gleam.

"You know I can't."

Virom watched the exchange, wondering how much influence one of the Three exuded upon those who came in contact with him. From his limited understanding, he knew each of the brothers were the avatars of different emotions. Amongeratix inspired hatred, greed, and fear. Tannus the opposite, for how else could he have swung the loyalty of a man of Falchi's caliber? Sorrow remained a mystery, appearing at whim and throwing the natural order of the universe into chaos.

"Admiral Falchi," he found himself saying, "would it be possible for me to meet with Tannus? I confess to admiring his principles, from a strictly religious perspective."

"Cardinal, I don't control who he sees. His power is beyond me," Falchi explained. "However, I shall inquire."

"I can ask for no more. Thank you."

Torgast's eyes narrowed on him. "Cardinal, we have more pressing matters to attend. A host of nobles, junior clergy, and administrators from beleaguered planets have come seeking asylum. While they are being vetted to determine loyalty, I must acknowledge their skillsets will greatly amplify our ability to control this sector of space. Several planets have offered to join us, pledging their resources and support at least through the duration of the war. My question to you is what should we do next?"

Khe-Zhehan clasped her hands over the table and leaned forward. "My plans are known. I am set to deploy to a secure location where a fleet of dreadnaughts and support craft await. We will attempt to break the blockade surrounding Vau Prime before Amongeratix arrives and pick up the survivors of Strannan's armies already being evacuated."

She no longer advocated for besieging the capitol planet, abandoning the quest as madness. Her earlier attempts ended in failure, forcing her to scatter her fleets across the stars and bide her time. Khe-Zhehan now believed she had enough strength to complete her chosen mission and rescue loyalists. It was a gamble, but one they needed to take.

Noticing their concerned looks, she added, "My fleet leaving will not diminish the defenses here. Admiral Falchi has accumulated enough ships to provide support and deter our enemies from launching an all-out assault. With luck I will suffer minimal losses and return with a tremendous boost to our combat power."

"I still think the risk is too great." Torgast shook his head. "You are the senior Guard and carry an unparalleled level of command—we need you, Admiral."

"We need the manpower more," she countered. "General, the army and citizens in our burgeoning little empire are in capable hands. I trust no one more than Falchi, and now yourself. The Cardinal has resumed weekly sermons, administering to the faithful and our infrastructure grows. This is a critical moment in our evolution. One requiring we go our separate ways."

Glowering over the unspoken implications of what her mission promised, Torgast had little choice, or say. By saving the remnants of General Strannan's army, they acceded to the fall of Vau Prime and the central power hub to the entire universe. "Is there any other pressing business?"

After having nothing more to discuss, the council broke. Torgast wasn't comfortable with any of it, knowing too many moving pieces left them exposed to treachery. The chances of missing a key element or failing to discover subversive elements before they struck heightened with each reduction of their total force. Still, Torgast had a job to do, and he'd be damned if he failed while the others busied with their own avenues of endeavor. They were all responsible for this phase of the war.

Hours later and still conflicted over their meeting, General Torgast arrived in the main prison. Inside were hundreds of dissidents, rebels, and threats to freedom. They presented the worst of humanity and, if left to him, would all be drifting lifeless and frozen through the eternity of space. Doing so was akin to the tactics used by his enemy however, and he was no butcher. While most held no redeemable quality needed in modern society, there was one locked away in solitary confinement with the power to influence those not yet fully committed to their cause.

He found Virom waiting at the main guard station. Both were cleared and escorted through the maze of winding, windowless corridors. A pair of Guards led them to the elevator bank and followed the pair six levels underground, where the worst of the worst were kept. Trials were already underway for many, but a limited number of qualified judges produced a backlog that would take years to get through.

The Guards brought them to the end of a narrow corridor, darkened by a flickering ceiling light. Torgast scowled, suddenly unprepared for what came next. He took a steadying breath and remembered their purpose.

Torgast looked at his friend and asked, "Are you ready for this?"

"Ready? Yes, though I fail to see the point of it. He will not change his views nor abandon the principles of his training."

"Doesn't mean we can't try." Torgast gestured for the Guards to open the door. "Wait here. No one comes to this level. No one."

He and Virom entered the cell. They found him sitting on a dirty mattress with a lone pillow. A used blanket was crumpled up at the foot. His hair was long, unkempt. His fingernails crusted with the grime of almost half a year of incarceration. The once proud uniform that inspired fear on a hundred planets was soiled, torn in several places. Torgast noticed the fresh spot of fabric where the notorious symbol of the Inquisition once rested.

"Dowan Mun, we have come to talk," he said.

Despite being fed regularly and provided enough water to prevent dehydration, the Inquisitor was gaunt and weak. He eyed them with mistrust. "What is there to talk about? I proved my worth during the final stages of the war. What was my reward? A cell so far underground I've forgotten the taste of sunlight on my skin. Endless rounds of interrogation with no clear direction. Tell me, General Torgast, what do I have to say to you?"

Forcing a chuckle, Torgast scrapped his teeth over the top of his lower lip. "You murdered your partner and attempted to sell us out to your masters on Vau Prime. Perhaps the Inquisition handles treason otherwise, but this is my planet. My rules. Your efforts to end this campaign resulted in numerous deaths, leaving me to question your authenticity. Not one of those you claimed to attempt to coerce to our cause joined us or survived."

"That wasn't my fault!" Dowan shouted, trembling. "I did what I had to do to survive. Bela Cass was a madwoman intent on burning you all to the ground and using your bones for a throne. Without me you would be dead, and this planet lost."

"Your inflated sense of importance concerns me, Inquisitor. When did self-preservation become a guiding principle for your Order?"

"When I realized I wanted to live more than I wanted to serve." He stared Torgast in the eye, unflinching. "You claim you stand for the righteous, yet those with flaws have no place in your new world order. You—"

"We need more, Dowan," Virom interrupted, sensing the conversation peddling downward.

"Come to pray for my soul, Cardinal?" Dowan snorted. "I was a devout follower. Once. I adhered to the word of the gods, committing my every reserve to serving them and the Conclave. You have shown me the worth of faith. Leave me. The guards will be coming to escort me to the head soon."

Virom, gathering his courage, shuffled forward and sat on the edge of the bed. "Dowan, I do not condone mistreatment, but you must understand there are many here who would as soon see you slain publicly than get a fair trial. I cannot accept this, for it counters all I choose to believe. Can I tell you a secret? The most closely guarded secret in history."

Tensing, Dowan glared down at the Cardinal. He sensed a trap, but there was no purpose for it. He was a prisoner, with no allies and no chance for escape. "I have nowhere to go."

Virom patted the bed, waiting for Dowan to sit before speaking. "What if I told you the gods are a lie? A myth of convenience developed by our early ancestors to ensure tranquility during our most difficult time."

"What?"

Torgast whistled under his breath. Fear of this information spreading presented its own challenges, none of which he was prepared to accept.

"I am saying the gods are not gods. They ruled this universe, keeping our kind as slaves for their amusements and cruelties," Virom said.

"Why are you telling me this?" Dowan asked, confused and stunned.

"Because, my son, you need to know what is at stake and, it is my hope, discover the strength in your heart to do the right thing."

Dowan Mun crossed his arms, flitting his gaze between them as his mind struggled with this new knowledge and what it might mean to his future.

THIRTEEN

3215 A.G. (After Gods), *Behemoth*, deep space enroute to Vau Prime.

The stasis pod was a massive feat of engineering. Twenty feet long and half tall, it filled the workshop. Thick cables ran from the pod to a series of computer banks and control panels lining an entire wall. Steam hissed from beneath the pod, frosting the containment window. It was the finest device he'd ever created, and it was a complete failure. Amongeratix glared at his pod with unmitigated hatred before snatching the nearest computer console and smashing it against the wall.

Algiss Her floated at his side. Her crimson robes were out of place among the drab grey and black of the ship. She watched from beneath the sanctity of her cowl, silent and judgmental.

"Useless!" he raged. "All of it. I am no tinkerer like my brothers. My hands were created to destroy, not build."

"Perhaps we should go to the nearest planet and retrieve the pod instead of wasting time with failed machines," she suggested.

Amongeratix whipped his head around, dark hair flowing around his shoulders. "You mock me."

"It is a suggestion. Nothing else."

"The only pods I know have all been destroyed. Tannus is the only one who knows the locations of the others," he explained. "Not even my dear cousin has been given this knowledge."

"You have her. You have her blood and genetics. It is a matter of time until you build a suitable device to weaponize it," Algiss reminded. "Patience is required to proceed."

"Patience? I have spent the last three thousand years wallowing in patience," he sneered. "The moment of my ascension is at hand. My brothers have never been weaker. Humanity stands upon the brink of self-annihilation. All is ripe for my return, yet I am thwarted by these very hands. Am I to remain trapped by ambition?"

Drifting before him, she said, "Let the humans burn themselves out. They are inconsequential to your grand designs. Why waste energies pursuing a task they are eager to accomplish for themselves?"

"You forget your humanity," he cautioned.

"The Sisters may have been born to human parents, but the similarities end there. We are advanced in every way. Do not make the mistake of reducing our relevance to your cause. Your nightmare creatures may have brute strength, but they lack cunning."

She knew of the skulldaerth's weaknesses from detailed briefings by Sister Alessandra upon retrieving the reincarnation of Tolde Breed. Unsightly monsters bred for war and carnage, they lacked the ability to conceptualize, relegating them to a hammer instead of a sharp blade. Useful yet limited. Each of her Sisters were capable of enhancing his combat strength exponentially. He still failed to see that.

"They serve their purpose, as do you," he said, his voice a low growl.

Algiss kept her opinion private. They were still weeks away from Vau Prime, even with repairs to *Behemoth* progressing. Amongeratix's obsession with creating a working stasis pod threatened to steal their attention from the prize. She contemplated going behind his back and deploying a team of Sisters to the Inquisitor General to prep for their arrival but did not trust Alain Nye. He emulated everything she despised in humans, and men.

Their list of enemies grew. No doubt Ruma Zzein and the Order busied preparing for the final battle of Forever Night. Opposition armies gathered and grew. Their recent successes on Mannus Prime emboldened them. Though Presha Von sat in her chambers onboard the ship they lacked the key needed to kill planets. The pall of Kharsis diminished with each new horror unleashed upon the universe. As powerful as Amongeratix was, even he lacked the strength to defeat seven hundred planets.

"We need more," she said.

"More what?"

"Everything. The Conclave represents hundreds of planets with untold trillions of people. They are already at war, fighting for what they believe will be the fate of their society. Entire planets have mobilized armies for both sides and, despite the Inquisitor General's insistence that he will be the ruling authority, his sphere of influence fails to extend beyond the edges of the Vau system."

"Humanity does not concern me," Amongeratix said. "They are a pox. A race of slaves who have long forgotten their place. My coming will return them to their knees where they belong."

"If you execute your campaign correctly," she countered. "Allow me to deploy a team to Krenz to prepare the planet for your arrival."

"Out of the question."

"My lord, you are a myth to most of humanity. A tale meant to frighten children into obeying their parents. The influence of the gods has long left the universe. The Conclave has seen to that even while preaching the glories of your kind. The Inquisitor General is a creature of habit, consumed with gathering power. He will become pliable with the right people whispering in his ear."

Three thousand years and he failed to understand how the Conclave seduced the population into believing his people were gods. Secret bearers and liars, the robed cardinals proved themselves monsters in their own regards, holding humanity hostage to false idols.

Amongeratix steamed under the knowledge that, while his name sparked fear, it was almost irrelevant.

Alone again, Presha Von hadn't seen a living soul in days. The enigmatic witches avoided her, as did the one being she thought to hold her best opportunity to rise to power. Only Geres Auk arrived to bring her food and water, a chore he simmered over for he had grown beyond the petty concerns of the ruling council of Crimeat and their base drives. Presha feared him now, unsure when he might lash out and end her life.

But would that be so bad? She spent decades building her reputation and found herself at the bottom of the mountain. A failure. Gone was the haughtiness she once applied to her persona. She became a shell, suffering fragility she did not know how to cope with. Her designs to be a queen reduced her to a pauper begging for scraps. In another time she might have suffered from indignity. Today she was lucky to be alive.

The hatch opened and in swept a Blood Witch. Presha stared back, doing her best to remain impassive and unimpressed. Though their order stretched back to the foundations of the Conclave, she failed to see much use for them. In her estimation, this witch and those who'd sided with her failed rebellion, were little more than chattel for Amongeratix's war machine. Useful tools until they weren't.

"Come to gloat more?" Presha asked.

Algiss Her cackled with energy. Smoke drifted from several spots of her robes. "The only reason I don't incinerate you is because Amongeratix seems to believe you yet have use to him."

"How kind."

The witch waved her off. "He is a fool. A blind man can see you are dangerous, even in your weakened state. You deserve to be dead."

"I've been saying that for some time now," Presha replied. She stiffened, eager for the gift of release. "What promises did he give you? Whispered sweet temptations in the dark when no one listened? The difference between us, witch, is I know my worth."

"Because you have none." She sneered. "Come, Amongeratix wishes to speak with you."

Presha considered the woman. Proud, arrogant, yet ripe with turmoil and an inane need for validation. Had she been the same when she first fell under Amongeratix's sway? He was persuasive and terrifying. Lacking the charisma of his brother, the giant ruled with iron fist and the promise of eternal agony for all who failed him. Presha once believed him the answer to the universe's problems. The lie now haunted her.

"What more is there to say? Can he not allow me to wallow in my misery?"

Algiss rose higher, until her head was but a foot from the ceiling. "It will be my pleasure making you attend him. Give me a reason."

Defeated, Presha flushed the creases on her pants and followed the witch to the bridge. They found Amongeratix staring off into space. He ignored their arrival, focusing on the red and green tendrils of the Buta Nebula. Others viewed space as an infinite landscape filled with wonder. He saw naught but the cold void preventing him from reaching his goals.

Presha caught the staunch figure of Geres Auk standing beside the First Officer console. His back was to her for he had long abandoned his need to keep her alive. She'd noticed it first during their frantic battle in the fallen Inquisition prison on Prophet Isle. Any vestige of normalcy left him, devolving the man into a raving lunatic. Again she wondered at the power of Amongeratix and his ability to twist all around him to madness and despair.

"Lady Presha Von," Amongeratix intoned, "you once came to me in the hopes of ruling a planet." His voice was low, emotionless. "I offered you the universe at my side for one small concession. Bring me the key. Was I wrong to place my faith in you?"

Faith? What faith is there between a creature who did not know he should be extinct, and a woman blinded by arrogance? "I did what you asked. The Conclave interfered, forcing me to abandon my original plans."

"Is this true, Geres Auk? Is Presha Von a loyal subject?" Amongeratix asked.

Her former defender turned, a ball of muscles wound too tight. "To an extent. She did what she could to keep the weapon from falling into enemy hands."

"Not enough," he said. "Where is the key?"

"The Guard has it," Geres admitted.

Leaning forward, Amongeratix fixed him with a menacing glare. "Why is that, Geres Auk?"

The big man fidgeted. "I saw what was happening and knew I had to get out of there, with her. We couldn't let them take us. Not with the work left to do."

"You did not think to retrieve the key and complete your task? Leaving the most important piece of my grand designs in my enemy's hands while I sit in impotent rage at being thwarted yet again? Give me one reason why I don't vent you into space."

Unable to meet the glare, Geres turned his eyes down and awaited judgment.

"I thought as much. You have both failed me, though in all fairness I never sought your assistance, Geres." Amongeratix settled back into his chair. "Come closer. I have a task for you to redeem yourself, Geres Auk."

Obeying, Geres dropped to one knee and listened.

Capital District, Krenz, planet Vau Prime.

Dressed in confiscated uniforms, Julian stood watching the front of the Inquisition Headquarters with the criminal Edam Boone. Neither fully trusted the other, sparking intense conversations among their respective groups, yet both knew the only chance they had of preventing a complete takeover and annihilation of their people came from working together. Not a marriage of choice, both men wanted to do the right thing. Even if they were unsure what that was.

"I feel ridiculous," Edam announced for the tenth time. He slipped a finger between his collar and throat in an exaggerated show of trying not to choke.

Julian rolled his eyes. Not only did he agree with the thief, the idea of Edam Boone being an Inquisitor made him chuckle. Feeling at home in his Guard uniform, Julian said, "Relax, this is the only way we are going to get close to this area without being discovered."

"Has it occurred to you nothing about me says Inquisition?" Edam snorted.

"That's the beauty of the universe. We can become whatever we choose to be," Julian replied with a grin. "Are you ready?"

"No."

"Me either. Come on."

They slipped into the stream of foot traffic. Julian wore his rank with confidence while Edam had been instructed to look intimidating and avoid eye contact. Civilians and junior enlisted stepped aside. The sight of the Inquisitor uniform transformed to one of fear over the course of the war. Had he known, Edam Boone would have dominated the plaza.

Air traffic over the district was restricted and the pillars of light extinguished thanks to martial law. Redemption Boulevard, the shining jewel of Conclave accomplishment meant to inspire peace throughout the universe no more than a blackened husk of oppression. Julian's heart ached with the burden of watching all he'd fought for fading.

"What's it all for?" he muttered, gloves creaking as he clenched his fists.

"Welcome to my world," Edam said softly so as not to be overheard. "My people have struggled beneath the

Conclave's oppression long before you were forced to choose sides. There is no winner. Not from this."

Julian resisted the urge to remind him that he and his people were acknowledged criminals, most with bounties on their heads. Despite this, he couldn't disagree. Much of the greater universe was being kept from Vau Prime but it took little imagination to envision war raging across the stars as ideological lines were drawn. The thought of scores of planets tearing themselves apart, splitting families, and driving society to the breaking point rested heavy in his heart. Julian knew stopping the Inquisitor General offered the only chance for stopping the madness. But how?

Rumors of Strannan's shapeshifter failing to assassinate Nye disheartened him. He didn't understand how any sane person so close to completing such an important mission could just walk away before pulling the trigger. It was, in his estimation, the single greatest failure of the war. One capable of seeing democracy fail for good.

"I can hear your teeth grinding," Edam said.

Jarred, Julian stretched his lower jaw. "Sorry. I got distracted."

"Uh huh. What are we doing here again? I can't help but feel like my neck is sticking out for no good reason."

"Intelligence. We need to know what Kale is doing before he does it. It's the only way we can continue evacuating our people. I—" Julian stopped mid-explanation when he spied a nightmare stalking in their direction. General Mobus Kale, a man he'd never met, provided an imposing figure. Resplendent with his robotic arm, Kale was a massive mountain of a man. His uniform bore the stains and scars of a long campaign. Not one to hide behind his rank, the general prided himself on leading his forces into battle. Julian found he couldn't take his eyes off Kale.

Kale halted before them, imposing in every regard. He eyed them, quietly evaluating both. "Captain. Inquisitor. Where are you going?"

"General, we have been reassigned from operations in the Warehouse District to prisoner escort," Julian said, falling back to his Guard persona without missing a beat.

Permanent sneer deepening, Kale said, "Too many good officers are wasted on useless assignments. Both of you come with me. I need capable leaders for this mission."

"General, we have orders—" Edam started.

Kale spun on him, looming over the smaller man. "Did I not make myself clear? Your orders have changed. I am deploying to the low continent to eliminate Strannan's rabble shortly. Return to your commands and report back to me within the hour. You are hereby assigned to me until further notice."

Julian snapped to attention and saluted, not trusting his voice. Kale returned the gesture and stormed off, retinue in tow, leaving the stunned pair in their wake. One of the senior enlisted following Kale turned to stare at them. At Julian. A knowing look passed between them before he turned and resumed his pace.

"We need to move. Now," Julian uttered under his breath.

Not arguing, Edam led the way.

Zevistya Spaceport, Low Continent, planet Vau Prime.

Since the raid on the communications shed, their prisoner had done everything in his power to undermine the failing army. Moral dropped daily. Desertions increased. The will to fight dissolved as factions developed. Losing Strannan had been the nail in the coffin. Nothing the interim leadership did to fill the power vacuum worked and Apontee understood this. He turned his poisoned tongue on every set of guards assigned to him, swaying several to his cause and prompting their replacements. An entire company's worth of Guards had collected their gear, drew supplies, and left in the middle of the night.

Jash Abernath shook his head as another set of guards passed by the tent. "We should have shot him."

Bryn Mal, rubbing a hand over the healed stomach wound, shot him an angry glance. "We've been over this, Jash. Killing him only serves to prove he is right."

"Maybe he is, what difference does it make? We are losing combat power and finding ourselves low on supplies with no hope of escaping the situation." Jash held out his hands in exasperation. "What else can we do other than wait for Kale to drop the hammer?"

They were interrupted by Gedrick entering the tent. Lines creased his face from new worries.

"Keeping him here is growing increasingly dangerous," Gedrick announced without pause. He ambled to a makeshift shelf and poured a cup of black caf. The oddly human drink was the one vice he allowed himself. His single link to humanity.

"That's what I've been saying," Jash agreed. "What can we do with him?"

"Not for me to decide," the shapeshifter replied. "A new commanding officer needs to be appointed. One who has the best interests of the command at heart, not necessarily by virtue of rank. We cannot sustain many more losses."

"We never should have come down here," Bryn growled. "We should have taken our chances in Krenz. What has it all been for, Gedrick? The battles. The raid on Tatarast? The deaths. It wasn't supposed to be like this. We were his crack division. Saviors of Vau Prime and the Conclave. Seems to me all we did was make it worse."

Relishing thc bold flavors trickling down his throat, Gedrick leaned his head back against the wall and closed his eyes. "That depends on how you choose to look at it."

"What do you mean?" Jash asked.

Gedrick took another swallow. "Yes, we may have been dealt a significant blow to our operations here with Davith's death, but that was unforeseeable yet perhaps inevitable. Our enemies are strong and grow bolder daily. Strannan had a price on his head the day the Cardinal Seniorus was assassinated. His death, while regrettable, has provided the rest of the universe with the opportunity to rise against Alain Nye and his pet killers.

Bryn shook her head. "And?"

"Every day Nye's spent fighting us is one where he cannot bring his full military might down on other planets. How many lives have been saved because of our efforts? When I was with Matthias I saw the beginnings of a great resistance movement against the Inquisition. Yes, the violence is widespread. Yes, worlds have burned. But others have thrown off the yokes of their would be masters."

"That does us no good," Jash muttered. "We're going to die down here."

"Very likely, and you should be ashamed for thinking of yourself when millions across the universe suffer under tyranny,"

Gedrick scolded. "You have all done admirable work and should be proud for what you've accomplished with so little."

Bryn rose, preventing Jash from further whining. "He's right. We're Guards. Defenders of the universe. Not some militia rabble on a backwater. We've executed General Strannan's intent to the letter. Just because we've suffered a string of setbacks doesn't absolve us of our mission. The people must come first."

She fixed Gedrick with an accusatory glare until he withered and turned away. Message received. If he'd succeeded in killing Nye like the plan called for they might not be in this predicament. She was also wise enough to know it no longer matter. Not now. The only way to move was forward. Always forward.

"What's your big plan?" she asked him.

Breaking into a smile, the first genuine emotion he'd allowed himself since getting to Utan Husk a moment too late, Gedrick said, "I have intercepted traffic from the Prekhauten Orbital Station that a fleet of unknown size is heading for Vau Prime. There is panic in the local navy. Rumors of none other than Khe-Zhehan herself coming to liberate us."

"A fool's errand. Even she lacks the strength needed to break Nye's hold," Bryn countered. "There must be another reason."

"Perhaps, but what if she intended on evacuating what loyal forces she could?" Jash speculated. The faintest flicker of hope was creeping into his eyes.

"To what purpose? We know there is a communications blackout. She has no idea what is left or where," Bryn said. "It's more likely a ploy to draw us into the open so Kale can finish us off. I don't like it."

"Our enemy has no reason to believe we are on their comms channels," Gedrick said. "I don't see any reason for subterfuge. Besides, it doesn't fit Mobus Kale's operating policies."

"Doesn't mean someone above him hasn't decided to intervene. Kale is a destructive force. One Nye might need to reel in before he loses control," Bryn theorized. She frowned. "Jash, how about taking a team of techs down to the commo shed and see if you can pick up anything else?"

"But you just said…"

"I know what I said, and I know what needs doing. This might be a trap, but we can't take the chance to be caught with our trousers down," she said. "If the Admiral is coming for us, I'd like to be prepared."

"Fine."

Defeated, the younger lieutenant headed off to collect his team. Bryn waited until he was gone before saying to Gedrick, "I like him, but he still hasn't figured it out."

"Figured what out?"

"That we're already dead. If what you say is true, we've done our part for the universe. I wouldn't mind a little down time, but I can't see Kale allowing us offworld. We're going to die down here, just like the Rengu heretics."

"Your fatalistic view does not help our situation," Gedrick scolded. "You must focus on retaining this army intact and get as many offworld as possible. There will be no more chances."

"I know, but I'm not in command, Gedrick. All I can do is take it to whoever we decide will lead us."

"There is another matter," he told her.

"That being?"

"What of the cells Strannan left behind in Krenz? Surely not all have been eliminated or we would have seen an invasion force down here."

"I wish I had an answer for you," was all she managed before snatching her rifle and heading to the senior officer's mess to meet with the others struggling to hold the army together. She wasn't looking forward to her report, nor their responses. No one wanted to be in command and she couldn't blame them.

Sorrow's Fortress, planet Inselcor.

Centuries of solitude left him bitter, fractured. With naught but his automatons for company, Sorrow often talked to himself. Secondary personalities developed, leaving him at war with himself. He never expected that. Nor had he expected to find the god hunter stalking Amongeratix's lower levels. Barely escaping with his life, Sorrow blazed home as fast as possible, taking care to alter his direction and course several times to confuse the god hunter. His singular worries of stopping Tannus and Amongeratix before they tore the universe apart compounded with this development.

Pulling his gaze from the lava flows, Sorrow stalked to the command room and keyed his brother. He needed to know, before it was too late. Tannus' image flickered to life with a concerned look on his face.

"Brother, to what do I owe this disturbance?"

Sorrow stiffened, uncomfortable with the tone. "We have a new problem: Akin Brohl has awakened."

"The god hunter?" Tannus hissed. "Impossible. He has been lost for centuries."

"I stumbled upon him on Antil and barely escaped with my life."

An eyebrow rose. "What were you doing snooping in our brother's castle, Sorrow?"

"That is my business. Akin Brohl must be dealt with," the Bloody Man shifted the subject. "He threatens us all."

"The god hunter has ever been a thorn, but he has his uses. What if we could direct him after Amongeratix?"

"What makes you believe he is open to compromise? He is an abomination capable of but one emotion."

Tannus exaggerated a sigh. "Everyone has a price, Sorrow. We can turn him to our side. Make him work for us."

"He is consumed with his mission, Tannus. You invite ruin. I only survived by fluke," Sorrow argued. "You did not see him. However long he has slept, Akin Brohl now returns to complete his purpose. He will not rest until we are *all* dead."

The finality of his tone sparked new thought: Perhaps the universe would be a better place with the last of their taint removed. Humanity could finally evolve, into whichever direction their hearts led. It wouldn't be perfect, but the influence his kind continued to wield burdened mortality with the inescapable conclusion of never being good enough.

"Calm yourself, Brother. Akin Brohl has hunted our kind to extinction. He is diligent and imbued with unnatural fervor thanks to the Oracle, but he is not unkillable," Tannus explained. "Nor is he unreasonable. Think, Sorrow, why has he avoided the three of us for all this time? He has had multiple opportunities to kill each of us yet here we stand. Why?"

Pursing his lips, Sorrow replied, "It appears his self-imposed truce is ended. Else why should he have reason to attempt my life?"

"A mystery, to be sure, but not one posing immediate threats," Tannus dismissed. "Let him hunt Amongeratix. Perhaps he is what is needed to tip the balance and finally end our war."

"He is still our brother," Sorrow whispered. "He deserves one of us to end his life … You, Tannus. This has ever been your crusade. None of us wanted any part in it. If only you hadn't defied our father in such a way."

"That no longer matters." Discomfort edging his tone, Tannus added, "What matters not is how we arrived in this predicament but how we move forward and end our struggle. The universe is tired, weary of our crimes and petty squabbling. We have been reduced to caricatures used to celebrate holidays and worse. Don't you wish to be free again?"

"I don't know how."

"Brother—"

Sorrow ended the transmission. He'd done his part. Tannus was warned. What happened next no longer weighed on his conscience.

He admitted that he was tired now. They all were. The longer their war stretched the less they became. A hollowness grew inside, deep within what remained of his soul. It was the one torment he never shook.

Closing his eyes, the Bloody Man let his thoughts drift back to a time the universe forgot.

They stood before the throne, heads bowed in supplication to their father, ever glorious in his power. Sorrow cast sidelong glances to each of his brothers. Tannus, the proud champion of righteousness whose hubris blinded him to the true workings of their empire. Amongeratix, vicious and naturally bitter. Taller and stronger than them, he embodied an unnatural rage capable of bringing all to ruin. And himself. The middle son oft forgotten when it came to the affairs of state. This alone allowed him to tinker, exploring different avenues of interest while his brothers drifted closer to inevitable conflict.

This day was not one of those.

Seated alongside their father were the lords and nobles of the ruling houses. Elder members of an austere society. To their father's right sat an empty chair, for mother never partook in such meetings. Rengu sat on the left, his stern visage deeming and accounting.

Sorrow often felt their uncle had unfinished business, but what? He was a man of few words and swift action. a slayer of untold numbers. How could any being live with such vivid hate?

"Why have you come before me, oh sons of my heart?" the father asked, his voice booming throughout the golden hall.

Windows one hundred feet tall stretched from the floor to the cusp of the domed ceiling. Alabaster pillars decorated the marbled floor. Elevated some meters, the seats of the council spread across half the chamber in a wide semi-circle. Birds sang from lofty perches high above, judging events that would soon come to spark a turn in all they knew.

Tannus lifted his head, proud in the cast of light and shadow. "Father, it is not an easy request I bring to you and the council but one that must be addressed in light of all transpiring among us."

Grumbles drifted from those gathered. Baleful stares and uncomfortable shifting.

Nonplussed, their father said, "We have had this discussion before, Tannus. This is not the time to speak of the humans."

"When else would it be? They have served us for generations, slaves in all but name. Father, our empire threatens to crumble from within. War is coming. What further use do the mortals have? They cannot withstand the tide of battle, nor do they have the strength to stand on their own. They will suffer and die while we tear ourselves apart."

"Humans are a stain upon this universe," Rengu interrupted. "Better they went extinct than remain underfoot."

Tannus took a step forward. "If we are so mighty, so just in our righteousness, why have we kept them down for generations? Life deserves to be free."

"The mortals serve their purpose, as do we, Tannus," Father said. "Do not think that because you are my son you may stand before this council and decree our shortcomings to suit your nature. This matter is ended. Leave now before I lose my patience."

Sorrow heard the intake of breath and closed his eyes. There would be no turning back. Not now. The die was already cast.

"I will not," Tannus announced to all assembled. "We are the stewards of the universe, guardians of life and spirit. What right have we to bring those deemed lesser to ruin? Let the mortals go so they might not be caught in our foolishness."

Outraged, Father jumped to his feet. "How dare you! This is no mere familial gathering, Tannus. We are the rulers of the universe. Our word is law. MY *word is unquestionable. You dishonor my name and your brothers with your pettiness. Do not speak again or I shall be forced to take action."*

Yet Tannus refused to back down. "Do what you must, Father, for I shall remain silent no longer. We are not monsters. Mortals have rights. Give them a planet and strike it from our archives. It is the only way to stay my tongue."

Trembling now, Father cast an accusatory finger down at his sons and uttered his proclamation.

Sorrow opened his eyes, tears filling them. "Why Tannus? Why?"

FOURTEEN

3215 A.G. (After Gods), Slums of Erdef City, planet Romalle.

Security teams swept through the less developed areas of the city for a second time hoping to catch the Cardinal's killer through a false sense of security. Tensions continued rising. No further murders were committed since that single night of terror, yet they were no closer to finding or identifying the culprit of those either. It was decided that Riles Tenaru had gone to ground. None of her known associates knew her whereabouts nor were they forthcoming with relevant information. It was as if she had disappeared.

Using this knowledge, Riles crept through allies, spent her nights in cold, abandoned backrooms and condemned houses on the outskirts of town. She scavenged her meals, relying on the generosity of those select few she trusted. She stole what she couldn't find. The noose drew tighter. She knew time had all but expired and still there'd been no word or summons from Lady Emmest DeMauve. Riles caught whispers of a failed assassination attempt on the Lady, a city in panic. She needed to escape and, with Emmest inexplicably out of the picture, that meant one thing.

"It's time," she told Nemineon as they sat perched along the edge of a two-story building.

Legs dangling over the side, they shared a quick meal of roasted fowl and day old bread and watched for signs of approaching patrols.

Relief flooded through him. Nerves frayed from being on edge, Nemineon swallowed the dry bread and wiped his mouth with the back of a hand. "Are you serious?"

She nodded. "What else can we do? The city is tearing itself apart trying to find me."

"That's not going to stop just because we leave."

"I know, but I don't have a choice. I don't want to spend my last few days in a cell while half the city prepares to watch me die. Maybe Hargan can help, maybe not."

Nemineon stared at her, wondering what happened to the carefree woman he once knew and had fallen in love with. In her place, Riles Tenaru transformed into a hardened figure incapable of trust. She'd grown cynical, desperate in ways he hadn't imagined. In many ways, Nemineon found himself afraid of her, for her.

"The tribes will accept us, though it won't be easy," he cautioned, unsure how he'd become the advocate of reason. "We will be forced to atone for our transgressions."

"I'd rather that than hang for sport because they can't find the real killer," she shot back. "You don't have to come with me."

"We've been through this, Riles. I am just as much of a target as you," he replied before breaking into a soft grin. "Thank you for that, by the way. I always wanted to be a fugitive."

She winced. "I could always knock you out and leave you tied somewhere. Tell the authorities I betrayed you and fled. They'll question you for a little before letting you go. There's no need for both of us to suffer because I was in the wrong place."

"What kind of friend would I be to let you do that?" he asked. "Like it or not, we're in this together, Riles."

She clapped a hand on his knee a few times and said, "You're a good man."

"I'm an idiot is what I am."

Tolde, Gando, and Luma stood beside each other, sharing their knowledge of recent events galaxywide and the implications for the people of Romalle. Ragan sat by the window, feeling out of place. He struggled with being here and would have stayed on Wexanos if not for Tannus' subtle encouraging. This did nothing to alleviate the angst spreading through him.

"Hargan here."

Conversation faded, all eager to hear what followed. Ragan glanced the investigator's way.

"Are you certain?"

Backs stiffened. Heads turned further to stare. Silence settled.

"I'll be right there. No one does anything until I give the word. Am I understood? Hargan out." Turning to the group he said, "We need to move. They have located the suspect and are surrounding her now."

"We can't risk letting her go into custody," Luma Kai blurted. "Not with a potential traitor in your ranks."

"You think I don't know that? Inquisitor, I'm no happier about this than you and if we don't get to her first this will all have been in vain."

Tolde clasped his hands together. "He's right. We need her if there is any chance of solving this mystery."

Glowering at Hargan, Luma asked, "What's the plan?"

A twinkle entered the investigator's eyes that made Ragan a little uneasy. "Leave that to me. Load up with whatever arsenal you feel you need. We leave in five."

Left with little choice, they prepared for battle.

Luma Kai's misgivings grew. Never one to trust blindly, she found Hargan's manner too easygoing, as if he were either in on the scam from the beginning or had intimate knowledge of events yet to come. She vowed to put a round in the back of his head should he betray them.

Emmest DeMauve swept into the City Board chambers unannounced. Rather than dress appropriate to the difficult times, she chose to present an image of a woman with no fear. Her golden dress and ornate jewelry left little imagination to her legacy of opulence. Strength imbued through conviction and Emmest was the building storm.

"Good morning," she announced, her sing-song voice echoing through the chamber.

"What is the meaning of this? We are in closed council," Damal barked. "Security!"

"Sit down, Damal. I am in no mood for games. Eiters, Kasop. Good to see you all here. I do hate repeating myself."

Flustered, Damal sank back into his chair with a creak.

"Lady DeMauve, this is most unusual. We have important matters to discuss," Eiters said. "Please make this quick."

Emmest resisted the urge to slap the false smile from Eiters' face. "Good. Now that we have the pleasantries out of the way we can get down to business. As you are aware, there was an attempt on my life recently. The assassin paid for his sins and, to my dismay, I learned of several other people of influence having been eliminated just in time for your vote on whether Romalle enters the war or not. Convenient, don't you think?"

"Who told you that? The vote has not been announced," Kasop said with a frown.

"Please, Kasop, I am a woman of means. If you knew half of what I do your head might explode," Emmest chided. "Who is responsible for these assassins? I would very much like to speak with them."

"What leads you to believe we are responsible?" Damal asked.

"Damal, I never intoned you were, but little transpires in this city without the board's knowledge. Surely Hargan or your Inquisitor have some leads by now."

"Matters are still developing. We are not at liberty to share information in the middle of an open investigation," Eiters began. "Perhaps it would be best if you confronted Hargan directly. I'm sure he will be more than willing to assist you."

"I figured I'd cut the middleman and come directly to the source. It would be a shame if I went to the media with complaints of the vaunted City Board withholding pertinent information and endangering the lives of all citizens by delaying the investigation, failing to quell unrest, and exhibiting a decided lack of common sense." Emmest hummed. "Perhaps the time has come for a new board. One who will place the needs of the people before their own pockets."

Damal shot back to his feet, meaty palm slapping the table. "How dare you come before us with accusations and slander? I will not sit for this. Lady DeMauve, we tolerate your eccentricities out of respect for your late husband but the line ends there. Retract your statements or—"

"Or what, Damal? Expose you for the fraud you are? Or did you think your private coup to sway Romalle on the side of the Inquisitor General was a secret? I can ruin you with a blink of my eyes. You do not know fear, nor wrath. I can teach you. It will be my pleasure."

At their shocked silence, Emmest DeMauve stared down the three people capable of saving or damning their world. She'd collected enough dirt on each to see them buried in an early grave and, in her estimation, more than one deserved it. The City Board was a den of serpents. Each member served for far too long, prompting the question of term limits to circulate. Emmest knew those in power grew corrupt the longer they were in charge. This needed changing if Romalle had any hope for the future. She decided the time had come to remove these obstacles and restore a measure of order and honor to her planet, before it was too late.

Eiters, desperate to salvage what she could, said, “Damal, please. This posturing gets us nowhere. The only way forward is through developing a working relationship and fundamental understanding between us. Lady DeMauve is a woman of immense influence. One can ill afford to stand against us, especially now.”

“Thank you, Eiters, though I fear your pleas fall on deaf ears,” Emmest intoned, trying not to scoff. “Damal knows how his vote will be cast, as I’m sure each of you do. Tell me, when will Romalle languish beneath the boot of the Inquisition? Is Gando preparing the Prekhauten detail for the arrival of reinforcements from Vau Prime? It takes little imagination to see waves of recruiters sweeping through our cities, drafting able bodies who have no desire to march off to war. Will you be satisfied knowing generations of our youth, the best and brightest of us, go to their slaughter in a war we have no business in?”

“Nonsense. We have a civic duty to support the Inquisition,” Kasop argued. “Romalle has stood with Vau Prime for centuries, never wavering. Why should this change now? The Inquisitor General proclaims heresy at the highest levels of Conclave and is doing his part to ensure the continuation of our civilization. I do not believe there is malice in his heart. He will root out the heretics and allow for the peaceful rebuilding of the clergy to guide us into the future. Where is the harm in this?”

“The harm is in the means, Kasop. Alain Nye is a monster, should the reports be true. Tens of thousands lie dead because of his need for power. A need that could easily spread to those deemed opportunistic. What point is there in involving Romalle in a war that will be decided half the universe away?”

“As I said, we must do our part.”

“Indeed. What has been promised to you, Kasop?” she asked. “What spoils of war has Nye vowed upon victory?”

Face darkening, Kasop held out his hands. “I seek only to serve our people. I’m sure you can understand.”

"I understand more than you know," Emmest retorted. "This meeting is done. Thank you for your time and your service to our people." Provoking them revealed more than she anticipated as well as confirmed her fears. She needed to act swiftly to stop them from making the worst mistake of their lives.

"You don't trust him," Tolde said. It was more statement than question. A voicing of concern over their mission.

Rifle in hand, Luma stalked through the darkening alley. "No, I don't. Neither should you. We are beset by enemies, Tolde. Can't you feel it? This world is ready to burn. We need to do what we came here for and depart before it's too late."

"Investigator Hargan has done nothing to arouse my suspicions," Tolde cautioned. "We cannot treat the local law enforcement hostile until provoked."

She squared on him, halting him midstride. "Tolde, you are forgetting everything we were taught as Inquisitors. Trust no one, especially not ones who are producing limited results in finding your brother's killer. How much more do you expect to push us before the cracks form?"

He opened then closed his mouth, choosing to remain silent. They were on the edge, forced into one desperate situation after the next. Tolde knew Luma struggled with much, from the loss of identity to accepting his impossible resurrection. A strong woman, there was but so much she could endure. He sympathized with her and might have sided with her if not for the agony his lifetime of service produced.

"All the more reason for us to get this Riles woman first," he said. "Gando vouches for Hargan, but that doesn't prevent information from falling into the wrong hands. Find Riles and we force our enemies to the defensive." He paused, searching for the right thing to say. "Luma, I know we have not seen eye to eye since my death, but that does not mean I am not behind you. We are still a team. Never forget that."

She offered a clipped nod, and the pair continued their pursuit of their prey. The three-dimensional image projected from the device attached to his wrist picked up heat signatures nearby. For all they knew every signature was an armed combatant ready to give his life to the cause. Caution being prudent, the Inquisitors slipped into hunting mode. Soon the open spaces funneled into tight alleys similar to the one they were ambushed in. Tolde thanked Sister Alessandra for taking Ragan with her. His inexperience would put him in danger, for Tolde expected this operation to take a nasty turn.

Switching their safeties off, Tolde and Luma entered the warren of alleys and cramped streets where the lower social classes lived. Grime smeared the broken cobblestones. The air grew heavy, fetid. They heard doors slamming. Shutters closing. The scurry of boots as the innocents hurried to avoid the approaching storm. Schematics from his wrist display showed a strong force on the opposite side of the district, pushing deeper into the warren.

A loud smack to his right made Tolde jerk to the side. He caught the trickle of dust and small pebbles, following the trail back to the rooftop of the tenement building across the street. He saw two figures hurrying to the stairwell on the opposite side of the building. Instinct took over. He gestured and Luma took point, entering the tenement with the silent grace of a predator. Tolde followed, pausing to check the street to ensure they weren't being followed.

"I should be with him.".

Sister Alessandra remained silent, choosing not to reprimand Ragan. He was young, inexperienced, and she was gradually coming to accept his presence. Removing him from Rastarok went against the Order's policies, and she still struggled with understanding why she'd done it, but her heart told her Ragan had an important part to play before the end. Before Forever Night. It proved a cruel twist of fate for Ragan represented the purity a large portion of the universe had forgotten.

At her silence, Ragan sighed. They were perched atop one of the taller buildings in the district, the Blood Witch a devouring angel overseeing all in sight. Ragan marveled at her diligence. What little he understood of their Order, left him awed and frightened in unequal proportions. Alessandra had done all within her power to keep him alive, though at great cost to their missions. His mind often thought back to the budding friendship of Paradise Tear. She promised him a better future but was lost to an evil he failed to comprehend.

Now he stood beside the Blood Witch to he owed an unpayable debt, waiting for a man who took a chance on him when no one else would.

"I'm sorry, Sister," he whispered. "I shouldn't have said that."

"We all have our parts to play, Ragan. Worry not over who does what and trust all proceeds as planned," she said. Her hawkish gaze swept through the streets. "And I have told you repeatedly to call me Alessandra."

He blushed; thankful she couldn't see him. With another sigh, Ragan resumed watching. The comms device in his ear felt uncomfortable yet kept him connected to the other team. He couldn't help but sympathize with Tolde, though he failed to fully understand how the man he knew as Tobas died and was resurrected. The universe proved much larger than Ragan imagined, casting all he knew in a spiral of doubt. Now he stood upon the edge of a dilapidated building in the outskirts of a city so unlike where he was raised waiting for a man he'd grown to appreciate find the woman rumored to be his brother's killer.

"How much longer do you think it will be?"

"Until she is found and secured."

The finality in her tone said enough. Glum, Ragan averted his gaze, unsure what he was supposed to be looking for.

Riles and Nemineon ran for their lives. Scores of officers swarmed the district, cutting off possible escape routes. Desperation made strange bedfellows while stripping her of a lifetime of aspirations. Realizing nothing was to come from her meeting with Lady DeMauve, Riles found she had little choice other than to flee into the far deserts. Romalle wasn't a large planet, but the City Board knew better than to cross the tribes. Now, with time running out, she wasn't sure she could reach them.

The first sign of approaching law enforcement aircars sent her scurrying, dropping what remained of her meal. Riles' heart thundered. She hadn't been this scared since nearly being apprehended by the Cardinal's killer. The tiny blaster tucked in her belt felt insignificant. She might incapacitate one or two but lacked the charge to enable their escape to Nemineon's waiting transport on the outskirts of town.

The rooftop door slammed behind them, the sound lost beneath the heavy tread of their boots on the stairs. Riles went first, unsure what she might find upon exiting the building. Her network had dried up. Those once staunch friends going to ground, turning their backs on her when she needed them most. Not that she blamed them. Mounting pressure by the City Board drove wedges between friends, reducing surviving friendships to the greed of coin over loyalty. Having this knowledge on her conscience, Riles chose exile.

They reached the ground floor and hurried down the poorly lit hallway to the backdoor. Riles pressed against the wall, shoving Nemineon against the far wall in the event hunters awaited on the other side. While there were limited instances when the patrollers and investigators opened fire on their quarry, she wasn't willing to leave today to chance. Failing to steady her breath, Riles cracked the door open and peered outside. She blinked as the dropping angle of the sun caught her eyes in blinding fashion.

Natural shadows peppered the immediate area. However, Riles failed to spot any lurking foes. No time to waste, she nodded to Nemineon and they hurried into the open. Sounds of approaching patrollers knocking on doors and shouting demands through loudspeakers echoed through the alleys. The hunters were coming.

"Where is the aircar?" she asked.

Nemineon took a moment to gather his bearings before gesturing to the right. "This way, come on."

He started running, forcing her to follow before she was ready.

"Nemineon, wait!"

He didn't hear her, or he chose to ignore her.

The promise of a life of torture or worse spurred him forward, reckless with the desire to escape and live. So it was he who charged around the corner and slammed into a pair of undercover Inquisitors. The woman shoved him away before he toppled them both, sweeping his legs out from under him and bending his right arm behind his back by the thumb and twisting hard enough to produce a yelp.

"Let him go." Riles came around the corner, immediately pointing her blaster at the woman.

The returning glare froze Riles. "Or what?"

"I'll shoot," Riles said, though it came out more as a question than firm defiance.

The Inquisitor glared. “No, you won’t. Lower your weapon and you both live.”

“How can I trust you?”

“She’ll kill your friend without second thought,” the other Inquisitor said. “I, however, need you alive.”

Riles caught the glint of sunlight reflecting from the muzzle of his barrel pointed at her head and her heart sunk. She lowered her blaster in defeat.

Damal sat in silence. The debacle of a board meeting ending in raised voices and thinly veiled threats. He blamed DeMauve’s intrusion for the chaos. Matters had been proceeding according to his plans until she stormed in with inquiries and supposition. Where he once stood upon the precipice of coercing his fellow leaders into following his lead and joining the war on the Inquisition’s side, Damal now found himself beset on both sides. All fell into ruin because of one person—a person who should have died. He vowed not to make the mistake again.

Unable to focus, he drummed his pudgy fingers on his desk. His eyes were closed, head tilted back. Emmest DeMauve was now his largest obstacle. The one unaccounted factor preventing him from proclaiming himself regional governor of Romalle and pledging fealty to Alain Nye’s new order. The lure of power beckoned, pulling from what little remained of good conscience and a sense of doing right by the people who elected him. His naivety long since evaporated, Damal wanted unmitigated power and was willing to do everything possible to achieve it. Even if it meant murdering the most influential people standing in his way …

Images of closing his hands around Lady Emmest DeMauve’s slender neck and crushing until her last strangled gasp of breath rattled from her lips flit through his mind. She, of all people, presented the greatest challenge to his plans. How the assassins failed proved concerning, for he’d hired the best in Erdef City.

Thoughts swirling, he contemplated subverting the Inquisitor, perhaps using one of the clergy at the temple. The pompous fools were ever arrogant in their insisted worship of the gods. Eager for coin and adoration, they might slip into his twisted machinations with the proper amount of force. Damal ruled out Hargan. The man represented the old Guard.

There was another option, but it would leave him financially ruined long enough for the carrion eaters to swoop in. Without any way of telling how long the civil war might extend, Damal couldn't afford to hire one of the Vaumagian assassins, despite their noted success. No. He had no allies and little time. He needed to speed up his timeline.

"So be it, DeMauve," he said aloud. "You handled one assassin. I wonder what you'll do against an army. Not even you can stop the storm coming for you." A chime threw him back to the present. Face twisted in frustration, Damal barked, "What?"

"Sir, your next meeting has arrived," his attendant said through the intercom.

In no mood for political doublespeak, Damal cracked his knuckles. "Send them in."

Behemoth, deep space, three days to Vau Prime.

"I am placing my full confidence in your ability to see this task through. We stand at a decisive point. The universe is ready to fall—all it requires is a subtle push from us," Algiss Her addressed her chosen few who would spread their message and influence on the highest reaches of power on Vau Prime.

Her gaze penetrated the shadows of hoods, questing the fractured souls of the women before her. All volunteers, they represented the most zealous of her new Order. Women with little compunction, who were willing to do whatever it took to achieve their ends. Three Sisters marching into the teeth of a monster who believed his own bullshit. Algiss scoffed at the notion of a mortal man attempting to assert authority over one of *hers*. The time was fast approaching when mortals would no longer rule on their comfortable thrones far from conflict enjoying luxury while the universe suffered.

Floating before them, conscientious enough to display authority to reinforce the idea that she had been right in her attempted coup, Algiss raised her hands.

"This is the moment you were created for. One the annals of history will mark as the turning point for us all.

Twist the Inquisitor General. Push him to the edge and open the path for Amongeratix to descend and take his rightful place as ruler of the universe. Do this for every Sister who has ever suffered, bled, or died for a cause not of their choosing. For the women and young girls mistreated by humanity, ostracized for being different. Those executed for the sin of living outside of religious constructs. Heretics they name us! This day is the beginning of the end of our unjust persecution! Today, Sisters, you assert your rightful dominance over the pathetic mortals and their misbelief in deities—Go."

Imbued with the strength of raw fervor, her disciples swept from the hall, heading for the landing bay where a fueled shuttle sat ready to take them to their destinies. Algiss Her watched with rapt focus, for they were the first weapons in her private war against mortal man. The catalyst for revenge, the Crimson Sisterhood stood poised to ascend.

Turning, her gaze settled on the hulking madman brought aboard by Presha Von. Covered in sweat, eyes blazing, his chest heaved. Algiss spied the madness lurking within. He was a useful tool, a blunt instrument in a war requiring precision. Nothing more.

"Do not let harm come to them, Geres Auk," she warned. "Or I shall flense your flesh and bring ruin to your mind and body. Perhaps when I finish, I shall feed your soul to the creatures of the deep, their appetites are forever wet for human suffering."

He growled through clenched teeth. "I take orders from my master, not a witch."

She lashed out, unconscious of the power she unleashed. She struck the giant in the center of his chest. Grunting, Geres took a step back as pipes burst in the walls. The deck at his feet melted, curling up around him. Warning sirens blared to life with sparks from sliced power conduits raining down from the ceiling. Fingertips blackening from the magic, Algiss stared down the larger man. She relished unleashing her full power. Wounds on his chest bubbled and blistered. Swathes of hair were reduced to blackened stubble. His hate filled eyes offered no give.

"See that no harm comes to them, Geres Auk. I have spoken."

Presha Von, fallen lady of Lethendweil and outcast among the stars, sat on the cushioned bench pressed against the bulkhead. Dull lights flickered, casting the cell in a realm of shadow. A draft of stale air circulated. Many of *Behemoth's* primary systems operated on suboptimal conditions since the raid. She wished those brazen few she had heard about succeeded. Such creations belonged in nightmares, not coursing through space under foul purpose. Shuddering, she turned to stare at the being chained to the table.

She didn't know why Amongeratix insisted she explore the ship. Presha knew it was a test, but to what end? She lacked the funding and powerbase necessary to prove her worth under his flag. The renegade witch was right. She was little more than a failed attempt at achieving his goals.

"You are her, aren't you?"

Jarred back to the present, Presha took a deep breath and replied, "Yes."

The blonde giantess' penetrating gaze judged Presha, reaching deep into her soul in search of … what? Without power or influence, she was naught but a hollow shell of a woman. What did Paradise Tear hope to discover in the tumultuous recesses of her mind?

"That's it?" Presha asked as anger took her. "No comments or threats? No promises of ill will or a violent demise? Accusations of hatred, perhaps?"

"What purpose would those serve?"

Presha threw her hands up. "Everyone else seems to find value in it. Go ahead. Promise my soul an eternity of torment for my crimes!"

"What torture could I provide greater than that which you give yourself? The burden upon your conscience is deserved, yet there is still hope for redemption."

Tears broke free. A torrent of pent-up emotions Presha spent years ignoring burst free. Her body wracked, threatening to double over. She was nothing more than a broken girl desperate for a father's attention and mother's love. And had neither. "I… I murdered an entire planet. Billions of lives gone because of me," she whimpered. "I don't deserve to live."

"No, you don't, but I don't have the power to give that you," Paradise Tear replied. "Nor would I wish to. You must spend the rest of your life atoning for the crimes perpetrated on Kharsis."

"Better I end that life now and be done with it," Presha countered between sobs. The thought of remaining a servant to the madness of Amongeratix promising eternal agony shook her to the bone. “I am not cut for this life, giant.”

“You are the product of your choices, nothing else. There is little point in debating the right and wrongs of it, nor is there need to lament what you once desired.”

Defeated, Presha sank back, wrapping her arms around herself. “What else is there?”

“The opportunity to atone.”

The matter-of-fact delivery stunned Presha. Any promise of a better future remained elusive, though the opportunity to right past wrongs was inspiring. She wiped the tears from her face then the sweat of her palms on the stained pleats of her skirts and rose. A determination long forgotten steeled her gaze. “Thank you.”

Paradise offered a sad smile. “What will you do?”

“What I must,” Presha replied. “If, gods willing, I can help you escape I will.”

“Better you killed me and saved the universe.”

Unwilling to answer that, Presha bowed and left.

Nestled into his command throne, Amongeratix stared into the unending expanse of darkness. Space soothed his nerves, calming the storm perpetually raging deep within. He hadn’t always been filled with hatred, but after countless centuries he knew no other way. His singular driving thought revolved around killing his brothers and laying claim to the universe, as was his birthright. A right stolen by Tannus’ arrogance.

The chime resounded across the bridge, drawing both attention and ire. Eyes narrowing, he ground out, “Well?”

The officer, a sickly woman with pale, mottled flesh and enough enhancements to reduce her humanity, spun her chair to face him. “My lord, it is from Vau Prime. The Inquisitor General wishes to speak with you.”

Amongeratix waved and the holoimage flared to life. “You disturb me, Inquisitor General.”

“My apologies, my lord but there is an urgent matter I must bring to your attention.”

“I am not a creature of patience, mortal.”

Nye avoided eye contact as he mumbled through the rumors of a grand evacuation in the works, detailing how his people continued locking down the planet to reduce and eliminate all enemies before they could escape. Amongeratix found little concern, seeing the report for what it was, a desperate attempt of a man who knew his relevance was all but expired and willing to do whatever it took to remain in power. Still, news of approaching enemy warships capable of further wounding *Behemoth* disturbed him. He was not ready to defend his new throne, yet.

"This cannot stand. Listen to me, Inquisitor General. I have much for you to do before my arrival."

Horror spread across Nye's face as Amongeratix continued speaking.

FIFTEEN

3215 A.G. (After Gods), PGN *Solstice*, enroute to planet Wexanos.

Gripping the armrests as her ship rocked, August shouted over the rising panic on the bridge, "More power to the engines!"

"Captain, we'll risk outpacing the escorts," her First Officer answered. "The corvettes are too heavily engaged to breakaway."

Trapped in a losing scenario, August knew she had no choice but to stand and fight. They'd run into a well-developed ambush on the edge of an unnamed asteroid belt, the fragmented remains of a long dead planet, shortly after departing the Mannus System. How the enemy knew where her heading remained a mystery, though she had her suspicions.

Surveying the tactical images filling the main screens, she watched the battle unfold. A carrier lurked somewhere in the unseen while smaller ships and close to thirty single pilot fighters swarmed her battlegroup. One corvette listed, burning as internal fires threatened to implode the ship. She'd witnessed several escape pods jettison only to be picked off by opportunistic fighters with little morals. Infuriated, August knew she was helpless. The remaining escorts were separated, forced to fight individual battles. Whoever commanded the enemy force proved their intent. She knew, as did the others, that once the corvette escort were nullified there would be little preventing the enemy from picking the *Solstice* apart one shot at a time.

Slamming a fist down, she was trapped by obligation and duty. "Reverse engines and prepare a starburst with the ventral guns. I want these fighters cleared away. We need to get the corvettes back into formation—it's the only way. Odir, relay orders to the corvettes. Have them conduct a tactical disengagement and collapse on us."

"Aye, ma'am," the First Mate acknowledged and began transmitting orders.

Warning sirens went off; August tensed.

"Hull breach on deck thirteen. Fire suppression teams are responding."

"Weapons! Target the nearest enemy ship."

"Captain, we won't last long with our hull integrity compromised," Odir leaned over and whispered.

"Thank you, First Mate," she muttered and glanced up. "Have the Marines standby to deploy."

"Ma'am?"

"If there's the opportunity to take one of their ships and turn it against them, we need to take it. Otherwise, we're already dead."

Odir stiffened. What she proposed amounted to suicide for the Marine boarding teams, despite being trained for such events. Swallowing hard, he clicked the intercom. "All Marine boarding teams report to your shuttles. Standby to deploy."

She imagined the chaos raging below decks. Men and women, some wounded or worse, frantically attempting to salvage the ship while gun crews launched barrage after barrage. The deafening roar of cannons, deep space lasers, and chaff bouncing through the outer levels combined with the screams and shouts of people doing all they could to survive. *Solstice*. She found the confliction oddly amusing.

"Enemy frigate rolling into firing solution. They have us locked," the tactical officer announced.

August nodded. *So, this is it*. "All hands brace for impact. Weapons, shoot down as many of those missiles as possible and cut a hole through their screen. First Mate, launch the Marines."

His protests were cut short by the determined look in her eyes, Odir gave the order.

Solstice lurched. Small caliber ion guns erupted with anti-ship defenses. Unable to do more than watch, August relied on the training and professionalism of her crew as multiple actions took place simultaneously. A flight of anti-ship missiles fired from the portside batteries, racing across the vacuum of space toward an enemy battle cruiser. Chaff and defensive weapons erupted on the starboard side. Brief detonations flared across the tactical readouts announcing at least partial success in stopping the enemy barrage as a flight of boarding pods rocketed away. Realtime monitoring showed her the interior of each pods, her Marine's faces concealed behind the deathlike visors on their helmets. She held her breath, counting the moments until the first pod struck the enemy ship forward of the landing bays.

A flight of enemy fighters, desperate to prevent the capital ship from being captured, raced after the pods but it was too late. Their ion rounds fell short even as the last pod crashed through the cruiser's hull. August watched her Marines rush from the pods. Weapons fired from both sides. Bodies fell. Soon the acrid haze filling the corridor obscured her view.

"Captain! Enemy cruiser is engaging engines. The other ships are preparing to disengage!" Tactical shouted.

"Odir, get those Marines out before we lose them. Do it now!"

The main screen showed the corvettes converging and meting out a ferocious barrage on the nearest enemy ship, turning the ambush. Enemy fighters too slow to evade the withering crossfire from the combined ships exploded in brilliant flashes before space reduced them to darkened bits of debris. Slowly the corvette screen pushed back. August ignored the lesser action, focusing on the desperate bid for her boarding parties to escape before it was too late. Should they remain aboard the enemy cruiser when it jumped their fates promised to be brutal.

One pod launched. Then a second. She continued holding her breath. A third tore free from the cruiser, trailing a spreading cloud of debris. August waited but the final pod remained clamped in place. A gnawing feeling spread through her stomach. One screen switched over to the Marine's head cams—the remaining warriors were locked in an intense firefight with their enemy components. One fell, the back of his helmet a gaping hole oozing smoke and gore. For each wound they received the Marines doled out unprecedented fury. Enemy soldiers dropped en masse, unable to withstand the grim determination of men and women desperate to survive. The feed abruptly cut, leaving August staring at a black screen.

"Enemy cruiser has jumped," Odir said in defeat.

Silence dominated the bridge. The impossibility of losing a full squad of Marines to the depredations of their enemies rocked many crewers with unease. Unwilling to meet their empty stares, August turned her attention to the dwindling battle. She still had people in harm's way and, until they were secured aboard, and the enemy presence negated, duty demanded she focus on the present.

"Get those pods back in the hangars," she ordered. "First Mate, open a channel to the corvettes. I want every trace of filth left behind destroyed."

"Aye, Captain."

August finally released the hand grips and looked up to her second in command. "Odir, I want a complete list of names as soon as the Marines reboard and are debriefed. We cannot allow our friends to fall without remembrance."

"Yes, ma'am."

Governor's Palace, planet Dalafar.

Junior Inquisitor Alpof marched with the surety of a man convinced he was right. A squad of Guards followed, resplendent in their combat armor and weapons held in the ready position. The echoes of boots stamped through the pristine halls. Menials and low-level government employees were brushed aside as the squad passed. Alpof enjoyed the sensation of being feared. The heady intoxication offered him promises of a better world where all his desires came true. He owed his allegiance to Alain Nye and the Inquisition, not the backwater provincial governess of an inconsequential planet. This action felt right. Felt justified.

"Step aside," he ordered the Governess' private security watching over her inner offices.

They exchanged a look before paling. Handheld blasters and minimum wage offered no protection from heavily armed Prekhautens. Nodding to one another, they complied.

Alpof pushed the doors open with a grand sweeping gesture. Before giving his Guards a final look. "Wait here. I won't be long."

They formed ranks, securing the entry point and protecting against possible incursion. Alpof closed the doors behind him as he swept into the office. Instead of finding a shocked old woman seated behind her desk he found Adris Moscasco standing with her hands clasped behind her back, staring out the rain-soaked windows.

"How may I help you today, Alpof?"

He stiffened. "That's Inquisitor, Governess. I believe we both know why I'm here. Don't make this difficult."

"Get to the point, Alpof. I am busy woman."

Bridling under the disrespect, Alpof jabbed a finger at her. "Governess Adris Moscasco, it has come to the Inquisition's attention you are working to subvert Conclave authority, aide the insurrectionists, and establish a singular point of rule for the planet Dalafar. You are hereby placed under arrest in the name of the Inquisition."

Rather than cower beneath the trumped-up weight of his accusations, Moscasco feigned a yawn and glanced at him. "Is that it? I would have thought you might concoct stronger threats. Your lack of creativity is almost insulting."

"This is not a game, Adris. Soon you'll be bound and shuttled off to an Inquisition prison where, gods willing, I shall have the pleasure of overseeing your interrogation." Madness shined in his eyes. "I have been looking forward to this."

"I'm sure you have, but I don't think I will let you arrest me today."

"I don't recall offering you a choice."

At this she turned, a predatory glare twisted her face. "No, you didn't. Neither am I. Alpof, you are brash, foolish, and far too young to understand how this universe works. Do you truly believe the Conclave will let you abduct me? Dalafar is a loyal planet and you and I both know there is no sustainable evidence for your charges. Even should you take me away I won't stay long and then, then dear *Inquisitor*, I shall unleash a wrath upon you not even your precious Inquisitor General can save you from. Get out of my office before I forget my manners."

Alpof trembled. His right hand dropped, whipping his sidearm out and pointing it at her chest. "I will not be talked to like a child! You are now my prisoner. Another word and I'll execute you on the spot. Turn and place your hands behind your back."

"Shoot me, you sniveling little coward. Prove to the universe how useless you are. Go on, I dare you."

His finger slipped into the trigger well, dancing over the cold metal trigger. She hadn't expected him to be so bold. The madness contorting his face deepened and she saw her life ending, not in the way she imagined.

A commotion in the antechamber drew their attention. Moscasco breathed a quiet sigh as Alpof pulled his finger clear and turned to meet the disturbance. The office doors slammed open and in stormed Captain Donab.

"Stand down now! All of you. Guards, return to your barracks and await my orders," he growled. Spittle flew from his mouth. When none of the Guards moved, he stalked to the nearest one, snatched him by the neck lip of his armor and pulled his visored face closer. "I said now."

The Prekhautens saluted and scurried off to await the punishment that was sure to come.

Donab spun on the Inquisitor and fixed him with a menacing glare. "What is the meaning of this?"

Alpof, unable to control his emotions, shouted, "Do not interfere with Inquisition business, Prekhauten. This is my operation!"

Donab's expression hardened. Over a decade of service, including combat experience, left him with little ability to suffer fools, especially impertinent ones still wet behind the ears. He ignored the Inquisitor and asked, "Governess?"

"It appears I am being arrested on charges of sedition and heresy," she replied, her eyes fixed on Alpof's blaster. "What is a woman to do?"

"I warned you," Alpof snarled.

Donab moved fast. His fingers curled around the young Inquisitor's throat. "And I'm warning you. She is the ruler of a free world under Conclave jurisdiction. The Inquisition has no authority to conduct such operations without the consent of the clergy."

"We … are at … war," Alpof gasped.

"Drop your weapon or you'll learn what war really is." Tightening his grip, Donab projected his dominance until Alpof reluctantly opened his palm and let the weapon slip to the floor. With an angry shove, he released his grip and stood between the two.

"Governess, these are serious accusations. I would be remiss if I left this matter to chance. Would you be willing to accompany me to the Guard station so I can ask you some questions? While I have no doubts to your loyalty, there are some who clearly view you as a threat to stabilization in these unprecedented times."

She smoothed out the wrinkles on her checkered patterned blouse before responding. "Captain, this is acceptable. I'm sure we can get to the bottom of this issue and be back to our business in no time."

"Thank you," Donab said.

"She is my prisoner, Guard." Alpof sneered. "Vau Prime shall hear of this. You won't go unpunished for your insolence."

"You tax my patience, Alpof. The Inquisition does not have authority over the Guard. You know this. Run back to your masters if you must. I'm sure the Inquisitor General will be delighted to hear of your failure."

"This isn't over."

"No. I don't suspect it is." Donab paused, expression thoughtful. "I am taking the Governess down for questioning. If she is innocent, she will be set loose at once. If she is guilty, she will be remanded to local law enforcement to await trial. We must stand by the rule of law. Else we are no better than the insurgents threatening our society. Step aside."

Left with no choice, Alpof obeyed, watching as Donab and Moscasco strode calmly into the antechamber, past a lone woman sitting behind her desk across the hall. They spoke in hushed tones causing several men and women to poke their heads into the corridor, only to hurry back into their offices upon spying him leering from the doorway.

A pall settled over Dalafar's ruling body. Alpof required revenge.

The door closed behind the Captain and the Governess and a woman shut down her computer before proceeding for a side exit.

"What was that all about?" Donab asked once they were alone. "I told you he was dangerous."

"He's grasping at straws, Donab," Moscasco replied. "Alpof claims he has proof of my treason against Vau Prime."

Donab stopped her with a gentle grab of her forearm. "Does he?"

"Proof? No."

Feeling gut punched at the look in her eyes, he muttered, "Adris."

"I have made no overt moves against the Conclave, nor do I wish to plunge Dalafar into civil war. Everything I have done is for my people." She paused, picking his fingers from her one at a time. "Everything."

"The Inquisition has every authority over the Guard, and you know it." Donab shook his head. "I can keep you safe for the time being, but it won't be long before that snake reports back to his superiors. Then you will be in real danger, Adris."

"I'm sure it won't come to that, Donab." She rubbed his fingers on her forearm. "There are events in motion that I couldn't stop if I wanted to. All will be fine. Trust me."

"Why do I feel you're going to be the death of me?"

She winked. "It makes life worth living, don't you think?"

"What do you mean she's been apprehended? By whom?" Annalilly demanded.

The skin beneath her scalp tattoos rippled, darkening as familiar anger returned. One she hadn't felt since the Vaumagians attempted to murder her and Fies back before Kharsis. The others gathered around, listening to the exchange but unwilling to intervene and risk provoking her ire further.

Tempest held up her hands. "By one of yours. The Inquisition attempted to arrest her for treason, but Captain Donab arrived just in time."

"Donab?" Fies asked.

She nodded. "He's the garrison commander. A simple man but one of honor."

"Shit."

Annalilly rolled her eyes. "Let me guess."

Holding up a hand to hold her off, Fies winced. "He was my first platoon leader."

"Of course he was."

"It was bound to happen," Quint added. "We've been in the service so long I'm surprised we haven't run across others we know."

"It's a complication we don't need," Fies snapped.

"One we have to deal with so suck it up," Annalilly countered. She focused back on Tempest, asking, "Where is the Governess being held?"

"Captain Donab took her to the command center. It is well guarded, though perhaps not from a vengeful Inquisitor."

Annalilly folded her arms. "Lucky for us we happen to be Guards."

"In civilian clothes," Haggle chimed in. The dark look on his face left little to the imagination. "We're not cut for this assignment."

"You must help her. Governess Moscasco knows too much about the insurrection. Once the Inquisition begins torturing her you will all be in danger," Tempest urged. Her voice rose, shoulders trembling.

"Lady, we've been in danger since this war started," Annalilly muttered. "This ain't nothing new."

Fies stepped between them. "We're here to extract the Governess. Rest assured we'll do everything within our power to see her returned."

Lowering her eyes, Tempest quietly asked, "What if you can't?"

Annalilly stiffened. "We got a plan for that too."

Concealing his apprehensive look, Fies asked, "Tempest, do you know any small Guard storeroom or outpost? Enough with armor for a small team?"

"I can find out, though I don't see how that helps." Tempest disliked the rogue nature of these Guards, seeing them for malcontents and misfits unworthy of wearing the uniform. They fit the description of insurrectionists, with low moral compasses and a seedy nature befitting escaped criminals rather than the defenders of the weak and innocent. The idea of Moscasco being wrong arose. Dalafar prided itself on loyalty to the Conclave, giving the new Inquisition no reason to suspect treachery. She suddenly found herself struggling with keeping true to the Governess' plans.

"Relax, our enemies know we are here but not why," Fies explained. "We just need a few official uniforms to sneak into Guard headquarters."

Annalilly jabbed a finger at him. "You're not going anywhere. Or did you forget Donab? You get made and we're doomed."

"Not necessarily. No one knows we're on the other side," Fies countered. "As far as they know we're on a layover before joining our unit forward on another campaign."

"I don't like it."

"You don't have to," he said. "Me, Quint, and Hollis are going in. I want you and Beve on overwatch. Haggle, you take Desril and Palco and establish the fallback. Jolent, you know what to do. The rest of you condense and get the ship prepared for launch. We leave as soon as we return with Moscasco. Questions?"

There were none.

Fies forced out the breath choking his lungs. Sweeping his gaze over each, Fies saw the lines of exhaustion, the scars, and haunted looks too many of them bore. They were one step away from quitting. Their actions went far beyond what the Guard was expected to do, and they knew it. Yet for all the raw emotions on display, he knew they bore quiet resolve to see this mission through. They wanted to end the war and restore order to a universe gone mad—it was, in his opinion, a humble dream.

"Keep your heads on a swivel for the duration of this one," he told them and turned to Tempest. "Ready?"

She jerked back a step, eyes widening. "Me? What do you expect me to do?"

"You're going to get us into the Guard house," he said with a smile, watching her face pale.

Great Library, planet Wexanos.

"I have doubts, Fistel."

The admission stunned the Chief Librarian. After a lifetime of service, decades championing Tannus' private guard and collecting as much knowledge as possible in the planetary archives for the eventuality of the Conclave's collapse, Fistel failed to recall ever hearing his lord speak so. Dire implications aside, he struggled finding words of encouragement to belay the building tension. "My lord, you have been a beacon of righteousness for so long. All your thoughts and plans have led us to this point."

Tannus smiled softly. “Just because I am immortal doesn’t mean I’m infallible.”

“Self-doubt is ever the curse of greatness.” His head bobbed within the pale-yellow hood all librarians were to wear when not in their quarters.

“One might accuse you of placating me, Fistel.” Much thought and energy went into selecting each Chief Librarian. Tannus, ever meticulous, mastered the process through the years. Each chosen was expected to run not only the library but the planet when situations dictated. Fistel had yet to let Tannus down.

“You and I both know better than that,” the Chief Librarian replied.

Tannus appreciated the familiarity with which Fistel approached him. “What news have you then?”

Fistel cleared his throat and shifted his weight to the other leg. “The Grand Mistress awaits you.”

“Put it through to my study and see I am not interrupted.”

Fistel bowed and left.

Worry clouding his mind, Tannus slipped into his study and activated the holoscreen; Ruma Zzein’s image filled the center of the room.

“Lord Tannus, to what do I owe this conversation?”

Ever cordial. Ever diplomatic. She was a far cry from the bedraggled woman he rescued before the Fall. Strong and defiant against the darkness surrounding them, Ruma was the rock upon which waves crashed and broke. A fact making this conversation most unpleasant for him.

“Akin Brohl is awake.”

Her face remained impassive. No emotion. No betrayal of inner thought. “That … is impossible.”

“Under normal circumstances I might be inclined to take your word, but Sorrow does not lie. He clashed with the god hunter on Antil IV while rummaging through our brother’s castle. According to Sorrow, he barely escaped with his life.”

“The god hunters were all destroyed a thousand years ago.”

He failed to remind her it was a program that never should have been enacted in the first place. Magically altering mortals to superhuman levels and providing them with murderous intent almost saw his plans wiped out throughout the years. “Apparently not. This presents a wrinkle in how we proceed.”

"Akin Brohl was ever the staunchest believer," Ruma said. "He alone eliminated over a score of your kin before disappearing. All these years I'd thought him lost, fallen like all the others. Did Sorrow say how he survived?"

"Would he?" Tannus scowled. "Brothers we may be, but we have not been close since birth. All Sorrow said was the god hunter was coming for us."

She remained silent for a time, contemplating various futures. There was no denying the god hunter's usefulness should he set on the proper course. The chaos Akin Brohl provided brought a distinct advantage to the battlefield. One they sorely needed. "I wonder if setting him loose against Amongeratix might not be the best course of action. With the mission to scuttle *Behemoth* a failure there is little capable of stopping him from reaching Vau Prime."

"Should Amongeratix succeed he will turn that planet into another Occanum, but it will be humanity's death nell this time."

"We must seek every advantage if we are to prevent a reign of darkness."

"We tried that before." Tannus crossed his arms, anger flashing in his eyes. Rising, he began to pace. "Not only did it backfire, it resulted in the near full destruction of those we tried to save. I cannot risk losing everything to a fanatic remnant of days long past. Akin Brohl is a problem, Oracle. One I have no desire to personally address."

"Meaning it falls to me to solve old problems I helped create?"

"We do as we must," Tannus told her. "Still, there is some merit in your suggestion. Should the god hunter succeed in killing Amongeratix he will spare millions of lives and help bring this civil war the humans are determined to fight closer to the end. Can it be done?"

"Why do you care so much about the humans, Tannus? They are little more than irritants to your legacy," Ruma asked without expecting answers. It was the old game they played.

Though he had an answer, Tannus doubted it would satisfy the Grand Mistress of the Order of Blood Witches. For how could simplicity placate one with such lofty titles? His devotion to her, slavish at times, further deepened the rift between himself and his kind. One incapable of closing. "I think I shall keep that to myself. There are many secrets in this universe, Oracle. Allow me to retain but one."

He felt her stare. That eternal questioning look she cast upon all who entertained her. Ruma Zzein was many things, forthcoming and accepting not among them.

"You have earned that much," she admitted. "I shall attempt to bring Akin Brohl to heel, but he was ever the most zealous of them. You understand I can make no promise?"

"I expect none," he told her. "Thank you, Oracle."

She laughed, an unexpected sound akin to glass breaking. "After all you have done for me, thanks is not required. I owe my life to you, Tannus. That debt shall never be repaid."

Her image faded, leaving Tannus alone with his thoughts. How could he explain his change of heart? The breaking with his father and their tyrant-like ways? Even to one he'd known for millennia, one born with the power to alter the course of the future and help the universe discover true freedom unlike ever before? Would Ruma Zzein remain dedicated to the course if she knew the truth?

Insurrectionist Fleet, transit between Mannus Prime and Vau Prime.

Admiral Khe-Zhehan dedicated her life to preserving the integrity of the Conclave. She'd been a firm believer in the gods since childhood, devout in prayer and accepting the doctrine without question. The revelation provided by Tannus rattled her, casting her mind into turmoil even as the universe burned around her. She'd felt trapped between factions until the disaster at Hawker's Gate. The maniacal fanaticism evinced by those loyal to Alain Nye, not the rule of Conclave, rattled her convictions. She failed to understand how anyone could so willingly lead whole chunks of the population astray in pursuit of fleeting power.

Losing Admiral Fhi and the *Righteous Fury* left her in command of a ragged fleet desperate for answers. The survivors looked to her for guidance, casting her course for the duration of the war. Khe-Zhehan used her experience and genius for tactics to turn defeat into a string of hard-fought victories. The effects proved instantaneous. Ships defected the new Prekhauten command, flocking to her flag as tyrants tightened their grip on Vau Prime. Pressing her advantage, the newly minted admiral drove a wedge into the enemy fleets and expanded her campaign.

Then came the summons from a man she both trusted and respected. She and Falchi had come up through the ranks together, often competing for the same position until she was promoted to rear admiral. His call to join him on Mannus Prime in the wake of a major ground victory provided Khe-Zhehan the spark she needed to advance her agenda. She vowed to remove Alain Nye and the upstart Mobus Kale, a man she reviled. Wheels turned. She needed to make a statement, declaring open war on those who opposed the failing ideals of the Conclave. The gods remained dominant through much of the universe, and she was in no hurry to slash the curtain of lies. Not when entire civilizations had been built upon the idea.

Now, thru fate or divine intervention—she refused to abandon the concept of gods or the power of faith—Khe-Zhehan found her calling. The desperate cry of trapped souls on Vau Prime, the tattered remnants of the late Davith Strannan, called for aid. Who was she to ignore the needs of thousands who could be best used on different battlefronts? Convincing the others of the need to travel to the core system took little effort. She was the ranking naval officer. Hers was the only word they needed. Torgast and Falchi agreed on salvaging what remained of Strannan's army. Word of his death shook them hard as Nye had it broadcasted across the stars in a propaganda hit job.

Gathering her chief lieutenants, Captains Targus of the *Vice* and Vestiri of the *Lance*, Khe-Zhehan detailed her scheme to swoop into Vau Prime airspace undetected and rescue as many of their compatriots as possible. One hundred ships joined their armada, broken down into three attack groups. She trusted her captains implicitly, knowing they were each capable of handling whatever assignment given.

Standing on the bridge of her flagship, the remodeled *Revengence*, Khe-Zhehan ignored the grey hair, the deep lines cutting through her flesh, and the ache of age nestled in her bones. Today she was the harbinger of light to a world plunged in darkness.

Resplendent in her uniform, she stood with utter surety, her right hand and most trusted advisor at her side. She stared out the main screen at the massive fleet spread across twenty thousand kilometers. Perhaps not the best fleet the navy ever assembled but the ones who had the most to give and everything to lose.

Without looking at the weathered man beside her, Khe-Zhehan ordered, “Captain Affernee, engage engines.”

“Aye, ma’am.” He turned to speak, “Attention all ships, this is Captain Affernee, fire engines and prepare to launch.”

His deep voice rumbled over the echoes of a hundred cheers. The time had come to return the fury upon their traitor brothers.

SIXTEEN

3215 A.G. (After Gods), the low continent, planet Vau Prime.

The bottle shattered against the wall, breaking into a thousand pieces. What liquid remained trickled down in a growing dark stain. Curses were shouted at the top of his lungs, venting frustrations stretching back years. Tired, Gedrick Silk slumped to the floor, drooping his head between his knees, and wept. Not for himself, though the shapeshifter often wondered how he'd gotten himself in such dire straits, but for those brave men and women who placed blind faith in a man only to be led to their doom. He knew, even as the others refused to accept, no help was coming. There would be no grand finale to their plight. Mobus Kale and his sprawling military complex would come for them and when he arrived it would be with the force of a thousand storms. The end was nigh and there was nothing any of the could do to prevent it.

Frustrated, he knew it would take little effort to slip away in the quiet hours of the night. The army remnants had grown lax in their daily duties. Guards often deserted when their friends weren't looking or showed up for their watch drunk. Discipline crashed beside morale. Charging Colonel Apontee, once hero of the Prekhauten Guard, with treason compounded matters. A divide continued growing. Half wanted to stand and fight, half to cower in the shadows and pray Kale missed them. Both stood upon the precipice, already teetering over the edge and Gedrick remained powerless to help.

They'd attempted passing him off as Strannan. He matched the mannerisms and voice but failed to inspire the confidence required of a fighting force in the field. Not that Gedrick blamed them. They were tired, ready to forget their oaths and flee to whatever end fate decreed. The fighting spirit had extinguished. And still he could not bring himself to abandon them. For each weakness, Gedrick discovered a strength, buried under the weight of tomorrow. The army may be finished, but Strannan's legacy demanded justice—he stayed for that.

"Gedrick? Are you all right?"

Using his palms to wipe his eyes, Gedrick lifted his head. "Fine. Just venting some frustration. Go away, Jash."

Ignoring him, the young lieutenant stepped into the communications shed. He was in his early twenties, but the weight of experience turned him into an old man. With barely a year in service, Jash chose his side after watching Kale's officers execute a group of Guards in the aftermath of the raid on Tatarast Island. Each had been loyal to the uniform and the institution, yet Kale ordered them gunned down for negligence and gross incompetence. It was not the Guard Jash thought he'd joined.

Then he met Bryn. Mal was his opposite. Confident and aggressive, everything a Guard officer was meant to be. Thankfully for him, she wanted no part in Kale's war. Vowing to fight against the rising tyranny, Bryn convinced Jash to join her and, along with a score of other dissatisfied officer and noncoms, deserted. They found Strannan and set about proving their worth. Though Jash continued feeling left out, a misfit among an army of misfits, he knew this was his home.

Looking down on Gedrick, Jash spied the drunken glare. That haunted appearance of a man pushed beyond his limits. Glass fragments peppered the floor, and the backs of his sleeves were wet. "Gedrick, the others can't see you like this."

"I miss him, Jash Abernath," the shapeshifter said after stifling back another wave of tears. "He treated me like a son, and I failed him. Now I have failed all of you."

"You didn't fail anyone, Gedrick. Being asked to kill someone in cold blood is easy for those who aren't behind the trigger. The ones who don't have to look in their target's eyes and feel the clench of their stomach when realization dawns that this is his last breath."

"You have done this?"

"Well, no."

Gedrick broke out into laughter. "You are an idiot, Jash Abernath. But you make a good point. Killing is a vile deed. One my kind seldom partook in. We were a gentle species, in our own fashion. Then humans came and exploited us for our unique abilities. It wasn't long before we became our own oppressors, selling ourselves to the highest bidder. I couldn't do it. Couldn't become a monster of illusions and false personality. So, I came across Davith Strannan. He offered me a home. A place to return to no matter what life threw at me."

Jash bobbed his head and sat beside him. "He was a good man."

"The best of us," Gedrick agreed. "And I failed him. If only I had the courage to do as he asked, perhaps this would not be happening."

"There's no way to know that," Jash cautioned. "I've only killed a few people, and those from distance, but even then, I lacked the spirit for it."

"Killing Alain Nye was not my problem."

The rumble of thunder in the distant hills threatened an approaching storm. Jash blinked, wanting nothing more than to find a cot and sleep it away. "What was?"

Gedrick looked him in the eye and said, "I did not want to die."

A score of senior officers and noncoms filled the empty flight briefing room. Designed for pilots, there were cushioned chairs and enough technical equipment to facilitate a proper military briefing, had the generator not given out two nights earlier. Instead of cooling away from the sun, they sat in pools of their own sweat.

Bryn Mal cleared her throat before barking, "Attention!"

Men and women snapped to their feet. All talk died as their new commanding officer strode into the room and took his place at the briefing lectern. Colonel Freyote was respected and liked by many of his previous commands. Highly decorated and groomed for promotion to general, Freyote represented everything the Prekhauten Guard was meant to be. His uniform was impossibly stained, his boots worn. The sun baked his flesh a golden hue. When he stared at you, he conveyed both understanding and authority. He was, they all agreed, the person to replace Davith Strannan.

"Take your seats," he ordered. "I'll make this brief. We have received word of streams of refugees fleeing Krenz. Many are coming here under the mistaken belief the low continent is secure because it has already been razed by

Mobus Kale. They are mistaken. General Strannan may be gone but we remain the thorn in Kale's side. Once he finishes crushing our insurgent cells in Krenz he will undoubtedly turn his attention to us. The arrival of civilians complicates our warfighting ability. This cannot continue."

"Excuse me, sir, but how are we supposed to protect these civilians when we cannot police ourselves?" Major Onof asked. A known confederate of the disgraced Colonel Apontee, Onof provided an obstacle to a peaceful transition of power.

"Major, I suggest you remember your place. It is only by the good graces of your peers I did not try you alongside your boss." Freyote fixed him with a withering glare before continuing. "He has a valid argument, however. We are fractured. Ready to break into a million pieces that have no hope of ever being put back together. Kale's elite units will storm in here and annihilate us with little energy if this continues. How do we fix that?"

Silence. The uncomfortable rustling in chairs as all refused to look him in the eye. Freyote noted the mannerisms of each, quietly gauging who he could count on and who was an empty uniform. With limited options, he knew what he needed to do.

"Let me rephrase that. I am not looking to turn this command into a committee. My service record speaks for itself. I have never lost a campaign, nor left a battlefield to the enemy. This action shall be no different. If Mobus Kale wants us, he can come and get us, but he will pay dearly for every step of ground he takes. We have been beaten, thrown back in so many ways, yet here we stand. Defiant. Spitting in the eye of those who would call themselves our betters.

Murmurs filled the room.

"Today is the start of a new campaign. One not based on gain of ground or attrition. Today we begin the fight of our lives. Nothing will stop the refugees from arriving. You all know the situation in Krenz has grown dire. These men and women are not fighters, nor should they be expected to become so. Our charge is the same as it was upon the foundation of the Guard. We are defenders of the universe. Failure means the death of untold numbers of civilians, and I will not stand for that. Not while I draw breath."

Those who returned his gaze weren't the best in uniform, nor the brightest, but they were the legacy of Davith Strannan. "You were all chosen for this command because General Strannan saw in you the very fire he bore himself. We are going to make our stand here. We are going to hold off Kale and his army for as long as it takes to get the incoming civilians to safety. Am I clear?"

Heads nodded. One or two oaths of affirmation echoed back.

Freyote wasn't impressed and slammed a fist on the lectern. "Ladies and gentlemen, this is our most desperate hour. Cells left in Krenz are funneling their way to us as we speak. They present much needed reinforcements and supplies. This is not finished. We are the best at what we do, and righteousness is on our side. I want accurate headcounts and weapons and ammunition status updates to me by the end of the day. Am I clear?"

The shocked looks that had haunted them for so long reduced as each of the assembled met his gaze. Freyote found resolve among them. They knew there was little chance of surviving the approaching storm, yet his stern reminder of who they were, what they were, inspired them in different ways. "Dismissed," he said and offered a crisp salute before marching away to the growing murmurs at his back.

Freyote found Gedrick Silk waiting in his makeshift office. The shapeshifter made himself comfortable in the chair behind the desk. Unused to working with Gedrick, Freyote frowned upon seeing the red veined eyes and grime-stained face staring up at him.

"Gedrick Silk. General Strannan spoke highly of you," Freyote greeted. "I'm afraid I'm not seeing what he did. You smell of urine and worse. You haven't bathed in far too long and the stench of alcohol is almost nauseating."

Wiping his mouth with his index finger and thumb, Gedrick said, "My apologies, but these are trying times."

"That doesn't give us the leeway to fall by the wayside. Not when so many continue looking to us to lead them."

"I'm not a leader. This was never my war. I owed a debt to Davith. Nothing more. With him gone there is no place for me among your army."

Freyote slid down into the smaller chair by the door and sighed. He flexed his right hand, eager to reduce the arthritis flareup in it. "That's where you're wrong. Plenty of these boys and girls in uniform look up to you, though you may not notice it. You represent the embodiment of all Strannan sought to accomplish. So long as you remain among us you provide inspiration. Not even I'm foolish enough to ignore that."

"I'm not the man you believe me to be," Gedrick insisted.

The last rays of sunlight thrust into the office, cascading across them. "None of us are, but that changes nothing. We are in this until the bitter end, win or lose. Stay with us. Help me rebuild morale and I will be in your debt. If we manage to live through this, you can go where your heart desires. No questions asked."

Gedrick often wondered what made men follow others. What inherent quality did they possess marking them apart from the masses? He never believed Strannan better than the rest, despite the admiration of his subordinates. What then? He didn't know, but there was comfort in Freyote's words. "I will stay, though I doubt you will be able to make good on your promise. We are all likely to die down here."

"That is possible," Freyote agreed. "Thank you."

Rising, Gedrick walked over and offered his hand. They shook, a silent agreement between men locked in a war neither wanted, and couldn't escape.

Gedrick stopped in the doorway and asked, "You didn't mention the approaching rescue fleet. Why not?"

"I didn't want to give them false hope."

Prekhauten Guard Staging Grounds, Tatarast Island.

Mobus Kale stood upon the balcony surveying the new Guards in pristine formations below. They were fully armored with state-of-the-art body armor and provided the latest assault rifles. Faces concealed behind their helmets, they represented the next line of defense in his personal war. He caught the stench of mechanics as a fleet of assault ships hovered over the parade field. Howitzers and tanks specially fitted to operate in urban environments sat in perfect lines behind the infantry. They were the First Special Division, and they were his. The sky turned crimson as the sun dipped below the horizon. It looked like blood—the promise of the future.

The lust for power inspired Mobus' thirst for violence. He should have been drummed out of the service long ago, or never admitted in the first place. Yet he made a career of slipping through the cracks. One tough assignment after the next propelled him through the ranks until he achieved his only goal; the total leadership of the Prekhauten Guard, replete with the ability to reshape it in his image, designed to operate on his principles. Soon they would become a scourge to the universe and the First Special Division would lead the way.

Snapping to attention, Mobus presented his finest parade salute. Roars went up from ten thousand throats. Every man and woman in the ranks loyal only to him. Company commanders and platoon sergeants barked orders and the division ground into action. Battalions headed off to their initial assignments. The army lurched into motion. Trained well by the best drill instructors on Vau Prime, the First Special Division readied for its first test: The systematic elimination of all insurgent cells and the final securing of Krenz.

Soon all Krenz would know the cost of harboring fugitives.

Soon the city would burn.

Krenz Underground.

Panic gripped the makeshift headquarters. Men and women snatched what they could, precious items each thought they needed to survive the coming purge. Edam Boone took in the scene with distress. His network operated on thieves' honor. A sticking point of pride between the law-abiding element and the criminal underground. Watching them abandon the principles that had seen them through so much over the past few years wounded him. Not that he blamed any. The promise of a violent demise softened the strongest man. Most of his people were gone, leaving the warehouse a haunted skeleton of better times. Those special few, his core supporters, remained, helping where they could, judging when appropriate. It was a sad demise of a once promising network of the best of the worst Krenz had to offer.

"Where did it all go wrong?" he mused.

"Blame me if you like," Aliz said.

She and Julian walked up to him. The looks on their faces told him all he needed to know. "I don't profess to understand much of Zoraq Darc's concepts, and never considered myself a leader, but he proved a good judge of character. You did not cause this, Aliz. I fear the foundations were laid long ago by men with hate in their hearts."

"Edam, you have been a breath of fresh air in dark times," she said softly.

"Not quite how we planned it, eh Captain?" He gestured to the group of criminals rushing off to find whatever fates waited.

Julian felt defeated. All their plans dashed by the unexpected deployment of an entire division. He and Edam got several thousand civilians and more than a few rogue Guards and insurgent cells out before the curtain fell, but not enough. "We should have done more."

"Yes, but to what end? More lives would be lost and our enemy that much stronger," Edam countered. "There's no point in wasting your life, Julian. Not for this."

"What now?" Aliz asked.

"This little operation may be coming to a close but there are other endeavors out there for me. I have the benefit of blending in no matter where I go, unlike the good captain here. I am an everyman, whereas he will always be a soldier, no matter how long he's been out of uniform. Do not worry about me, Aliz. I have a feeling all will turn out just fine for me and my cohort."

She caught the twinkle in his eye. "You already have a plan."

"Of course I do! What sort of criminal mastermind would I be otherwise?" He winked. "Take heart, Aliz, all is not lost. We gave those bastards a good run, didn't we?"

"A bloody nose, no more."

"Better than nothing." He smiled then. "There are many forces at work in the universe. I don't believe Alain Nye and his marauders are the only ones. This may feel like the end, but the war has far to go. Seven hundred worlds are far too many to conquer. The universe will rise up when they learn of the slaughter sown here. Opportunities will abound for us all."

"You plan on continuing your criminal enterprises?" Julian asked.

Edam sighed. "In some cases. You've shown me there is more to life, Julian. I have found my heart these last few months. Helping people escape Kale's wrath feels right. Wherever I wind up I have a feeling my unique services will be most welcome."

"You are a good man, Edam Boone," Aliz said, patting his arm. "I am proud to have known you."

"This isn't over yet," he replied. "We still have a few tricks to play before the noose tightens. Captain, are your people prepared for one final fight?"

Julian rubbed his jaw. His ion rifle swinging under his shoulder. "I figure we've already bloodied their nose, might as well knock out a few teeth."

"I knew I liked you!"

Julian flashed an embarrassed look to Aliz and said, "Great minds and all."

"What have you two concocted without me?"

It was Edam's turn to pat her arm. "The less you know the better, Aliz. Suffice it to say we are about to bring a world of hurt down on our new enemies."

Third platoon, seventh company, First Special Division, spread out as they'd been trained. Relying on proven tactics, they established interlacing fields of fire, spread three meters apart and lined the sides of the buildings to avoid enemy fire. They did everything right from the moment the transports stopped, and the heavily armed infantry debarked. Each was filled with righteous vigor, comforted by the knowledge of doing what was best for humanity. Inculcated lies promising to rid the cancer threatening the rule of Conclave imbued them as they deployed to their first combat zone. In theory, this should have been enough.

Private Zims felt his hands moisten and was thankful for his gloves. Dropping his rifle on his first op wouldn't do much to impress his sergeant and would serve to make him the ridicule of the platoon. He'd joined the Guard out of necessity. From one of the poorer farming communities, Zims believed the Inquisition as it excoriated the insurgents, blaming them for destruction of property and the wanton death spreading. He believed in order and eagerly escaped his life to do his part. The Conclave meant everything to him. Who was he to deny them in their time of need? Kissing his mother goodbye and giving his father a firm handshake, Zims headed off for basic training.

His heart hammered. Nerves played havoc. No amount of training prepared one for that first thrill of an ion round whizzing by. The anticipation killed him. Zims grew up around guns, often going hunting in the predawn hours with his father. He made himself think of this as a hunting trip. Nothing special. Nothing out of the ordinary. His instructors told him to dehumanize the enemy in his mind, reducing his capacity for empathy—it didn't work now.

Zims felt the cold press of the building at his back and tried not to look up, focusing on his mission and assigned sector of fire as his squad shuffled down the street. Hundreds of windows leered down on them. He felt small and knew an insurgent could be waiting behind anywhere. Ghostly torments of hundreds of rifles unleashing upon him while he was exposed threatened to freeze him where he stood.

"I got movement to the right. Seventh floor."

The distorted voice crackled through his helmet speakers. Zims' breath caught in his throat. This was it. His baptism by fire. Gripping his rifle tighter, he glanced up. Every window was dark, their reflective properties casting shadows like missing teeth. He questioned if whoever spoke misread the situation. He failed to see how anyone could accurately notice the tiniest flicker of movement when faced with so much.

Zims forced out a sigh of relief—

The explosion tore half of his body away. He'd been standing a foot off to the side, never noticing the concealed device dug into the walkway. His last sight was a string of detonations up and down the street.

War had come for the First Special Division in glorious brutality.

Julian stared up at the rising clouds of black smoke, choosing to ignore the screams of wounded soldiers a street over. The ground trembled from shockwaves still rippling through the district. Unlike civilian emergencies, the Guard handled mass casualties without the attention of sirens or unnecessary vehicles and personnel. Until the area was cleared of further traps those caught in the blast range needed to care for themselves. Julian silently hoped enough line medics were taken out by the blasts to reduce the survivability rate among the wounded. He traded part of his soul for it and, at least for the moment, could live with that. The rustle of uniforms and equipment behind stole his attention away from the carnage.

He counted down, the others clustered around him anxious in wait. A squad of his best, survivors of numerous ambushes and certain death situations, waited to enact the second phase of his operation. One the enemy would never forget.

The chrono in Julian's helmet beeped as it hit zero. "Initiate phase two. Time now."

A trio of armored aircars raced by. Confiscated civilian vehicles, Julian borrowed some of Edam's finest welders and mechanics to transform them into combat vehicles. Julian saluted the heavy gunners standing in the rear cargo compartment, their double barrel heavy machineguns charged. He admired the handiwork of the installed swivel mounts giving the gunners 360-degree access, but it was the bank of six menacing black tubes jutting up from behind the gunners keeping his attention.

Soon enough, the enemy would share that interest.

Alain Nye slammed a fist into the desk. The datapad at his fingertips sparked through the cracks on the screen. Sycophants and acolytes thronged in a half circle by the main doors. None looked up. Only Mobus Kale met his vitrified glare. The general loomed over the desk with bloodstains on his uniform.

"How?" was all Alain managed.

Grinding his teeth, Mobus replied, "The insurgents used improvised explosive devices to create initial casualties, relying on Guard doctrine to draw in additional forces before launching a barrage of point detonating mortars and heavy ion guns."

Alain failed to imagine the chaotic scene. No matter how many reports he read or debriefings he attended, he found no substitute for the smoke of battle, the screams and cries of the wounded, and the daze etched upon each survivor.

"Casualties?"

Mobus stiffened. "Thirty-seven dead, one hundred fourteen wounded. At least thirty of which are not expected to survive the night."

"How is this possible? You assured me we were on the verge of winning."

Poison dripped from each word, powerful enough to force the beleaguered general back a step. Redoubling his demeanor, Mobus answered, "They used weapons confiscated during the raid on the Island. My troops were still green, unblooded. They had no way of being prepared for such underhanded tactics."

The first inklings of panic set in. Decades of scheming, eliminating obstacles and competition, worming his way through the corridors of power to achieve the ultimate rank stood in peril. Alain Nye dedicated his life to this singular purpose with the goal of becoming the reigning dominant power in the universe. He felt those dreams crumbling, slipping away as dust between his fingers. Ruin. All blasted to utter ruin for underestimating the fervor of his enemies. Mobus Kale's continued incompetence in dealing with the insurgency rattled him to no end. With the added weight of Amongeratix approaching to reclaim his rightful throne, at least in the false godling's eyes, Nye's empire promised a brutally swift demise.

Recognizing the perils of his chosen path, Alain wondered how he'd fallen prey to the manipulations of Amongeratix. The Three were never meant to rule, leastwise not the human empire. They were relics, useful tools propagating the Conclave, but nothing more. Striking a deal with Amongeratix became the equivalent of selling his soul when he'd been blinded by the desire of power. The Inquisitor General used every advantage to press his agenda, laying waste to storied traditions and institutions to reshape the universe in his image. He questioned now if Amongeratix had further use for him when the dust of this war settled.

"Your new army falls well short of promised expectations, Mobus. This is most unsettling. Perhaps I was wrong in selecting you for command."

"Give me free reign to shut down this city and the insurrection dies," Mobus all but shouted. "I mean complete control. The low continent can wait until Krenz is properly secured."

"We've had this discussion before. I am not willing to let you raze Krenz because of your vainglorious pursuit. A measured approach is needed, especially with this rumored fleet bearing down on us," Alain snapped. "Keep up the pressure. Drive them from the city but never forget this is the seat of the universe. I will not have this city, nor its population caught in the crossfire. Keep your collateral damage to minimums or it will be your neck swinging from the noose. Am I clear, General Kale?"

Hatred flared, bright and threatening in the general's eyes. "Perfectly."

Waving his hand, Nye ordered, "Everyone out."

Mobus Kale led the way, storming off like a caged animal waiting to escape. The others bowed and shuffled behind, a trailing remnant of human dignity. Low level dignitaries and junior clergy twisted in Nye's image followed. He watched until the last woman was lost from sight. Thoughts swirling, he summoned his aide and ordered the next meeting. Nye found too much of his day spent in a pointless string of meetings resulting in limited advances. Glancing at the cracked datapad, he rolled his eyes. Three planetary governors from backwater worlds he'd never heard of were scheduled to discuss opening new trade routes with Inquisitor support.

The doors hissed open but instead of government officials Nye felt his stomach clench as he laid eyes on a hooded woman in crimson robes floating into his office. At her back strode the largest mortal man he'd ever seen. Feral looking, the only item missing was a cloak of pelts. Nye shrank against the wall, spying the swish of crimson robes in the hall, recognizing them for the abominations they were.

"Inquisitor General, my name is Sister Evangeline. I come on behalf of the Crimson Mistress and Lord Amongeratix," she began.

He squinted, eager to pierce the veil of shadow beneath her cowl but the sorcery surrounding the woman proved too powerful. Each time he thought he glimpsed her flesh his eyes were drawn to another place. Witchcraft. Their arrival on Vau Prime shouldn't have gone unnoticed yet here they stood, predators come to see his compliance.

"I was not made aware of your dispatch," Nye managed after clearing his throat. "Why has Lord Amongeratix not contacted me directly?"

Drifting close enough the hairs on his arms stood on end, Evangeline said, "He is pressing other concerns enroute to this planet. I'm sure you understand, his vision is vast, patience endless. We were deployed to prepare this city for his arrival. I trust this will not be an issue?"

Nye regained a measure of composure. "Of course not, though I would inform him the planet is secure and all is in readiness for his great coming. Perhaps I should contact him directly and explain."

"He does not have time to deal with this matter," she replied, and edge hardening her voice. "The degeneration of the Conclave and subsequent authorities is well known to us. While you pedal your brand of truth and justice here, the rest of the universe erupts in civil war. The only reason Amongeratix has not reprimanded you yet is because his attention is focused elsewhere."

"We've come to fix your shortcomings," Geres Auk snarled over her shoulder.

Nye stiffened. "Who is this … beast?"

Geres lurched forward, reaching for the power axe strapped across his back. "The one who'll take your head."

Evangeline held out her arm, staying the giant. "Easy, Geres. This is not the moment." She looked back at Nye. "Inquisitor General, this is Geres Auk. He is an associate of sorts and has been involved in this war since the foundations on planet Crimeat. He and I both act in the name of those above us." She came closer still, allowing him to see her yellow stained eyes for the first time. "Meaning you are at our disposal until Lord Amongeratix arrives."

"This is my planet. I make the rules here. Amongeratix was invited on my behalf, not to supplant me upon his arrival. Deals were made. Oaths sworn." Nye leaned forward, knowing any display of fear meant his inevitable defeat.

"Ones I'm certain will be kept, in due course," she soothed. Darkness returned to conceal her face. "This meeting was mere courtesy, Inquisitor General. Nothing more. My colleagues will find adequate quarters within your command complex and guide the Inquisition through the final stages of preparedness for His coming."

"I could have you arrested before you left this office."

"What a waste of good soldiers that would be," she replied. "I think we have gotten off on the wrong foot. Understandable, all things considered. We interrupt your busy schedule with unexpected announcements. Ones meant to inspire renewed vigor amongst you and your confederates. It is no wonder our messages are crossed." She hummed.

"You, who have nestled deep within the confines of your minor empire with delusions of grandeur, incapable of seeing the truth sweeping across the stars, are out of touch with reality. Beyond the paltry gravity well of your precious Vau Prime my lord has been waging constant war against his brothers and those who remain defiant. Thousands die daily while you pretend to be in control. The

Conclave has lost authority. Your Inquisition no longer holds the fear it once had and the Prekhauten Guard is a mockery of revolutionized militant factions fighting one another. But please, enlighten us as to how you intend on presenting Amongeratix the keys to his new empire."

Alain Nye, plotter of a thousand schemes, had become a despot ruler so eager to come into his own he'd abandoned all he sought to preserve. He was little more than a mockery of once proud aspirations.

"I thought as much." Evangeline's voice dripped smugness at his failure to reply. "I expect a private detail assigned within the hour. I am to have unrestricted access to all relevant command centers and intelligence briefings starting today. You have an insurgent problem, I understand." At his wince, she continued. "Very well, Geres Auk and the remaining Sisters will be dispatched to the front lines in support of what combat units you have in place. They will root out your insurgents like vermin and ensure this city is secure well before Amongeratix arrives."

"When is he expected to make planetfall?"

Evangeline fixed him with a baleful glare. "Within the week. Matters are coming to a head, Inquisitor General. The human war shall end, and all focus will go to the eternal war against his most hated brothers. A new day dawns. One your kind shall never forget."

SEVENTEEN

3215 A.G. (After Gods), Erdef City, planet Romalle.

Lady Emmest DeMauve was many things, patient not among them. Dressed in loose leather pants and a forest green blouse, she stood before her captive, doing her best to ignore the sight of blood trickling down his ankle to the accumulating pool at his feet. He was the third man she'd apprehended, all professed minions of her least favorite board member.

Emmest understood the urge to remove rivals when making a bid for control but had a difficult time discovering why she was on his radar. She'd built a world around presenting an aloof, grieving widow incapable of mischief. Damal certainly hadn't penetrated the charade. The man's focus centered on his future, not the insignificant rantings of what amounted to little more than a ghost among society.

So why her? Why now?

Her victim's soft whimpers drew her attention. Pursing her lips, she crouched before him, ensuring he looked into her eyes. His face was streaked with grime, sweat, and blood. One eye was swollen shut. The other open wide in horror.

"I can make this all go away, you know. All I need is a name. Give me what I seek, and I shall forget I ever saw you. Don't you want to see your family again?" She traced a manicured nail up the top of his thigh. "I'd give anything to see my husband again. He's been gone so long. My heart aches in the lonely night … Give me a name. End this pointless suffering. I beg of you."

Blood frothed on his lips. He gave a curdled sound, incoherent. She knew she had him. The others never broke, choosing to die on their vows. Their bodies were tragically placed around the city where Damal couldn't help but notice. Any enjoyment she took in breaking them fled with the lack of information she desired.

Emmest stared into that eye, searching, questing with silent enthusiasm. Her reward was a subtle nod. Cracking a thin smile, she patted his thigh and rose. "There, see, I knew you could be reasonable." She plucked a knife from the table beside them. It was already littered with bloodstained implements. Cutting the gag, she jerked the cloth down.

He stretched his jaw, running the tip of his tongue over the space where two teeth once sat. Fear filling his eye, he stared at her. The first inkling of resurging anger echoed deep within the iris, enough for Emmest to question if she needed to find another victim. Again.

"The name," she demanded a second later. The blade danced an inch from his face.

"Lostan Fidiuos."

She flinched. The information broker ... What qualm did he have toward her? They were reduced acquaintances at best, having crossed paths but a few times. Lostan preferred operating in the shadows where he bent information to his purposes. She'd never wronged him, nor gone looking for the man. It was an unspoken arrangement. Her fingers curled tightly around the hilt. Emmest had been thrown to the wolves.

She traced a mental path back to the assassination of Cardinal Breed. Never a believer of coincidence, Emmest saw the pattern. Influential figures were being removed. Ones capable of altering Romalle's future. But by whom? Damal was self-centered and ambition but far from what she'd call brave. The others were little better. She feared more developments across the stars held sway over the internal politics of the City Board. A game was afoot, and she'd been thrust onto the board as a player.

Mind clouded, Emmest stepped away.

"Wait," the man croaked. "You said I'd see my family again."

She spun in midstride and, marching up to him, swept the blade across his throat. An arc of blood splashed against the smeared wall. He gargled, gasping for breath.

Emmest frowned in disgust and wiped the blade on his shirt. "And so you shall. Give them my regards."

Trapped. The one room had one viable exit point and that was closely guarded. A bank of windows on the far wall were not only too small for either of them to fit through, but they would have to get through too many of their captors. Escape seemed impossible, forcing them to bide their time and hope their captors made a mistake.

Riles found it distressing and confusing. She knew she and Nemineon ought to be behind bars in a cell, or dead. The entire law enforcement department seemed to have crowded the streets in their biased manhunt. Certain death hounded her steps for days, straining her mind and draining her energy. Tired and pushed to the brink, she'd been on the cusp of escaping back to the tribes where succor warred with atonement only to run into the collection of people who didn't belong together.

She studied them, searching for cracks in their solidarity. The man and woman, clearly partners, were intimidating but not her immediate concern. The boy, barely older than her, knew he wasn't meant to be here. Who he was intrigued her and, despite her staunchest efforts, Riles found him mildly attractive. Cursing her lack of focus, she centered her gaze on the floating woman. Of them all, this was the one she feared. Raw power radiated from her, churning Riles' stomach. One wrong move and Riles had no doubt this woman would make her pay for it. Best to sit still and see why they'd rescued her from the police and secluded her deep inside the city center.

The others in the group she recognized. Chief Investigator Hargan provided a ragged appearance similar to having spent the last few days on a drinking binge. She'd seen the type before. Easy marks but with sharp edges if you moved too slow. The Inquisitor was the definition of authority. Strong, bold, he paced like a caged beast. Riles wanted nothing to do with the Inquisition, or the woman in the gossamer robes.

"We must do something," Nemineon whispered.

Riles give him a disappointed look. She knew that, yet she also knew neither had been bound. They sat freely in chairs and had been provided water and a meal of steamed meats and fruit. She'd seen enough friends and neighbors locked up without one receiving similar treatment. They wanted something from her and weren't sure how to get it, potentially making it an advantage.

"Be quiet."

"The boy is correct yet acting on the brashness of youth will see you both incinerated where you sit."

"What are you?" Energy cackled off the woman's robes, sending miniscule jolts throughout the room.

"My name is Sister Alessandra, a disciple of the Order of Blood Witches."

"A witch!" Nemineon moaned.

Riles jabbed an elbow to his ribs. "I thought you were myths used to frighten children."

Alessandra drifted close enough that sparks lit upon Riles' clothing. Leaning down until the fringe of her hood touched the young girl, she asked, "Do I frighten you?"

Tears welled in her eyes before Alessandra drifted away. Point proved.

"Thank you, Sister Alessandra," the slender man with tired eyes said. "What do you know of the Cardinal's assassination? Why is everyone looking for you?"

Riles shifted, uncomfortable with the direct questioning, while patting out the smoldering bits of her clothing. "Why don't you ask what you're really thinking?"

"Did you kill him?"

No build up. No intensity. Only the pale shade of failing compassion so many passed upon her through the years. Built upon a life of hardship, Riles learned to read people early on. The man confronting her now reflected a hollowness she hadn't felt. One burrowing into the forgotten places of her soul, threatening to overwhelm her if she let him.

"No."

Tolde said. "We need to discover the reasons behind his assassination. It may prove the difference in your world going to war or not."

Hargan scratched the stubble on his cheek. "Riles, this is the Cardinal's brother, Tolde. He's not here to condemn you. He just needs answers."

Needs and wants, the distinction did not go unnoticed. Riles liked to think herself astute, yet the cloud of intrigue smothering the group of offworlders left her senses reeling. "He looks nothing like the Cardinal."

Her response produced a flinch. The subtle withholding of breath and terse looks shared.

Leaning close to Gando, Hargan said, "I didn't know we were heading for war. What aren't you telling me?"

"The City Board is voting on whether to remain neutral or join Vau Prime," he said after the wall of questing stares from the others grew too much. "Should they side with the Inquisitor General armies of Prekhauten Guards will deploy to Romalle and use it as a staging base for this sector.

An entire generation stand to be drafted to put down the insurrection."

"That bad, huh?" Hargan joked.

"Worse," Tolde said. "The war continues spreading. Entire planets have been rendered lifeless. The Inquisition has become twisted and polluted. Innocents are rounded up and burned. As if that wasn't enough, the cult of Rengu grows. We are beset on all sides. Despite this, our allies flock to hidden bases scattered across the stars. People are fighting back. The tide turns but it isn't enough. Every defeat suffered, each planet lost, provides the enemies of humanity with more fuel to cast upon their fires."

"Why Romalle?" Riles let curiosity get the better of her to speak. "We have no military. No great wealth of resources."

"Strategic value. Your planet sits upon the edge of a major shipping lane," Alessandra replied. "The Inquisitor General needs Romalle to facilitate the quicker transition of planets to his cause. The world you know stands upon the precipice of total transformation into an industrial and military machine. Your fields will be plowed under. Your cities turned into camps. Change will be instantaneous as your leaders bend their knee and feed the Inquisitor General's hunger. It has happened before."

The color drained from Riles' face. She tried and failed to imagine her world as a tortured landscape of machines and factories. Friends, families, even the strength of the tribes swept under the tidal wave of destruction painted so vividly by the offworlders. "I feel sick."

"The Inquisition does not care," Alessandra asserted. "We must discover who murdered Tolde's brother to prevent your world from falling."

"I wish I could help, but I've already told you everything I know," she protested. "The man who tried to snatch me wore a uniform."

"Doesn't mean he was one of mine," Hargan grumbled.

Tolde lifted his eyes. "We also cannot dismiss the possibility. Not until each of your people are properly vetted."

Puffing out his chest, Hargan blustered, "Do you know what you're asking? You want me to abandon the trust I've spent years cultivating between my department and the population. I'll risk losing every gain."

"While standing to increase your approval from the masses," Gando countered. "Think of it, Hargan. Finding the true killer, unproven plot aside, will not only reestablish your authority but take this planet further away from the war."

"Meaning I'd be a hero."

"I wouldn't expect a statue."

Hargan snorted and ambled off.

"Riles, I need your help," Tolde urged, softening his voice. "Help me solve my brother's murder."

She nodded, clipped and stunted. "I'll do what I can, but you should know there is no promise worth making."

"I don't need other than your word," he replied.

"What about me?" Nemineon asked. His voice rose to a shrill.

Gando stepped forward. "You get to stay here with us. Wouldn't want you going off and getting yourself killed, would we?"

"Here, I thought you might like some."

Riles looked up in surprise as Ragan handed her a steaming cup of caf. She found him attractive, alluring in an alien way. His youthful innocence could easily be misconstrued as ignorance, though she found the simple act comforting. Too many in this city snubbed their noses, turned their heads when she passed. The insult forced her hand, shoving her down roads she'd never considered with little other opportunity. The great lie of the universe was the future was open for all.

Smiling, Riles accepted the mug. The aroma struck a moment later and she rolled her eyes in delight. No one could say the Inquisition provided anything but the finest for their field agents. Bubbles formed against the back of the mug as she blew before taking that first sip. "Thank you," she groaned.

"You're welcome. I figured you've been through enough today and I'd want someone to do the same for me."

Riles resisted the temptation to shoo him away so she could enjoy the drink in silence. Acts of kindness should never be repaid unjustly, her mother used to say. "Most people around here don't think so."

He sank into the battered leather chair across from her, absorbing the way her dirty hair framed the soft angles of her face. "I guess it's like that all over. Folks on my planet did the same. I spent more time being chased by the prefects than enjoying my childhood." He smirked. "By all rights I should be in a jail cell."

"You don't act like you do."

He hummed. "I wasn't so different from you. Outcast. Unwanted. I ran the streets for a time before being sent on a mission that changed everything. I still can't believe I've survived everything we've been through."

Riles found herself wanting to know more. This strange and enigmatic young man presented her with the one factor she'd longed for, hope. If he escaped his lot in life, then so could she. "Is that how you wound up with them?"

"More or less," he replied, his gaze settling on Tolde. "Tolde took me in, made me feel like I belonged. Once we'd completed our quest, I was presented the opportunity to leave my problems behind and discover a better life. How could I say no? The days have been filled with unimaginable danger and horror, but I've seen so many wonders I would never have gotten the chance to if I'd said no."

"You guard your words, Ragan." She wanted to know more. To discover what impossible quest he might have been assigned and the circumstances leading to his escape from the dregs of society. To learn more about him, admitting to herself she was charmed.

Suddenly ashamed, she cast a sidelong look to the dozing Nemineon. He'd been there through the good times and the bad, never once shying away from watching her back. Yet for all the familiarity he offered she'd never felt the tug on her heart. Riles once determined she and Nemineon were destined for one another, fate forcing them closer into an unnecessary relationship. Then in stepped Ragan and her meticulous world shattered.

His cheeks tinged pink through the scruff already growing. "Sorry. Force of habit. If you knew a part of what we've done you wouldn't want to talk to me."

"I think I would."

At his smile, Riles busied herself with the rest of her caf. Lowering her eyes, she did her best to ignore him. It had been a long time since she last felt like a woman and, despite her crumbling resistance, she discovered a quiet truth in his eyes.

"Rag—"

A commotion broke out across the room, stilling her words. She watched as Hargan and the Inquisitors marched up to her.

Determination twisted their faces. Riles snapped her mouth shut, thankful for the interruption. Words, once spoken, could never be taken back.

"Riles, if I brought you data files with images of every officer under my command would you be able to pick the man you saw?" Hargan asked. A hint of desperation lingered in his gaze. One suggesting he was out of answers.

Riles felt a surge of adrenalin. Could she? She'd replayed the event a thousand times during those quiet moments sleep refused to come. Each time she got closer to seeing his face, but the image remained blurred. "I think so."

While she didn't know if she could, she questioned if she wanted to. Inviting the killer back into her life after spending weeks attempting to flee amounted to little more than raw madness. She'd be exposed, vulnerable like never before and, despite the strength in her protectors, be forced to look over her shoulder for the rest of her life. However short that might be.

Hargan puffed a sigh of relief. "Good. Stay here. I'll be back later this evening."

He made it to the door before stopping and asking her, "How's the caf?"

Riles blushed and avoided Ragan's searching gaze.

Night had fallen by the time Hargan returned to his office. Normal duties conflicted with his personal quest. After a quick stop at the Boards' chambers, then a meeting with a pair of local factors to help settle a boundary dispute, Hargan removed his cap and stumbled into his building. Most of his officers were gone for the night. The others were out on patrol. Heightened security since the rash of assassinations pushed his people to their limits. Lacking funding to hire and train additional personnel, Hargan met the harsh realities of his situation with a foul temper.

Slinking into his desk chair, the well-worn cushions absorbing him with intricate familiarity, Hargan tipped his head back, closed his eyes, and sighed. Lack of sleep combined with the unexpected arrivals of Cardinal Breed's brother and his people conspired to keep him running ragged. He didn't remember the last night of sound sleep he'd gotten, nor the last full meal. His body ran on fumes at this point. Tired and frustrated, Hargan felt the need to discover the killer and put this case to rest. Before it destroyed him.

That thought in mind, Hargan activated his computer and accessed personnel files. A shadow caught in the corner of his eye, drawing his attention. Then there was a rustle of clothing in the hallway. Hargan glanced up, peering through glare of the screen but the lights had gone out in the rest of the building. "Hello? Who's there?"

The squeak of a boot on the freshly buffed floor set his arm hair on end. Darkness swirled in the hall, enticing him. Hargan narrowed his eyes and unsnapped the holster. His fingers curled around the familiar handgrip, but he did not draw the blaster. Knowing his nerves were on edge, he didn't never hear the end of it if he shot one of his own people out of paranoia.

"Who's out there? Answer up."

The answer came in a flash of movement and the sizzle of multiple rounds blasting. Hargan cried out, pitching back out of his chair and to the cold floor. The last thing he heard was boots running.

Behemoth, nearing Vau Prime.

"You return to torment me or yourself?" Paradise stared at the smaller woman standing before her. The giant felt no sense of closeness her cousin had with the humans. She'd never considered them much as a species before the war and avoided them once the war broke out. Thousands of years in statis softened her views but Paradise remained wary. Knowing Presha Von might be a pawn in Amongeratix's long game, had her keeping her tongue.

Presha held out her hands and shrugged. "There is no easy answer for that, is there?"

"No. I suppose not. Why have come back? Did my beloved cousin send you?"

"He does not know my whereabouts." Presha swallowed. "I doubt he concerns himself with me after my failures."

Content to let the woman speak her truth, Paradise remained silent.

Emboldened, Presha took a step closer. "Did you mean what you said earlier? Can you help me?"

"Help you how? I am in no position to grant wishes, Presha Von."

"You could be."

The admission caught Paradise off guard. "I don't see how. These restraints are sealed through blood magic, and you lack the ability to set me free."

Peering back over one shoulder, Presha stiffened. She'd been monitored since arriving, even if no one admitted it. It wasn't Amongeratix she feared, not any longer. That honor went to the fallen witches.

Her voice fell to a whisper. "I'm not a sorceress. What can I do to counter the acts of magic entrapping you? I may be willing to help, but do not think I trust you. Your kind has been nothing but a curse in my life for too long. How do I know you are any better than Amongeratix?"

"Why else would I be in chains?"

Presha backed away. "You would say that, wouldn't you though? I'm not fool. Despite what *he* believes. My star has risen, burning hotly across the universe even as I wallow and diminish. Your golden tongues have ways of swaying us. Binding us to your bidding as if we were naught but slaves."

"You were."

The admission froze her. She'd longed to understand the relationship between mortals and gods, never once believing … "What do you mean?"

Paradise sagged. "When we ruled the universe, your kind was bred and made to serve. An entire species of servants who bled, died, and struggled under the burden of our demands. Yours wasn't the first, but it proved the heartiest species. We kept you as chattel for our amusement."

"Why would a god do such a thing?"

"Because we are not gods."

Presha collapsed, falling to the cold decking where she wrapped herself around her drawn knees, even as her mind reconciled with previous suspicions. "I don't understand."

"Presha Von, we were never gods. Older, eternal, but never deities. Our origins were lost, even back then, but the truth is we rose to become the dominant species in the universe and ruled with an iron grip. Our tyranny knew no bounds. At least until Tannus stood up to his father and dared question the king in front of the entire court. His hubris proved the catalyst leading to our ultimate demise. But a few of us remain and I fear our end swiftly marches toward us."

"How am I supposed to process that knowledge?" Presha blurted out. "How do I accept it's all been a lie? All of it!"

"What choice is there? There can be no going back, not after your eyes have opened," Paradise consoled. "We must accept these facts for what they are and adjust our lives accordingly. You wallow in grief for events three thousand years before your creation while I remain trapped by them. It was my people I betrayed. My people I watched slaughter themselves at Occanum and my people I helped Tannus save. What is your grief of having the truth revealed compared to having played a role in the extinction of an entire race?"

"We are not so different," Presha offered after a long period of silence. Flashes of her efforts on Kharsis, when she'd been caught in the illusion of Amongeratix's promises, surged to offer fresh torment. More than once she contemplated stepping into an airlock, but an unspoken power whispered for her to remain strong, to stay for a while longer. Her story was not yet complete, though for what purposes she yet served remained hidden.

"Kharsis," Paradise concluded.

The death of an entire planet continued reverberating through space and time. The cosmic screams of millions ripples across the fabric of reality, threatening to tear a hole in the veil between real and abstract. Though Paradise lacked the intimate knowledge of how such a deed felt, she understood the pain and torment. For she had been a useful pawn in Tannus' game, helping hide and condemn her people to an eternity of forever sleep. The comparisons awakened a bond. A sense of kinship missing for so long she'd forgotten how it felt.

Tears flowed freely down Presha's face. "I … I didn't want to do it. I've never killed anyone before, leastwise not like that. My manipulations were my own. Always focused on improving my position. I never wanted … All those lives…"

"Rest in the webs of your conscience," Paradise finished. "Judgement shall come for you in its own time, but there is an opportunity for atonement. Do not let the weight of your sins carry you to the grave, Presha Von. One final chance to prove your worth and deliver justice to those responsible for twisting and using you for their own conceits."

"Amongeratix."

"Among others," Paradise agreed.

Regaining her composure, Presha pulled herself off the deck and flattened the wrinkles from her skirts. "He is the last. The others once seeking to use me are dead."

"What must I do?" Presha asked.

Knowing she needed to proceed cautiously, Paradise took a moment to clear her throat. She was dehydrated and hungry. Her body ached from the cruel ministrations Amongeratix allowed his witches to inflict upon her. Yet despite this, Paradise Tear desired revenge and saw her instrument. "Help set me free, and we shall end my cousin's reign once and for all."

PGN Flagship *Revengence*, edge of Vau System.

The fleet powered through space. Silent assassins come to deliver their vengeance on the planet they once called home. Tens of thousands of men and women aboard one hundred ships racing to their inevitable conclusion. At least Admiral Khe-Zhehan saw it as so. Shaking the thoughts of doom proved more difficult the closer the fleet got to Vau space. Responsible for every soul under her command, she knew many would not be coming home. Their sacrifices, should her mission meet success, would not go in vain however, for success meant the salvation of countless soldiers and civilians desperate to escape the growing nightmare on Vau Prime.

Standing on the bridge, hands clenched into fists, Khe-Zhehan studied the tactical readout screen. Blue markers denoted her ships. Cruisers, carriers, and smaller support craft arrayed around the *Revengence*. The fleet was large enough to break most worlds and blockades, but the admiral was no fool. She knew her enemy had ample time to prepare his defenses. The promise of slaughter high was high.

"Entering the fringe of the Vau System, Admiral," the ship's First Officer called.

Khe-Zhehan closed her eyes. "Very good, Commander. Captain Affernee, give the order to the fleet."

Grizzled with more years of experience than she recalled, the veteran captain of her flagship stood rigid, jaws clenched. “Aye, ma’am. Comms, open channel to the fleet.”

Computers whirred to life and the static hum of an open channel filled the bridge. Crewers stopped moving, turning to watch this singular moment that would forever define their lives. Khe-Zhehan had full faith and confidence in them and knew there might never be another experience in their shared lives coming close to the immensity of the following words.

“*Revengence* to fleet, slow to impulse and assume defensive array. Launch fighters. Ground forces board your shuttles and prepare to deploy,” Affernee barked.

Acknowledgements chirped back.

Khe-Zhehan and her crew watched as the ships of the fleet shifted positions, forming a string of wedges with interlocking fire sectors. No point in the immediate area was safe from the thousands of cannons, bombardment engines, and ship to ship batteries. Gunports opened, their barrels jutting forth like broken teeth.

Satisfied, Affernee turned back to the admiral. “All ships reporting in and ready to advance.”

“Very good, Captain. *Revengence* in the lead. Open a new channel to the fleet,” she replied.

Affernee offered a clip nod and clasped his hands behind his back.

“This is Admiral Khe-Zhehan. I won’t bore you with the standard prebattle speeches. We are here for one purpose only: to rescue as many of our fellow Guardsmen trapped on the planet as possible. We are not here to engage in full combat.” She paused, allowing her words to sink in. “That does not preclude you from taking action when necessary. All enemy ships who move to intercept or deploy in firing positions will be dealt with.” She paused, purposefully making eye contact with each of her bridge crew.

“Make no mistake. We are facing men and women who have the same training, discipline, and tactical prowess as ourselves. The Prekhauten navy has long been the standing space power in the universe. What comes will be a test of untried proportions. I have no doubts about your ability to execute your missions. Lives are counting on us. Break the blockade around Vau Prime and get to those on the ground. May the gods watch over each of you. Khe-Zhehan out.”

The transmission ended, leaving a morose bridge crew awaiting orders. Most were survivors of the ambush at Hawker's Gate when Khe-Zhehan assumed command of the loyalist fleet. Burdened by the weight of fallen comrades and broken promises, she met the gaze of each in turn, staring deep into their eyes with silent reassurance. Moments like these were rare, even for fighting people. They knew what she asked of them, the heavy sacrifice their actions meant on this day.

"It has been an honor and privilege serving alongside you these long years. Whatever end may come today I have full faith and confidence in your abilities. You are the pride of the fleet. Nothing else needs saying." She swallowed the lump in her throat. "Captain Affernee, take us in."

Snapping to attention, Affernee tilted his head. "Aye, Admiral. Helm, set course for Vau Prime, target set one. Tactical, sound general quarters. Bring the ship to full alert."

Revengence lurched forward, the rest of the fleet following.

EIGHTEEN

3215 A.G. (After Gods), Eger City, planet Mannus Prime.

Cardinal Virom sat in the dark, brooding over recent actions. He remained confused and, though he'd never admit such aloud, afraid of the future. Too many wheels were in motion, robbing him of the ability to see through the morass and find a moral compass once more. He never imagined rising to the head of a splinter organization built upon the ruins of the Conclave, yet here he was. Thrust into his position out of necessity. Countless souls looked to him for guidance as their understanding of the war and what it meant for the universe developed. He felt like an island in a sea of madness with no sight of salvation.

Gnawing on his conscience, Virom struggled with the idea that he had become more than a mere planetary representative. A lifetime of humble piety threatened to be subsumed by what his peers and companions all but demanded of him. He felt the change. The shift in the cosmic sands as the winds of war blew fiercer with each passing day. Decades of faithful service weren't enough, he begrudgingly admitted. More was required. Virom knew what must be done and was loath to make that commitment.

Clicking the light on his desk, Virom blinked as his eyes got used to the brightness. The day already in full swing, he deliberated remaining closeted in his personal chambers, of which had conveniently been moved into the governor's palace as the foundling government established and reorganized itself. Duties notwithstanding, Virom knew he would never get used to the countless souls scurrying by each day with displays of reverence.

"Humble and pious my ass," he grumbled and slipped into his freshly laundered robes of state.

Sighing his frustrations to an empty room, Virom steeled himself for another day of endless meetings, confusing political doublespeak, and military planning he failed to understand. His one saving grace lay in the friendship with General Torgast. They'd begun tepid, a companionship forced upon each when the war came to Mannus. And though they failed to see eye to eye more times than not, Virom had grown fond of their conversations as much as his ability to bounce ideas off his military counterpart.

Virom did his best to avoid the masses as he made the daily migration through the winding corridors of power. It still wasn't enough. Functionaries and menials threatened to stop him, even as the lure of fresh caf and breakfast pulled him closer to the mess. Stomach growling, Virom waved, smiled, and offered clipped prayers and blessings so as not to sound rude as he scurried past. Entering the mess, now all but deserted from the morning rush, he filled a mug of caf, had a modest plate of eggs, bacon from an animal he didn't recognize, and toasted bread. Fresh fruits stretched across one table in every color imaginable. He wondered if the main army ate this well in garrison but, selfishly, abandoned those thoughts as the first swallow of hot caf slid down his throat.

"One might think you've grown accustomed to the niceties of life."

Closing his eyes, Virom took another swallow. Only after the last grasp of warmth passed into his gut did he address his guest. "Hasn't anyone told you not to interrupt a man before he's had his morning caf?"

"I already have one mother, don't need another," Torgast retorted. "May I?"

Virom gestured to the empty bench across from him and opened his eyes. "You look particularly haggard this morning."

"Picked up on that, eh? Sometimes I wonder what got into me to accept this position."

"Truer words have never been spoken, my friend," Virom agreed. "How goes the war?"

Torgast winced as he helped himself to a slice of bacon from the cardinal's plate. "Minute by minute. We're almost at the point where I need to start turning people away. Our supply lines are stretched to capacity. Finding qualified noncoms to train the recruits is proving difficult as more frontline units are transferred to the other side of the planet in staging bases. Food, ammunition, and uniforms are at a premium. Even with the addition of Falchi's units we lack the vehicles and cannons, fliers, and drones to launch an effective offensive when the time comes."

"I was understanding equipment was being funneled in," Virom said between mouthfuls of now lukewarm eggs with a decided green tinge. "Is this not the case?"

"It is, but not at speeds to keep up with the influx of recruits. In short, we're screwed unless another miracle lands in our laps." Torgast reached for another piece of bacon and had his hand slapped for his efforts.

Jabbing his fork, Virom said, "That might be a problem I can solve."

"Angels on our shoulders?"

"In a manner of speaking. We're set to meet with the delegation of government officials from the nearby systems this morning. I'm sure I can convince them to see the righteousness of our cause and lend their support."

Torgast snorted. "Cardinal, I'll kiss your feet if you can make that happen."

"Miracles are my specialty."

The room filled quickly. Over a score of senior leaders, policy makers, and rulers from ten different planets introduced themselves and helped themselves to the bounty Mannus Prime provided. Some wore gaudy robes of state marking them more performer than politician. Others, those select few understanding the value of keeping opinions private, stayed on the outskirts watching, listening. Virom marked these as the ones he needed to win over as they were the true power players in the room.

A Marine corporal announced his arrival and the noise dropped to manageable levels one might appreciate. Virom gestured to the patchwork of tables filling the center of the room forming a large square. He preferred a round table where no one person might feel more important than the rest but those were in short supply thanks to the war. Torgast found his place beside him. Ambassador Treil from planet Tanap on the other side.

"Ladies and gentlemen, I wish to thank you for coming in person, understanding there are many constraints demanding our time," Virom began once everyone was seated.

"Constraints that might otherwise not be necessary if not for this war," Treil offered abruptly. "Cardinal, I am sure we can afford to skip the unnecessary platitudes and pleasantries. We all know why we are here. Let's get to the point."

Pursing his lips and biting back a retort that would have made his mother blush, Virom conceded, “Very well. Here it is. We are faced with the unenviable position of planning for the end of the war. What happens when Vau Prime is defeated?”

“You sound convinced this will happen,” a slender woman in a golden dress said. “My sources indicate the Inquisitor General is not slowing his campaign. For every world you liberate, another falls to his will. It has devolved to a war attrition.”

“As to be expected when two sides of equal training meet, Minister Phaesl. Our victory here has liberated every system for parsecs,” Torgast said.

“To what end? Those systems are still confronted by a dire choice: Either join the war or wait for it to come to their worlds.”

It was then Virom realized she had lavender eyes. “Minister, were it my decision there would be no war. Our peoples could return to their lives free and without worry. Alas these dark times fall upon us. Dreams and wishes mean little in the face of rising oppression. The question is not who wants a war but who will do the right thing when it is needed most.”

Folding his arms, Treil scowled. “The esteemed cardinal from Mannus is correct. We are forced into an impossible position and left with but two choices. Stand by and do nothing or fight. I have no desire to pick up a rifle but if sending aid to General Torgast’s forces will help bring this conflict to an end it is the least I can do.”

“Ever the nobleman, eh Treil,” a pompous man of great girth derided. “I am Yazie, the official representative of the Kings of Storbor. My lords have bidden me to express their distaste of this war and the proposed solutions I have heard already. Storbor is a small planet with limited natural resources. We have no standing military force, nor have we a wish to be occupied by one.”

“Why are you here if not to lend support?” Phaesl spat. “This is a council of war, not for scared little men unwilling to meet their destiny.”

He pointed an angry finger at her. "I know you, Phaesl. You speak with both sides of your mouth. Ware to any who would place their trust in you, mistress of snakes."

Rebuked, she sank back in her chair, glowering.

"Enough of this," Virom snapped and rose. "This group represents the majority of power in this sector of space. A force strong enough to repulse our enemies and turn the tide of battle in our favor once and for all. Already our military forces are deploying on actions deemed high priority. Should they return successful, we will have the keys to launching a counteroffensive all the way to Vau Prime."

Torgast added, "He's right. Military actions are underway as we speak and, though they remain classified, we have every reason to believe they are capable of turning the course of the war."

"Why then are we here and not on our homeworlds?" Treil asked.

"We need support. Thousands of able-bodied volunteers arrive daily. My sergeants are working diligently to turn them into some semblance of a fighting force, but we lack weapons, uniforms, vehicles, and more. With your support that can and will change."

"What assurances will you provide in return for our aid? Monetary compensation or perhaps some sort of trade agreement?" Yazie asked.

"Longstanding trade agreements can be arranged," Virom conceded. "We have every desire to see each of our planets find sustained success in the war's aftermath. But first we must get there."

Treil joined him standing. "Tanap will offer what aid we can. You have our support, for the immediate future. But Cardinal, no gift comes without cost. We shall seek to find recompense for our efforts."

"Such will be given once terms are decided upon," Virom agreed. "That goes for all of you. The foundations of this alliance will be based on mutual understanding and the spirit of cooperation, much as our initial foundings on Vau Prime once dictated."

"Cardinal Virom, we are all well versed on what the Conclave once offered us, but those days have been replaced by greed and corruption. None of your order has stood up to the rogue Inquisitor General as he campaigns to brings ruin to us all. What has become of the vaunted Conclave in these dire times?" Phaesl demanded.

Expecting the assault did little to diminish its potency. Virom's love for his order conflicted with the passion welling deep within for the fledging freedoms many planets now discovered. His brethren, those still loyal to the founding ideals, were forced underground lest Nye's pogroms find them. Weaker willed Cardinals bowed in supplication to the Inquisitor General, unwilling to voice objections while giving in to their inherent flaws and avarices.

"I have been assigned to Mannus for the entirety of my career. As I'm sure many of you know, we are independent from the moment we are ordained; so long as we continue adhering to the Conclave's guidelines and traditions. My focus has always been here, on the people of my world. The actions of the Forum and Cardinal Seniorus have little impact on planetary clergy."

"Cheap excuses in the face of societal catastrophe," Yazie sneered.

"Perhaps," Virom said. "But are you to be held accountable for all your masters decree? Would you stand trial for their indulgences while they sit comfortably in their ivory towers or do you have authority to treat with matters as they arise, disconnected from the kings of Storbor?"

The Minister from Orlei cleared his throat before Yazie could retort. "You all know me and what I represent. I have come to know our esteemed cardinal over the past few days and respect his opinions and ideologies. The Conclave rules through proxy, allowing each of us to develop our worlds as we see fit in accordance with their designs. That does not mean Virom should be put to the fire for wearing his robes of state. Rather that he be embraced for taking a stand in the face of rising tyranny." Standou looked around at each before continuing.

"We stand upon the precipice of a unique opportunity. The Conclave is lost. We must accept this. Even if the war ends according to our designs the rebuilding of Vau Prime will take a lifetime. Who is to say whether the Conclave, Prekhauten Guard, or Inquisition will survive in their current iterations? What I do know is new leadership will be necessary. Leadership born in this very room by each of us. Give Torgast his supplies and equipment. Fuel the engines of war. For once the smoke clears and society can at last rebuild a new dawn awaits. We are that dawn."

Failing to keep his disappointment from showing, Virom cleared his throat. "Thank you, Minister, but this is a discussion of logistics, not of filling gaps in leadership."

"I but bring the idea to the table," Standou said with a smile. "Orlei is with you, Cardinal. Whatever we can provide for the effort, though the matter of leadership moving forward remains to be settled."

A wave of agreement and promises of support soon followed as the others fell in line. Virom being no fool, he took it for what it was, a band of opportunists with visions of power.

The shuttle touched down on Eger City's main spaceport. A hundred passengers disembarked. Some wore peasant garb and carried all their possessions in one bag as they answered the call to arms. Others were in government official uniforms or in the clothes of high society fleeing the ravages of war on their homeworlds. Only one failed to fit in. Trapped between peasant and noble, he was older and tired. Lines creased his face, spots filled the backs of his hands. His age reflected through dulled eyes as he hobbled down the ramp.

The man stopped at the edge of the tarmac and breathed deep. Intoxicating smells of industry and nature warred within his nostrils. The open air of what he viewed as an uncivilized planet enticed him, for it was a far cry from the stagnation of his previous location. Here was a planet untamed, ready to be developed under the heavy focus of his visions. The crowd thinned. Ground crews waved them off before the shuttle launched. A glance skyward showed him the dull underbellies of several descending vehicles. Whistling a tune, the man stalked off in search of a ride to the governor's administratum. There was much work to be done and little time.

Tinus Har had come to Mannus Prime and with him the dreams of a future.

Central City, planet Dalafar.

"This isn't going to work."

Fies rolled his eyes for the tenth time, longing for the silence of working alone behind the anonymity of his helmet. Still, Quint had a point. They were marching into the wolf's den with little intelligence and a fool's chance of success. He glanced at the more haggard addition to the platoon, unable to correct the man. Only

Hollis seemed nonplussed by their situation. The hint of an eager grin lifting the corners of her mouth.

"Saying it doesn't make it better," he said.

Jelin Quint chuckled and tugged on his uniform blouse to get a better fit. The uniforms Tempest absconded with were the best she could do given the circumstances, as were the standard sidearms of garrison soldiers.

"Oh come, LT, it's almost like playing dress up," Hollis chimed in.

"Are you insane?" Fies asked.

Her grin spread from ear to ear. "Don't I have to be? We're on an enemy controlled planet. Our chances of success are low, almost too low to count on. We either go out in a blaze of glory or we slip through the cracks and somehow find a way succeed. Either way, it's out of my control. Might as well have fun doing it."

"I never should have said yes," Quint muttered.

"Hollis, maybe you should stay behind," Fies suggested.

"Where's the fun in that? You know I'm damned good at what I do, sir. Let's go in there, crack a few heads and see what happens."

From the small stool across the room, Tempest watched and listened to the exchange with rapt attention. She never understood what made men and women place themselves in harm's way on purpose, though after seeing Governess Moscasco work wonders in her position over the last three years inspired her. The trio before her however—

She jerked from her thoughts when Quint leaned close and said, "You know they gave me a name back on Mannus after I lost my entire company. The Madness. How would you like to go through life being known as a crazed man with a hair trigger? To be fair, I would have killed any and everyone in my path during the days following."

"How did you overcome it?" she asked.

"I almost didn't. Took to seeing what was at the bottom of a bottle for a while." He rubbed his jaw. "A good man took me in, cleaned me up, and gave me purpose again. Men like me don't get second chances, so I took it and never looked back."

Her heart warmed to his story for reasons she failed to understand. “We all deserve second chances, sergeant.”

An eyebrow rose. Images of his brother lying beaten in the mud tormented him. “If you say so.”

“How did you wind up with this lot?” she asked, eager to change the subject.

“Poor decision making,” he replied with a snort. “I was sent to coordinate their attacks on the enemy lines from a second front. Turns out they liked me enough to offer me a job. I jumped at the chance of getting back on the line, thinking it might do me some good.”

“Did it?”

“That remains to be seen. If we survive this.”

“Oh, come on, sarge! How about a little optimism,” Hollis complained, grimacing. “We’re the fucking best of the best or we wouldn’t be here. We go in, grab the governess, and beat feet outta here quiet like ghosts.”

“I like her,” Tempest admitted.

“Uh huh.”

“Everyone ready?” Fies asked.

“Enough.”

Hollis flashed a thumbed up before double checking her blaster’s power charge.

“Right. Does everyone know their roles?”

Quint stretched, loosening his shoulders in anticipation of what came next. “Let’s do it. The sooner we get this over with and get back to Mannus the better. I’m tired of smelling like fish.”

“You haven’t even eaten one since we’ve been here,” Hollis replied.

Quint held up a finger and glowered.

“All right, enough of this,” Fies snarled. The time for games over, he needed them focused and ready to act. “Tempest, you’re up. Lead us in.”

“I thought you’d never ask,” she said with a smile and hurried to the door.

“They’re moving,” Annalilly said and lowered her binos.

Beve grunted, barely flinching from behind his light machinegun. Not that she expected more. The heavy gunner, already disgruntled from having to lower his caliber and stopping power for the mission's sake, took taciturn to new levels. Despite years of working together, Annalilly failed to find any connection with him other than his professionalism and dedication to the fight. Men like that were handy when shoved against the wall. They just didn't make great conversationalists.

She watched a pair of flies chasing each other across his forehead, landing on the bridge of his nose and he didn't budge. Annalilly wondered what made the man tick, marveling at his iron discipline and lack of concern over the ill-reputed hygiene of the insects.

"Where are you from, Beve?" she asked, deciding to bridge the gap. With nothing else to do until the mission either went south or Fies and the others absconded the governess, she figured she might as well live up to her role of platoon sergeant.

"Does it matter?" he replied. "The Guard is home. Always has been. Always will be till the war ends or I do."

Stunned by the number of words spoken at once, Annalilly narrowed her eyes. She realized his admission did little to remove the stigma surrounding him nor improve her feelings toward him. Perhaps keeping their relationship professional was for the best.

"I liked it better when you didn't talk," she admitted.

Beve grunted again and resumed his watch.

"Once he gets started, he won't stop," Haggle told them.

Desril scowled and shook his head. Together they watched as Palco continued cracking his knuckles. The sound akin to breaking rocks echoed throughout the small room the trio confiscated for their fallback position. Haggle remained amazed by the massive hands on the man. Working in the mines proved grueling work but produced giants like Palco. Not very bright, Palco made up for it with unusual vigor and a passion for doing a good job.

"Will you fucking stop," Desril ground out. "I can't take anymore."

Glancing up, Palco offered his best confused look. "Eh?"

"Your hands! Stop cracking your godsdamned knuckles already."

"Oh, that. Can't help it. Old habits and all." His sheepish grin, tinged with crimson, spread. "Working the mines left us with a lot of time on our hands. Sorry. That wasn't right. I had to find something to do when I wasn't breaking rocks, so I started cracking these knuckles. Feels good. Lets me stretch my hands out and keeps em from hurting."

"Hurting?" Haggle asked.

"Thritis. Mines is no place for soft men."

"You mean arthritis?"

"Sure. What did I say?"

Haggled sighed. "Never mind. Just give it a rest, will you? We're going to be here a while and I don't think any of us need another reason to get jumpy."

"If you say so, sarge."

Desril breathed a sigh of relief and went back to sharpening his combat blade. Soon the harsh scrapping sounds replaced the cracking of knuckles, and the cycle started all over again. Silently cursing Desril, Haggle hoped Fies and the others hurried. He didn't know how much more he could take. If rank had its privileges, this wasn't it.

Quint admired Tempest's composure. Any other person this close to treason's doorstep might have wilted under pressure. Knowing her neck was at stake, she marched into the Guard offices with the authority of her own. Several junior Guards stepped aside as she entered, giving the false impression she commanded the arena. Quint remained impressed when the duty officer stopped and questioned her arrival. She didn't flounder. Perhaps if times were different and their situations more manageable he would have pursued her, but practical men seldom enjoyed the carefree visions of the future. Their odds currently weren't looking great.

Needing a distraction, he focused on the faces of nearby Guards. Thus far he'd yet to find one he recognized, which didn't say much considering the millions in uniform spread throughout the universe.

Fresh concern sprouting when thinking of who Fies knew, Quint focused on the task. Get in. Grab the governess. Get out. Unscathed. What could go wrong? His pulse quickened. A nervous tick from early years in uniform he'd never shaken. Resisting the urge to curl his fingers around the comfort of his rifle, Quint stiffened his back and marched forward with false authority.

They were halted by a junior sergeant at the intake desk. His youthful vigor betrayed his lack of experience. In Quint's opinion, this often made for aggressive, unstable behavior. He refrained from snorting. Bad things happened when people believed their own bullshit. Quint's eyes widened when Tempest strode forward, having expected Fies to take lead.

"Sergeant, you know who I am. I am escorting these gentlemen to the governess' cell." Her voice was strong, confident.

Taken off guard, the sergeant balked. "Ma'am, I don't have you on the authorization list. You're going to ha—"

Curling her hands into fists, Tempest lifted to the balls of her feet and fixed him with a withering glare. "You misunderstand me, *Sergeant*. I'm not asking. This is a matter of universal security. These men have come from Vau Prime on orders from Prekhauten command."

Grey eyes flitted between them.; Quint could see the wheels turning. That inkling of doubt threatening to sink their operation and lock them away for the rest of their mortal lives.

He took in the immediate area. A trio of Guards loitered off to the side, quiet in their conversation. They were unconcerned with them, a byproduct of having grown comfortable during their extended planetary assignment. Recorders affixed to the ceiling corners covered every inch of the room with hidden security monitors concealed somewhere near the building center. Quint figured it wouldn't take much to subdue the personnel on hand and secure the entry point if it came to that, but the odds of holding diminished with each passing moment.

"I'm going to have to clear this with my superior," the sergeant insisted.

The sound of teeth grinding set Quint on edge. Tempest, refusing to back down, leaned close and lowered her voice. "If I don't get these two in to see the governess immediately it will be your head on a pike at the dock. Or perhaps I should summon Captain Donab. I'm certain he would enjoy being pulled from his busy schedule to address your shortcomings."

Paling, the newly commissioned sergeant lost much of his bluster. "I'm just trying to do my job. There are reports of rogue agents on Dalafar, ma'am."

"I understand that but I also have a mission to accomplish. With the governess in custody someone has to run the planet," she replied, the edge slipping just enough.

Fumbling under her softened gaze, a visitor's pass was produced and the sergeant gestured for her to continue.

Quint trailed after Tempest, unwilling to look the younger man in the face lest he giveaway his revulsion at how easily the man collapsed under the flirting of an attractive woman.

Marching through a pair of reinforced doors, the trio were soon past the front desk and worming into the bowels of what Quint deemed his worst nightmare.

"Well done," Fies whispered as they carried on.

Tempest, loose hair swishing wild across her shoulders in stark contrast to her business attire, shrugged. "It is a game I've been forced to play too many times. Men always fold. Always. Besides, I think I enjoy watching them squirm."

"Never easy, is it?" Fies smirked.

"Never should be."

Quint trailed behind. He'd never been one to understand women, maybe that's why every relationship he had ended in failure, usually with him on the losing end. After a while he abandoned the foolish quest to settle down and marry and devoted himself to the uniform and the cause.

After clearing his throat, Quint asked something that had been bothering him, "What now?"

The other two stopped, turning to give him varying looks. Tempest appeared flustered while Fies attempted to discern what Quint was after.

"What do you mean? We get the governess like planned," Tempest said.

Quint shook his head. "Not that part. The other part. We're here. We got in past their defenses. Now what?"

"I don't understand what you're getting at?" Tempest cocked her head. Her left foot tapped, eyes scanning different parts of the hallway in search of surveillance devices, and worse.

Giving her a deadpan look, Quint asked, "How are we supposed to get out? We can't shoot our way out and your original plan of convincing the Guards to let us walk out isn't going to work."

"Fuck," Fies whispered.

Nonplussed, Tempest led them without falter. She remained weaponless and, in the face of overwhelming danger, fearless, prompting silent admiration. In comparison, Fies and Quint grew jumpy the closer to the target the got. Neither were able to dismiss their honed instincts. Their heads remained swiveling, hands itching to grasp and draw their sidearms if for no other reason than for familiar comfort. Compounding the confusion, the desk sergeant hadn't insisted on any accompanying Guards to see them to their destination. Suspecting a trap, they quickened their steps.

Much to their surprise, they found Governess Moscasco's holding cell unguarded.

"Are you sure this is it?" Fies asked, pausing.

Tempest pursed her lips, eyes narrowing. "Yes. Now, unless you have any other pointless questions, we need to get in and get out."

"I hope you have a plan for that," Quint muttered.

Shooting him her best glare, Tempest pushed the button and the door hissed open. She stormed in without pause, forcing them to follow. Whatever they'd expected to find was a far cry from the truth.

Moscasco sat on a cushion divan pushed against the far wall beneath the lone window. Storms thundered outside, reminding them of the fury Dalafar repressed daily. A carpet, stained from too many boots and too little care, centered beneath the small interrogation table in the middle of the room. Though if this was meant for breaking subversives it was all but forgotten. Food and drink filled the table, along with a small stack of books.

The governess looked up, peeling her face from the limited glimpse of the outside world her window afforded. "It appears my fate is determined. That was faster than I thought."

"Governess, we are here to get you out."

Eyes widening, Moscasco said, "Tempest?"

Quint exhaled the breath he hadn't realized he'd been holding. He studied the woman seated before them, finding little to get excited over. The pinch of her nose suggested a severe demeanor, though he supposed such was necessary considering her position. Thin lines of grey sprouted through her hair, poorly disguised since her capture. Her clothes were rumpled, and bags clouded her otherwise dazzling eyes. Yet for all appearances, she appeared defiant. Quint took that as a good sign.

"What are you doing here?" Moscasco asked after sweeping forward to give Tempest a hug.

"We've come to get you out of here," Tempest repeated. "We must hurry. This ruse isn't going to last long."

"It lasted less than you think," a man's booming voice came from behind them.

As one, Fies and Quint whirled, hands dropping to their weapons.

There, in the doorway going unnoticed until now, stood Captain Donab. His hands were clasped together at his waist. The older Guard searched their faces, ignoring the women. Donab had been expecting a measure of foolishness from Tempest. The woman, who's true name escaped him, was a thorn in his side from the moment he'd first been assigned to Dalafar. It was the men in Guard uniforms, imposters most likely, drawing his attention.

Donab took in the wear of their uniforms, the way they stood. Their hands clutched their sidearms, still holstered, waiting for the opportunity to strike him down. Unable to move his hands without being shot, he waited. Then recognition dawned. His mouth twisted. Eyes narrowed.

"Fies? Is that you?" he asked. "What in the name of the gods are you doing here?"

Quint rolled his eyes. The game was up. He drew his blaster and leveled it at the captain in one swift movement. Whatever else happened, Donab would die first.

NINETEEN

3215 A.G. (After Gods), PGN *Solstice*, enroute to planet Wexanos.

The silence aboard the bridge matched the emptiness in her mind. Sharlyn August watched the stars drift by, the countdown still going on the distance clock, yet she saw nothing. Since escaping the ambush two days ago her mind had become consumed by the guilt of sending her soldiers to die. In retrospect, she decided, deploying boarding teams to the enemy ships shouldn't have happened. August ran the scenario back through her mind countless times, until the barrage of names and faces became unbearable.

She felt, more than heard, her First Mate sidle up beside her command chair. August refused to meet his gaze, already knowing how the conversation would engage. Odir was a good man and might have been a better friend if not for the divide of rank and uniform. Trusted and liked by the crew, he complimented her skillset the way every good ship captain needed. For that, August remained grateful.

"Captain, this has gone on long enough."

"Odir, we've been through this."

"Aye we have, and it is having a damaging effect on the crew. We know how much you care for us. It's our turn to care for you."

She snorted, unwilling to trust her voice at first. "It was my call. My responsibility. Their lives were entrusted to me. How can I inform their families that my actions led to their deaths?"

"They were professional Marines in the Prekhauten Guard, ma'am. Each one of them knew what they were getting into. Don't think for a moment they didn't. This war has gone on long enough we all know the deal." Odir's infliction rose with his voice. "For you to do anything other than celebrate their dedication to the cause does them a grave disservice."

Rebuked, she slumped back into the well-worn cushions of her chair. He was right, of course. Every man and woman in uniform knew what they were involved in and only a few backed down, scampering off in the middle of the night while former comrades continued fighting on the line, watching friends fall, then celebrating victories and dealing with anguish over defeats. The weak were weeded out by this point, either through combat or cowardice.

"What would you have me do? There are no words capable of bringing them home. No modicum of comfort I can offer through apologies."

"That is where you are wrong. You are the captain of this vessel. The one voice every crewer and Marine seeks before we engage. Your words matter as much as your deeds."

August closed her eyes in a vain attempt to ignore the situation. Pursing her lips, she said, "You are a cruel man, Odir."

"I am what the universe has made me," he replied. "Captain, the Marines are waiting for you. Any further delay threatens to undermine your authority."

"Meaning they will rebel?" she asked, at last opening her eyes.

He shifted, a frown spreading. "Meaning they will obey your orders without question though many might harbor a cancerous lack of respect."

Slapping her palms on the worn leather armrests, August rose. "You know, there are times when being in command is more burden than reward. I swear, if we make it through this war unscathed, I am resigning and never going to be in charge of another soul for the rest of my days." At his silence she added, "Very well, lead on."

Concealing his amusement, Odir stepped back and allowed his captain to exit the bridge.

"We're not children, ma'am. We can take it."

August paused, taken off guard by the frankness of Talore's comment. The Marine, bitter with the loss of his friends, remained stalwart in the face of adversity. She hadn't known what to expect, but it wasn't this.

They listened to her words, emotionless faces staring back. The occasional tear welled; not one fell. She admired their tenacity. Their resolute professionalism. Trading away one's life in the name of others they might never meet was no small ask, yet this understanding did little to assuage her guilt.

"I appreciate your honesty, Sergeant, but those Marines died because of my orders."

"Captain August, no one can predict how a battle will develop. Those Marines fought with honor and sacrificed themselves in the promise of creating a better universe. Do not diminish their deaths by minimizing the action." The defiance in Talore's gaze dared her to counter him.

August knew a losing proposition when she saw it. She shifted her gaze to the rest of the Marine contingent. "It is my great honor to serve alongside you. Each of you is a credit to your organization and the temerity of the true Prekhauten Guard. You are the reason I continue to fight. Continue dedicating my life to the cause and am willing to sacrifice myself in the name of liberty and justice.

"The actions of two days ago rest on my shoulders. I made the call to board the enemy craft. You went without question. Staunch defenders of our way of life. To you, and those who fell, I owe my deepest gratitude. We entered this war without understanding. There was no way to know how sides would fall out or who we would meet on the opposite end of the barrel. This civil war is a travesty on all we hold dear and will become a defining moment for our species for generations to come."

She paused, trembling from the raw emotion threatening to burst free. "This I swear unto you: From this day until the end of the war I shall not tire, not relent, and never forget who it is keeping this ship secure. Sergeants and junior officers, it is by your blood and determination the rest of us are able to perform our duties. This war may be planned on levels far above your paygrade, but it will be won through your deeds.

"The names of the fallen will be engraved upon the Wall of Honor. Forever remembered by all who pass. All Marines will immediately enjoy a well-deserved day of downtime." Murmurs of approval rippled through the ranks. "We will be arriving at our destination within the next day. Once there I expect each of you to be ready to leap back into the fight. This war is far from over. Victory or defeat is no longer in our hands, but I vow to you to stand by your side until the last shot is fired. You have my loyalty, my commitment, and my undying gratitude for all you do." She looked around once more before finishing her speech. "Company commander, take charge of your people."

A gaunt faced captain stepped forward and snapped a crisp salute. "Aye, ma'am. Marines, fall out and commence twenty-four-hour standdown. Dismissed!"

Cheers spread through the assembly deck as the Marines dispersed into smaller groups and disappeared back into the winding corridors of the *Solstice*. Several came forward to shake her hand or offering a clipped nod. Soon the deck was clear of all but August and Odir.

She glared at his beaming smile. "All right, out with it."

"See, that wasn't so hard." Odir broke into a grin. "Trust your crew, Captain."

"I should have you scrubbing pots in the galley for this, Commander" She tried, failed, to sound stern. "Still, there is no denying the power of proving yourself among subordinates. Thank you, Odir. I do not deny my heart dreaded this moment."

"We are all human, ma'am. We all make mistakes," he replied. "They needed to hear this as much as you needed to say it. Giving them a day off went just as far as accepting responsibility. That was an unexpected touch."

"Never underestimate the power of a day off," August said. Stifling a yawn, she asked, "What's next on the agenda? We'll be entering Wexanos space soon enough. I can't wait to get this damned weapon off my ship. We've been a target since Crimeat. It's time we went back on the hunt like the predator this ship was meant to be."

Falling in beside her, Odir said, "As it so happens, Admiral Falchi has requested an updated status report. It seems our betters on Mannus Prime are concerned over the recent assaults on our wellbeing."

"Let's not keep the old man waiting. It wouldn't be seemly for a ship of the line captain to fail to report."

Low continent, planet Vau Prime.

"That makes another two hundred. At this rate we won't be able to last if Kale returns to finish us off."

Gedrick Silk listened the lament of Jash Abernath before asking, "How many active fighters remain in our army?"

Jash threw his hands up. "That's almost impossible to tell. The army started dissolving right after General Strannan died. Colonel Apontee's coup attempt fractured things further."

"We took care of that," Gedrick pointed out.

"Too late to stop it," Bryn Mal said. "Small units, squad sized and above have been slipping away since his arrest. What combat strength remains must be less than a thousand. Not enough to protect the influx of civilians and stop Mobus Kale from rolling over us."

"Meaning we are in a dire predicament."

"Meaning we're fucked."

Cocking his head, Gedrick studied his young counterparts. Until he came around the Guard, Gedrick seldom heard profanity. Humans, unlike his kind who concealed their feelings, were fast to express their emotions with little regard to the listener. He decided to shift the conversation. "How many civilians have fled Krenz?"

Jash produced a datapad. "Twenty-three thousand by last count, but that number is assumed. With small transports arriving daily up and down the coast and the runners sneaking through the blockade there is no real way to track accurately."

"The one figure we can track is our dwindling resources. This airfield wasn't meant to sustain large numbers. Food is running out, even with the limited supplies being funneled to us from Captain Julian and his cells. Water isn't an issue as long as the purification equipment stays running. The one thing we have plenty of is ammunition."

"Too many people. Not enough food. No one to use our ion charges on," Gedrick mused at their predicament.

Bryn snorted. "Ain't life grand?"

"We're still alive and our enemy has yet to turn his eye on us. That is what matters now, Bryn Mal," Gedrick said. "Have we heard anything on Captain Julian?"

"Communications have been spotty for the past week. Last word was Kale was tightening the noose at the direction of the Inquisitor General. We don't anticipate the insurgent cells to last much longer before a total collapse."

"They knew what they were getting into when they volunteered for the mission," Gedrick reminded. "We must look to the civilians first. Our priority has to be evacuating them to safety."

"Our recon element has secured a small airfield on the far side of the continent, closer to the pole. Most of the buildings are in disrepair due to the inclement weather but there is proof of use," Jash said. "Reports of pirates and smugglers operating out of the far south have plagued the Guard for years before the war. Activity is lessened but it remains a viable solution provided we can produce enough transports to move that many people."

"The way will be perilous, no doubt," Gedrick quested. "Is there a chance to make it on foot?"

"Not unless you want to risk half of them dying along the way," Bryn said. "The land shifts to rock and snow two day's ride south before becoming an arctic wasteland. The passage is easy enough on vehicles."

"Vehicles we don't have," Jash snapped.

Gedrick, clasping his hands behind his back, paced in thought. He grew desperate to salvage something of this nightmare. Every human life saved offered the chance for redemption he needed to eliminate the guilt within. Failing to take the risk and assassinate Alain Nye when he had the chance haunted him. It took every ounce of common sense left to convince himself he was not the catalyst for the ruination coming down on them. That Nye and the civil war would have continued even in his death. Legitimate as that sounded, he couldn't fight his conscience and win.

"Have personnel meet every incoming shuttle or transport. Direct the pilots to the south," he ordered. "Abernath, get the numbers on what we have to move these people and how soon we can get a convoy moving south. Mal, I need you to organize a detail and have the refugees prioritized. Families with small children should go first. Anyone who has military expected remains behind."

"They won't like that," she countered. "There will be riots or worse the closer we get to Kale's assault."

"None of that will matter if rumors of Amongeratix's impending arrival are true," Gedrick replied. "We use what Guards we can to ensure the peaceful transition. No violence unless there is no other way."

"What about Julian's teams?" Jash glanced up from the datapad.

"Captain Julian will have to fend for himself for the time being. They are trained to fight. These civilians are not."

Bryn stifled a yawn. The sun had set, bringing sweeping chill with it. Pain from her wounds still haunting her, she rose and stretched. "It's a plan. Better than what we've had. Who's going to take it to Colonel Freyote?"

Jash felt the heat of eyes staring him down and held out his hands in protest. "Oh no. Not me. He's determined to hold this army together until the bitter end. You expect me to go in there and tell him we're falling to pieces?"

Gedrick sighed. "No, Jash Abernath. Your admission will spin him the wrong direction. I shall go." The two lieutenants had grown much during the past year but remained ignorant of too much.

"Brave man," Bryn muttered.

"There is nothing to fear from Freyote. He is a good man with the weight of the world on his shoulders," Gedrick replied. "He will see reason and do the right thing."

Jash shook his head. "Still doesn't feel right going behind his back like this, not after the Apontee affair."

"We are in a desperate position. Trust Freyote as we must trust each other."

Krenz, planet Vau Prime.

Smoke trickled from the barrel, dissipating before the body struck the ground. Julian spared a moment to glance down at the corpse. He'd long grown inured to the glazed look of confusion often etched in the eyes of his foes.

The harsh realities of combat, accentuated by endless amounts of time spent at the sharp end of the stick, transformed Julian into a hard, often brutal man. He wasn't alone. Every Guard fighting for their place in the new universe became reduced, less than what they had been before the first shots fired. They laughed at death. Forgot the pleasantries of modern society. Julian assumed it was the same for their enemies, those men and women who'd abandoned their principles and fallen for a lie. Not that it mattered.

At the end of the day, dead was dead.

“Come on, we need to move,” Edam Boone urged from his covering position across the street. The criminal bore a wild look, betraying his inexperience with a violent world.

They’d stumbled into a poorly designed ambush not an hour earlier. A squad of what he assumed to be raw recruits lay in wait for him and Edam Boone. Had they been seasoned their odds of survival would have been lower.

Once the last of them fell under his merciless blaster fire, he realized the damage had been done. No doubt word reached back to their battalion command and control and support forces were already being dispatched. Soon this district would be swarming with more Guards than they were prepared to handle.

Julian scanned the immediate surroundings. Wise enough not to let his guard down, he scampered through the field of strewn corpses, carefully avoiding the spreading pools of blood. He still looked into each face even though his conscience screamed at him. How many of the bodies were once his friends? The thought sickened him despite his best efforts to insulate his spirit. Each body he passed whispered to him, begging him to join them. Face blanched, he picked up the pace until he slammed against the wall beside Edam and caught his breath.

“You have a death wish, my friend,” the criminal commented.

Julian snorted. Perhaps he did. Blood spattered his already stained uniform. His boots were worn to the limits. Grey hairs streaked his once impressive head of dark hair. The lines under his eyes, creasing his cheeks and forehead suggested a life far harder than the one his mother envisioned. Every muscle in his body ached from repetitive firefights, ambushes, and sleepless nights. He was, Julian decided, too old for this.

“How much longer can we continue like this? The noose tightens daily and, even though we continue evacuating our forces, the enemy is becoming increasingly wise to our tactics. Julian, I don’t wish to die here. Not like this.”

“Life seldom gives us choices, Edam. We fight until we can’t, or the last transport escapes south into the night.”

Shaking his head, Edam said, “Zoraq Darc once tried convincing me to move to another planet to head up his expansion efforts. I refused, saying this was my home and I had no desire to visit other worlds—I regret that decision.”

"If it's any consolation, I've no doubt this war has spread to the farthest reaches of Conclave control. Vau Prime may be the focal point, but it is a pebble cast into the greater ocean. Even if we get offworld there is little guarantee of finding peace."

"You can be depressing when given the chance."

"What can I say, comes with the job. Did you set it?"

Edam's eyes narrowed. "I did, though it sits will me. What if the device is tripped by innocent civilians?"

"We are in the heart of one of the enemy's most loyal districts. There are no innocents here."

Conflicted, the criminal handed over the detonator. "As you say."

Julian felt for the man. They'd been companions since Zoraq Darc's former top lieutenant took him and Aliz in. An uneasy alliance formed, and all Julian brought was the promise of a violent demise should they be caught. Yet instead of fleeing, Edam drove his people deeper underground, burrowing beyond the reach of Mobus Kale's vengeance. Joining forces with the insurgency might had pronounced their doom but it was better than the alternative. Or so he told himself.

Julian thumbed the activation switch and was rewarded by a net of flashing red lights spreading across the immediate area. One hundred tiny mines, each packed with enough charge to kill in a three-meter radius, spread out like a web. Motion activated, they would detonate at chest height. The Guard called them 'sweepers' and he loathed their use in urban settings. Practicality overrode his hesitance. This was a war of attrition and he entered it on the losing end. Still, Julian learned one invaluable lesson early on. He learned that fear went much further than the sting of an ion rifle. Fear made soldiers reluctant. Kept them from unleashing their potent fury at the onset of an action. Fear was his most important ally. One he wielded with utter surety.

Inquisition Headquarters, planet Vau Prime.

Alain Nye glared at the Blood Witch. She presented an impossibility of reason. A creature of magic that should not, by all rights, exist. Yet a growing number of women were sent to the haunted abbey on the Acumensiis Comet to undergo the ritual transformations of their Order. He despised them and their necessity.

Longstanding allies with the Conclave, the witches were consulted and brought in when matters of heresy threatened the greater good. He'd seen their work during the first attempt to recapture Amongeratix decades ago. That witch fell, but others soon swarmed the Conclave in a great purge. He vowed, upon assuming the office of Inquisitor General, to avoid them altogether and destroy their comet once it became prudent. Now he was being told to work hand in hand with the aberrations. Nye's stomach churned.

Studying the crimson robes, so flat and aggressive compared to the standard gossamer of their Order, Nye wondered what fell powers were strong enough to transform these women into what he regarded as monsters. The cruelty in Evangeline's eyes simmered and fear threatened to override his sense of purpose, for this was no mere witch. This was an eldritch entity capable of wanton destruction once unleashed. How many more did Amongeratix have at his disposal and how many remained loyal to the Grand Mistress? With no way of knowing, Nye decided to bide his time and wait for the opportunity to remove this threat to his ascension.

"I fail to understand the reason for this visit," he said after wetting his lips.

Hands clasped behind her back and her face all but hidden in the shadows of her cowl, Sister Evangeline considered him. Weak, like most human men, he represented the reason she and those like her were not welcome among society. The reason they were treated like anathema and outcast among the stars. Mothers and fathers willingly abandoned them to the predations of space lest they suffer the curse of magic in their villages. Evangeline had been a girl of five when the power first manifested. Teased by one of the boys, she lashed out. When she awoke, she was covered in gore. That was the last time she was home. Vowing to reap vengeance upon her family should she ever return, Evangeline became a creature of darkness.

"It is not my position to question Amongeratix," she replied. "He has ordered myself and Geres Auk to prepare you for his impending arrival. Whatever designs he has for you are his alone. That should suffice for you, Inquisitor General."

Feeling the sting in her tone, Nye struggled to maintain composure. "I am not questioning his designs, witch. I fail to see why he felt the need to send one of your kind as the advance party. Vau Prime is prepared to welcome him and lead us into the next stage of this war."

Her robes shifted as she cocked her head. "Perhaps you misunderstand. Lord Amongeratix does not require your assistance. Nor does he accept you have pacified this world accordingly. I am here to ensure you do not fail. The growing insurgency creates a unique problem. One he wishes solved before arriving."

"General Kale is dealing with the situation."

"His efforts have been woeful, else Vau Prime would already be clear and ready to accept Amongeratix."

"Matters are progressing on schedule. General Kale's forces are whittling down our enemy. Their leadership is dissolved and what remains in Krenz fights to hold on all while praying for a salvation that will never come," Nye defended. "I have personally neutralized the authority of the Conclave and subsumed command from the Cardinal Seniorus. Soon enough their order will be eliminated. What more would you have me do?"

"I have no interest in your success or failure. It is Amongeratix's intent to transform this planet into his seat of power through which he will rule the universe indefinitely. Your priests and cardinals offer little interference as it is, but your renegade armies threaten all he has sought to achieve," she replied. "The recent disaster on Mannus Prime is evidence enough that our enemies remain strong, emboldened. They must be crushed decisively if there is any hope of a swift transition."

Glowering at her, Nye slapped a palm on his desk. "Then perhaps Amongeratix would be so kind as to send his vaunted cadre of witches into the field to hurry this matter along. Once Vau Prime is secure, the outlying systems will fall in line or perish by their own designs. Kharsis is example enough."

Evangeline paused, just enough to let him know he'd struck a nerve. The Crimson Sister floated higher, the breeze of her movement shifting the hem of her robes. "That is acceptable. Show me your enemies, Inquisitor General, and I shall make them regret their indiscretions."

A thin smile crept across his weathered face as he outlined his plans. With luck, he'd solve two problems at once.

Animosity filled the space between them. Clenched fists and leering gazes threatened undisguised violence. These two titans, apex predators in their own realms, brought worlds to heel yet there was room for but one now. Which one might prevail should they come to blows? The stalwart general hungry for power and filled with vitriol or the barbarian from a backwater world convinced he was destined for more than mere mortality?

"Got a problem?" Geres Auk bristled under Kale's gaze.

"Perceptive, aren't you?"

"I want to break the bones in your face. Pulverize your flesh into an unrecognizable mess no surgeon can repair. Is that perceptive enough or shall I continue?"

"I welcome the opportunity," Mobus Kale taunted, flexing his bionic arm. The whirl of gears filled the space between them. "You might be a worthy challenge, but one easily defeated. The stench of your primitivity is arousing. Let us fight and see who wins, eh?"

Geres cracked his knuckles. "I welcome the opportunity, but I have been given my orders."

"Ah, a pet I see. Very well. Stay on your leash, barbarian, lest your masters turn their wretched gaze upon you." Kale found in Geres Auk the lone opportunity to test his martial prowess. No opponent to date had proved worthy of his personal interventions. Geres' refusal writhed him in frustration even as countless foes lay dead beneath the heels of his armies. The insult wounded him too.

Geres rose and crossed the distance between them. His breath steamed on Kale's face, so close the general spied ragged strips of chewed meat wedged in his teeth. "I have no master, unlike you, soldier boy. Take off your rank and meet me fist to fist. It's been too long since I last pummeled my enemy. I shall kill you and wear your face around my neck like a trophy."

The absurdity of the image aside, Mobus Kale wanted nothing more than to acquiesce. One factor held him in check. The lone mitigating response to any act of violence perpetrated upon his supposed allies. Stepping back, he measured his next words. "There is no need for this tone among us today, barbarian. We are on the same side, bound to destroy our enemies together." He paused. Teeth bared. "But make no mistake. Once the moment arises where I am no longer obligated to perform at the whims of others, I shall take great delight in removing your stain from existence. Until that day we must remain allies."

Uncertainty crept into his gaze, for Geres Auk had been fooled by fancy words before. His time with Baron Scura and the now defunct Presha Von rendered him distrusting of all but the power of Amongeratix. He jabbed a finger in Kale's chest armor. "Make no mistake, I will kill you."

"I look forward to it."

The door swished open and out stepped the Crimson Sister with the Inquisitor General at her side. They paused, staring at the two men with undisguised curiosity. One found opportunity. The other weakness. Neither were pleased.

"Come Geres Auk, there is work to do," Sister Evangeline hissed and drifted off.

Grinning like the savage he was, the barbarian kept his gaze upon Mobus Kale until turning the corner.

"Something I should know about, General?" Nye asked with arched eyebrow.

"Nothing that won't sort itself out."

"Good. We have much to discuss."

Kale followed him into the office without further comment.

Main space route to planet Occanum.

The ship shuddered as another salvo of low powered lasers struck aft. Chunks of fuselage broke away, burning up in the harsh reality of space. Swearing, Akin Brohl brought his ship into a spin, desperate to avoid being blasted into debris. Warning lights and alarms screamed throughout the cabin. Fearful of losing air pressure, the god hunter came out of the spin and dove down. Far ahead, there in the void, loomed his destination. One he might not make. Whoever piloted the assaulting craft was both cunning and ruthless. He knew all it took was one well placed shot and his long life would end.

His assailant had yet to hail: to proclaim their identity would at least offer a moment's respite. Unused to being on the receiving end of withering punishment, it dawned on Akin he was being toyed with. His foe, whoever that may be, was better armed and had enough military prowess to ensure the last of the Blood Witch's experiments joined his fallen brothers. He wondered what the cold embrace of eternity felt like—then his ship was struck again.

Fresh alarms wailed. He was losing power. The main engine blinked red on the control panel. Reaching Occanum seemed impossible, forcing him to make the one concession he had never done. Drawing a calming breath, Akin Brohl opened a channel between ships; static replied.

"Hostile vessel, cease and desist your aggression. I am losing power. Stand down."

"I am all too familiar with your tricks, god hunter." The snarl reverberated throughout the cockpit.

Akin tensed. He knew that voice, but it was impossible. Weren't they all gone? "Grand Mistress?"

"Akin Brohl, you have served my Order for many centuries. The time for your final assignment is at last at hand."

He paused, drumming his fingers on the control panel. "I am doing so. My hunt for the final three is in motion. All will be taken care of soon."

"There is a new purpose you must undertake," Ruma said, her voice measured, clipped. "The time to set aside the past is here. I need you to turn your focus elsewhere."

"You created us for singular purpose, did you not? Why the change now? When I am the last?"

"Can your craft make it to Occanum?"

Akin checked the control panel. It would be close, but what choice was there? "Well enough."

"Good. Transmitting coordinates now. There is one who wishes to meet with you in person."

The transmission dropped, leaving the god hunter wondering what he was about to get himself into and whether he could get back out if it went south in a hurry.

TWENTY

3215 A.G. (After Gods) Erdef City, planet Romalle.

Lostan Fidiuos ran for his life. Since aligning with Damal, his life had devolved into a series of near-death experiences. The self-styled information broker lived with numerous regrets. Most failed to materialize while a scant handful returned to hound his steps. Providing City Board member Damal with information he subsequently used to undermine the rest of the board and, it appeared, assassinate a cardinal and senior detective, was the final nail in his coffin. Yet it was not the local authorities concerning him. No. His stalker was one of far deadlier purpose and nefarious intent.

Slipping through the narrow alley, Lostan grimaced as he scrapped his back against the rough stone. Gone were the luxuries of his position. The nice clothes. The expensive aircar. He had a fortune in secure accounts scattered through planetary and interplanetary banks but knew none of it would free him of his predicament. Hurrying, he gained the end of the alley. Pressing against the wall, he stuck his head out just enough to view both sides of the street.

Darkness was marred by the dull orange flicker of streetlights, this part of Erdef City was sparsely populated. It was the sort of neighborhood people went to conduct business they didn't want known. City patrols seldom ventured into the tight, winding corridors of tenement houses and abandoned warehouses. Normally it was the perfect element. One Lostan knew like the back of his hand. This night he feared it wouldn't be enough. Not against her.

She became the bane of his existence after the failed attempt on her life, and he had nothing to do with that. Lostan knew her well enough to never wish to cross her. Those who did often disappeared, or worse.

Lady Emmest DeMauve was a formidable opponent with shady interests few realized. Rumors circulated of a penchant for dabbling in the occult. Heresy by Conclave standards. While he placed no faith in rumor, Lostan knew better than to underestimate her. Yet here he was, a target—her target.

Part of the wall above his head burst apart, fragments of stone and mortar falling around him. The stench of superheated energy curled his nose hairs before he heard the shot. Ducking instinctively, Lostan sprinted across the street without looking.

And ran into the barrel of a snub nose blaster.

"Don't move if you know what's good for you," a male voice growled.

Unable to control the trembling, it was all Lostan could do to not wet himself. Never a brave man, he longed for a return to anonymity.

Lostan raised his hands over his head. The chase was over but there yet remained the possibility of salvaging his life. That all depended on the fickle mood of Lady DeMauve. He winced at the sound of lithe footsteps coming up behind.

"Lostan Fidiuos. I am most disappointed," she began.

"Lady DeMauve, I can assure you I—"

She leaned close enough that he felt her hot breath in his ear. "I can assure you I don't care."

He closed his eyes, waiting for the final blow. Instead, he caught the whisk of her trousers then the clip of her boots as she maneuvered in front of him. Eyes open, he took her in. Having only seen her once before, from a distance at her departed husband's funeral, Lostan marveled at her inherent beauty while struggling to reconcile the raptor-like nature of her demeanor. Beauty and lethality in unusual combination, she was every bit the threat he feared.

"An attempt was made on my life and that of my closest confidant," she stated, gaze never flickering. "Why? Who pulls your strings, broker? Give me a name."

His mouth closed as soon as he opened it. No promise of salvation? No threats on his life for the insult of his silence? He braced himself, replying, "Lady DeMauve, I had nothing to do with that! I brokered a deal with Board Member Damal to ensure he had the votes to keep Romalle out of the war and helping him assume control. There was no mention of assassinations, leastwise not against you or your house."

Her eyebrows went up despite the passive expression remaining in place. She'd known of Damal's duplicity and lust for power but hadn't suspected him of going so far as to rig the game.

Another visit was in order, this time in a clandestine manner. "Why should I believe you?"

Confusion crossed his features. "What benefit is there in my lying? I have no desire to wind up dead in the streets, a message for those who dare cross your path."

"Your life or death is no longer in your hands. The gods do not listen to your pleas. There is only me and I am not known for forgiveness."

His face paled. The prospect of death suddenly too real to ignore. "Please, Lady DeMauve, you must believe me. Damal wants power and did not confide any future plans in me. If he is the one responsible for attempting to murder you, I was not made privy to it. You must believe me."

"I am tired of people telling me what I must and mustn't." She waved him off. "Tell me what information you passed to the esteemed Damal and I may spare your life. Quickly. I have no time for dithering. My patience is a finite resource and I have little to spare for the likes of you, gutter snake."

Lostan Fidiuos told her everything … until he could no longer speak after his tongue was cut out.

"Where are we supposed to go? There is no place safe left in this city," Riles protested. Her diminutive size countered the severity of her stern gaze and folded arms.

"This is not a secure location," Gando told her, his voice calm, controlling. "We don't know what Hargan told his assailant, if anything, before he was shot. They might very well be coming for me next and then you."

Tolde listened to the exchange, weighing all angles before intervening. "Riles, you are the key to all of this. If you are caught or killed, we will never learn the truth of my brother's murder nor discover how deep this conspiracy reaches. Keeping you alive is paramount to this entire operation."

"You're placing a cruel burden on me."

"That happened the moment you stumbled upon the murder," he replied even as he wished there was another way, one not involving using her as bait. She reminded him of himself at that age. Headstrong and unsure where she stood in the grand scheme. Admiring her temerity, Tolde lamented her necessity. A long life stood before her, if she made it through the impending storm. He vowed, privately, to give her his best efforts.

"Hasn't she been through enough?" Nemineon asked, head in his hands on the worn couch across the room.

"Your question is irrelevant. Our enemy does not care for her hardships endured. They know she exists and will stop at nothing to eliminate her before she can divulge what they assume she knows," Sister Alessandra said. "Want matters little in games of power. You would do well to remember this as we progress, lest it becomes your neck in the noose."

Stifling a wail, Nemineon fell silent.

"The Blood Witch is right," Gando said quickly to quash any remaining doubt. "Riles, we can protect you, but not from this location. It is too exposed with too many avenues for our foes to assault."

"Where are we supposed to go, Inquisitor? Nowhere in this city is safe for us," she protested.

"I don't know," he admitted.

Nemineon lifted his head. His eyes were streaked red. "What about the tribes? We were on our way there when you captured us."

"Rescued," Ragan countered. Riles' tight smile his way made him swallow the sudden lump in his throat.

"We can argue semantics once we are safe." Tolde frowned. "Gando, what did you have in mind?"

Scratching the stubble on his chin, Romalle's Inquisitor thought for a moment. "I really don't know. I might have suggested the law enforcement center but with Hargan's assault…" He let the thought fade, the wound still too fresh. They didn't know if Hargan was going to survive. His wounds were severe, and he was now under full guard in the medical facility.

A warning chime sounded. The outer perimeter had been tripped. Hands reached for weapons.

Ragan hurried Riles into the relative cover of Gando's bedroom. His look was pinched with displeasure as he tried to reconcile his growing interest in her. Nemineon followed behind, a constant reminder of how slim Ragan's chances were.

Flanking the door, the Inquisitors readied for an assault. Tolde and Luma formed two points on the same side, producing what would be a withering crossfire deadly to any seeking entrance through the front door. Gando waited on the far side, completing the triangle. Only Alessandra remained in the open. Her magic abilities protected her from mundane human weapons.

Tolde clicked his safety off and waited.

A second chime sounded, quickly followed by the singsong voice of Emmest DeMauve. "Inquisitor Gando, let me in. I must speak with you. It is a matter of utmost urgency."

Disbelief rippled through the defenders before Gando came to his senses and allowed her to enter.

Damal walked through the government building with a perpetual snarl. So close to accomplishing his goal, his efforts were being dealt with an endless string of setbacks. Murders, fires, Hargan in the hospital and doubtful to recover, and now whispers of Lostan Fidiuos wandering like a tongueless vagabond. He'd been taken to the sanitarium for observation while medical officials debated the severity of his case. Damal found little issue with the information broker remaining locked away, for his own good of course. That the man was missing his tongue went far in calming Damal's fears, yet he'd never learn the truth over whether Lostan spoke his secrets.

With the walls closing in, Damal decided the time had come to force the issue and resolve Romalle's fate for good. Opposition mounted against dragging the planet into the war. The recent rash of murders left the population shook. Once filled streets now lay empty. He couldn't blame them. The thought of being gunned down, or worse, without warning drove a wedge of terror into his heart. Losing control of the situation, Damal's best chance for convincing at least one other board member was now.

He also needed to discover who was responsible for Hargan's shooting before fingers pointed his way. The prospect of ending up like Lostan chilled him, but without knowing who was responsible for cutting the man's tongue out Damal had no avenue to pursue. Men like the information broker made a career of building powerful enemies and keeping secrets. Secrets that might damn Damal if he wasn't careful. His decades on the board left him with a developed, robust network he could now turn to. Competent operatives in every level of government and corporations. An idea sparked.

Soon Damal sank into his office chair and withdrew the datapad from a secret compartment under the main desk drawer. Waiting for it to power up, he spun the chair around and stared out the window at the darkening sky. Blowing out the breath he hadn't realized he'd been holding, Damal rubbed his aching temple. Too much. It was all too much. He tensed at the sound of his door hissing open.

"Damal, is this a bad time?"

He winced and swiveled the chair around, his face a mask of pleasantry. "Eiters. Not at all. What is on your mind today?"

She leaned against the doorframe, one hand behind her back. "It has come to my attention you haven't been yourself lately. Not that I blame you. So much is happening in the city it is difficult to focus on one trouble spot. We must be overly cautious these days. Wouldn't want to end up like poor Hargan."

"He did his job," Damal replied. "Has there been any update on his condition?"

She shook her head. "No. He is a most resilient man but that is not enough to stop an assassin's blaster. Kasop is scared witless, though he won't admit it. Our esteemed colleague is convinced we are next."

"Not wholly inaccurate. Too many prominent figures are either dead or in hiding. This vote on Romalle's future holds us all in chains," Damal said. Frowning, he scratched the corner of his mouth. "Perhaps we should take precautions."

She waved him off. "We've endured storms before, Damal. Kasop is paranoid. Nothing more. Of course, there is a degree of accuracy in his judgment. If Hargan hadn't been shot, we could have the entire force on the streets hunting down the assassins responsible. The population won't stand for inaction much longer."

"Riots in the streets," he mused.

"What's that?"

"Eh? I said riots in the streets. What do you propose we do? I doubt Kasop is willing to listen to reason given the current circumstance."

Eiters broke into a grin and brought her concealed hand forward. A small bottle of golden-brown liquor jostled. "There are times a stiff drink solves matters when deep thought can't."

"Drinking on the job? That's not like you."

Her shrug matched the wildness in her eyes. "No better time to escape my comfort zone than at the end of the world. Do you have glasses?"

Suspicious, he gestured her in and produced a pair of crystal glasses. "I am always prepared. Come, sit. Be my guest as we discuss the future of our glorious world and the city board."

Grinning, she accepted the invitation and poured.

Damal brought the glass to his lips, middle finger tapping the rim before asking, "What do you have in mind, Eiters? We are not close confidents, nor do I recall ever sharing pleasantries outside of official functions."

"Can we not bond through harsh times?" She smiled demurely. "We are contemporaries, Damal. It is our job to understand each other and work for the greater good. Naturally we have personal agendas that might or might not conflict."

"Naturally."

"I am offering a peace between us until this matter of assassins and referendums is settled." She hefted her glass. "This is hundred-year-old brandy from the Phidis System. Very rare. Very expensive."

"To your health."

Eiters tipped her head and watched as the brandy slid past Damal's lips, tracking the bump in his throat as he swallowed. Once he finished his drink, she set hers down and rose, smoothing the wrinkles from her dress.

"What is the meaning of this? Were I a lesser man I would take insult," he fumed upon seeing her glass untouched.

She offered a sweet smile caught between sympathy and regret. "Oh, Damal. You were always far too trusting. Know that what I did was for the best. Romalle must move forward and you, dear friend, have been hindering me for far too many years." She headed for the door. "Goodbye, Damal."

He opened his mouth, ready to snap but no words came. His throat constricted. Sharp pain stabbed through his abdomen. Spittle foamed in the corners of his mouth. Eiters watched from the doorway until she could bear no more and left him.

Another problem had been solved but a new one arose. With Damal removed Eiters needed to figure out how to pin the assassinations she consigned on him before eyes started searching through the shadows for the true culprit.

Satisfied the others were secure, Gando led Tolde and Luma to the hospital, careful to remain in uniform lest their enemies spy weakness. The Inquisitors strode with righteous authority, bound and oathed to the Conclave and all the once austere body stood for.

Tensions were rising across the city. Small riots broke out in response to the recent murders. Fear gripped the population despite the government's best efforts. As a result, many areas went unattended. Trash blew down wind swept streets. The stench of refuse grew stronger in the midday heat.

Tolde frowned. He failed to understand the base emotions of the masses. Why would any civilization be so willing to devour itself at the first sign of trouble? Did the threat of war promise such terror in their feeble hearts?

"Are you certain leaving them with this DeMauve is the best course of action?" Luma asked, jarring him.

Gando huffed. "If you knew a fraction of the tales surrounding that woman you wouldn't ask. I am confident no harm will befall them."

"Even after an assassination attempt in her home?" Luma pressed.

"More so now—she has been awakened. I pity whoever is foolish enough to attempt a second attempt on her life."

Tolde repressed a shudder. The nature of his career kept him running in circles with killers and murderers. Emmest DeMauve might have been the worst. She presented a noble image on the surface, but a darkness lingered just out of touch. Curiosity gained the better of him. "Who is she?"

"A person one does not question, or willingly mess with," Gando answered. "I have been stationed here for many years and have yet run across another as cunning or manipulative as that one. She is a waiting viper. A fearsome enemy but also a staunch ally depending on which side of ire you land. We are fortunate. Her eye is fixed on other targets."

"For the moment," Luma muttered.

They entered the hospital moments later. A pair of uniformed officers stepped aside upon seeing their Inquisitor uniforms. Gando led them to the information desk where they were given a police escort down the hall to Hargan's room. A second pair of guards flanked the door, prompting Tolde to question if they were protecting the stricken detective or ensuring he did not wake up.

Once inside, they found Hargan swaddled beneath heavy blankets. Tubes and hoses attached to machines were inserted in his nose and mouth. A steady hum of machinery, accompanied by the rise and fall of an artificial breathing apparatus told them he was alive. The room was dim, heavy curtains drawn closed. A sterile smell assaulted them.

"He's still alive," Gando said in relief.

"As it is," Tolde said and took the empty chair at his bedside.

Gando picked up the datapad clipped to the footboard and scanned through the documents. A twinge of sadness struck, clipping his voice. "He was shot three times at close proximity. Somehow the killer missed his vital organs, though narrowly."

"Good fortune shines upon your friend," Tolde said. "I'm assuming all digital recordings in his office and hallways were scrubbed clean?"

"And we don't have the authority to investigate," Gando agreed.

Luma scowled. "Doesn't the Inquisition stand above local law enforcement?"

"It does, but this is not a matter of heresy," Gando reminded. "Our mandate is to root out heresy before it contaminates the population, not investigate personal matters. Even for friends."

"There must be some channel we can work through," Tolde insisted. "The Inquisition is fragmented. Separate factions are growing within. This civil war tears the fabric of our mandate apart."

"Giving us the wiggle room to slip through the cracks," Luma concluded. "Gando, can you get us audiences with the city board?"

"To what end?"

Tolde wiped a palm on his trousers. “We must assume whoever did this is part of the greater conspiracy. They knew Hargan was getting closer to discovering my brother’s killer and struck.”

“The question remains, who is responsible and why,” Gando replied.

“I think it’s safe to assume the culprits are working to pull Romalle into the war,” Tolde said. “Who on the board has a vested interest in the matter?”

“All of them from what I’ve seen,” Gando said. “They are each greedy in their own regard. Damal wants the world and remains frustrated while the others thwart him. Eiters is sly, but ambitious. She has quietly amassed a fortune through second party munitions contracts with the Prekhauten Guard. Kasop, he is a different animal. I’ve yet to determine his motivations, though I consider him the weakest of the three. He plays to the whims of his constituency.”

“Marking him the consummate politician.” Luma frowned, pushing the lock of curled hair from her face. “Men like that are dangerous.”

“They are all dangerous.”

“Can we arrest them quietly on trumped up charges of suspicion of heresy?”

Gando shook his head. “Not if we want to escape this mess alive. There is no way of determining where the loyalties of the law enforcement and local Guard contingent lie. We could be slaughtered.”

“There is a chance Hargan,” Tolde gestured to the prone man with his chin, “knows who is behind this. We cannot afford to let him die.”

“That might be out of our hands,” Gando said. “He was shot in his office, making the possibility of one of his subordinates the culprit exceedingly high.”

“And they protect him,” Luma said.

“Leave that to me,” Tolde offered. “I will ask Sister Alessandra if she can protect this room with magic. Keeping Hargan alive is paramount to our future.”

“All right, what’s our play?” Luma asked. She pulled her gaze away from Hargan’s unnaturally pale, almost sickly flesh.

“Misdirection. I go to the board with claims of suspicion of heresy in Hargan. That should give me access to his office and allow us to squeeze the board members,” Gando replied. “We do this right and combining the knowledge Lady DeMauve provided about the information broker, we can crack this case open and put an end to it once and for all."

Tolde silently reevaluated his feelings toward Gando. Until arriving on planet he had all but forgotten the man, then old rivalries flared the moment they spied one another. Seldom one to hold grudges, Tolde chose to bite his tongue instead and was glad he had. Gando proved a stalwart ally as conspiracies began unraveling. Admitting to being wrong never sat well with him.

"If the enemy has turned the local Guard contingent, we may be in for more than we can handle," Gando commented after a brief silence.

"We have an advantage they won't expect," Luma said. Her face became a dour mask. "We have a Blood Witch."

The rush of footsteps in the hall drew their attention. Hands went to weapons as the three prepared for battle. They caught hushed tones laced with panic then the sounds slowed in passing. Curious, Ganda opened the door, scanning the hall in time to catch a pair of orderlies turning the corner.

"What's going on?" he asked the guards on duty.

"It's council member Damal. He's been assassinated."

Behemoth, approaching the Vau system.

The mechanical hiss and hum of countless ancient machines keeping the monstrous warship operating droned without end. It was a callous sound. Numbing. Incessant. Countless souls had been driven mad throughout the centuries, succumbing to the fervor and sacrificing themselves deep within. The machines ground on. The victims rose. Ghosts chained to the ship prowled the lower decks.

Presha Von refused to venture further than her meager living quarters. The ship scared her on levels she failed to understand. She walked as if a dagger pressed against her throat. The promise of a violent demise quickening her step from the moment she stepped out of her cabin to when the doors sealed her in. No stranger to the arcane, Presha knew better than to mess with those eldritch powers binding the universe … until Amongeratix.

The whisk of her slippers striding on faltered confidence was lost under the ship's drone. Her robes prevented the chill of space travel from burrowing into her bones. Presha knew time had become her opponent. The one mitigating factor threatening to consign her soul to the depths of *Behemoth* for all eternity.

She rounded the last corner, heading for Paradise Tear's cell. To her surprise, there were no guards. No hidden threats waiting in the shadows for signs of treason. Hubris she once enjoyed, but no more. Amongeratix failed to consider any being on his ship capable of betraying him and, even if they should, there was nowhere to escape to. This made Presha's task all the harder.

Paradise Tear raised her head at the sound of the door opening. Her once lustrous golden hair now greasy and plastered to her sweat soaked flesh. Red-streaked eyes stared at the lithe figure returning for another visit. She'd been there on Kharsis at the end and knew Presha Von for the villain she was, yet time conspired to turn enemies to allies.

"It pleases me to see you," Paradise croaked. Cracked lips accented her parched throat.

"You look terrible."

The comment sparked a laugh. "The cruelty of my captor knows no bounds. It is a gift of his uncle, for never a more wicked man has ever existed. Is all prepared?"

Presha took a seat, wringing her hands. The tiny hairs on the backs of each stood on end, accompanied by the nervous tapping of her foot. "I believe so. My shuttle has not been touched since I docked. Amongeratix doesn't have the time for people like me it seems."

"He never has," Paradise replied. "Arrogance is his trademark."

"My people call that believing your own bullshit," Presha said. "I've seen others like him, though none so violent in their ambitions."

Sadness crept into Paradise's eyes. "None like him have existed since the creation of my people."

"How does one create a god?"

"We are no gods. Older, yes. Immortal, perhaps. But gods? No. There are none who would claim that title. Humanity was led to believe this to provide purpose through their struggles after earning their freedom. It is no easy thing starting a civilization from scratch." She shook her head. "No, Presha Von, the gods you were raised to believe in were little more than hated filled beings who had forgotten their purpose."

"You-you said you were created. By what?"

"That is a difficult tale. One you might not understand."

"Try me."

Paradise licked her lips. "The first generation of my kind were born from dying races spread across the stars. Each was the sole survivor of their tribe who endured a series of trials forging them into what they would one day become. None knew this at the time. Only that they were compelled to keep going."

"What power in the universe is capable of destroying a society in one breath and giving eternal life in the next?"

"It has no name. It is primordial. We long suspected it was the first sentient being in the universe. A vast and misunderstood entity at the center of everything. Many theories arose from scholars and skeptics, but none were ever confirmed. My uncle and his fellow rulers captured the entity after a long and twisted hunt. They lied and coerced it into a cage at the heart of what you know as Occanum.

"There they made the seat of their empire and my kind flourished. We spread across the stars, building a society on a hundred worlds. Those races we encountered we brought into the fold, but good intentions seldom survive the lust for power. One by one the lesser races were devolved into slavery, many going extinct as my uncle and his ilk consolidated their power. When our civil war began, humanity was at last set free."

Presha's throat went dry. Prolonged exposure to Amongeratix, and now Paradise Tear, altered all she once thought she knew. The prospect of unlimited power still active on a dead world capable of rendering all life extinct filled her with dread. "What happened to this power?"

"It is dormant. The final battle of our civil war happened on Occanum, as you may know. There what remained of our armies battled to the last, even as Tannus, Sorrow, and I hurried to save as many of our kind as possible before the end. The primordial power is trapped in the heart of that dead world."

Presha stiffened. Her eyes widened in terror. "Paradise, what would happen if Amongeratix discovers this and awakens the power?"

"He'll slaughter everything and start over."

The admission echoed softly off the walls before settling on the fringes of Presha's soul. She once dreamed of taking it all, but her story took a twisted course leaving her little more than a defeated shell of failed potential. She felt cornered. Trapped like a wild animal knowing it was doomed. Yet when she looked upon Paradise Tear she saw the tiniest sliver of hope. A way out of a losing situation. "We are almost at Vau Prime. He will move on the Inquisitor General and usurp control of the universe. With the planet and Conclave under his thumb there will be nothing capable of stopping him from returning to Occanum."

"Hope is not lost. There are powers at work against Amongeratix. Once capable of thwarting him," Paradise reassured. "Get me back to Tannus and we change alter the course of the future. I swear this, Presha Von."

"Redemption as promised," Presha whispered.

"Redemption as promised."

Ensuring the door was secured, Presha rose and began unlocking Paradise's restraints. The only chance of escaping *Behemoth* was by fleeing before they reached the protective Guard fleet surrounding Vau Prime. She estimated mere days before that happened.

TWENTY-ONE

3215 A.G. (After Gods), Capital City, planet Dalafar.

It took every ounce of willpower not to pull the trigger. To eliminate the threat before it became a problem. Fies learned early on to not wait for his mind to reconcile with his gut. Moving from one firefight to the next honed his instincts. He liked being alive and wanted to keep it that way until he was old and grey. The man before him with eyes so wide they threatened to burst and a gun to his head stood between him and that dream.

"Fies, what are you doing?"

"This can go one of two ways, Captain. Either I kill you now and be done with it or you let us go, with the governess, and pretend you never saw me."

"Neither sound amenable," Donab replied. "You are committing treason. Put down your weapons and stand down. This is your only chance. I am not a forgiving man."

Tempest slid beside Fies and glared. "Captain, I know you to be honorable. You and I both know the governess is only here because of that imp Inquisitor."

His gaze flickered between Tempest and the soldiers flanking her. "Imp or not, I do not have the authority to order the Inquisition around."

"Didn't stop you from arresting her."

Donab made a face. "You are?"

"None of your business," Quint said with a scowl.

Moscasco threw her hands up. "Enough of this empty male posturing. Captain Donab has done me the courtesy of keeping me from being taken by the Inquisition. If not for his interference I would already be enroute to Vau Prime and whatever fate that vile Alain Nye has in mind. Tempest, I appreciate your concern and assistance, but I am quite safe where I am."

"Can you lower your weapon now, Fies?" Donab asked.

"I shouldn't. This isn't adding up."

The prospect of killing a man he once respected and having the entirety of the Guard station hemming him in clashed with his mission directives. Donab was a liability. One he could ill afford to escape. The matter required delicacy, which wasn't about to happen with a pair of hostiles waving weapons around.

Giving Quint a clipped nod, Fies holstered his sidearm.

"There, you see, we can all be reasonable," Moscasco said. "Captain, as much as I appreciate you keeping me from harm's way, I must question how much longer we can maintain the charade. These people are here at my request. It has become untenable for me to remain on Dalafar. These gentlemen are escorting me to safety. If that is all right with you."

"You place me in a dangerous position, Adris." Donab scowled.

"No more so than I," she replied. "Donab, I like you. We've enjoyed a quality working relationship I have not duplicated with any other Conclave representative since assuming my position. Don't spoil that by shipping me off to an Inquisition prison."

Folding his arms, he leaned back against the nearest wall. "Even if I did allow you an escape, what's my out? Alpof may be a prick but he's still an Inquisitor. I don't imagine being afforded the luxury of feigned ignorance after your departure. He's already demanding your head and sending back to Vau for official orders for your arrest. Once that happens, I won't have the authority to keep you."

"All the more reason to let her go," Tempest insisted.

"Tempest, my hands are tied."

"Because you let them be. Captain, what happens when word spreads you allowed their most beloved governess to become a prisoner of the Inquisition, accused of heresy or worse? The planet already stands on the edge of a knife. A subtle push in either direction sets the pendulum swinging, thus ensuring our plunge into chaos and violence. Do you want to be the man responsible for bringing the war to Dalafar?"

"No, but I also don't want to be in an interrogation cell beside the governess either." Grunting at the impossibility of his situation, Donab focused on Fies. "What are you doing here? Last I heard you were a hero for your actions on Crimeat."

"A lot has changed since then," Fies told him. "We don't have time to rehash all that's occurred since the war began. Just know I am trying to do the right thing here."

"By absconding with the governess to foment a wider spread among the planets?"

"By trying to save as many lives as possible before it all crashes down." Fies sighed. "Donab, how long have you been assigned to Dalafar?"

"You mean have I been in combat in the past three years," Donab countered. Emotion, regret perhaps, flashed through his eyes. "The answer is no. I've been here for almost five years. There has been no combat in this sector, and I would like to keep it that way for as long as possible."

"We have. We've been at the front of this war from the beginning. I've lost friends, slain foes, and watched entire planets die." The quiet admission was laden with guilt. "But the winds have shifted. We are building a sizeable force capable of defeating the Inquisitor General and restoring order to the universe. The governess is one of the missing pieces we need to advance. Enough life has been lost already, don't enable the enemy by allowing for more."

Donab regarded his former subordinate. Headstrong but likeable, Fies represented the best of them. Once, long ago, he envisioned grooming the young soldier to take his place. It was by mere chance Donab suffered an injury pulling him from the line mere weeks before the unit was assigned to Inquisitor Breed on Crimeat. What followed devolved into years of regret. For not being with his people. For missing his opportunity to prove his worth on the field of battle. For everything. Instead of a proven combat leader with invaluable experience, Donab was reduced to an administrator on a world yet to feel the sting of the spreading war.

"I always liked you, Fies," he said. "I assume, by the way this grizzled veteran defers to you that you have risen through the ranks?"

"I've been promoted a few times. Admiral Falchi saw fit to promote me to lieutenant," Fies confirmed. "I preferred being on the line. Squad or platoon sergeant suited me just fine."

"As did the lack of total responsibility, I'm sure." Donab offered a thin smile. "Any of the old crew still around?"

"Most of them. We've lost here and there."

"What about that crazy one. The one with the tattoos on her head?"

Quint snorted before falling silent.

"Annalilly. Yeah, she's still there. A platoon sergeant now," Fies answered before scowling. "You're deflecting, Donab. I don't want to kill you, but I will if you don't give me a choice."

"Good thing for you I don't want to die today," Donab said. "How's this going to work?"

Silence filled the room. Consideration never once entering their thoughts as Fies and his team prepared for extraction. Now with Donab wrenching their plans, they were cast in an unenviable position.

"My dear, Donab, it would kind of you to escort these gentlemen to their ship, with me in tow of course." Moscasco's light tone brightened the mood. "Let us escape and no one needs to be the wiser."

"Those are conflicting ideations, Adris. My people see me escorting you anywhere and I'm good as dead."

"Captain, we are in a desperate position," Tempest inserted. "One way or another, the governess is leaving Dalafar, tonight. You can help or be part of the problem."

"I still haven't heard a viable solution."

"Come with us," Fies blurted before realizing it. "You're a good leader and a better man. We can use you in the coming fight."

"What are you doing?" Quint hissed. "We can't trust him."

"Relax, Quint. I know what I'm doing." Fies cleared his throat. "Donab, I know you don't support what Nye is doing and if I told you what his next move is you might not believe it."

"My absence will be noted before long."

"What if I told you the Inquisitor General has allied with Amongeratix, who is enroute to Vau Prime as we speak?"

Donab shook his head. "Impossible. The Three are a myth."

"I wish that were so." Sadness edged Fies' voice. "I've been working with Tannus for almost three years now. He can stop his brother from destroying the universe, but not without our help." He stepped closer. "Come with us. Don't be part of Nye's twisted vision."

"The Conclave is already being dismantled," Moscasco added. "Those cardinals not aligned with Nye are being rounded up and executed. Others fall in line, spreading his brand of filth and torment. If left unchecked, Nye will burn it all to the ground, remaking it in his dark image. Be the better man, Donab. For your sake."

"I don't know if I can, not without abandoning my men," Donab admitted. "Adris, are you certain you can be an example for other planets?"

"Yes."

The single word awakened him. Donab stiffened, remembering old pride he'd assumed gone since his deployment to Dalafar. There was promise again, though perhaps not for himself. "What about the people of Dalafar? You risk exposing them to revenge after you leave."

"Some matters cannot be helped," she replied. "Without me here there is no need for the Inquisition to care. The people do as they're told. One or two may disappear, but I have every confidence this planet will remain as it is." She looked away. "I am leaving for them."

"Make up your mind, Donab. We don't have time for this," Fies urged. His hand falling back to his blaster.

Donab's gaze bounced between a woman he respected and a man he'd trained. "I—"

Junior Inquisitor Alpof fumed. A naturally vengeful man, he reveled in the freedoms allowed his station. Men and women, heretics and traitors, fell beneath his brand of ire. The Inquisition enjoyed a unique freedom in the universe, more so now that the Conclave was all but disbanded and the Prekhauten Guard wholly subservient to the Inquisitor General. Alpof longed for the day when he controlled entire sectors, not the backwater Dalafar whose sole contribution to the war effort was location along the major shipping lanes.

Trapped, forgotten, on the water planet and perpetually stinking of fish, or worse, Alpof sank inward until he became naught but a twisted reflection of forgotten promise. Hatred was his tool. A weapon against friend and foe alike. Inexhaustible and calculated.

Alone in his offices, the junior Inquisitor plotted against the one person on Dalafar thwarting his every move: Governess Adris Moscasco. Visions of torturing her, breaking the woman until nothing but a husk of emotionless flesh remained, inspired his perversity. Alpof grew up under the heavy blanket of rejection from every woman ever passing through his life, starting with his mother. The only kiss interesting him now was one of retribution through violence.

A storm raged across the ocean, trembling the floating city with each thunderstrike. Built upon massive support columns buried deep in the planet's mantle, each city withstood the battering elements, from freak storms to the push and pull of the tides. How any remained afloat was a mystery sparking little interest in Alpof. They could all sink into the ocean for all he cared. And good riddance. The pedestrian way of life on Dalafar failed to inspire greatness, or mediocrity, in his opinion.

Flinching as lightning struck the tower to his immediate front, Alpof' scowl darkened. Oh, how he hated this world and all upon it. A fire sparked upon the domed city roof, spreading through electrical circuits and conduits. Fire control units would soon be enroute, but for now the roof burned. The dance of flames reflecting in his eyes, Alpof reluctantly pulled away from the growing conflagration as he had other matters to attend.

His central frustration stemmed from Guard Captain Donab absconding with the governess mere days before Alpof intended on arresting her for heresy. The Conclave may be little more than a broken shell, but the Guard remained a powerful, separate entity. He couldn't override Donab anymore than the soldier could he. Locked in a stalemate, Alpof struggled finding legal recourse to free Moscasco from the Prekhauten Guard to then secure her for the Inquisition master torturers.

Alpof slipped into his utility blouse, careful to adjust the blue tinged rose on his lapel and stormed into the hall. His path was blocked by a pair of Inquisitors and a decrepit looking man unable to meet his gaze. Glancing at his wrist chrono, he cursed. "I don't have time for this."

"Sir, this man claims to have information," the female Inquisitor said.

"Everyone has information. Most of it is useless." Alpof stepped to the man, enjoying how he flinched.

Threadbare clothing and the stench of having not bathed in some time, the man wore an ill-favored look. He'd seen the type before. Skulking between shadows in search of an easy mark or an undeserved handout. These were the dregs of society. The people burdening the Conclave with their laziness and lack of productivity. Were it up to him, Alpof would have them all in uniform and dropping behind enemy lines on the nearest battle world.

Personal displeasure notwithstanding, Alpof gestured with his chin. "Make this fast."

"S'rry, Inquisitor, sir," the man mumbled. His fingers fidgeted, eyes dancing across the bland hallway. "But I seen the gov'ness. She was being taken out of the Guard station."

"The governess? Are you certain?"

"Saw what I saw."

His leather glove creaked as his hand curled into a fist. "Where was she being taken?"

The man shrugged. "Down t'ward the dock I imagine."

"We have a team searching for her now," the second Inquisitor said.

"That's not enough! I want all available forces deployed at once," Alpof roared. "That woman is not to reach any transport. Am I understood?"

Saluting, the Inquisitors hurried off.

Alpof blinked away the building rage before remembering the man before him. "Yes?"

"Was hoping to get paid."

A flash. The whoosh of air. The distorted grunt of pain. Falling, the informant struggled to catch his breath as Alpof snarled, "Get out of my sight before I have you arrested and dismembered in front of your family." He rushed after the Inquisitors—a traitor needed catching.

Government complex, Eter City, planet Mannus Prime.

The miniscule portion of his day allotted to private reflection already diminished, Torgast reread the names on the datapad, again, before setting it on the aged wooden desk and getting to his feet.

A few minutes later he found himself in Cardinal Virom's office waiting for the man to arrive. Word had come from Dalafar via a shaky network of spies and informants not wholly vetted—they needed to talk as Torgast's mistrust ran deep but he lacked choices.

Bright rays of golden sunlight filtered through the rows of ceiling high windows. The fractured heat felt good on his face. The last days of summer were dwindling, promising the chill of a long winter. Torgast looked across the low roofs of the city proper, spying the first hints of changing leaves in would otherwise be a peaceful time.

"Ah, Torgast. Good morning," Virom greeted coming into the room. The wild gleam in his eyes matched the hurried wave of his hands. "Come. Come. Sit. We have much to discuss," Virom gestured to the empty divan by the bay window overlooking the city. Far to the west sat the sprawling army base and hastily constructed landing pads.

Torgast couldn't help but smile as he sat. "Cardinal, I haven't had my caf yet. You are borderline psychotic at the moment."

"Eh?" His face pinched. "No breakfast? It's nearly lunch."

"Your point?"

Settled back into his chair, Virom clasped his hands and said, "I trust you have heard the news from Dalafar and are here to chat about them."

"Only rumors."

"Bah! Rumors have ways of becoming truth."

Crossing his legs, Torgast said, "They still have to get offworld and back into space. If what Fies reports is accurate, the local Inquisitor is worse than Cass or Dowan. I don't like their odds, Virom. Too much can go wrong."

"Trust in Jelin Quint to see them through. He's a good man."

"One of the best we have," Torgast agreed, "but he's not in charge and one man cannot affect the entirety of the mission."

The cardinal cleared his throat. "You really need to eat. Especially for what comes next. Garnering the votes will not be easy."

Torgast blew out a long breath sounding more like a sigh. "How many?"

"Seventeen. Most of them will remain silent while a handful, the usual suspects I dare say, will bicker and blow hot air."

"They defer to you. Have you had private meetings with any of them?"

"With all of them! I've talked and listened until my ears threatened to bleed."

"It's the enormity of the task. Virom, are you certain this is the proper course of action? Should we fail…"

"It won't matter," Virom concluded. "Vau Prime has grown corrupt beyond salvation. And with Amongeratix about to assume control we must plan for all contingencies. The surviving planets will need a new form of government to keep them safe. What we are attempting might well prove the tipping point in the war."

"While exposing us to every blow Nye wants to throw at us. We are outgunned and they now have one of the Three in their midst."

Virom's eyes lit up. "As do we, General. As do we."

Having never laid eyes on Tannus, or any of the Three, Torgast found difficulty in accepting the notion of immortal beings pitching in for the cause. Imaging titanic beings clashing over the fate of the universe felt foolish, childish. Torgast prided himself on being grounded, an implacable drive keeping both himself and his people alive through their darkest moments. "Until he materializes, I won't hold my breath. I prefer placing my faith in tangible beings."

Cocking his head, Virom stewed over his words before replying, "Perhaps I can quell your doubts. There is someone I want you to meet. He has been influential for our side from the first shot fired and, I believe, promises to be a powerful combat multiplier."

"Who is this mystery man?"

Chuckling, Virom pressed the intercom button on his desk. "Able, please send him in."

"At once, Cardinal."

"I wanted you two to meet before we become swallowed by the den of power-hungry politicians and professional bureaucrats."

Torgast's eyes narrowed but he remained silent as a slender man entered the office. A familiarity settled over the room, one he knew intimately as he took the measure of the man standing before him. Tall, light in frame yet honed, a haggard look clung to his eyes. Lines creased his face and hands. This was a man who had seen much, too much. A veteran. An asset. He stood.

"General Torgast, this is Matthias."

They clasped forearms in the manner of soldiers. "You're a military man," Torgast approved.

Matthias said, "Once, but no longer."

Virom waved off his words. "Matthias is a retired sergeant major and the very same squad leader who accompanied Inquisitor Breed on the early assignment to recapture Amongeratix. He has been at the front line of this war from the start."

"Thank you, Cardinal, but I must accept my current position." Matthias blushed. "General, I've heard good things about you and what you accomplished here."

"Something tells me you were on planet during the final campaign," Torgast said after overcoming his awe and returning to his seat. Matthias was a legend among the Guard. A true hero in a time of villains. Having him among the fledgling army would go far in boosting morale, and more.

Matthias took a seat in a nearby chair. "I did my part, yes. I would have departed but Cardinal Virom is a most insistent man."

"He is at that."

Virom shrugged. "What can I say? I'm a man used to getting his way."

"Bringing me to my next question, what are you hiding up that crimson sleeve?" Torgast asked.

"That, my dear general, will be shown at the proper moment."

"Uh huh. Very well." Torgast hummed. "Matthias, it is an honor to meet you. Thank you for sticking with us. Hopefully together we can end this war and start rebuilding."

"I'll see what I can do, but I'm just one man."

Virom's gaze flitted between them, a knowing twinkle in his eyes. "Nonsense. Matthias is more than a veteran presence. He is the link between us and Tannus."

Torgast's jaw set. Tannus. Another myth. "Will he help stop his brother?"

"He's working on it, along with Sorrow," Matthias replied, choosing to keep the word of Paradise Tear secret until he understood Torgast's motivations clearer.

"You present a dire situation, Matthias. One I have no desire to indulge in."

"Our desires no longer matter. This war may have been started by Alain Nye's greed, but it has been conducted at the behest of the Three for the past two years. I cannot speak on the future, but I will say events are in motion that will either damn or save the universe. We can win, but not without everyone working together."

Torgast puffed out his breath. "By selling our souls to the Three? Beings who have no place in our universe."

"General, I'm not here to try and convince you. Whatever our actions become, they do so without the regard of the Three. Just know we have powerful allies working in concert with our regular armies. It won't be easy, but we can win."

Sensing a turn in the conversation, Virom rose and headed for the door. "Gentlemen, I'm afraid our time is up. The restless herd is no doubt wondering why we are late. Let us not disappoint them further. We stand on the precipice of history. This will long be discussed as a seminal moment for humanity. I am eager to see which side of the discussion it falls on."

PGN *Revengence*, edge of Vau system.

"Prepare all direct fire weapons to repel fighters and smaller escort frigates. I want firing solutions plotted on the larger capital ships."

Echoes of the commands raged across the bridge as personnel hurried to comply. The fleet had emerged from space at the edge of the Vau system and was immediately detected by enemy forces. It took three days for the two fleets to meet.

It was time.

"Admiral, the fleet reports ready to engage. Awaiting your orders."

Unable to pull her gaze from the stars and growing orb that was Vau Prime, Khe-Zhehan wrung her hands. Out there among the stars waited a fleet of equal size. Mere pinpricks of darkened metals almost lost against the backdrop of space.

She slowed her breathing, an old trick learned during the crucible of her academy tests, but reality and training clashed within her.

"Launch the fighter screen and fire on their battleship. There's no point in waiting."

The *Revengence* rocked as a salvo of ship to ship torpedoes blasted from the port side. Three squadrons of single man fighters followed as flashes of light erupted like waves of fireworks on Celebration Day.

"All hands, brace for impact. Air defense, target and engage."

Warning lights flared, bathing the bridge in angry red. Khe-Zhehan watched as numerous explosions flared, quickly dissipating in the hard vacuum of space. Outer shields prevented the ship from sustaining major damage. She forced herself to stop grinding her teeth as real time imaging filled the main screens. Her patience was rewarded. Enemy air defense shot down most of the torpedoes, but a handful struck their targets. The battleship flared, breaking apart midships. A second flight of thirty-meter explosives slammed into the open wound, striking deep into the ship's heart. It took little imagination to hear the screams of crewers. She'd weep for their souls later.

"Admiral! Incoming ship signatures!" the First Officer shouted.

"Tactical, pull it up."

Tensing, she watched a score of Prekhauten ships emerge from the deep space lanes and commence firing—on her fleet. Stressed communications flowed between ships, presenting the illusion of panic. Smaller ships broke formation, desperate to avoid being killed without barring their fangs. Khe-Zhehan watched the intricate dance of metal beasts. Flights of fighters swept in between to counter enemy fighters.

The dogfight began in earnest.

"What other tricks do you have in store for me I wonder," she muttered.

Without knowing her counterpart, Khe-Zhehan reduced her strategy to guessing. Far from effective, she needed more information to form a grand strategy that would not only see them to victory but help retrieve Strannan's shattered forces before Nye sealed his grip on Vau Prime. The slightest hint of desperation crept in, gnawing at her confidence and weaving holes in her plans. "Captain, deploy battle group A."

"Aye, ma'am."

A frigate and escorting corvettes broke away from the rear of the battleline and flanked the new arrivals. The barrage of fire was fierce, even as enemy ships broke contact and attempted to reengage with the direct threat. She knew it was too late. In their eagerness to claim quick kills for Mobus Kale, the enemy ships wrote the epitaphs of their own demise.

Freshly promoted Rear Admiral Drean watched as his opponent's fleet drifted deeper into his trap. Never having commanded fleets in combat, Drean allowed overconfidence to guide his hand. The reserve strike force waiting just out of orbit struck like a fist—until it didn't. Drean watched in muted horror as his best tactic, one he'd used numerous times over the course of the war, faded to twisting wreckage and pointless deaths. Slamming his fist on the command chair, he trembled with rage.

Khe-Zhehan proved an honest opponent, one he longed to shame since she first denied his promotion to Captain several years earlier. That hatred simmered until finally being set loose on the woman herself. Yet for all his fervor, he lacked the experience.

"Bring all capital ships about and head directly for *Revengence*. I want no traces of that ship left," Drean bellowed.

The crew obeyed, though whether from terror or duty went unspoken. Drean cared not. Those failing to obey orders were shot or voided into space at his discretion. Taking example from the ruthless efficiency of Mobus Kale, Drean became a self-styled tyrant among his ships. That vitriol turned hatred saw him hunt down and destroy countless foes and led him to his own command. Revenge stinging, Drean hungered for the humbling of Khe-Zhehan until it clouded his judgment.

Racing toward the enemy fleet, he gripped the arm rests of his command chair until his fingers blanched and tiny cracks in the fabric formed. Ship to ship fire increased. Smaller, more agile craft managed to evade the heavy fire while the larger, more ponderous craft absorbed the punishment with metal groans. Plumes of oxygen flared through cracks into space. Bodies and debris followed. Ships died without fanfare on both sides.

Drean imagined Khe-Zhehan staring across the void at him. Her small eyes pinched with despair. So intent on his need for revenge, he failed to—

Khe-Zhehan sank back into her chair as her crew watched the enemy flagship burst apart under the combined assault of six frigates. With the heart of their fleet ripped out, surviving ships attempted to break and flee back to the protective ring of the remaining fleets heeding Mobus Kale's call.

"Captain, I want every ship destroyed or disabled," she barked. The shrill of her voice cut through tension's ebb and flow.

"Aye, ma'am," her First Mate responded. "All battle squadrons, proceed with hunter-killer operations. Break off and execute at will."

The battle for the edge of Vau space faded to small dogfights and desperate survival attempts. Soon the main travel routes to Vau Prime were open. At the end awaited the prize. Khe-Zhehan only had to navigate an impenetrable gauntlet of steel teeth and a million men and women eager to destroy her. She'd know the gambit desperate from the initial planning phases but there seemed little choice. Kale's armies were pinching the resistance to extinction. Every life she saved robbed the enemy of the one thing he wanted: total victory.

The tiny fleet regathered and raced toward its destiny.

TWENTY-TWO

3215 A.G. (After Gods), Great Library, planet Wexanos.

The majesty of the dawn went unparalleled. Having witnessed the spectacle on a score of planets, Sharlyn August found no comparison to the vermilion swathes of Wexanos as the distant sun crested the horizon. How any planet could remain so pristine after thousands of years of occupation, especially against the backdrop of the spreading war, left her with chills. Whatever else Tannus was, or claimed to be, he was the master of his domain and a fitting caretaker of the great library world. There was no denying his influence. The planet teemed with life in harmony and balance. She found it remarkable.

Much of the weight burdening her dissolved the moment she arrived and delivered the artifact to Tannus. His yellow robed librarians immediately took control of the object and scurried away to deep planetary catacombs few had access to. And good riddance. The object many dubbed a planet killer caused more trouble than it was worth. She'd lost too many lives hunting it down and escorting it to Tannus and feared the stains on her conscience might never be removed.

The air on Wexanos held healing properties, or so Fistel, the Chief Librarian, claimed when he first spoke to her. Who was she to deny brief moment to rest?

August tilted her head back, basking in the first warmth of the new day despite the troubles swirling through her mind. Much had been accomplished but there was more to do. She feared the war bordered on entering a dangerous stage. Whispers of Amongeratix arriving on Vau Prime all but sealed humanity's fate, for evil seldom rested. Little of that concerned her. What did concern her was that with her mission complete, she still hadn't received follow on orders, nor was there a rush to return to Mannus Prime and reenter the fleet. The simple truth was she, along with her crew, were tired.

"On a clear night you can see half the galaxy from the observatory."

Tensing, August turned to find Fistel standing nearby, hands clasped before him. She hadn't heard him approach. She looked away, saying, "It's funny. I spend my life among the stars, yet I seldom find time to appreciate the enormity, or grandeur."

"A human failing. We often overlook what we see, taking it for granted until it is too late."

She nodded sagely, closing her eyes. How much had she missed since the war began, or before? There was undeniable beauty among the stars if one chose to look. Forced into a constant string of engagements and pursuits, August and the crew of the *Solstice* grew calloused to their surroundings. "A shame. This world is beautiful. How has it remained so for so long?"

"We are meticulous with our security, Captain. There is no record of Wexanos in the Conclave databases, nor has there been reports or actionable intelligence suggesting this world exists. I'm sure you can understand why."

She did. Sadly. The Conclave was ever eager to hook their fingers into all it purveyed, absorbing cultures and unique identities into the grand collective. New worlds were discovered and quickly subsumed under the auspices of Conclave, often before the indigenous population understood what was happening.

August opened her eyes, searching skyward through the thin wisps of transparent clouds. "You know, I think I would like to see the night sky from here."

"I'll arrange for you to have the observatory tonight. Privately of course."

"Thank you."

"My pleasure," he replied with a smile. "But all good things come with a price, I'm afraid."

"Another human failing?"

"Beyond my control," he said. "Lord Tannus is expecting you in his private study."

Of course he is. Enjoying the final kiss of warmth on her face, August sighed. "Let's not keep him waiting."

"A wise decision," Fistel said. "Follow me please."

They hurried through the library. August once marveled at the majesty and serene beauty on display. This trip afforded little opportunity for it. She counted the footsteps echoing in her mind as the halls blurred by. She stood before Tannus before she knew it.

"Ah, Captain August. It is a pleasure being in your presence once again." Tannus beamed at her, his smile genuine. He remained seated, choosing to present a less intimidating figure than his twelve-foot frame suggested. His face was a blanket of scars and age lines. Immortality held many advantages, graceful aging not among them.

The slender starship captain took the proffered seat and drank from the crystal glass of water before replying, "I wish I could say the same, lo… How am I supposed to address you?"

The knowing look he gave her suggested he'd been through such before. "Tannus is fine. Though Fistel insists on addressing me as lord. I assure you I am far from noble and certainly no god. I am, above all else, just a man."

"Unlike any man I've encountered."

"Indeed. Larger, longer lived, but I bleed, succumb to emotions, and eat just as the men of your race," Tannus told her. "Pleasantries aside, I have summoned you for purpose."

Her face pinched. "I am supposed to return to Mannus Prime after delivering your artefact and ensuring it is secure."

"An unenviable task, no doubt." His head bobbed. "Thank you for bringing me the item. Had it remained loose our foes would reap a terrible toll on the universe. Now, my brother cannot use it. Your losses suffered on your quest are well known to me and I lament each soul committed to the void. War is the cruelest master of all."

"Thank you, Tannus. We are professionals, dedicated to serving the greater good. Death is a constant companion in our line of work, though it seldom serves to dwell on it."

"How true." Sadness choked his voice. Countless souls were lost throughout the course of the last three-thousand-year war and he held himself accountable for each of them.

"I'm sorry," she blurted upon witnessing the pain in his eyes.

Tannus waved her off. "No worries, we all have burdens to bear. The reason I called you here is one of utmost secrecy, and importance. I have been in contact with Admiral Falchi, and he has agreed to lend me your services for a special mission."

"I'm not following." August tensed, unable to comprehend how the admiral so willingly dispensed with one of his most experienced crews when they were needed most. The rational part of her knew if Falchi authorized the move it was necessary, but the realistic part contained behind her rank screamed at the injustice of being assigned to an elder being long worshipped as a god.

"You and your crew will transfer to my ship and escort me to an important meeting that may well decide the fate of the universe," he explained. The stern delivery left no room for doubt, or an opportunity to back out.

"What of the *Solstice*?"

"Your ship is formidable, but I am afraid my size will not make for comfortable passage." He smiled. "That and the planet we seek is not in your star charts."

"I see … My crew will need time to adapt to new systems. How soon are you looking to depart?"

"Immediately."

She'd grown accustomed to military urgency, even when such was unrequired, but there was something in his tone setting her on edge. August knew of a company of Guards who were in Tannus' employ, stricken from the rolls and now acting independently. Veterans all, they were rumored to have been the first unit to uncover the heresy on Crimeat. Was this to be her fate as well?

"Tannus, you ask the impossible. How am I supposed to acclimate my people to your ship with no time?"

"They will manage. I've taken many of your operating systems and integrated them into my ship's design. Weapons, tactical, communications, and navigation are all compatible with standard Prekhauten Navy ships of the line."

She pursed her lips, choosing her next words carefully. "I don't suppose we have much of a choice in this?"

"In short, no. The mission you are about to embark upon is as important as the one you just concluded," Tannus said. "Sharlyn, we stand upon the precipice of success or demise. I will do all within my power to stop my brother from laying low the universe. That includes confiscating you and your crew." He paused, seeing her tense. "Though I would much rather have your willingness at my side. I have long learned the value humanity brings and, though our lifespans are incomparable, appreciate the efforts you and your people continue delivering."

"That is small comfort, all things considered."

"It is all I have to give. Now, are you with me or not?"

She opened her hands, head slightly lowered. "Doesn't seem like I have much of a choice. Permission to inform my crew?"

"You need no permission from me. Full operational authority aboard the ship lies in your hands. Consider me a passenger."

She offered a clip nod and rose. "Very well. I shall begin transferring my crew and supplies to your ship at once. We will depart on schedule."

"Is he out of his fucking mind?" First Mate Odir raised his voice upon hearing the news.

Several crewers nearby paused, unsure how to react to their normally placid first officer threatened to launch into a tirade. Others stayed busy moving equipment and gear from the *Solstice* to the massive *Brightstar*, an ancient and venerable ship that took to the stars long before any of them were born.

August concealed her grin. "Orders are orders. It seems we have become the admiral's go to crew for unenviable missions."

"There's an understatement. I don't suppose there's any way around this?"

"None. Tannus assured me the risk is negligible."

Odir snorted. "That's not reassuring, Captain."

"It wasn't meant to be. Look, I don't want to do this anymore than you, but we need to move. The sooner we depart the sooner we can return to Mannus Prime."

"I never imagined being on the front lines would be preferable to whatever this shadow concealed mission is." Odir closed his eyes and took a deep breath. "Did he say where we were going?"

"I didn't ask."

"This gets better and better." Odir groaned. "Very well, Captain. I'll have the ship primed and ready to depart with all haste. You wouldn't know if this is a combat op would you?"

Her sharp glare was his answer.

Alone for what he surmised would be the last time in an impossibly long existence, Tannus sank into the well-worn cushions of his favorite chair. Sunlight warmed his face, prompting him to tilt his head back and close his eyes. Quiet moments were few and far between. The longer this iteration of the war dragged on the more drained he felt. Regardless of whether his words provided the necessary catalyst for open war or not all those years ago, Tannus proved to be the lone factor capable of saving what little remained of his once proud society. The burden of guilt rested on his shoulders despite the wealth of common sense he held.

Events were barreling toward an inevitable conclusion. He felt it in his bones. How would it end though? Amongeratix certainly held the advantages of strength thanks to the capitulation of Alain Nye and his violent takeover of the Conclave and Prekhauten Guard. That deficit forced Tannus to consider alternative solutions. Ones he'd been loath to enact for far too long.

A chime disturbed his ruminations.

Slowly opening his eyes, Tannus voice activated the communication array. "Oracle. It has been too long since I last heard words of encouragement from you. Have the cosmic tides shifted at last?"

"Lord Tannus, ever have you placed your faith in me though I once begged you not to," she replied. "Much is changing. Almost too fast for me to keep up with."

"I have felt the same for a very long time. My soul is stretched thin. I fear I have not the strength to finish this."

Silence echoed back, as if mocking his singular moment of humanity. Tannus frowned, knowing Ruma Zzein selected her next words with focused intent.

"You are the backbone upon which all hope is built. Humanity is a fickle species. They need guidance. That higher authority to seek when times become dire. Were it not for the belief in gods and the promise of eternal salvation associated with such their fledgling empire would have collapsed long ago."

"How many know my name? Or believe me to be a tangible figure? I have been relegated to legend or lumped under the moniker of the Three. Any individualism, born through myth or reality, has been lost." He shook his head. "The times are changing, Ruma. My kind does not have long for this life—I ensured such when I placed those final survivors into stasis."

"Perhaps placing those chosen into stasis was not the correct decision," she countered.

Tannus' face darkened. "I have thought long on this. Those I rescued were the best of us. Thinkers and builders, more prone to listening to their hearts than picking up the sword. All save one. It was a dream that I might one day resurrect my people, stealing across the stars to find an uninhabited planet to rebuild society as it should have been. More the fool I."

"Blessing and bane. Your brother seeks to slaughter the last of your kind. Imagine if he sought to turn them to his cause instead. What would seven hundred of your people accomplish if they were set loose upon the universe with hatred in their hearts and Amongeratix's barbed whips at their backs?"

"The universe would burn."

"It already is. War spreads unchecked. Though we rally star systems and a ragged band of heroes to our cause we are hard pressed to stop your brother. As it stands now, he will reach Vau Prime, likely supplanting the rogue Inquisitor General and establishing his new reign."

"Which is why I must do what I am about to."

"You still seek then to enlist the god hunter to your cause?"

"What choice do I have? Vile as your creations were, they served their purpose and were good at what they did. Akin Brohl is the last chance I have to shed Amongeratix's blood on the hands of another."

"You have burdened yourself for too long over your brother's fate. You are not responsible for his hatreds."

"Am I not? He would not have been unleashed on the universe if not for the defiance I showed our father."

"He writhed in hatreds long before the first shots were fired," Ruma scolded. "Do not believe you were the problem. Amongeratix ever longed to be the first son. To earn your privileges and authority and supplant your father's will when the time came. It is time for you to rise above your shame and become the man your father wished you to be, Tannus. This will be the last war. I have foreseen it."

Silence settled over the room as each pondered the meaning of her words. Truth threatened to undermine what confidence remained.

"How does it end?" It was the same question his thoughts returned to time and again.

"The future is clouded. I cannot see victory or defeat. Fate, it seems, has no desire to reveal its hand."

The finality in her words settled like a cold chill. Immortality meant little in the face of the unknown. Perhaps he deserved to die. To be forgotten forever save for a random passage in a book cloistered away. He'd caused enough damage by stealing lives over the course of the long campaign against his brother to earn whatever fate lay in store. Tannus long accepted his place at the end of the road. Should death claim him that would be it.

"I am departing for Occanum within the hour," he informed her, shifting focus. "It is my intent to convert the god hunter to my cause. Should that fail, I will take *Brightstar* and meet *Behemoth* over Vau Prime myself."

"You will not be alone," she replied. "You have friends, Tannus. They will be with you at the end."

"Let us pray it does not come to that. I cannot bear the guilt on my conscience any longer."

"You and I both know our choices have been dictated for far too long." She offered a small smile. "Sail well, Tannus."

"Thank you, Oracle. I will be in touch."

Sail well. That remained to be seen. His faith in humanity unwavering, Tannus knew August and her crew would discover the best way to man his warship. Eventually.

Low continent, planet Vau Prime.

Gedrick watched the blue-white engines flare to full power as the convoy carrying the first wave of refugees away from the beleaguered planet lifted into the clouds and open space beyond.

Word of a major engagement at the edge of the system imbued the rebels with hope, little as it may be. With the threat of continued battles, the enemy fleets were in disarray and they hurried to open escape routes previously sealed. Daring pilots and those eager to put the traumas of Mobus Kale's purges behind took to the sky at the first opportunity. Gedrick applauded their audacity and wished each luck. For himself, he was heading into the heart of darkness. Not the end he envisioned, but one becoming inescapable. Brave men and women were dying at the behest of the fallen Davith Strannan. If he could rescue any, he considered his pending sacrifice worth it.

The shapeshifter stared skyward until the last engine light flickered and disappeared. Three thousand souls crammed into the tight holds, squeezing into every available inch of space over his head. He longed to be with them. To be anywhere but here.

Gedrick hefted his bag, one filled with a few meager belongs left to him, over one shoulder and turned for the waiting shuttle that would sneak him into Krenz. It was, he knew, the last stage of an impossible journey. Eyes cast downward, he saw the shadows stretching toward him before he heard their voices.

"This is how you're saying goodbye?" Bryn Mal accused. "Sneaking away without a care for your friends?"

"What she means to say is we are going to miss you, Gedrick," Jash Abernath said, scowling at his counterpart. "We couldn't have done any of this without you."

Gedrick's heart warmed as he looked at them. "I did what I promised Davith I would. Your cause is just and this," he gestured skyward, "is a noble deed worthy of his name."

"This is what we call running with our tails between our legs, Gedrick." Colonel Freyote commented dryly. "We have much to thank you for, even if it is a full retreat bordering on panic."

Gedrick cocked his head. "I don't understand."

"You're saving lives," Jash whispered. "It's not how they are saved that matters."

"Is it worth it?" Gedrick asked.

The subsonic roar of engines engaging with full power rippled across the skies.

Freyote nodded. "Many of them will stay in uniform and rejoin the fight from Mannus Prime. Others will slip away and hope to find a measure of peace on their homeworlds. This war will go on, regardless of either. I hope you find the solace you need. I really do."

Freyote extended his hand, and, after a moment, they shook. Gedrick appreciated the man for his candor, suddenly wishing he'd gotten to know the new commander better. His care for what remained of the fighting force on the low continent remained, even as he headed into the jaws of the enemy. The respect went both ways, for Freyote knew he wouldn't be in command without the support of Gedrick and the young lieutenants.

"Before you go there is one last thing I need to do." Freyote cleared his throat. "Lieutenants Bryn Mal and Jash Abernath, attention."

They exchanged a confused look but snapped to without comment. The clink of metal dropping into Gedrick's hands drew their gazes.

"It has come to my attention that this army needs quality leaders. Ones who have proven themselves in the crucible and are willing to do whatever it takes to ensure stability and survival. You two are hereby promoted to captain, effective immediately. Gedrick, if you would do the honors."

Unable to keep his grin from stretching across his face, Gedrick stepped to Jash and removed the rank pin from his collar. He looked Jash deep in the eyes, chest swelling with pride. He placed the new rank into the soiled uniform fabric and smoothed the blouse over. Beside them Freyote performed the same with Bryn.

"You are a good man, Jash Abernath. One I have come to look upon as family. It has been a privilege working with you, watching you develop and become the man you are today," Gedrick told him before withdrawing his hand. "Stay safe. Get these people to freedom and never forget where you came from. This is what is important." He cast a side glance to Bryn and said, "Don't let him mess this up either. Davith would have been proud of you both."

"Thank you, Gedrick," she mumbled. Her eyes grew heavy with tears.

Not trusting his emotions, Gedrick said, "I shall miss you both—goodbye."

They watched him stalk off, departing into the sunset like a hero of old. Only when the shuttle launched did they return to the pretend semblance of normalcy.

Freyote cleared his throat, drawing their attention. “Gods willing he will survive this storm. The universe needs people like him. His fate, however, is no longer in our hands. We need to get the next convoy moving. The influx of refugees continues growing and we will be hard pressed to evacuate them before Kale arrives.”

“I’ll see to it. The second convoy should be staging now. All we lack is pilots,” Bryn said.

“We must trust our faith, my friends,” Freyote told them. “Pilots will come. We are doing a good thing here. I intend on maintaining the status until enemy forces swarm over what remains. Will you stand beside me?”

“Yes sir,” they answered in unison.

“Good. Let’s get back to work. It won’t be long before enemy scouts start arriving.”

Eger City, planet Mannus Prime.

Controlled chaos dominated the city. Waves of junior diplomats and interplanetary representatives scurried to the capital building with missives and pleas from their homeworlds before returning to their shuttles. Newly christened security forces lined the main avenues despite the promise of violence being low in the aftermath of the campaign earlier in the year. Commerce and gaiety returned to the shopping districts. With employment rising and the low tax rates being maintained there was little reason to remain trapped under the dour blankets of oppression once threatening the planet. The atmosphere of the people was one of hope.

New construction spread throughout the outskirts of the city as immigrants and wave after wave of newcomers seeking a better life flooded Mannus. Most of the new arrivals came willing to earn their place. Many joined the ranks of the military, replenishing losses sustained from extended combat. Others filled in across the civilian sector. Efforts were made to limit the number of government officials, knowing too well the dangers of a bloated bureaucracy. The fledgling coalition council was determined to avoid the trappings of Vau Prime.

In the endless shuffle of crowds, forgotten by the rest of the universe, the deposed Cardinal Seniorus walked. His clothes were stained and unassuming. Gone were the brilliant crimson robes of state. Tinus Har knew there was no going back. No return to the halls of power he once sought to dominate through an ill-fated alliance with Alain Nye. The clergy, for his efforts, was all but destroyed. Their ranks emptied as priests, monks, and cardinals were imprisoned or executed for treason. Tinus refused to acknowledge any role played in the pogrom. His goal had been to strengthen the Conclave, not push it to the brink of annihilation. The results were a far cry from his dreams.

Now destitute and abandoned, Tinus Har sought to carve a new path to glory in the fledgling halls of command here on Mannus. The spark of inspiration struck during his harrowing flight from Vau Prime. Hounded by those once sworn to fealty, he narrowly escaped the transit to deep space. Listless and adrift among the stars, he thought hard on his next moves. Where to go. Who would accept him. The list, already thin, depressed sharply the more he gave it thought.

Then word reached him of the insurrection on Mannus and the rising tides of power coalescing where defeat should have reigned. It was here he decided to make his play. One final bid to recreate what was lost. For Tinus Har there could be only one outcome. The alternatives saw his ashes scattered to the winds of abject failure. His name cast down as one of the greatest villains in human history. Fueled with the twin desires of revenge and redemption, the fallen cardinal used what little authority remained to his name to slip through the crowds.

He came upon the long bridge crossing what amounted to a moat from old times, though the modern architects claimed the flowing water was meant to be tranquil and a sign of peaceful times to come. He was surprised to find it unguarded save for a pair of predatory soldiers scanning the crowds from the security of their guard towers on either side of the open road. None seemed overly concerned, prompting Tinus to wonder how secure Mannus Prime was now that it had transformed into a military staging base for what promised to continue a devolving conflict.

It wasn't until he reached the far side of the bridge where a squad of Guards manned a checkpoint complete with security sweepers and digital scanners. He found it odd, knowing the value in security lay at preventing potential enemies from reaching the main doors. Wisdom dictated the checkpoint should be on the city side of the bridge, giving reinforcements time to act should any nefarious deeds arise. Scoffing at the supposed brilliance of the fledgling council, he halted, waiting for his turn to be called forward from the growing lines.

"State your name and business," a stern captain with twin scars running down the left side of his face demanded.

Handing over an identification passport, Tinus paused and said with a practiced lie, "Davos Imhl. I am an envoy from planet Ghosis and have an appointment with Cardinal Virom."

The captain handed the id over to an equally grizzled sergeant who ran it through the scanner while another soldier scanned Tinus' body for concealed weapons or explosives.

"He checks out, sir."

Tinus accepted his false id and tucked it away in the folds of his robes.

The captain waved him through.

Exhaling a sigh of relief, Tinus hurried past the barriers and waiting soldiers. Stepping into the newly minted capital building, he couldn't help but be impressed. Far removed from the grandeur of Krenz, the rebels of Mannus Prime went to great lengths to portray their competence and willingness to lead by example. Lost amidst the endless rows of paintings and statues were people from a hundred worlds, all come to seek out a new life from the uncontained ashes of violence spreading. He felt hope in the air and, for a moment, almost gave in.

Tinus stopped to ask directions a handful of times before winding through the labyrinth halls. He was surprised to discover no suspicion as he passed. No raised alarms of promise of detainment for who he was. How could these people be so ignorant? Did they forget war threatened all or had he been insulated among the top tiers of Conclave while the rest of the universe moved on? The questions plagued him until he found himself standing in Cardinal Virom's antechamber. A sneer crossed his face. The audacity of this man to assume a leadership position contrary to the Conclave, contrary to him, brought a sour taste to Tinus' mouth.

Humiliation, however, tempered his judgment. Cast down and ostracized by the Inquisitor General, Tinus Har reluctantly accepted his reduced role and, despite being thankful for escaping Vau Prime with his life, devoted his energies to reclaiming a measure of semblance of who he was meant to be. If that meant further debasing himself in front of this lowly cardinal stuffed with delusions of grandeur so be it. A short while and forced argument over his fraudulent appointment with Virom's scheduling clerks later and he was ushered into audience with the man who would supplant a king.

Virom clasped his hand, gripping tight enough to grind the bones, and smiled. "Welcome to Mannus Prime. I'm afraid I didn't catch your name."

"Davos Imhl from Ghosis," Tinus lied.

Offering his guest a seat, Virom settled into his chair and interlaced his fingers over the desk. "Now that is interesting. I was unaware a second envoy had been sent. All very unusual considering I already met with Davos Imhl from Ghosis. Perhaps you should tell me who you are and why you have lied your way into my office before I have you dragged away in chains."

Paling, Tinus flicked his tongue over his lower lip. "You already know who I am, Virom, else you wouldn't have allowed me to enter."

The doors hissed open and a squad of Prekhauten Guards in full battle gear marched in, the scarred captain at their head.

"You didn't really think one of the most wanted men in the universe could go unrecognized here, of all places, did you?"

"What are you going to do with me?" the deposed Cardinal Seniorus asked, cuffs appearing on his wrists.

"That remains to be seen. Take him away."

Brightstar, high orbit over planet Occanum.

Captain August felt his presence before he addressed her. Tannus emerged upon the bridge to stand beside her. He'd contentedly let her pilot the ship, having her handling all normal duties of a captain. Thus far the alliance between them was working. The *Brightstar* had reached Occanum without incident and settled into orbit to await his orders.

He stared at the dead world, an uneasy feeling dancing through the pits of his stomach. How long had it been since he'd last been home? Occanum. Homeworld of the gods. A bitter, dead rock where nothing grew and never would again. It was the one place in the universe there was no legitimate reason to go to and the only place he needed to be right now.

A second ship loomed on the horizon. Smaller yet equally lethal. Tannus knew he looked upon his Sorrow's ship and took mild comfort from the knowledge he had joined them. It was the third and smallest ship already descending planetside that bothered him. The god hunter. Akin Brohl. The one being in the universe who wanted them all dead and held the power to ensure it happened.

Too late to back out of their fated meeting, Tannus cracked his knuckles. "Captain August, would you do me the honor of accompanying me to the surface?"

She didn't really have a choice. "It would be my pleasure. Might I suggest a detachment of Marines for security?"

"They won't make any difference. This is work best left to my brother and I."

Disturbed by the admission, August turned to her first officer. "Commander Odir, you have command."

"Aye ma'am."

Satisfied the ship was in capable hands, August turned to Tannus and said, "Shall we?"

TWENTY-THREE

3215 A.G. (After Gods), Erdef City, planet Romalle.

Heart thundering, he struggled to beat back the rising tides of fear threatening to change his mind and send him fleeing back to the safehouse. No stranger to violence, he'd discovered a critical truth these last few weeks. While he'd proven he could handle his own, he preferred drifting through the days anonymous and without conflict. Life might not be kind, but it could be molded to fit his needs. The only problem was he didn't know what he needed. Confusion rippled through him the moment he laid eyes on Riles. Owed loyalties to Tolde and the others only extended so far and, stranded on a foreign world that didn't want him, Ragan felt trapped.

"What have I gotten myself into?" he muttered, hoping not to be heard as they crept through filth smeared alleys away from prying eyes.

Riles glanced back over her shoulder. "What?"

His cheeks flushed crimson. "Nothing. Keep going." He focused on her back, noting the shape and definition of her legs. The curve of her shoulders. It was no secret, leastwise not to her, Ragan found her attractive. But that's where it ended. He fawned over her, presented impossibly hopeless doe eyes, without knowing where to go or what to do next.

Much to his embarrassment, Ragan had never been with a woman. Life had other ideas, shoving him down roads he'd never dreamed of before depositing him on Romalle in the midst of a brutal string of murders and hidden power plays. The former street thief often thought how matters might have been different if he'd never been set loose from his jail cell by the Blood Witch. Dead at the end of a rope or stumbling around the streets without hands, no doubt. Perhaps leaving Rastarok was in his best interests after all. Otherwise, he never would have met Riles.

Thinking of her produced odd sensations deep within. Inexperience left him bereft of knowledge, further complicating those fledgling emotions attempting to assume control. Ragan felt warm, childish with excitement he still hadn't figured out, and more awkward than at any other point in his life. Did she feel the same?

The question plagued him. He needed a sign. Validation. Anything to prove this wasn't a childhood crush careening out of control. Yet the universe answered him with silence.

"Come on, it's clear," Riles hissed over a shoulder and slipped around the corner.

Holding his sigh, Ragan followed.

The sidearm on his hip felt foreign. He'd come from a world of swords and magic. The ability to harm or kill another accurately from distance bothered him. Mankind spanned the universe in a vast empire, but it seemed more focused on devising new methods to harm itself than to evolve. Displeased as he was with the weapon, he was no fool. Too much had gone wrong since leaving Rastarok, he could no longer be empty handed.

The three of them, he kept forgetting the almost complacent Nemineon trailing behind, hurried down the street. They approached the edge of town and, if all went according to plan, the waiting transport to get them into the wilds and the tribes. Ragan remained dubious. Nothing had gone right since they arrived planetside. Throw in blindly trusting a woman with assassin written all over her and he knew, if they survived, Tolde was going to give him more than an earful. Ragan felt like every eye in the city was upon him. Watching. Waiting. Left with no choice, he ran.

Running for their lives, they failed to spot the lone figure marking their every move. He scowled as he guessed their intent. He needed to act fast before the chance of stopping them disappeared. Tonight was a night for bloodwork. Drawing his darkened blade, the man climbed down from his rooftop blind and followed. The hunt had begun.

"They did what?" Tolde struggled to keep his emotions in check. Face red from building rage, his clenched fists trembled at his sides.

Emmest DeMauve uncrossed her legs and made a show of stifling a yawn. "Relax, Inquisitor. I know what I am doing."

"What you have done is sent them to their deaths. None of them are capable of fending off the avalanche barreling toward them."

"Riles is a tenacious young woman, Tolde. I'm not concerned with her abilities."

"You've killed them all."

Exasperated, she threw her hands up. "What else would you have me do? Our investigations have led to nothing but dead ends. Your brother's killer is still out there, and we are running out of time. Besides, they are not alone."

Folding her arms, Luma asked, "What do you mean? Who is watching them?"

"A friend." The slight hint of mischief twinkled in Emmest's dark eyes. "We are wasting our time worrying over them. They are well taken care of. Should they escape the city unharmed they will find succor among the tribes, where Riles is from. Instead, we should focus our attention on Hargan. He is a stout man but remains the primary target. Once his assassinator learns he is alive, they will come to finish the job."

"Gando has that covered," Tolde mumbled thinking of Ragan and the others still. Had he been here he never would have agreed to the plan. Which was precisely why he hadn't been consulted.

"Inquisitor Gando is the acting representative of the Conclave in this matter. As such, his hands are tied. There is but so much a man in his position can accomplish without his deeds being reported back to Vau Prime. Correct me if I'm wrong, but even with the schism among your Order there is still a system of checks and balances that must be adhered to."

Tolde rubbed his jaw, knowing that he'd lost the argument and was blowing nothing but hot air. "You're right, but that doesn't make what you instigated right."

"Who said this was a matter of right?" she replied. "We are trying to prevent the war from reaching Romalle. Our goals are the same, though our means differ. I am not your enemy, Tolde."

Sister Alessandra swept into the room. The shimmer of her robes, combined with the space between the bottom of her slippers and the floor, presented an ethereal appearance. No matter how many times Tolde worked with the Blood Witches he had yet to become comfortable in their presence. If Alessandra noticed his flinch, she kept it to herself.

"Lady DeMauve is correct," Alessandra announced. "Our backs are to the wall. Every day we fail in our quest brings this planet closer to open war. The Grand Mistress foresaw this before we departed. There is no alternative for success. I believe by discovering your brother's killer we will not only avenge his death but uncover a deeply rooted conspiracy driving the political winds of Romalle."

"What are you saying, exactly?" Luma asked with a frown, tired of the pointless argument preventing them from taking action.

"Luma Kai, it is simple: Find the killer and save the planet."

"Right, no pressure," Tolde muttered.

He felt rather than saw Alessandra cock her head beneath the cowl. "You misunderstand. There is every pressure to ensure we do not fail."

Barely avoiding rolling his eyes, Tolde wondered what it was like being human yet having no connection to your own race. Was every witch a similar product? Despite their ocean of differences, Tolde found himself beginning to like her.

Luma nodded. "So the question is where do we allocate our time? Do we follow Ragan and the others, or do we go to Hargan? Regardless of how this plays out, I am not fond of either choice."

"Fondness has no place here, Luma," Emmest said, her voice light but laced with implied threat. "As I said, Riles is being well looked after. While I do not believe the mastermind behind this affair will strike directly, they will send their most capable people to finish the task."

Tolde stiffened. "How can you know that?"

"I let word escape Riles saw your brother's killer before she escaped."

His face paled. "You're using her as bait."

"Completely."

"Does she know this?"

Clearing her throat, Emmest leveled her gaze and said, "Yes."

"This is madness!"

Lady DeMauve's true compassion dictating her moves remained hidden from those around her. She yearned to fill the void left by her husband's passing. Instead of finding love, she discovered intrigue. Playing behind the scenes, Emmest worked to destabilize the corruption of the city board while placing the needs of the downtrodden and the poor ahead of her own. She took no reward other than seeing powerful figures burn in a pyre of their own making. Enjoying the game for what it was, she couldn't help but feel the spiral of many threads coming to a twisted conclusion.

She waited for his rant to fade to barely legible whispers before speaking. "Tolde, you must understand, I will do everything in my power to keep Romalle safe from your war—yes, I said your war. We do not seek conflict, nor do we have standing armies or navies. Romalle has always been peaceful. To watch it collapse under the weight of the Inquisitor General and his banal demands or from the well-intended occupation of those forces loyal to your cause is unacceptable. I will help you find your brother's assassin and you will assist me in preventing the remaining board members from finding the necessary votes to join Vau Prime. Once complete it is my sincerest wish to part ways in friendship and, I hope, never to see any of you for the rest of my days."

Frustrated, Tolde resigned himself to this fragile plan. "Fine. What's our next move?"

Lady DeMauve gave him a conspiratorial smile and detailed what she had planned … Tolde wished he'd never asked.

The beeps and hums of the hospital machines spun a maddening symphony. Thunder pounded in his skull; a subtle reminder of how close to death he teetered. Medications stalled the wall of pain from consuming his weakened body. Crude prevented him from opening his eyes. What he found most disturbing was the incessant tingling in his fingertips. Unable to move and drugged enough to be incoherent, Hargan exhaled as deep a breath as he could and sank back into the oddly hard mattress.

Flashes of memory danced behind his eyelids. A dark figure entering his office. The brightness of the blaster and the burning sensation in his chest and arm. Logic suggested he should be dead. Whether through stubborn need or his assailant being a poor shot, at close range, he still drew breath. Hargan did his best to concentrate, but the medication left him weak and sluggish. Frustrated, the investigator settled back into uncomfortable sleep.

Bouncing between fits of consciousness, Hargan had vague recollections of nurses and doctors coming and going. Food and water were fed intravenously. Any sense of humility evaporated the moment the orderly first entered to empty his bedpan and clean him. A prisoner in all but name, Hargan did the only thing he could. He endured.

At last able to stretch and move, to a degree, Hargan raised his arms above his head and drew a deep breath. The murk of an endless cycle of drugs faded, though the pain remained. His fingers still tingled but there was nothing for it. He wiped the corners of his eyes clean and stared up at the ceiling for the first time since being admitted. Finally, he could think. Not of himself, but of his friends. Had they been targeted as well? Were any still alive? His hands slid under the pillow with the intent of interlocking his fingers to stretch. Instead, they touched upon the slightly warmed metal of a small blaster.

A weapon? Where did that come from? More questions sprang to life, all leading to one inescapable conclusion: He was not out of danger and at least one of his friends yet drew breath. Emboldened with the information, Hargan's fingers curled around the pistol grip. From feel alone he determined it was standard police force issue. Guessing the power pack was fully charged, his mind ran through various scenarios. None of them ended well.

Whoever placed the weapon under his pillow understood the dangers and decided to give him an edge for survival. Prudence in his best interests, he kept the blaster in place. Without knowing who to trust among the hospital staff, the last thing he needed was one of them confiscating the weapon. Hargan yawned and settled back into a light slumber.

The door hissed open a short while later and Hargan stilled, trying to see into the pall of darkness that had settled throughout the room as night fell across the city. There'd been a time when he enjoyed the quiet anonymity of the night, right now he didn't. All of the staff announced themselves when they entered. This time he heard nothing but silence. Cracking his eyes open as thin as possible, Hargan watched as a man dressed in orderly scrubs paused to lock the door behind him.

Hargan's hand snaked up under his pillow and felt around for the blaster—he found only fabric. Frantic, he widened his blind search. His heart sped up as the stark realization that the end to his story would forever be linked with a hospital bed instead of going down in the line of duty. How insulting.

At last, his tingling fingertips grazed cold metal. Panic subsiding, Hargan gripped the weapon and thumbed the safety off. He waited, guessing the imposter would be unwilling to risk giving himself away by using an energy weapon. The man turned and Hargan caught the glint of light reflecting from the long, slender blade in his right hand. Murderous intent weighed the man's eyes suggesting he'd done this before. Hargan slowed his breathing, feigning sleep as his killer approached.

Reaching the edge of the bed, the killer paused to glance over his shoulder. He then placed a palm on Hargan's chest and brought the blade up.

Hargan coughed, giving the killer pause. In a clumsy move, he brought the blaster out and pointed it at the killer's chest. Hargan watched the man's eyes widen a split-second before he pulled away. The weapon fired. Twice. The first round took the killer in the shoulder. Blood and cauterized bits of flesh splattered the white blanket on the bed. The second round left a black stain on the wall to the right of the door.

Frantic now, the killer fumbled with the door lock. A third round struck his opposite shoulder, slamming him into the door just as he got it open. He took half a step into the hallway before Hargan's final shot caught him in the base of the spine. The killer collapsed in a paralyzed heap of whimpering flesh. Hargan kept his blaster pointed at the door but no one else came. Pain lanced his side. His eyelids fluttered, darkness creeping in around the edges. Blinking away the wash of fresh tears, he made out the figure of a large man entering the room with an assault rifle in the ready position.

Inquisitor Gando snorted. "Guess you didn't need help after all."

"You're an asshole, Gando." Hargan let his head drop back, chuckling and pressed the call for help button.

"I know." Slinging his rifle, Gando's head bobbed as he knelt beside the corpse and rifled through the pockets. As suspected, he found nothing. Whoever this man was, he was professional. The two men assigned to watch over Hargan were dead, their corpses in the hall. Gando frowned, stalled by another dead end until an odd bulge protruding from beneath the would-be killer's ribcage caught his attention. Leaning forward, he tore the body glove to reveal an unnatural rectangular spot just below the nipple. Invigorated, Gando drew his blade from his left boot and made a careful incision. Blood spilled in trickles over the bruised flesh, but he spied the glint of metal. Withdrawing the item, Gando rubbed the blood off and raised it to his face—an identity tracker.

The rush of footsteps scampering down the hall announced the arrival of hospital staff. Gando moved to intercept them and, he hoped, use his rank and authority to explain the body already cooling at his feet as he slipped the chip into his jacket.

"Run!" Nemineon shouted and shoved Riles down the narrow alley.

Confusion twisting her face, she opened her mouth to question him before spying the trio of armed figures emerging from the shadows. She still shook her head, unwilling to accept the inevitable.

He shoved her again. "Riles, they don't want me. You're the one they're after. Run. Take Ragan and get to the tribes. Go!"

Ragan's hands grabbed her lightly by the shoulders, silently urging her away. The intruders were getting closer, weapons raised.

Nemineon pressed his forehead against hers. "I'll be fine. Go, for both of us."

Ion rounds slammed into the buildings around them as Ragan dragged her away. She caught a high-pitch scream. Left to question whether Nemineon was injured or dead, Riles ran.

The huff of their breaths echoed in their ears, preventing her from knowing if their enemies pursued them or not. A crisp rifle shot exploded ahead of them.

They ran harder.

The end of the alley beckoned. Soft violet lights announcing the street beyond. The shadow fell first. Then the figure. Realization dawned. They were trapped. Weaponless. Hopeless.

Weeks of pent-up frustration finally breaking free, Ragan roared and charged. He was lunging for the man blocking the alley when Riles slammed into him from behind. They fell in a tangled mass. Squirming, he snapped, "What are you—"

Ion rounds slashed overhead in relentless fury. Riles pressed him down further then looked back down the alley, hoping to learn Nemineon's fate. Instead, she saw all three gunmen drop or pitch backward. Only when the last man fell and did not move again did the man before them cease fire.

"Riles, get off me!" Ragan shouted.

"Shut up. I'm saving your life," she hissed.

"You can get up." Showing no concern for the youths, their savior slung his rifle and drew a blaster as he stepped over them in passing. Once at the end of the alley his paused to place a round in each of the fallen gunmen before returning to where they sat. He extended his gloved hand.

Riles, distrust in her eyes, accepted it. It was then recognition dawned on her. "Ragan, it's all right."

Despite his misgivings, he let her drag him to his feet. "Who is he?"

She ignored his question and faced their savior. "I remember you. Mayn?"

He made a show of bowing. "Indeed. Lady DeMauve had me deploy ahead in anticipation of such an event. You're most fortunate I was in place. Those men were part of an offworld band of criminals and, I suspect, an integral piece in the murders of Cardinal Breed and the others."

"Who?" Ragan mumbled.

"Ah, my apologies. My name is Mayn. I am Lady DeMauve's chamberlain. Her right hand in affairs of the estate."

Still confused, Ragan looked back at the bodies. "With a crack shot by the looks of it."

"I serve my purposes." Mayn shrugged. "Now, if you are ready, we must depart. This was but one hunter team. There are others sweeping the edges of the city."

Ragan shuddered at the thought of armed bands of murderers scouring the city, in search of him. Of Riles.

"What about Nemineon?" Riles' voice was shaky, threatening to break.

Mayn paused. "Gone. There was sign of a struggle, but I found no bodies. If he lives, he will have gone to ground. That is best. These men are extremely good at what they do. Nemineon needs to remain in hiding until this matter is settled. I will have reliable friends search for him later."

Riles heard him but couldn't pull her gaze from the pile of bodies. Nemineon had been at her side through the worst times, refusing to abandon her no matter how perilous their plight became. To leave him now, without confirmation of his fate, sickened her. She, like most of the people of the tribes, prided herself on integrity. She also needed him by her side.

"Young Riles, we are not safe here. It won't take long for the others to figure out what happened. We need to move. Keep the offensive now that we have it," Mayn pressed.

Riles struggled to withhold her sobs. "This wasn't the plan."

"Plans change. Let's go. Time is running out." The last thing Mayn wanted to hear was Lady DeMauve reprimanding him for his negligence. He handed his blaster to Ragan, deciding the offworlder less of a liability, and brought his rifle back to his hands. Despite his feeble appearance, the elderly man wore the ferocity of a viper waiting to strike.

Lost in her daze, Riles followed him, Ragan taking the rear. The night was just beginning.

Behemoth, outer Vau system.

"Scanners are picking up a major engagement on the far edge of the system. Is this anticipated?" Algiss asked.

The image of Sister Evangeline flickered. "No. Enemy forces jumped into the system and engaged what little protection the Inquisitor General had in place. From what I've gathered there is a push to deploy additional fleets to stop them."

Standing behind the Crimson Mistress was the severe Ibrest who scowled at the news. "What is the disposition of the navy's forces in system? Surely Nye has amassed enough to end this threat before it grows."

"Unclear, Sister. The Inquisition has not seen fit to entrust me yet. Geres Auk and I have been relegated to pointless meetings of material and supplies. Tactics, troop movements, and fleet deployments have been kept from us."

Ibrest turned to Algiss. "It appears the usurper has not committed to our alliance. A demonstration is required."

"Not yet."

"Why are we submitting to this *human*? Together we have the power to overthrow his crumbling regime and emplace true power in the universe," Ibrest snapped.

Algiss frowned at the threat. Discipline was required, but not yet. "Lord Amongeratix has plans. It falls upon his shoulders to decide Nye's fate. We are here to support, not supplant."

"What of the battle at the system edge?" Evangeline asked. "Do I become involved?"

"No. Do nothing. Leastwise not until we arrive in orbit," Algiss answered. "Learn what you can and report to me. I need to know what we are being dragged into so I can advise Amongeratix appropriately."

"Understood, Mistress. How long before you make planetfall?"

"Two days at present speed." Algiss voice was dark with displeasure at the leisurely pace Amongeratix moved. It was as if he knew the risks and dangers amassing against him and didn't care to hurry destiny.

She cut the transmission before Evangeline or Ibrest could say more.

TWENTY-FOUR

3215 A.G. (After Gods), primary spaceport, planet Dalafar.

The recoil slammed into his shoulder as the shell casing ejected from the rifle. Jolent grinned through the scope when his target dropped. Choosing to avoid standard Guard issued sniper rifles, he enjoyed the pop of the antiquated gunpowder rifle. He felt an intimacy with the weapon in ways he seldom felt with other people. That relationship paid off on several planets, from Crimeat to Mannus Prime. Now it was paying off on Dalafar. Three enemy combatants lay dead several hundred meters from the escaping command team Jolent decided was foolish for infiltrating the opposing forces headquarters. Still, he admired their audacity.

A fourth target crept over the bodies of his compatriots with scarcely a glance down. Nestling back into the scope, Jolent almost felt sorry for the man. Weapon trembling in his young hands, he had no idea he was already dead. Jolent loaded another round and lightly touched the trigger. Calming his breathing, a feat remarkably easy for the sniper, he exhaled and fired. The round struck true a split-second before the crack of the shot snapped through the damp air. Four dead.

"Jolent, are you done playing around?"

Frowning, he keyed his headset. "Just knocking the rust off, Lieutenant. Four targets down. No additional units in my peripheral. You're clear."

Swinging his rifle in a practiced movement, he trained on Fies as he darted out from cover. With him was Quint, a man Jolent both admired and found frustrating, the firebrand woman Tempest, and two strangers. One he assumed to be the now defunct governess. The other looked to be a Guard captain—Jolent kept his scope trained on that one.

"Moving."

A flicker from a second story window at the end of the block caught his eye. Jolent spotted the wave of a curtain before a slender barrel poked through. A bright white-blue flash traced a sizzling line from the room to the street. Jolent fired twice for good measure. The shooter was silenced. Scanning the perimeter for more targets, Jolent took relief in seeing all five of his people still on their feet.

"What the fuck was that?"

Quint's voice bore the hardened edge of a man used to killing. Jolent scowled. "Unseen shooter from the second floor. He's neutralized."

"Try not to let it happen again," Fies snapped.

"Roger." Jolent lifted his finger from the trigger and tapped the side of his rifle as he decided whether to broach the subject of the unexpected Guard officer in their midst. He supposed the addition would need dealing with, but later, after the team made it back to friendly space. Jolent wasn't the one to form a ruckus, choosing instead to let the rest believe him a man of little words and violent action. If they only knew he aspired to write his memoirs once this war finished.

Taking a moment to rub his eye, he turned his thoughts to Jers. How that man managed to survive as long as he had, with his dour attitude and growing sense of doom, was a mystery to him. Jolent didn't have a problem with his former squad leader. Jers proved himself a fierce warrior on several occasions, but he lacked the aggressiveness to see him through to the very end. He hoped Jers found the peace his soul needed, even if it came at a cost to the squad.

Frustrated with his thoughts, Jolent focused back on the Guard captain. All it would take was a quick squeeze of the trigger and the problem vanished before it got worse.

"Are you sure these are the right people?" Moscasco asked Tempest through winded gasps as they hurried down the side street cutting over the main avenue to the docking pads.

Tempest repressed a grin. Nothing in her wildest imaginations compared to the thrill of being hunted by embittered Guardsmen and Inquisition henchmen. They were being shot at and she had just seen another pursuer fall—her giddiness spiked. "Does it matter, Governess? These are the soldiers we were sent. I trust them."

Adris Moscasco cast a sidelong glance at her assistant, silently questioning her judgment. Mind in turmoil, she hurried along with the others. There seemed little doubt her assigned Inquisitor wanted her dead. The security risk of her defecting alone was worth the effort playing out around them. No doubt the entire city would be alerted shortly. The sooner they reached the escape craft the better. Having Donab provided a small measure of comfort she lacked with the foreign soldiers. But the cost for him being with her was high. She knew, even if he didn't, he'd never be able to return to his garrison. Alpof would enact his vengeance and have the man tried and executed before the end of day.

"Trust should not be given freely, Tempest," Moscasco whispered. "We do not know their true intent, nor should we accept them with blind faith."

Tempest kept moving. She'd seen the true character of the men and women risking their lives just by being here. Stalwart, loyal to the old regime, and willing to throw themselves in harm's way for a woman they'd never met, a political refugee no less, the Guards represented what Tempest believed the Conclave should have aspired to, not the filth of Alain Nye's new reign. Deciding it prudent to keep her mouth shut, Tempest knew the only way for Moscasco to fully understand was through surviving this gauntlet and reaching the fledgling government on Mannus Prime.

"What of Donab? How can you be certain he won't turn us in when it benefits him most?" she asked eventually asked Moscasco.

The responding glare was answer enough. Tempest concealed a grin as her employer unwittingly revealed her true feelings for the beleaguered Guard captain. She opened her mouth to comment when the group slowed and huddled against the nearest wall.

"Alpha team, we have problems."

Fies rechecked the power charge of his rifle before taking a knee. "Talk to me."

"Enemy elements are setting up a roadblock less than twenty meters from your position. Looks like Inquisitors and hired thugs."

Annalilly's report chilled him. The shuttle was less than a few hundred meters away according to the navigation system at his side but with a host of enemy ahead and who knew how many trailing behind the possibility of being captured or killed grew higher. "Can you neutralize?"

"Possibly."

"Do it. Take them down and retreat back to the shuttle."

"Roger that."

Grinning like a savage, Annalilly flexed her trigger finger. She lived for moments like this—the reduction of humanity to its basest form as a contest of wills played out. No stranger to violence, the platoon sergeant offered a silent prayer before remembering the gods were lies. Instead she placed faith in a full power charge and her natural aggressiveness. She glanced at each of the others with her. They nodded in reply, though she spied the fear lingering in their eyes. She understood that, though failed to respect it. Each had been with her through more battles than any Guard was expected to endure. They were survivors. The best at what they did. She needed to remind them.

"We move quick. Strike fast and eliminate every target with fury. There are no friendlies before us. No innocents. Gun them down so we can get off this fucking fish smelling rock."

Beve grunted, hefting his light machinegun like a newborn. The others, having already collapsed their positions in anticipation of the mission going sideways, drew deep breaths in a pointless attempt at calming their nerves. She wanted to lash out, remind them of who and what they were. Or perhaps it was a silent reminder of what she needed to hear. Tough as she was, Annalilly couldn't help but fret over Fies and the rest behind hunted down like animals.

"Jolent, what's your status?"

"Moving."

Satisfied, and used to the taciturn sniper, Annalilly clicked her safety off. "Let's move."

"What's the plan, El-tee?" Quint asked. He couldn't stop flexing his arms, an old habit born in the fraught moments before his first firefight years ago. Already blooded with his new platoon, his sole concern rested in the man Fies insisted was an asset. He cast sidelong glances at Captain Donab, questioning whether he should eliminate the man now or in the fog of battle.

Fies frowned before steeling his expression. "Same thing we always do. Kick down the door and stir the nest. Ready?"

Quint wanted to say no. That he didn't want to march into an ambush with a smile on his face and a song in his heart. He'd already lost one company and vowed to never let that happen again if he could help it. "What about the governess?"

"Captain Donab, will you keep them safe while we handle this?" Fies lowered his barrel, his intonation clear to the rogue captain.

Swallowing hard, Donab nodded. "As I can. Are you sure this is the right play? Alpof's people will be ruthless. They don't fight by our rules, Fies."

"Which will make killing them easier." He turned to Tempest and Moscasco. "Governess, if you will be so kind as to remain with the captain until we're done, I would appreciate it."

"You mentioned that snip Alpof had people coming up behind us. How are we to be any safer here?" she asked.

"She has a point," Tempest added before any objections were raised.

Fies wished Annalilly was beside him, if for nothing else than her rapid-fire wit and inane ability to solve tense situations with a glare. Fies handed over his sidearm to a woman clearly versed in its use. "I still don't like this."

Tempest checked the power charge and slid the action bolt forward, ready to fire. "Lieutenant, you worry too much."

Eyes wide, Fies gestured down the street. "Let's go before I lose my nerve."

Jolent ducked under a vicious swing and launched an uppercut into his assailant's stomach. Rewarded with the whuff of air leaving, the sniper sent a kick into the side of the man's knee. He fell with a crippled gasp as Jolent's combat blade stabbed through the side of his neck. A red rope trailed the knife as it ripped free, and the sniper was back on his feet and scrambling for cover.

Several ion rounds struck the wall behind him, blasting apart the thin metal with unrepented fury. A pair of bodies decorated the staircase to his chosen overwatch position. Unfortunately for him, the local Inquisitor's goons anticipated his move. Jolent was forced to run and gun his way closer to the shuttle. A stray round clipped his shoulder from behind, nearly pitching him to the floor.

Jolent tucked into a combat roll and hurried around the corner before the shooter got lucky. Growling at his misfortune, he felt behind for the entry wound. Lances of pain swept through him as his gloved fingertips touched the cauterized flesh. Bits of clothing were burned into the wound. Fresh anger consuming him, Jolent snatched his rifle off the floor and went hunting. He hadn't been the prey since his early days in sniper school when instructors delighted in taking him and his classmates out with regularity.

Haze from the brief spurt of ion fire fogged the room. Jolent crawled over the corpses to a firing position and began scanning windows for his attackers. Three were open but there was no sign or shooters. Jolent blinked against another wave of pain. Fear of infection or internal injuries drove him on. The last thing he wanted was to die on a world reeking of fish. He chuckled at the thought of friends and family wafting their noses as they passed his coffin.

Movement drew his attention. The slightest hint of a curtain shifting. Silent as death, Jolent shifted his rifle and dropped behind the scope. The tip of his index finger landed on the trigger, waiting. Seconds later the grim black rifle barrel slid into the open.

"Got you," Jolent snarled.

He squeezed the trigger twice. The rifle seeking him fell out the window. Target down. Vengeance satisfied, Jolent flipped the safety on and slipped his rifle across his back. Confiscating an assault rifle and extra power pack from one of the dead, he hurried to get back in the fight. His family was in danger.

Beve's dark face was lit up from muzzle flashes as he unleashed a stream of automatic fire into the unsuspecting enemy personnel thinking they held the upper hand. Far from the borderline psychotic of his platoon sergeant, he did what he did because he was good at it. Not that slinging a machine gun took special talent, just muscles and a strong stomach. Unlike his peers, Beve never kept body counts or campaign records. The only thing mattering was surviving. That, he took seriously. And currently the heavy weapons specialist was unleashing his full fury on those seeking to harm him.

A pair of Inquisition shock troops pitched backward, their innards shredded by his volley. Taken by surprise, the ambushers fell back. Their flimsy defensive positions overwhelmed by superior firepower and a squad of Guards driven by desperation. Choosing to let Annalilly reap her unique brand of mayhem, Beve settled in for raw destruction.

She fired three rounds into the chest of her nearest attacker and was rewarded by the puff of blood and the confused look on his face as he fell. Pushing forward, Annalilly ducked under a hail of ion rounds. Madness reflected in her eyes. Each shot enhanced the lightning bolt tattoos on her scalp. A second target made the mistake of poking her head out from concealment. Her body dropped, half her face missing.

Instincts taking over, Annalilly scanned the bodies. Poorly trained and ill-equipped, she deduced they were little more than hired thugs. The insult infuriated her further. Searching for her next target, she found herself standing in the middle of the carnage, a tiny figure amidst the haze and small fires spreading. She counted ten corpses. None of which were the local Inquisitor.

Beve lumbered up beside her, admiring his work. "That was fun."

She shot him a glare as he smiled. "I did all the work. Double check to see if any of them are still alive. I don't want to get shot in the back."

"Roger, Sergeant."

Annalilly looked down the now empty corridor. The landing pad was only a few meters away. All she needed now was Fies and the others to arrive so they could make good their escape.

"Haggle, get the shuttle prepped to depart. We're out of here as soon as Fies gets his sorry ass back."

"You got it, Sergeant," his reply cackled over the handheld comms unit.

Satisfied she'd done all she needed, Annalilly turned back to Beve and glanced at her chrono.

Echoes of gunfire barreled down the street. Fies picked up the pace, eager to reach the rest of his team and escape with their package. He sensed the city rising against them. A tide of violence threatening to wash over them with the full authority of the twisted Inquisition. He'd heard rumors of how the Inquisitor General inspired his minions to greater acts of depravity in his quest for ultimate power. How many friends languished in Inquisition prisons? How many others were already dead for following their sworn oaths of duty? Fies didn't know how much longer the war would drag on, but the desire to be on Vau Prime when they finally toppled the usurper kept him warm on cold nights.

Leading his group single file, they hurried through the remaining streets to reach the landing pads. He smelled the carnage before they saw it. An acrid haze clinging to the air, held down by a thin blanket of mist caused by weapon discharge. Stepping over scattered debris, weapon trained to his front, Fies stalked into the engagement area expecting the worst. Instead, he found almost a dozen bodies—none belonged to him.

"Holy fuck," Jolent mumbled from his right.

"Fan out. Check the dead. I don't want any surprises."

Quint shouldered his rifle and drew a sidearm. "What do you suppose happened?"

"Annalilly."

Fies felt Tempest sidle up to him and scowled. The last thing he needed was a distraction. The young assistant was vibrant, filled with the enviable energy of youth and being exposed to her first firefight. She meant well, but she was a mere smokescreen for the raw power that was her boss. Adris Moscasco was a woman, Fies believed, capable of changing the universe.

"I'm impressed," the Governess said nearby. "A pity our dear Inquisitor isn't among them."

"We're not here to kill anyone, Governess," Fies replied. "The sooner I can get you aboard the shuttle the better. For all of us."

"I know, Lieutenant. I know." She laid a comforting hand on his upper arm, mindful of his need to maintain weapon control. Though each body before her presented a threat, they were still her citizens. Twisted and subverted to malevolent causes, but citizens nonetheless. Her heart ached at the wound caused by Alain Nye's greed, and she feared worse was yet to come once she fled. Try as she might, Moscasco saw no other way out. This war had to end and if she could hasten that end and help facilitate the rebuilding who was she to ignore it?

"Not a soldier among them," Donab remarked.

Quint returned. His face grim and determined. “None of ours. We should keep moving. The others at our back will be pressing in and wondering why they can’t hear any gunfire soon.”

Snapped back to reality, Fies squared his shoulders. “Right. Let’s move.”

They scurried through the battleground, avoiding already drying pools of blood and bodies. Fies couldn’t help but admire his lover’s handiwork. Sooner or later there was going to be a reckoning. No one could get away with the sheer amount of carnage she did without paying the consequences. When that day came, he vowed to stand by her side, even if it killed him.

“You make too much noise,” came Annalilly’s hoarse voice from the shadows less than twenty meters from their last location.

Fies closed his eyes, relief spreading across his features. Duty conflicted with emotion as he tamped down the urge to hug her. They’d made it. The shuttle was nearby and there was no sign of enemy agents. “Did we lose anyone? The whole damned city is rising up.”

“Everyone is aboard. Jolent got a little beat up, but you know him,” Annalilly cocked her head, taking in the governess and the Guard captain. “Ah, Fies, what’s going on?”

Fies followed her rifle to Donab. “He’s fine. We used to work together. Now he’s helping us get the governess offworld.”

“Which isn’t going to happen if we continue standing around thanking each other for staying alive,” Moscasco snipped.

“She has a point. You talk too much,” Annalilly added.

Rolling his eyes, Fies gestured toward the shuttle. “Let’s move.”

“That’s far enough.”

A stern, shrill voice shouted from behind. Fies and the others spun, weapons raised, and discovered over a score of armed and armored men and women. Each wore the black of the Inquisition and bore the look of hardened killers. Luck, it seemed, had run out.

"Alpof," Moscasco hissed.

The junior Inquisitor stepped forward, sidearm pointed at her. "Governess, you didn't really think I was going to let you escape, did you? I've had people watching you for months. The only thing sweeter than capturing you is discovering the depth of your conspiracy. Now I have you all. A neat package to send to the Inquisitor General." He almost preened. "Weapons down. Let's not make this messy."

Donab took a step forward. "Alpof, this isn't—"

"Quiet, traitor," Alpof interrupted with a sneer. "I've taken enough from you and this bitch. You and these renegade Guards will face the torturer's tools once you arrive on Vau Prime. The governess, I'm afraid, isn't going to make it that far."

"You were always a little worm of a boy," Moscasco taunted as he raised his weapon.

Madness gleaming in his eyes, Alpof said, "Goodbye, Governess. I've been waiting for this moment for a long time now."

His finger curled over the trigger. The weapon fired twice.

Donab jumped in front of Moscasco and took both rounds in his chest. The Guard captain grunted as he pitched back. The front of his uniform stained with widening red circles. Moscasco cried out.

Sensing his victory, Alpof took a step forward. "Enough of this," he snapped. "Donab was a fool, but you, Adris Moscasco, are a cancer needing to be removed. He damned himself, but his sacrifice will go unanswered."

He raised his weapon again—

The shot echoed off the walls. Smoke drifted in small clouds from the trembling barrel in Tempest's small hands. A horrified look twisted her features. Her mouth hung open as she struggled to comprehend what she'd just done.

Alpof shared her confusion. He dropped his weapon and reached for the base of his throat. Fingertips came away covered in blood. A hole penetrated from his throat to his neck.

Fies and his soldiers opened fire. Ion rounds filled the space between the opposing forces. Bodies fell. Jelin Quint and Annalilly emptied their power packs with ruthless intensity, advancing on the enemy with deliberate steps. The enemy line wilted and then broke. It didn't save them. Several more dropped as they ran. Only a few survived the slaughter.

The Guards pulled up and formed a defensive perimeter in the growing silence. Annalilly glanced back over her shoulder to see the governess covering Donab's body, tears streamed down her face.

Fies reached over and gently took the weapon from Tempest. For all her exuberance, she exposed herself for what she truly was: a woman unused to a world of violence. Her shoulders heaved with sobs as he whispered in her ear. Once she quietened, he gestured for Hollis to escort her to the shuttle.

When no one moved, Fies said in a smooth, quiet voice, "Governess, we need to move. This little scrape will draw attention and there is the possibility of our enemy returning in greater number."

Between sobs, Moscasco said, "He was a good man. He didn't deserve this."

"Donab kept his honor. Don't let his sacrifice be in vain."

Moscasco's face hardened, as if a switch went off. She reached down and closed Donab's eyes before planting a kiss on his forehead. Rising, she smoothed the wrinkles from her clothes. There would be time to mourn, for Donab and the countless millions already lost in this war, but first came an hour or reckoning. She vowed to set the universe on fire for as long as she could. "Very well, Lieutenant. Get me out of here."

Fies stiffened. "Yes, ma'am. Quint, Annalilly, collapse back to the shuttle."

"What about him?" Quint gestured to Donab's body.

"He stays here, amongst his enemies. Let them see the power of righteousness and tremble," Moscasco ordered.

No one questioned her.

Behemoth, Vau System.

Presha Von struggled to calm her nerves. She'd planned and waited, patiently accepting her fate while straining to be released from it. It was during those quiet moments of torment she realized a truth long forced down: She'd been a prisoner for years.

Since accepting the lies told by her father and ascending to the first iteration of the dark council on Crimeat. From there she bent the wills of the lords of Lethendweil to championing the resurgence of Amongeratix as he sought to make his final war on humanity. Then what? What was she after it all fell apart? She was little more than a stooge to be used and discarded when her value ran out. The thought sparked newfound fury. Even facing certain death, Presha knew she needed to do everything she could to ensure Paradise Tear escaped.

Moving with what little authority she had, Presha marched down the darkened corridors with her head high and shoulders back. The whisp of her robes echoed, mixing in with the voices. Too many times since arriving she caught whispers of anguished funneling through the walls. She felt the pain of those lost souls accumulated over the course of millennia. Now that Amongeratix was aboard and in full command of his ship the darkness swelled.

Naught but a handful of decrepit automatons performing maintenance marked her passing. Presha's confidence grew the closer she got to the holding cells, and she remained thankful for the skeleton crew and reduced compliment of Blood Witches. The vast size of Behemoth and limited number of living bodies placed the odds in her favor, if slightly. The soft scuff of her slippers on the deck raised the hairs on her arms. Nerves getting the best of her, Presha hurried the final stretch. She paused to check for watchers and hit the door switch.

"I was starting to think you wouldn't come."

The voice froze Presha just inside the threshold. Not Amongeratix … it was the last sound she wanted to hear. She slipped a hand inside her robes for the concealed blaster at her waist. A blast of wild magic struck the wall by her head. Sparks singed her face, lighting stray hairs. Stunned, she jerked back.

"Your little toy won't protect you," Algiss Her taunted. "Go ahead. Shoot me if it makes you feel better. I'll burn you to cinders."

Mouth trying to coordinate with her mind, Presha managed, "He doesn't want me dead. You can't kill me."

"Can't I? Lord Amongeratix is many things, attentive to those who serve him not among them. You didn't really think you'd just stroll in here and release the prisoner, did you?" She scoffed. "You will die and no one will remember your name. Ironic, isn't that? One of us shall rise while the other becomes little more than dust to be swept aside."

"Do you ever grow tired of your voice?" Paradise Tear asked from her bondage behind the Crimson Mistress. "I've lived over three thousand years and been forced to listen to countless others just like you. All pompous and arrogant in your actions but lacking the one thing you need to evolve—morality."

Taking the bait, Algiss turned to confront the giant. "Lesser daughter of better sires. I shall deal with you in good time."

Paradise broke into a feral grin. "Once my cousin lets you slip your leash?"

Energy cackled over Algiss' knuckles in tiny flames. She raised her finger, jabbing it toward Paradise's face at the same moment Presha fired. Taken off guard, the Crimson Mistress pitched back into the bulkhead as Presha emptied her power charge.

A roar filled the chamber, overpowering the blaster report and the crack of magic whipping wildly through the air.

Paradise Tear broke her bonds and lunged at the witch. Outnumbered and suddenly overpowered, Algiss unleashed her full power at the giant. Magic splashed across Paradise's chest and arms, melting away to malignant energies absorbed by the ship's walls.

Hands clenched to fists, Paradise struck to crush her but the witch retained her wits and slipped aside a split-second before. Recognizing a lost battle, Algiss Her fled. She knocked Presha into the wall on her way out, her robes blurring into a kaleidoscope of colors trailing away through the gloom.

Finishing her escape from the leather straps, Paradise paused to check the corridor before kneeling beside Presha. The smaller woman was dazed and burned but still conscious. "Can you rise?"

Presha attempted to nod. "I can do whatever I need to if it gets me off this damned ship."

Admiring her spirit, Paradise helped her to her feet and began the long trek to the landing bays. Only when they were on the way did it occur to Paradise that she had no idea whether there were any crafts aboard worth flying, much less knowing where they were in the universe.

They gained the outer doors to the bay she thought Amongeratix boarded through. Paradise ached for a weapon, anything to combat the witches skulking on *Behemoth* or her cousin, yet none presented themselves. Frustrated, she resigned herself to using her fists and weeks of pent-up aggression. "Let's move."

Smoke issuing from her robes, Algiss slid beside Amongeratix as he watched the shuttle pull away. There was the twinkle of endless stars reflected from his eyes. Hands clasped behind his back, he chewed on the corner of his lip. She knew better than to disturb him during these introspective moments. Wrath proved a terrible thing.

"Your magic was ineffective," he mused without looking at her.

"None worth noting," Algiss bristled. "She seemed immune."

The sound of his bones snapping as he rolled his shoulders echoed across the bridge, louder than the whirl and hum of the computers and machinery. "You need more than your limited abilities to contend with my kind."

"Was it wise to allow her escape? I could have killed the woman had you allowed it."

"Presha Von has purpose yet and the tracking beacon on the shuttle is active. We will not lose them." Confidence imbued his tone. "My cousin will return to Tannus, and I will at last learn the location of his sanctuary."

Algiss Her saw the multitude threads pulling into one great strand as enemies and allies converged. Forever Night, the long prophesized end of the universe was at last arriving and she stood as one of the architects.

TWENTY-FIVE

3215 A.G. (After Gods), Krenz, planet Vau Prime.

They'd been on the run for three days. The lack of sleep, food, and solace wore them down to broken men and women desperate to survive.

Sirens and alarms rang throughout the city. Panic gripped the population, for word had spread. Amongeratix, nightmare of a hundred generations, was coming to claim his throne. Fires raged unchecked as chaos settled in. Those few still determined to maintain order were overwhelmed by the surge of violence. Lawlessness turned friend upon friend as waves of shock troops and hired thugs moved across the city. For all his faults, Mobus Kale was a thorough man.

"We lost another safehouse this morning. I'm down to less than fifteen people."

Julian winced at the now commonplace news. "Sel, do what you can to keep them alive but don't sacrifice yourselves for no reason."

"We're not done fighting yet. We can't be," Sel replied with determination.

Julian shook his head. "The city is lost. The best we can do is get to one of the escape points and head to the low continent."

"And then offworld."

Wraith-thin, the former lover of the most powerful woman in the world showed her age. Wrinkles and spots decorated her flesh. Dark circles were a permanent fixture around her eyes. She stood on the edge of breaking yet remained defiant. Against all odds. It was to her they looked for comfort, for that subtle reassurance there was yet hope even when wisdom suggested otherwise. Even now, at the impossible end, Aliz refused to accept defeat.

"What choice do we have?" Julian asked despite seeing the fire in her eyes.

She pursed her lips. "You are right, of course. We've shed enough blood; lost enough friends these past few years and our enemies continue growing stronger. How could we have contended with the rise of Mobus Kale and the depths of his depravities?"

"The man is a monster," Sel hissed.

"Created by a corrupt system and set loose from his restraints," Aliz agreed. "He is but the symptom, not the cause. Alain Nye has either lost all control of his special pet, or fully approves. Regardless, we are doomed if we remain on Vau Prime."

A trio of explosions rumbled across the city as if to emphasis her point. None flinched, for they'd become immune to the horrors of war as Kale's noose tightened.

"So we need to escape while we still can," Sel said. "What of Boone Edam and his people? Can we still count on them to help?"

Julian and Aliz exchanged looks before Julian answered, "Doubtful. Any aide he was prepared to give has dwindled during this last press. He is willing to provide us transport offworld however."

"If we can rally on his private landing pad," Aliz added.

"Which is far from certain. Enemy patrols are securing every major port and egress from the city. More and more flights heading south are being detained," Julian said, leaving out the rumors of shuttles filled with innocent civilians being shot down over the ocean. "We're running out of time."

"This is it then? We accept our fate and let Nye ruin the universe?" Sel asked.

Aliz laid a comforting hand on the younger fighter's shoulder. "No but sacrificing ourselves here is pointless. There are other worlds to regroup on. We retreat, we rebuild, and we return with the authority given to us by the gods. I vow that will life still flows through my veins I will not rest until Nye is overthrown and order restored."

"Captain Julian, we have a situation."

The call on his headset interrupted them. Julian stiffened, instinctively reaching for his rifle. "What is it?"

"We've detained a man who claims he is here to see you. Said he used to work for General Strannan."

Eyebrow lifting, Julian asked, "Did he say what his name is?"

"Silk, sir. Gedrick Silk."

"I thought you were safe halfway across the universe by now," Julian said as he clasped hands with the shapeshifter.

"I was but had to return. I owe much to Davith and will do anything to keep his name alive."

"Does that include rescuing strays?" Aliz asked.

A thin smile crept across his face. "Mistress Aliz, you are many things. Stray not among them. You are the very reason I am here."

She flinched. "Why me? There are plenty of more deserving people to focus your attention on."

"Promises were made and I will not slink away in the night," Gedrick told her. "Aliz, there is a terrible darkness coming. Amongeratix is already in the system and approaching Vau Prime."

Sel snorted. "He's a myth. A fairy tale meant to keep children in line."

"He is more than that. I have seen the results of his deeds across the universe. Amongeratix is very real and will bring humanity to its knees should he assume control. Alain Nye knows not what he is dealing with. The Inquisitor General thinks he can control the beast. He cannot."

"What are we supposed to do?" Aliz asked. Her hands trembled as visions of her beloved city in ruins danced behind her eyes. She cursed Nye under her breath. His greed threatened the foundations of civilization.

"I have a ship waiting at an undisclosed location. I can take you far from here, all of you."

Julian's shoulders dropped. "And go where? Last I heard the war had spread across the universe. There can't be any safety left."

"The war has spread, but so has Nye's enemies. Planets are standing up against his reign. Civil war spreads, even while we struggle with trying to maintain control here. From what little we have been able to gather, thanks to the communications blackout, is a splinter group of political leaders, cardinals, and ranking military are forming a new ruling council to counter Nye's powerbase. They have won a great victory and are assembling to defeat Nye and end the war. But with Amongeratix here, at humanity's very heart…"

Enough darkness choked the world. Adding further promises of torment served no point. Gedrick studied their faces as each absorbed the information. He wished there was more to tell and, no doubt, there was, but it had been too long since he last stood upon the foreign shores of Wexanos with

Tannus and the others. His loyalty to Strannan trumped all. What little he'd gleaned from stolen transmissions and his covert assignment inside Inquisition headquarters earlier in the year suggested a great movement was underway, capable of shifting the balance of power and restoring order to the seven hundred worlds.

"Vau Prime is lost," Aliz concluded with downcast eyes. "I can accept this. We've all known it for a year now. Lorenu is dead. Strannan now as well. What little remains is but the stubborn refusal to accept reality. I appreciate you risking your life to bring us this news, Gedrick. I do, but I am having a difficult time accepting this has all been for naught."

"Is that what you think this is? A cowardly retreat to distant stars while humanity suffers and burns? No, Aliz, I am not so callous as to suggest such."

She spread her hands out. "How else am I to take it? I am not a woman of great importance. No one outside of this circle knows my name. They never have. I am the woman behind the throne. A wife. A lover. A widow. What care has anyone for a broken old woman whose best years are far behind?"

Gedrick reached out and took her hands in his, feeling the callouses and grooves wrought from hardship. "Aliz, you are so much more than that. You are the vision of hope this fight needs. Let me take you to wherever this new council is forming and show you a new destiny."

"Even if we could get offworld there is still a planetary blockade in place," Julian said, joining the conversation.

"Admiral Khe-Zhehan has arrived with a fleet. They are engaged at the system edges as we speak. It's how we've managed to evacuate so many civilians on the low continent," Gedrick said and went on to explain the operation to save the refugees from Krenz and what little remained of Strannan's combat command. He felt minor relief upon seeing the first sparks of hope rekindle in their looks when he finished.

"You would take us to the low continent from here?" Sel asked.

"If needs be. Or we could rendezvous with the fleet directly," Gedrick answered. "The choice is yours, though I fail to see any allure of returning to the low continent."

Thoughts of his friends preparing for their final battle at the bottom of the world, against impossible odds, saddened him. Gedrick would have liked one more day with Bryn, Jash and the others.

"Are you certain we can slip through Nye's chokehold?" Julian asked. His tone grew stronger. Forceful.

"No," Gedrick replied. "All I can offer is my best efforts. It is far and the way perilous."

"Lorenu once told me nothing worth doing was ever easy," Aliz said after a moment. "Very well. Gedrick Silk, I accept your offer."

Explosions rumbled across the cityscape.

Planet Occanum.

It was a dead world. Most life obliterated as there were few survivors from that catastrophic time. Once the definitive rulers of the universe, they were reduced to little more than broken memories, transformed over time into the very gods humanity would come to worship and fear. The irony was not lost on Tannus. His defiance proved the catalyst to the final war of his kind. Now he was playing a defiant role again.

Thousands of years later, he had returned and alone stood on the precipice of a second cataclysm. Armageddon approached; he felt it in those hollowed edges of his soul. Perhaps it was all meant to end this way. Humanity. The gods. All turned to cosmic dust and forgotten, leaving the universe to rebirth and begin anew. Not one for understanding evolution, Tannus wondered if that might not be for the best. Both of their races seemed genetically disposed to erasing their legacies with blistering speed. Amongeratix accomplished this long ago for his kind, here on the former shrine world of Occanum.

For a moment, as he sat beside Captain August and her pilot shuttling down to the planet's surface, Tannus gave thought to waking up those seven hundred he'd saved in stasis before final preparations were in place. They held the potential to end the approaching storm before it washed over the universe. What would humanity do upon seeing seven hundred of their gods unleashed upon them? How would they react?

It would cause chaos for the Conclave was all but disbanded. Hundreds of cardinals and lower functionaries were dead or in Inquisition prisons. Twice that had gone into hiding, leaving a stalwart few to tend to their flocks. Brave, but foolish. The flocks wouldn't understand the appearance of their gods without help.

His spies reported the rising power on Mannus Prime and it gave him hope. Light remained to hold back the powers of darkness, even as Vau Prime fell, for he deemed the capital planet unsalvageable. Especially now that Amongeratix had arrived.

Wheels continued spinning. Factions played out. He'd done his part. Orchestrating humanity's best hope for survival. The Paladin continued her training with *Grimfurvor*. Agents were being groomed for their pending roles in the final battle, Forever Night as the Blood Witches named it, progressed. All loose threads were converging. Refusing to acknowledge the pressure in his chest, Tannus couldn't help but wonder if he missed anything.

Then the wildcard popped up, slowing his momentum. Sorrow's warnings came with ill portents. The last of the god hunters had at last awoken. Tannus once cautioned Ruma Zzein on their creation, deeming them uncontrollable killing machines lacking morality or vice. To an extent, he was proven right. Akin Brohl and those hundred like him swept through the universe on a crusade of vengeance. Hundreds of survivors from Occanum were hunted down and executed with ruthless precision during the waning days of the war when Tannus salvaged what he could of his kind. Their fervor came with a terrible price, for only Brohl remained. Would he be enough to slow Amongeratix so Elisa could fulfill her destiny?

The shuttle jarred as it touched down on the sandy bed of what was once Occanum's largest ocean. Enough time had passed that not even the bones remained, leaving a bleak landscape for as far as the eye could see. Tannus stared out the viewport. The last time he'd stood upon this planet there were massed armies, siege engines throwing devastation, and clouds of magic burning the atmosphere.

"We came here for what?" August muttered as she took in the emptiness surrounding them. She'd never seen a dead world, having only heard stories from the survivors of Kharsis.

"For the beginning of the end," Tannus replied. "This was once the jewel of my people's civilization. A world filled with jungles, oceans, and temples. Occanum served as our shrine. A place of pilgrimage all sought to experience during their lives. This was once a world of peace. Of promise." Warning alarms sounded, jarring him from his thoughts.

August scanned the radar screens and felt her heart quicken. "Two signatures inbound. One is a shuttle."

"The other?" Tannus asked.

"A fighter not registering in our database."

"The god hunter has arrived."

August tensed. "Do I want to know?"

He gave a sad smile. "It's probably better if you didn't. Wait here while I meet with Akin Brohl. It will not take long."

"What about the other shuttle? Who is on it?"

"My brother."

Color drained from her face as the prospect of confronting a second of the Three arose. She readied to alert the crew for combat before Tannus' soft grin soothed her.

"Not that one," he said. "Come with me. There is much needing to be discussed."

"Where is your oxygen mask?" she asked as she reached for hers.

"There is no need. The atmosphere is breathable, if slightly thin. We shall be fine."

Skeptical, August replaced the gear she had gathered and motioned for Odir to take over control. Tannus was already heading for the boarding ramp.

"Are you sure this is a good idea, Captain?" he asked her.

August snorted. "We are far beyond good ideas, Odir. Keep the engines warm and watch for treachery. His species may have died here but that doesn't mean I want to."

"Aye, ma'am."

Eger City, Mannus Prime.

Streets were filled with more humanity than Mannus was used to, thanks in large part to the anticipated first meeting of the fledgling New Council. Word spread like wildfire despite the subtle urgings for caution by the various elected officials and religious leaders. The need for secrecy did little to dissuade eager tongues, forcing local security forces to partner with the Prekhauten Guard to ensure the city was as secure as possible in the event of enemy infiltration.

Checkpoints and roadblocks were established at major intersections and around designated buildings. The new rulers went to extreme lengths to prevent this historic moment from devolving into chaos, or worse. Armed soldiers patrolled in squads with quick reactionary forces on standby at company and battalion headquarters. Aircraft circled the city, wary for unregistered crafts. Already a small handful of shuttles lacking official documentation had been forced to land at the nearest airfields under threat of being shot down. Nothing was left to chance.

Arriving dignitaries were funneled from their lodgings to the freshly minted Capital Center via underground tunnels away from prying eyes. Despite the rigid measures emplaced, it was certain the enemy had spies and agents among the throngs of civilians lining the major thoroughfares in the hopes of catching a glimpse. Still flags waved. Music played. Vendors hawked roasted meats. Eger City had never seen the like and everyone attending awaited memories.

The chaos inside matched that of outside. Guards watched from behind their helmet visors, rifles held across their chests, as officials and functionaries scurried about. Standing in his finest uniform, Rear Admiral Falchi inspected the immediate area surrounding the meeting rooms. Hands clasped behind his back, his low whistles were met with concealed grins and the occasional nod from the Guards he passed. He'd spent decades in military service, but never once had he bore witness to such spectacle.

"Have you ever imagined?" he asked the man limping at his side.

Retired Command Sergeant Major Matthias leaned on his cane as little as possible without pain. Mostly recovered from wounds sustained during the final campaign to liberate Mannus Prime, he'd been recalled to the city in what he surmised would evolve into more than a mere advisory role. Ever the professional soldier, his view of events failed to match Falchi's.

"I don't believe I ever wanted to. Standing formation for hours so some general or Conclave representative could inspect was torture enough. Why would anyone want to subject themselves to endless days of meetings?"

"There can be no progress without it, Matthias," Falchi chided. "We are the cusp of a new order, if it is done correctly."

"Doesn't mean it's best for the people." Matthias grunted. "How can we be sure the men and women in this meeting want what is best for the universe and aren't here for some self-serving agenda?"

"We can't. We must trust in them and remain watchful so that another Alain Nye doesn't resurface. This a dangerous time for us. The war can tip in either direction depending on what they decide these next few days."

Matthias shook his head. "It's been in my experience tyrants often start with the best intentions. I don't know how Virom is going to pull it off, but you can bet the people won't stand for another iteration of Conclave."

"Those are problems for others, Matthias."

They continued walking, now well beyond the small crowds of aides unable to attend the meeting.

Matthias longed to be back in the field with the soldiers. He understood them where he failed with politics, leaving him feeling an outcast in a game he was ill-prepared to play. His thoughts drifted to Fies, Breed, and the others. The gnawing guilt of retiring wore at his defenses. Feelings of abandoning his people when they needed him most mocked his dreams. Yet for each sensation of inadequacy, Matthias always wound up in the middle of important occasions, from the battlefield to the halls of power. Was this his fate or were the gods toying with him?

A young officer hurried through the thinning crowds after spying Falchi. Her golden hair felt obscene against the dull grey of her daily Guard uniform in Matthias' opinion. A look of relief swept over her face as she stopped before them and snapped to attention. His appraisal raised.

"Admiral, Cardinal Virom and General Torgast wish to see you immediately," she reported. "I am to take you to them."

Falchi passed a sidelong glance to his companion, questing if the former infantryman sensed any danger. "This seems rather odd considering the moment, lieutenant. Are you certain they meant before the meeting?"

She handed him a slip of paper. His eyebrow arched at the archaic missive, concluding there was but one reason for not committing the message to a datapad. "Very well. Let us see what they have to say. What say you, Matthias?"

The lieutenant flinched. "Ah, sir, I was told to bring only you."

He waved off her concern. "Nonsense. Sergeant Major Matthias is a valuable member of my council and known to all parties. Whatever they have to say to me can be said to him. Is that clear, lieutenant?"

Cheeks reddening, she gave a clipped nod. "This way, gentlemen."

"Ah, Falchi, come in and close the door," Virom invited upon their arrival. He paused, clicking his tongue on the roof of his mouth as he spied Matthias sidle in awkwardly behind. "You as well, Matthias. We could use both of your inputs for this matter."

"Cardinal, we came as soon as your messenger found us."

"Welcome to the party," Torgast said from his seat at the oval table dominating the center of the room. The glass in his right hand held a finger of amber liquid.

Falchi gestured for Matthias to sit and followed suit. "Torgast, always a pleasure. But something tells me I'm not going to like this."

Torgast motioned to Virom. "That's his department. I'm here for moral support."

"Yes, yes. No one wants to do the dirty work," Virom grumbled. "Admiral, I have an unexpected, dare I say unprecedented, situation requiring our attention. And before you ask, yes, this must happen now before the delegates begin their endless string of questions and prattle."

"That doesn't sound like you want to be here anymore than we do," Falchi commented.

"Show me a man who wants to be the center of attention and I'll name him a fool," Virom replied. "This goes far beyond whatever your suspicions are. All of you. Two days ago, I was approached by the acting Cardinal Seniorus."

The military officers stiffened, leaving Matthias the odd man out. The last he knew, Lorenu Phos was the final Conclave ruler before the insurrection. Whoever sat upon the dais was little more than Nye's puppet.

"The Cardinal Seniorus? Here on Mannus Prime?" Falchi questioned.

A dark look shadowed Torgast's eyes. "Was he arrested?"

"That is a, ah, delicate matter," Virom said. "Tinnus Har is in exile. Or so he claims. Right now, I am uncertain as to his true intent. The Conclave has been thoroughly usurped by Nye's people. I am led to believe most of my fellow clergy have either been arrested, executed for heresy, or are on the run. The disbanding of Conclave is a foregone conclusion at this point."

"Making him useless to us," Torgast down the last of his drink and folded his arms.

"On the contrary. He has insights into Nye's inner sanctum," Falchi countered. "Cardinal, is he willing to talk?"

"That depends on what you expect him to say. I suspect he'll talk out of both sides of his mouth. The man strikes me as a viper, desperate to lash out at whoever it perceives to be a threat. I hate to say this, because it goes against every fiber in my moral being, but we'll need to break him first."

"Ah, Virom, we don't condone torture. That's not our play," Torgast started.

"Who said anything about torture?" Virom balked. "We're not animals! He is a man of immense ego. Push him in the right direction. Give him what he wants to hear. Let him think he has the upper hand and he'll crack."

"You play a dangerous game, Cardinal," Falchi cautioned.

"Seems to be the only one we have available," Virom told them. He turned to Matthias. "What is your opinion on this? I've studied your dossier. I've heard of your exploits on the battlefield. You have experiences the rest of us can only dream of."

Licking his lips, surprised to find them dry, Matthias clasped his hands before him and rested them on the table. "Men like that represent the foulest part of the universe. They hunger power, eager to jump on the backs of those they deem invincible. This Tinnus Har willingly took the position in supplication to the Inquisitor General. He is the enemy. Pure and simple. Anything he says will be for his purposes. It might be best to take him up into high orbit and see if he can fly."

"Propositions of murder aside, I happen to agree with you," Virom admitted. "He has a loathsome presence, one I don't prefer to stain my hands with."

"Where is he now?"

"In a secret location nearby. Waiting on our collective decision."

"If he escapes if can ruin everything we have sought to achieve here," Torgast said.

"Which is why he won't escape. I have him under guard but would like you gentlemen to step in and assume responsibility." Virom sighed. "I'm an old man with far too much to worry about. We are on the cusp of forming the rudimentary outlines of a new universal government. Tinnus Har is a distraction, nothing more. His being here represents the total collapse of the Conclave … But that does not mean he lacks vital intelligence we require to win the war."

"I don't like this," Torgast said with a scowl.

"There is nothing to like. Our backs are to the wall and the hours draws short."

Matthias struggled with understanding the implications of their decisions. None of it made sense. Why would Nye's puppet come here and for what reason? Was this but a precursor to a larger subversive action? Rumors of Amongeratix arriving in the Vau system rippled through Mannus' population unchecked, even if most of the population proved unable to comprehend the true meaning behind it. His limited interaction with the Three inspired nightmares of unprecedented proportions. Humanity simply was not equipped to deal with the last remnants of the former masters of the universe.

"What do we do with him?" Matthias asked in the gathering silence. "We can't just let him walk free. Regardless of his current status, he was a willing accomplice to this insurrection. The best thing for him is a fast trial and faster execution."

"Killing him undermines what we are creating here, Matthias," Virom said after careful consideration. "Though, you present an interesting solution."

"In what way?"

Rising, the cardinal began pacing. "We don't know why Har is here. He could be a plant, or his intentions are genuine. Regardless, he continues to represent a threat. What if we let him loose?"

Torgast coughed, eyes widening. "You play a dangerous game. We should—"

"One we have little choice in."

Leaning back in his chair, Matthias said, "Give him enough rope to hang himself if that is his intent. Let him show his true colors by forcing his hand."

Virom cracked a thin smile. "Precisely. One way or another he will reveal his reasons for being here and we will be able to act accordingly."

"I still don't like it," Torgast fumed. "Might be best to send in a specialist and call it an accident."

"That's why I appreciate you, Torgast. You're always there to keep me in line." He chuckled. "Now, I think he might respond better to a pair of smartly dressed military men than a dusty old cardinal well past his prime."

Both dressed in formal uniforms, Falchi and Torgast exchanged looks before turning their heads to Matthias.

"We are both expected in this meeting," Falchi began. "Do you still fit in a uniform or has retired life been too good to you?"

Face locked between snarl and smile, Matthias felt the familiar gnawing sensation in the pit of his stomach that he hadn't felt since hopping in the main battle tank with the Shadow Hammers earlier in the year. "I knew I should have commissioned when I had the chance."

"Rank does have its privileges," Falchi noted dryly. "Try not to break him. I'll send you one of my best Marines to assist. He's a good man, though you might need to ensure he's unarmed ahead of time."

"Wonderful."

Side by side, Matthias and Asom marched down three levels to a private holding facility only Cardinal Virom and a few select advisors knew about. All cells were empty but one. Guards in civilian clothes warded the doors, staircases, and the exterior of the lone occupant. Virom left nothing to chance. So deep underground only a string of low-level lights lined the ceiling. The air smelled rank, fetid. Each footstep produced a sucking noise as the floor was loose dirt. Whoever designed this level had a cruel heart.

"Are you sure this is a good idea?" Asom asked. He wore standard combat fatigues to match Matthias.

Image fragments of the harrowing attempt to recapture Amongeratix when he was a young sergeant danced behind his eyes. A far cry from losing half his squad, Matthias never liked interrogations, even ones under the false pretenses of nicety. He snorted. “I’ve been asking that for about twenty years.”

They halted before the door and presented their clearance papers to the guards, who inspected them with extreme caution while eyeing the strangers. Satisfied the papers were in order, the guard sergeant handed them back.

“You have twenty minutes. No weapons.”

Matthias held up his empty hands. “We’re unarmed. It wouldn’t do to get in Cardinal Virom’s bad graces.”

“No, sir. It wouldn’t,” the guard agreed. Turning to his companion, he said, “Unlock it.”

Exhaling a deep breath, Matthias stepped into the cell. He hadn’t known what to expect when given the assignment. His service was mostly relegated to line units and, recently, special operations far from conventional terms. Dealing with cardinals and senior leadership felt as alien today as it did the first time the previous Inquisitor General presented him with a medal for valor.

Tinnus Har was a shell of a man. Battered and worn thin from his escape, the former Cardinal Seniorus retained the venom of a snake. Enough to give Matthias pause upon entering.

He stared at them without making a sound. Thinly disguised hatred reflected in his eyes.

The door closed behind them.

TWENTY-SIX

3215 A.G. (After Gods), Erdef City, planet Romalle.

Dusk settled over the city in a smoldering shroud. Oppressive clouds hung low over the buildings. Families hurried inside to lock their doors lest they be caught in the open. A thin wind slipped down the streets, whistling poison as they passed.

"It's been a long time since I saw a darkness this thick," Gando muttered.

He and Tolde stood on the small balcony to his office overlooking the heart of the city and lamenting on the devolving situation. Word of Warder Damal's death continued spreading despite their best efforts to prevent it. The official word was he choked to death, but the Inquisitors knew better. Thanks to the failed assassination attempt on Hargan, a plot was uncovered reaching deep into the pillars of power on Romalle.

"Seems all I can remember of late. It's the perfect night for what we are about to do."

Gando grunted, hand caressing the handle of his blaster. "We're playing a dangerous game with this one. Are you sure it's a good idea?"

"Evidence leads back to the church."

The corpse of Hargan's assassin provided just enough information to give them a new lead. Bereft of identification, the conspirators failed to take into account the Inquisition's facial recognition technology. Those responsible for Leganas Breed's death were about to feel the full weight of vengeance.

"I am uneasy with an attack on the Conclave, even if they are responsible for murder," Gando said with a strained look on his face.

"Justice falls upon those who deserve it," Tolde reminded him. "We are still loyal operatives of the Inquisition. Even if they have betrayed us all. Everyone deserves fair treatment."

"Even your brother's killer?"

"We have other problems to worry over," Luma Kai said as she joined them. The ion rifle in her hands hummed. "There's been no word from Ragan. I fear he is in over his head. We never should have left him to his own devices."

"Lady DeMauve is a capable woman. If she says she has assets in place we should trust her," Gando said, his tone hesitant.

Luma pressed. "You don't believe that yourself, do you?"

"Inquisitor Kai, there are times in life where we must place our faith in powers beyond our control. If DeMauve says she has it taken care of we must accept it. We are outgunned and too far behind our enemies to act in accordance with Inquisition mandates."

The tap-tap-tap of her boot sped up. "Whose side are you really on, Gando? You have yet to declare a side in this war."

Tongue snaking across his lower lip, Gando turned on her. "Inquisitor Kai, I am not willing to place my planet in jeopardy over impulsive actions. Romalle wishes to remain neutral, and I am doing all within my power to ensure it stays that way. I am no fan of how the Inquisitor General has destroyed our organization, nor am I willing to declare outright treason against all we are supposed to stand for."

"That's not an answer," she fumed.

"It's the only one I have to give," he snapped. "Help me solve this murder and stall the rising insurrection and return to your war knowing Romalle will not be part of it. You have my word."

His eyes bore into Tolde's, searching for a bond neither man felt. Old rivalries died hard, yet the trio was all each other had.

For the moment.

"They have departed."

Hargan grunted as he adjusted his position. Pain rippled through his chest and abdomen. He was healing, but not fast enough to join the mission. Scowling, he stared at the Blood Witch protecting him. Nothing about her made sense. "How do you do that?" he gestured to the gap between the floor and her slippers.

Bemused, Alessandra replied, "Its magic."

"Uh huh. Its fine if you don't want to tell me."

A hint of smile curled her lips. "It really is magic. There are some who are born with dormant abilities. Once identified, usually after far too many years of torment or ostracization from our communities and families, we are taken to the abbey and trained how to harness our powers and use them. Society brands us exiles. Dangers to humanity. The Order uses this to our advantage."

He nodded. "The less people know the more they fear."

"Not fear, precisely. We prefer the shroud of mystery. Makes it easier to be about our tasks."

"I was under the impression you witches … is that alright to say?" At her nod, he continued. "That you kept to yourselves unless there was no choice."

"We do. Our mandates imply we help humanity where needed."

His eyes narrowed. "Aren't you human?"

"To an extent."

Grunting, Hargan rubbed his thumb over the blaster handgrip and felt underprepared for the night to come. "We should be out there. Not cowering like fugitives."

"Be careful what you wish for," she warned. "The night only gets darker."

The crack of distant thunder emphasized her point, leaving a hollow sensation in the pit of his stomach.

A trio of hired guards, little more than thugs with outdated weapons and grim demeanors, patrolled the front of the temple. Lights were dimmed, suggesting no worshippers were within. Smoke carried the stench of burning wood and incense into the night. Wild dogs brayed down the street, accompanying the light coat of dust kicked up by the wind.

One of the guards, a burly man with shoulder length jet black hair and missing two fingers on his right hand, growled and started banging on the door. "Hey, how about we switch out! You've been in there long enough."

"Fuck off," a voice shouted through the closed door. "You drew outside duty. Earn your pay and leave us alone."

"You and me are going to have words once this is said and done, friend," he snapped only to be met by silence and the growing wind. "It's getting damned cold out," he added, shouldering his rifle to rub his hands together.

"Be colder in the ground. You heard our orders. We keep everyone out. No matter what," a second man replied behind him.

Snarling, the first said, "I didn't sign up for getting soaked. This storm promises to drench us out here."

"Beats getting shot at. We finish this job and head offworld. It's a big universe with plenty of wealthy marks."

"Aye. It—"

The first man dropped with a grunt, blood spreading across his chest. Stunned, the others stared at him.

The second man started to speak. "What—"

The remaining two men pitched backward as ion rounds sizzled into them, killing each instantly. From the shadows across the street emerged Tolde and the others. They dragged the bodies off lest passersby raise the alarm.

Tolde led them back to the doors, each Inquisitor pressing up against the building exterior. He gave Gando a nod and dropped to a crouching firing position.

Gando drew a deep, steadying breath before banging on the door. "Open in the name of the Inquisition."

The shuffle of boots was his only reply.

Gando risked pressing his ear to the door and caught the scurrying of feet. He closed his eyes as his hopes for avoiding more bloodshed evaporated. Guilt produced extreme measures. He was now certain those in the temple were part of the plot to assassinate Cardinal Breed and usurp governmental authority. "This is Inquisitor Gando. Open this door immediately or face the consequences."

The first shots burst through the thin fabric of the door, sending a shower of splinters and superheated energy into the street—Tolde returned fire.

The street lit up with bright blue-white energy. Structure compromised, Luma slammed her rifle butt against the remainder of the door. It swung open with a tired groan. She tossed a flashbang into the acrid haze choking the entry. The resulting spark and explosion elicited screams and cries of agony. Gando and Tolde charged in and discovered a pair of guards fumbling around. One had his hands pressed against his ears, trickles of blood slipping between them. The other covered his damaged eyes. Both were unarmed.

Gando kicked the legs out from the first, driving him to his knees and using the body as a shield in the event of additional shooters lurking within the temple. Tolde mirrored him, taking a moment to place restraints on his prisoner. A red line cut through the haze, tracking the back of the temple's main hall as Luma entered.

After a quick infrared scan, Luma cut the laser. “Clear.”

Tolde frowned. How could that be? Was the temple warned ahead of time? If so, by who? “Are you sure?”

“I didn’t pick up any additional lifeforms,” she confirmed.

Tolde whipped his prisoner around; the blinded man flailed. “Where is the priestess? Who told you were coming?”

Despite his pain and disorientation, the man remained silent.

Tolde gripped the man’s tunic tighter. “I’m not asking again. Where is Ingrid?”

Blood spitting from his cracked lips, the guard moaned, “Gone. She’s heading offworld where you won’t find her.”

“Which airfield?” Gando demanded.

A baleful laugh mocked him.

“Tolde, we’re running out of time if what he says is true,” Luma said.

Agreeing, Tolde ordered, “Secure these two. Luma, check the back offices for any clues to Ingrid’s whereabouts. We can’t afford to let her escape.”

Waiting for her to leave, Tolde pulled his prisoner close and said, “Now, you’re going to tell me who hired you or you’re joining your friends outside. Start talking.”

“Are you certain?” Hargan rubbed his stomach, careful not to irritate his wound. He and Sister Alessandra just received Tolde’s report, which he read aloud. Her shoulders slumped under the new pressures suddenly thrown on him. At his side, Sister Alessandra hovered. Her robes shimmered through a pattern of colors before settling on dark hues.

“They were too late. The temple was guarded but empty.”

“Where is our wayward priestess?” Alessandra’s voice boomed from within the shadows of her hood. Dangerous energy curled out from the edges.

“Supposedly heading for one of the local airfields.” Hargan frowned, glancing at his datapad. “But I don’t think so. It’s the obvious answer. She would know we’ll be targeting each them … No, Ingrid will seek to go underground. Dig deep where we can't find her."

"How can you be sure?"

"It's what I'd do."

"We must hurry. If we lose her, we might never discover how deep this conspiracy runs," Alessandra urged. A nagging feeling tugged at the back of her mind. She knew she was missing a key fact but failed to place it.

"We're not even supposed to be tracking Ingrid. Our mission is to confront the remaining warders and discover which one is behind this mess. The priestess is little more than a convenient diversion."

The cackle of electricity dancing off Alessandra's knuckles filled the room. "I grow weary of these mortal games, Hargan. We must act now and act decisively."

Catching Ingrid and exposing the corruption of the local temple meant nothing if he and Alessandra failed to learn the true perpetrator of Romalle's problems. Hargan worried about making the wrong choice. One false move and their scheme might unravel and plunge his beloved planet into war.

"We go to the board chambers," he said at last. "They must be stopped, above all else."

"Yes."

He snatched up the handheld. "Gando, Hargan. Do you read?"

"Go ahead," the Inquisitor's voice cackled over the comms channel.

"We're moving on the Board. Don't waste your time with the airfield. If my hunch is right, the priestess will attempt to flee for the protection of her benefactor then underground. Meet us at the city board chambers."

Mouth open to lessen the sonic force as the former Guardsman Mayn instructed, Ragan jammed his fingers in his ears as far as they could go without hurting himself. Not that it mattered. The crisp report of automatic rifle fire penetrated to the center of his skull, threatening to drive him mad. A slight ringing bounced between his ears, high pitched and irritating. He glanced over to see Riles in similar, if somewhat reduced, agony.

"Back door. Move," Mayn ordered as he ducked behind the ruined window frame providing cover.

Nemineon went first, having returned a short time ago. The confiscated blaster in his hand trembled, threatening to slip from his grip. For all the bravado he displayed, he'd never been caught in a firefight. He vowed to return to the tribes if he survived the night. City living clearly wasn't for him. He wondered if Riles would join him. The life they once envisioned seemed so far away now. A fading shadow lost to pointless dreams and dashed upon broken shores.

His thoughts swirled around her newfound fascination for the offworlder. Ragan was a simple man, no older than Nemineon, but he offered the experience of having traveled across the stars. How could Nemineon compete with that? His knowledge seldom expanded beyond the endless savannahs stretching across half of Romalle. What little he knew of the rest of the universe felt pale compared to all Ragan claimed to have endured over the last year. In comparison, he was little more than an uneducated child from a backwater world far from the center of events.

He glanced back at the pair. They seemed easy together, as if they'd known one another for years. Side by side, Riles and Ragan ran while Nemineon considered turning back and helping Mayn. It would be a last act of defiance to establish his position for Riles, hopefully showing her how much he cared for her.

The coward's tug in his mind gave him pause, forcing his legs to keep running forward. That tiny whisper told him he was no hero. No brave soldier dashing into harm's way to save the day. Nemineon realized that he was more interested in surviving and forgetting this nightmare than winning over Riles. A pair of energy bolts striking the wall inches above his head emphasized his point. He froze as bits of the wall crashed down on him.

"Keep moving or we're all dead!" Mayn shouted from behind. The older man unleashed a hail of rounds at their attackers.

Nemineon felt a shove and scowled until he saw the fear in Riles' eyes. Unexpected courage surged from within, and he pushed through the shattered door frame they had been heading toward, pausing to help both Riles and Ragan through. Once safe within the doorway, he watched Mayn with wonder. For his age, the former Guard retained his martial prowess and vigor, fighting like a man half his age.

A rush of emotions overwhelmed him. Latching on to the vein of courage, Nemineon stepped into the open.

"Nemineon! Come back!"

Riles' voice was all but drowned out under the increased fire. He wouldn't have stopped even if he'd heard her. A strange sensation he failed to recognize filled him. One capable of tricking him into believing he was invincible. Nemineon hit the wall beside Mayn and started shooting.

"Stupid kid, what the fuck are you doing?" Mayn bellowed without ceasing his assault.

"You need help!"

The blow of an explosion against the lower wall threw them back in a cloud of shrapnel and debris. Flames devoured all they touched. A second and third detonation trembled the entire building, sending a shower of dust and debris down from the ceiling.

"Nemineon!" Riles screamed again.

Ragan shook his head, clearing his vision even as his ears rang from the successive concussions. Spots dancing across his eyes, he watched Riles run toward the others. Crossbeams and chunks of ceiling were dropping around them, threatening to crush them in the collapse. Cursing under his breath, he followed.

They found Mayn partially buried beneath the rubble. Blood ran down the side of his face and a finger stuck out at an obscene angle. Groggy but still conscious, Mayn reached out for Ragan's hand and was pulled clear. Pain twisted his face, but he remained silent and gained his feet. Leaning on Ragan, he snatched up his rifle.

"Damned kids are going to get us all killed," Mayn grumbled as he was half dragged away from the scene.

"Where should we going?" Ragan demanded, ignoring the snarl in the Guard's voice.

"Down the hall and to the left. There's a back door leading down to a service tunnel." Mayn gestured with his chin. "Gain that and there's a vehicle waiting to take us to the secondary site." Increased rifle fire broke his attention. "If we make it that far."

"Where did all these people come from? I thought we were escaping?" Nemineon cried as Riles helped him up.

Mayn rolled his eyes. “You’re bait, boy. Nothing more. We’re trying to draw out the bad guys and put an end to this once and for all.”

“Bait!”

Riles said in hushed tones, “Quiet, Nemineon. This was the plan all along. You weren’t supposed to be a hero.”

“I want to go home,” he all but whimpered.

“So do I,” she said.

Ragan winced at the warmth in her voice. He knew then any thoughts of pursuing a relationship with her was naught but passing fancy. Once close to remaining on Romalle, for her, after the mission ended, Ragan saw with clarity again. This was no place for him. He still wasn’t sure what greater purpose the universe had in store for him, but it wasn’t on Romalle. Like a weight slipping off his shoulders, he gripped Mayn tighter as they began to move. They reached the door shortly and Mayn ensured the passage down was clear.

The older man produced a small, flat object from the side pocket on his trousers and handed it to Ragan. “Here, place this against the wall a foot from the floor after the others pass and hit the red button.”

Ragan took it, grunting at the unexpected weight. “Then what?”

Mayn grinned, blood covered teeth gleaming in the gloom. “Run like hell, boy.”

Pressing against the back door, Mayn hefted his rifle and waited for Riles to catch up. His gaze never left Ragan as the youth fumbled with the device before attaching it to the wall and doing as instructed.

“Inside, both of you. Trust me, you don’t want to be here for what comes next,” Mayn ordered.

Riles and Nemineon obeyed and slipped down into the darkness and musky smell of the forgotten tunnel system. Ragan hurried to join them as Mayn fired off a pair of well-placed shots felling their closest pursuer. Shadows of more mercenaries crowded the thin hall. Grin frozen on his face, Mayn continued firing as he backed into the tunnel and hit the button to close the door an instant before the explosion ripped the building apart.

Eiters sat and glared at the woman across from her, wondering why she entrusted the aging priestess. Astrid lent a frail appearance; a broken figure far removed from the lust for power she once imbued when the first thoughts of conspiracy came to Eiters. At the time she'd sought staunch allies for the change she knew needed to happen if Romalle was to gain respect throughout the sector and prove its worth. Enough planets were falling into shadow thanks to the growing civil war. Should Romalle share a similar fate it meant near economic and social disaster. Worse, if the Inquisitor General won the war they would be punished without mercy.

Eiters knew the church needed to be involved from the start, but Cardinal Breed was a proud man with a storied legacy among the clergy. His open defiance of the changes on Vau Prime suggested he would never submit to any coercion or subversion on her part. They also lacked a strong relationship he shared with other members. Eiters needed Breed out of the way to enact her plan.

Seducing Astrid with promises of power hardly proved worth the time. The priestess already possessed a corrupted spirit. She fell for the promise of running Romalle's Conclave faction and a healthy stipend. Matters became complicated from there. Eiters languished over finding the right mercenary crew to eliminate Breed as she worked to plant enough false evidence on Damal, using her guile and natural charm to blind her colleague into thinking what transpired was thanks to his doing. The fool. If only he'd opened his eyes a little more, he might still be alive. Eiters kept the smirk from twisting her face. Her plan had been going smoothly until the unexpected, and unofficial, arrival of Breed's Inquisitor brother.

"We need to get out of the city while we still can," Astrid repeated for the third time.

"You are prepared to abandon this course of action far too easily, Priestess. I thought you made of sterner material."

"They raided the temple! A trio of Inquisitors!" She struggled to stop fidgeting. "I have no desire to face the Inquisition, Eiters."

"They are of little concern. What bothers me is the ease with which you have given up. And, by doing so, you leave a trail for our friends to follow. Right to me. I'm sure you can see my dilemma."

"They were coming for me!" Astrid's voice became shrill. "Perhaps you don't recognize the penalties for suspected heresy."

"Against what precisely? The Inquisitor General has his own issues to deal with. I highly doubt the Inquisition is carrying out its mandate of old in the midst of this war." Eiters waved a hand lazily in the air. "No, these Inquisitors won't be an issue. Or they wouldn't have been if you'd remained in place."

Eiters regretted telling Astrid of her plans without developing a secondary trail for any poking noses to follow. She also lamented not having Hargan killed. The investigator proved too good at his job and harder to remove than anticipated. A shame he wouldn't turn to her side, but it was far too late for that now.

"What you fail to realize, Astrid, is I have factions in place across the city. As we speak they are hunting down and eliminating the witness to Cardinal Breed's murder. Board member Damal has been taken care of and the path is wide open for me to assume control of Romalle and dictate our future course of action."

"You're mad," Astrid's voice dropped to a whisper.

"Mad? More determined, I'd say. You've dedicated your life to banal service in the name of beings you've never met, nor can confirm ever existed." Eiters stiffened. Her tone bore a darkness that hadn't been there before. "My problem, and the one thing capable of leading our friends back to me, is you. I entrusted you with performing your role and turning the heads of both the Conclave and Inquisition. Instead, you flee at the first sign of trouble, placing me in a dangerous situation. You, my dear priestess, have become a loose end I can't afford."

Astrid jerked back in her chair. "What do you mean?"

"I believe the time has come to part ways. You're a liability, Astrid."

Balking, the priestess exclaimed, "So you're going to what? Kill me?"

"Don't be crass," Eiters replied with a chuckle. "I've ensured all evidence leads back to you. All of it. Breed's murder. Damal's poisoning. A document in your writing will be released proclaiming your resignation from the Conclave and attempt to subvert Romalle for your own designs. You will become this planet's largest villain. A victim of your own greed." She sighed at Astrid's gasp of outrage.

"I will admit to you having come to enlist my support. No one will believe you. How could they with mistrust of the Conclave already spreading? You will be tried, found guilty, and executed before the masses. All in the name of Romalle's continued prosperity." Now Eiters smirked. "Fret not, your death will provide the fuel needed to propel us into a new era where we shall become a dominant power in the system. Thanks to you, Romalle will be well-regarded in the halls of power of Krenz."

Pressing a button under the table, Eiters nestled into the cushions of her chair and watched.

Trapped against the wall, the priestess saw her world crashing down. A pair of guards entered the chamber and her hopes dissipated. They snatched her by the arms, pulling her from her chair and dragging her toward the exit. Wild strength came to her. Astrid wriggled free and drew one of the guard's blasters. She elbowed the man, producing a huff, and took aim at Eiters who, much to her amazement, hadn't so much as moved. "You bitch!"

Pain flared up her arm as the second guard punched the weapon free. Astrid felt tears break free as another blow crossed her face. Her left arm was twisted behind and jerked up with just enough pressure to make her gasp. Stunned, she tried to move. The first guard recovered his weapon, mumbled a quick apology to Eiters, and hurried to join his partner as they escorted the fallen priestess away.

Alone, Eiters sighed. So close to achieving her goals, there was yet more to do before she could claim the title of sole ruler of Romalle.

"You're going to pay for that, bitch," the guard beside her snarled in her ear once they were in the hall. "I'm going to have fun with you. Where you're going, no one will hear you scream."

Astrid's eyes widened, but her strength had fled.

They continued toward the last place she would ever see. Random thoughts swirled through her mind, rendering her little more than an emotional mess lacking the coherence necessary to win through her situation. They rounded a corner and jerked to a halt. Hair dangling over her face, Astrid made out three figures standing at the opposite end of the hall.

"Out of the way. This is Board business," the guard beside her ordered as the one holding her tightened his grip. "This woman is responsible for the murder of Cardinal Leganas Breed. Step aside."

None of the trio moved.

Tired of being hindered, the guard stepped forward. "I said move. There won't be a third warning."

"Let the priestess go," the man in the center ordered.

"On whose authority?"

"She is now a prisoner of the Inquisition."

Astrid stifled a gasp as she recognized those before her.

"I am Inquisitor Gando. Follow my commands and you may go home to your loved ones this night."

"If we don't?" the guard asked, too high strung to stop now.

"You don't go home at all," Gando finished.

The guard holding her, less excited than his counterpart, released her and stepped aside.

"What are you doing? We have our orders!" the first snapped after seeing the priestess on her own. He turned back to the Inquisitors. "We are acting on orders of Board Member Eiters. The Inquisition has no authority here."

Gando sighed. "That is where you are sorely mistaken."

In unison, they drew their blasters and gunned down the pair of Guards, careful to wound instead of kill. They fell with blood spots spreading on their thighs.

Thinking herself safe, Astrid ran toward the trio, only to find a blaster pointed at her face.

"Priestess Astrid, you are under arrest under conspiracy to commit murder and foment insurrection against the Conclave," Gando declared. "Tolde, Luma secure them please."

Tolde and Luma rushed ahead to secure the wounded guards in bindings.

"Please. Please, it wasn't me. I was being used," Astrid pleaded.

Gando scowled.

"You have to believe me," Astrid said, defiant in the face of imprisonment, or worse. "It was Eiters. She is behind all of it."

"Prove it," Tolde demanded. "Make me believe you weren't my brother's killer."

Astrid looked back down the hall. "She's in the private meeting chamber. She—she admitted to using me as a scapegoat."

Tolde gave Gando a clipped nod and leaned closer to Astrid. "Pray you speak true or it's the Inquisition for you, priestess."

The smell of urine, warm and pungent, filled the air as Astrid collapsed.

Using a crutch under his left arm, Hargan slunk his way through the back corridors of the board's main building. If his suspicions were correct, Eiters would be attempting to escape back to her safehouse where she would consolidate power and make her move to proclaim Romalle free from the Conclave and plunge the planet into the heart of the war. The Blood Witch at his side, radiating power through dangerous intent, filled him with the strength.

Eiters. He hadn't expected her at all. All evidence pointed to Damal. Frowning, Hargan retraced the steps of their investigation. Perhaps it was the former board member's inherent greed which blinded him from seeing the truth. Perhaps he hadn't wanted to believe any of the others were capable of subverting an entire planet to their whim. None of it mattered now. If what the priestess said was true via Gando's last communication, Eiters was responsible for Cardinal Breed's death, a string of violence and assassinations crippling the upper class, and a failed attempt on his own life. For that, she needed to pay.

"There is vengeance in your heart," Sister Alessandra whispered.

Hargan grunted, partly from the pain and partly in acknowledgement. Still, he needed to be seen making the last move in what he hoped would be the end of Romalle's political suicide. "Wouldn't you? This must end."

"It will, though I urge caution. You are an enforcer of the law. Not a brigand."

Chewing on the corner of his lip, Hargan's face darkened. "I understand, but if she so much as shows any sign of resisting..." Some things sounded better without being voiced aloud.

TWENTY-SEVEN

3215 A.G. (After Gods), Eger City, planet Mannus Prime.

It was a clear summer day with scant a cloud in the sky. Light winds tousled the trees, stripping a scattering of leaves across fields and into city streets. Flights of orange and purple martins zipped between buildings without pause. Yet for all the inherent glory in an alien world, Adris Moscasco failed to find the beauty. Her heart and mind remained focused on Donab and his sacrifice since they boarded the shuttle. She'd long suspected he harbored feelings for her but neither voiced them. And now he was gone. Another casualty in a pointless war. The weight dragged on her soul, threatening to undo all the hard work she'd accomplished over the past year.

"This planet is so different from ours," she murmured.

Standing behind her, staring out across the vast city stretching as far as the eye could see, Tempest continued to marvel at the sights and sounds of Mannus Prime. "And it doesn't smell like fish." She chuckled to herself, thinking of how the clothes they'd worn during the escape from Dalafar were taken and burned upon arrival.

Moscasco turned, eyebrow arched before breaking into a shallow laugh. "What would I do without you, Tempest?"

"Let's hope we never have to find out. I've received word our stalwart squad of saviors is scheduled to return to the line soon," Tempest said. "I have also arranged for a final meeting with them. An informal luncheon before you begin your duties in the new council."

"Thank you. They deserve our thanks, whether they choose to believe so or not. We are going to need more like them if we have any hope of winning this war," Moscasco admitted. "Are they in place?"

"They should be arriving as we speak."

Moscasco rose, pausing to stretch. Weeks aboard their tiny shuttle after a harrowing escape into one of the deep space routes left her feeling cramped, even in the expansive halls of the new government. "Come, let us give our thanks one last time to our new friends."

"I don't like wearing this uniform," Annalilly said with a scowl as she plunged a finger between her neck and the stiff collar constricting her.

Haggle replied, "I didn't think you still had your dress uniform."

She fixed him with a glare. "What do you mean by that?"

He held up his hands in mock defense. "Nothing. Just that we haven't been part of the Guard for some time now. It's a surprise any of us still has them."

She waggled a menacing finger at him and stalked off.

Soon they were seated in a large dining chamber off the main corridor of official apartments. Attendants scurried back and forth with tray after tray of meat, cheeses, fruits, and breads. Pitchers of homemade beer from a local distillery beckoned the soldiers. Sunlight filtered in through a wall of windows. If they looked hard enough, the Guards could see the edges of wide grasslands untouched by the recent war. Soft music played from ceiling speakers, leading many to believe they were in store for a formal reception.

"What do you suppose they want with us?" Hollis asked. She stuffed her hands in her pockets to keep from sneaking chunks of cheese to satisfy her rumbling stomach. "Are we getting medals?"

"I doubt it," Quint replied. "We'd be in front of a formation looking at a bunch of angry stares. This is either a reprimand or a thanks."

"Must be nice to get thanked for doing our jobs," Beve snorted and plucked a slab of roasted meat from the table. "This is good."

The door hissed open, and their hosts swarmed in. Fies spotted the crisp general officer uniform lingering behind Moscasco then another behind him and snapped to attention.

"Squad, attention," he barked.

As one, his Guards stopped what they were doing and turned to face Admiral Falchi and General Torgast.

"Stand easy, soldiers," Torgast said to ease the tension. "I believe you all know the Governess. She wished to have a last thank you before you depart on your next assignment. Eat and drink your fill, but I caution you all not to get drunk on duty. It would be a shame to lock our newest heroes away in the brig to work off a bender."

No one moved, making Fies proud. Clearing his throat, he said, "You heard the man. Relax and have fun."

"Never thought I'd hear him say that," Haggle whispered to Jolent.

The sniper stared at him before moving to grab a plate.

Once everyone was seated and enjoying their meals, Adris Moscasco clanged her spoon to her glass to get their attention. Conversation died down as all eyes turned on her. Her face reddened, unexpectedly succumbing to the surge of emotions as she took in this lone squad who dared take on an entire planet for her.

"I have known many Prekhauten Guards during my time in politics. They represented the best the universe had to offer. Men and women of impeccable character and quality. Alas, far too many decided it was in their best interests to continue their loyalty to the new regime and the Inquisitor General. For you to travel halfway across the universe just to rescue me, and Tempest of course, speaks volumes to who you are and what you represent.

"The uniform you wear is more than a badge of intent. It is a symbol of justice and freedom. I sit here before you humbled by your dedication to duty and the lengths you were willing to go. It is my honor to raise a glass to you. I know there are no words worthy of your heroism. Nor will anything I say return Captain Donab to us but that does not mean I won't try." She raised her glass. "To your soldiers, Lieutenant Fies, and to Captain Donab. May you continue shining your example to the rest of us as a reminder of all we can become."

They drank deeply of the rich red wine. More than a few teared up. Never had they been recognized for their actions in such a manner, for they were professional soldiers used to working in the shadows.

As the ranking officer in the squad, it fell to Fies to offer a response. "Governess, I think I speak for all of my people when I say we were merely following orders. Somewhere along the way we came to respect you, and Tempest, and consider it an honor to have helped you reach Mannus Prime. May you continue to serve the needs of the people and help restore order to the universe before it is too late."

"Good words, Lieutenant," she replied. "You should ask for a promotion. I'm sure the new Guard will have need of leaders of quality."

Before Fies could defer Falchi jumped in, "That is an excellent idea, Governess. Fies has demonstrated impeccable qualities under the worst situations since the war began. You may not know it, but it was his squad that was involved in the first battles of the war. Since then he and the Guards seated before you have endured more trials than any individual should have to."

Falchi rose, reaching into his trouser pocket as he moved to an open space. "Lieutenant Fies, front and center."

Fies winced but followed orders. He halted three paces away from the admiral and snapped to attention. A gesture from Torgast sent the rest of the squad to their feet.

"Lieutenant Fies, on behalf of the Prekhauten Guard and the new council of Mannus Prime, I hereby promote you to the rank of captain, effective immediately. We thank you for your service and continued devotion to order and justice. May you hold your rank long and continue living up to its lofty standard."

Applause broke out as Falchi removed the old rank pins and placed the new ones on Fies' collar. Had they been in standard fatigues Falchi would have pounded the rank into his flesh, but new dress uniforms were hard to come by. Instead, he shook Fies' hand and stepped aside so General Torgast could do the same.

"Ladies and gentlemen, Captain Fies," Falchi proclaimed.

One by one the squad filed by and congratulated the freshly minted captain. After the last one passed, Fies leaned close to Falchi. He was rewarded by the admiral handing him something. The formal part of the reception ended, and genuine merriment broke out in the form of awkward dancing and speckled conversation.

Moscasco made her way through the room, making a point to thank each of them. Though it was a joyful occasion, she eavesdropped on multiple conversations to gauge the value of Falchi and Torgast. A cursory glance showed Tempest doing the same, though with less enthusiasm.

"Congratulations, Captain. It is very deserved," she said after making her way to Fies.

Embarrassed, Fies nodded. "I'm sure it wouldn't have happened without you, Governess."

"Nonsense. I've spoken with each of your squad, and they all gave me the same answer. You are the definition of a true leader. A man who consistently places the needs of his people ahead of his own and balancing that with accomplishing the mission." She smiled. "I meant what I said. We need more like you to stop Nye and his war machine."

"She's right. I had doubts about your mission, but the admiral assured me you were the right person for the job," Torgast said after joining them. "Damned good job out there."

"Thank you, General, but I couldn't have accomplished any of it without my people. Especially Sergeant Quint. He has found his home with us and for that I am most grateful."

Torgast's gaze shifted to his former guard. "Quint's a good man. He's been through a lot over the past year. Losing him to the line was a blow for my command staff but I have a feeling it worked out for the best. Keep him safe and I guarantee he'll do the same for you." He paused, eyeing the room before focusing on Fies. "Report to Admiral Falchi first thing in the morning. You've earned the rest of the day off."

"Yes, sir."

Torgast and Moscasco excused themselves. Another meeting beckoned and the reception ended. Attendants began sweeping in to clear the room of plates, glasses, and leftovers. Soon the squad found themselves alone again.

Fies cleared his throat, summoning his best command voice. "You heard the man. Rest up and be ready for our next assignment. I want formation five minutes before the sun comes up." Reaching into his pocket, he produced his lieutenant bars. "Oh, and Sergeant Annalilly, I have something for you."

Her eyes widened and she stepped back. "Not on your fucking life."

Brightstar, enroute to Wexanos.

Over the course of three thousand years humanity carved out a substantial empire from the ashes of the old regime. It was a time of prosperity and unprecedented growth fraught with hidden perils. Chief among them was the feud between three brothers. Together, they were responsible for countless deaths and the desecration of numerous worlds. Vanity drove their motivations, poisoning their minds while gnawing away at reason and righteousness. What remained after their protracted conflict was little more than a shell clinging to the tattered fragments of reality.

Or so Sharlyn August once thought. Since discovering most of what she'd been raised to believe was little more than empty lies, she never envisioned how far from the truth they were. Seeing a twelve-foot-tall man perpetually weeping blood argue with his equally frightening brother while another looked on with murderous intent genetically imposed in his blood left her feeling inadequate for what was to come and unable to convey her thoughts to her crew.

She looked around the bridge, amazed by the massive space swallowing her. August guessed the *Brightstar* once held a bridge crew of a hundred in its prime. Those days were far removed. Shadows filled the bridge where life and light should have been. Prekhauten naval vessels carried much lighter crews, choosing the maximization of the individual over redundancy in positioning. Twenty of her people, veterans all, manned their stations, from weapons to navigation. Tannus insisted on keeping the transit routes back to Wexanos private lest the enemy discover his grand secret.

"You've been silent since we left Occanum."

August wiped her mouth, stifling a yawn before looking at Odir. "I don't know what to say. None of this makes sense."

"Because you are thinking rationally. What about this war leads you to believe we are in normal times? Our enemies murdered an entire planet, from people to the smallest insects. We've allied with pirates and have floating witches serving alongside us. Don't get me started on our host." Odir exhaled. "These are trying times, both for our willpower and our imaginations."

"At least you only have to follow orders."

Odir clasped his hands behind his back and resumed his stare out the main viewport. "I wouldn't have it any other way. I've been watching what command does to you—no thank you."

"You are ever the voice of reason, Commander," she joked. "How long until we arrive at our destination?"

"Half a day at least. The timing system is archaic at best. I've had crews working around the clock to update the technology. I won't miss being on this ship."

August didn't have the heart to tell him she doubted they would be returning to the comforts and familiarity of the *Solstice* anytime soon. Admiral Falchi's orders were vague. Until she received a formal recall back to the fleet, she feared they were now Tannus' permanent crew.

"Did you ever think to see the Bloody Man in person?" Odir asked suddenly. "I've gone over it in my mind repeatedly. How can he have survived for so long weeping blood like that? It's not natural."

She shuddered. Legend suggested he'd fallen victim to such despair over his brothers he skinned himself alive. Whatever dark magic sustained him millennia later shook her to the core. "As you pointed out, so eloquently I might add, none of this is natural. The entire universe has lost its mind and we reel to make sense of it all. I fear this may be the end of all we hold dear."

Fidgeting, Odir replied, "The Blood Witches call it Forever Night. The great ending of the universe. If you believe in such things."

"Perhaps it's better we let it all burn down. Whatever remains can rebuild, start fresh. Clearly all humanity has achieved since the fall of the gods has been for naught."

"Your assessment is far from accurate, Sharlyn August."

They turned at Tannus' arrival. He stormed onto the bridge with defined intent and the natural authority given to a man in his position.

"Lord Tannus, I did not expect you," August began.

"On the bridge of my ship? That seems uncharacteristically shortsighted of you," he chided. "And please, I have said this before, I am no lord. Tannus is fine."

He saw the same hesitancy in her as others who'd been in his service. Tannus found it an endearing trait among the best of humanity. He knew August by reputation before the mission to recover the planet killing artifact and discovered a great deal more about her in the time since. Though she didn't know it, he valued her opinion and her competency.

"What do you think of my brother?"

Odir's mouth dropped open, leaving August to respond. "He, ah, is an interesting person."

"A fool is closer to the truth." Tannus' voice dropped conspiratorially low. "Can you imagine the willpower it took to skin himself?" He paused, watching the horrified light filling her eyes. "I'm kidding, of course. My brothers and I each have flaws. What he did was out of love and desperation. Sorrow isn't the one we need to concern ourselves with. Erratic in the best of circumstances, he has our best interests in mind. Without his aid the Paladin would never have recovered *Grimfervor*. So, take heart, Captain. We are entering the endgame."

"Forever Night," Odir whispered.

Tannus eyed the man. "Yes, though I dare say the universe is far from ending. No, should I defeat my brother and finally win this war I will provide humanity with the reset it has been needing for too long."

"How does killing Amongeratix help stop the Inquisitor General's bid for domination?" August asked.

"There is more going on than you might guess," Tannus replied. Without knowing what Falchi or the others briefed her on he didn't want to open any fresh avenues for her thoughts to spiral down. Recognizing the fragility of her mental state after the meeting on Occanum, he wished to preserve their budding friendship.

"Everything transpiring is the direct result of your Inquisitor General having meddled with the wrong sort. This began decades ago, though neither I nor any in your command structure recognized it at the time. Alain Nye fell prey to my brother's whispering madness. Once the spark ignited there was no turning back. Now here we are. I regret this had to happen during your lifetime, but I am also confident in your generation's ability to process and handle these events. We are in a good position to defeat the darkness."

"Until it rises again," she muttered. "I've studied the histories. There is always a crisis, whether militarily or through faith. There is still the cult of Rengu to deal with."

Tannus waved off her concern. "A minor nuisance, no more. Zealots fueled by my brother to distract from his main thrust. With Amongeratix removed they will fracture and fade."

August wasn't convinced but held her tongue. "When this war ends another will pop up. It might not be for a lifetime, but my people will find themselves at the end of the rope once again. How can you promise not to be involved?"

He sighed. "Because I do not plan on being here by then. Once I am finished with my brother no one will see me again."

The finality in his tone chilled her. For one of the greatest powers in the known universe to admit his approaching end, even while keeping such end cast in shadow, offered little hope for the rest of them when they, she, needed it the most. "You mean to abandon us? After thousands of years?" she asked, lower lip quivering.

"Captain August, much of what you find occurring right now is because of me. When the war is over and the dust begins to settle, if we both survive, come and find me and I shall tell you a tale that has been twisted into legend. If your heart does not break, I will have overestimated your worth." He turned away. "Please inform me when we reach the Wexanos system."

He made it to the stairs when she called to him, "Tannus, who do gods pray to?"

Tannus paused for a heartbeat before exiting.

Eger City, planet Mannus Prime.

"He's ot going to break," Asom threw down his uniform cap and collapsed into the rickety wooden chair with an ominous creak. "This is a waste of time. We should be preparing for the coming offensive, not playing nurse maid to a broken old man past his prime and with little to no intelligence value."

Matthias didn't disagree. They'd been down to Virom's private dungeon numerous times a day for the last week without making any progress. Former Cardinal Seniorus Har proved a difficult subject more intent on playing games than providing any actionable intelligence the new council might use. "It doesn't help we're not interrogators," he admitted before joining the Marine at the small table. Matthias poured himself a glass of amber ale from the pitcher between them and drank deep. "Be easier if we could do it the old Guard way."

Asom's eyebrow arched. "I may not have as much time in service as you, but even I know the value of an old-fashioned beating, even if it is banned by regulations."

"The Guard always seems to find a way to get worse, doesn't it?" Matthias asked. "I suppose every generation says the same. How many times have we each heard how things were different in the old days?"

"More than I care to remember," Asom answered. "Now I'm at the point in my career where it's my turn to say it to the new recruits."

"Passing the torch."

After pouring his own glass, Asom frowned and asked, "How long before you want to head back down?"

"Let's give him a break. We've earned it. I say we finish this pitcher and head back to Falchi to see if he has any bright ideas."

"You want me to report to my commanding officer with alcohol on my breath?"

"We're on special assignment. If he says anything I'll take the blame. Besides, the admiral owes me."

They clinked glasses and said no more.

"Nothing?" Falchi asked, choosing to ignore the aroma of local ale seeping through his Marine's skin. "After all this time?"

"No, sir," Asom responded, suppressing a burp.

"I can't say that I'm surprised. Men like that think they're above the rest of us. He'll cling to his convictions for as long as he thinks he's useful. You could always take him into orbit and show him the dark side of space."

"Don't tempt me," Matthias said. "This man is a huge part of the problem. Breaking him isn't going to happen. Leastwise not any time soon. Not unless you want to start depriving him food, sleep, and water."

"We're not terrorists, Matthias. Stooping to our enemy's tactics ill serves our purpose. No, keep applying pressure. Let him think he's got the upper hand. Sooner or later he will slip. Play to his vanity. You and I have both encountered enough politicians and bureaucrats to know how this game is played. Push him. Be relentless."

Crossing his arms, Matthias shook his head. “I’m afraid that will prove a waste of time, and resources. There isn’t much more I can do here, Admiral.”

“Ready to depart again?” Falchi asked. The thought of losing one of his most valuable assets sat ill with him. “I won’t deny losing you will be a huge blow to morale. We need men like you to keep whatever this is we’re building going … There might a career in politics for you.”

“I’m not going anywhere yet, but history shows Tannus likes to deploy his assets with frequency.,” he replied.

Falchi smiled. “Meaning you’re open to the idea once this war ends.”

“Wouldn’t that turn heads? I’m afraid my talents lay behind a trigger.” Matthias shook his head, a wry grin on his face. “None of this helps with the Tinnus Har issue. If word of his being here gets out it might subvert the entire operation. He’s a dangerous man, Admiral. His tongue can twist your mind until you think it’s your idea. Let him loose and he’ll shift allegiances in the wrong way.”

“Has he given any indication why he’s here?”

“No, only that he believes he can help us defeat Nye.”

Asom added, “For his own selfish needs of course. He’s poisonous, sir.”

“Snakes often are,” Falchi agreed. “There is an opportunity here, however.”

“I don’t see what,” Matthias said. “Anything he does will only serve to further his goals. Which, we’ve gathered, are his return to power by any means necessary. He wants the throne back and will destroy anyone standing in his way to get it.”

“The man is more delusional than we thought. Rumor is the Conclave is bordering on dissolution under Nye’s mandates. With Amongeratix already in system and Admiral Khe-Zhehan’s fleet engaged I fear the old order is on its way out. Men like Har refuse to accept the truth of the moment.”

“Then we play it up for him. Make him believe he can return to Vau Prime triumphant once the Inquisitor General is removed,” Matthias suggested suddenly.

Falchi steepled his hands. “Go on.”

"How influential is this governess Fies and his people brought back?"

A glint sparkled in Falchi's eyes. "More than enough for what I think you've got in mind. Getting her to cooperate might be an issue. Virom and the others have already embraced her. What little time she has is devoted to establishing the authority of the new council and aligning neighboring systems. We've already seen the benefits of her knowledge and influence. Dozens of neutral worlds have declared for us, contributing their natural resources, supplies, and military assets for the coming fight."

"Let me see if I can pull Moscasco away," Falchi said. "When did you plan on leaving?"

"There's no rush, Admiral. I said I would help and will."

Falchi rose, smoothing the creases from his blouse in the same motion. "Very well. I will get back with you as soon as I can. In the meantime, I believe there are a few weary Guards eager to speak with you."

Matthias broke into a grin. "I'm sure there are. Thank you, Admiral."

Left alone for the first time in days, Tinnus Har had never felt his world so restricted. His robes of office were replaced by simple clothes. His facial hair was unkempt, his face itching from the constant burn. Grime collected under his fingernails and his teeth felt loose from the lack of proper nutrition and hygiene. Not that his captors bothered mistreating him. The fools. He despised their generosity. They fed him, clothed him, and gave him a bed to sleep in when they should have tortured him and disposed of the body. The difference, he noted, between the victors and the vanquished.

His only guests had been the former hero of the Conclave and a space marine who was as out of place underground as he was attempting to interrogate a prisoner. A laughable effort from those who he supposed were in a position of moral authority. So, Tinnus Har, deposed Cardinal Seniorus, sat patiently in his forgotten cell, waiting for the next time and then the next time before he broke his interrogators and finally spoke with someone having the intelligence and wit to trade information with him.

During his incarceration Tinnus learned to trust his senses more. He caught the clip of boots coming down the hall long before the guards turned the key and the outdated iron door swung open. The faint trickle of golden light poured in, now an old friend he longed to embrace. Tinnus kept his head down, refusing to give the odd pair the satisfaction of seeing the growing despondency haunting his eyes despite his best efforts to retain a measure of dignity.

"Back so soon? I'd have thought you were more than anxious to be done with me for the time being," he mocked. "What's wrong, Matthias, can't stand to feel the sting of failure?"

"I'm afraid the sergeant major couldn't attend this meeting," a woman's voice replied.

Tinnus looked up through strands of greasy hair. The woman standing before him, haughty in appearance and well-dressed, meant nothing to him. "I don't know you."

"There's no reason you should, other than now," she said. "My name is Adris Moscasco. I am, or was, the governess of Dalafar. Today, I am so much more. One might even say I am the final deciding factor in whether you ever see the light of day again, *Cardinal Seniorus*."

The title rolled off her tongue as an insult, causing Tinnus to flinch. He glared. "Why should I believe you? Dalafar is far from being the center of the universe. Your influence is more limited than you think, *Governess*."

She clicked her tongue on the roof of her mouth, a bemused look creasing her face. "Tell me, what was it like being Nye's puppet? You didn't truly think you were the most powerful man in the universe? Not after the assassination of Phos. She was liked and beloved. You did the bidding of a madman and when he no longer needed you, he discarded you like detritus." She sniffed. "Who is lying to who, Har? You fled Krenz in the night, little more than a fugitive with a price on his head. The true power in the universe wants you dead. I dare say needs you dead. Why else would you be here? You bring no value to what we are growing."

"I bring the only value," he seethed. Veins popped on his neck, reddening his face. "You don't expect this rabble to withstand Nye's assault once he turns his gaze here, do you? He controls the bulk of the Guard and all but a scattering of the Inquisition. When he is ready, Nye will unleash his military might, and that dog Mobus Kale, on Mannus. Not a single soul will remain alive once he finishes."

"You overestimate his chances."

"Do I? What if I told you he has already amassed a fleet of unprecedented size and the one factor he has been waiting on is finally arriving?"

Moscasco prodded. "Should I be concerned? We have a growing fleet of our own."

"Yet you lack the one thing capable of burning the universe down."

She struggled to keep the growing sense of dread from reaching her face. Anything to let Har think he held the upper hand. "What would that be?"

The answer was not what she expected.

"Shit," Matthias gasped after hearing the confession.

Asom, having little experience in the matter, gave him a confused look. "What? You don't really believe that? The Three are a myth."

"I wish they were," Matthias shook his head.

Memories rushed him again: His men dying as Amongeratix slaughtered them, first on the derelict ship and then again in the deserts of An'kuruku. Having witnessed the true evil plaguing life firsthand too many times, Matthias wanted to take his gear and find a place to hide.

The others studied him, cautious in their approach to the subject. Denouncing his fears did little to bolster confidence. Accepting it for what it was likewise. Of them all, only Falchi knew what the retired Guard feared.

"Matthias speaks the truth. We have encountered Amongeratix in the past," Falchi said.

Moscasco, of whom just entered the room, crossed her arms and stated, "There is more."

"There is. Since this war began both he and I have worked with Tannus. He is the one chance we have at defeating his brother, but even that remains a stretch. Amongeratix is an unstoppable force of nature. Aligning with Nye is the worst-case scenario for us."

Torgast groaned and wiped his face.

To his right, Moscasco struggled with accepting the truth behind legends told through the generations. Her faith rested in what she could see, not shadows in the night. To see these proud, experienced military men all but cower told her more than enough. They were in trouble. Until now, she found difficulty in believing the Three were more than conjured images, despite all she'd been told. "And is this Tannus willing to continue his support?"

"To the best of my knowledge. Even now he is working with members of the navy. Make no mistake, we do not control him. Nor do we order him around. He is in complete control. He helps where he best thinks it will serve his goals. While I don't think he is focused on Nye and our mortal affairs, he is determined to stop his brother. He will help."

"And he's not alone," Matthias added.

"What do you mean?" Torgast asked.

Matthias looked at each in turn, pausing to see the depths of their convictions lingering in their gaze, before saying, "There are two others, his kin, who stand beside him, but even they might not be enough. This is going to be humanity's ultimate test."

TWENTY-EIGHT

3215 A.G. (After Gods) Third planet from the sun, Vau Prime System.

Impacts rippled through *Revengence*. New alarms sounded with every weapons strike. The allied command ship groaned as bulkheads melted and twisted under the strain of prolonged combat. Yet for the beating she took, the old ship delivered more. The wreckage of enemy ships filled the space for hundreds of kilometers, drifting aimless until entering a gravity well.

The twin fleets continued pounding each other. Ships were crippled and disabled throughout half the star system. Evacuation pods weaved through withering barrages of long-range missiles and energy beams. Those unfortunate ones caught in the crossfire died instantly. Numerous ships on both sides were forced to withdraw from the line before suffering catastrophic loss. For the moment, neither side held an advantage.

Khe-Zhehan watched as her broadside cannons unleashed their full fury on an enemy frigate. The kinetic shells penetrated the already battered hull, blowing the ship apart from the inside. A flight of assault fighters swept in through the debris cloud as the lack of oxygen snuffed out the brief flames in the wreckage. She spied a trickle of bodies streaming out into space and offered a prayer. Despite being on opposite sides, they all once shared the same philosophy.

"Admiral, incoming signatures from our rear!" the tactical officer shouted over the din.

Scowling, she released her grip on her command chair. "Identify."

A detonation in the rear of the ship dimmed the lights, throwing several crewmembers to the deck. Smoke poured from the rear access wall. Security personnel rushed to extinguish the fires before they spread. A ceiling panel broke free, crashing down beside the helm station.

"All gunners, weapons free! Target everything in range," she bellowed. "Clear the airspace! I want control of this engagement area now!"

Her crew hurried about their assignments, coordinating the battle sphere throughout the nearly two kilometer long flagship. Armed with seven hundred kinetic cannons for ship to ship action, twenty-five dorsal and ventral high-powered lasers, and deep striking fusion missiles, *Revengence* was once considered top of the line. Khe-Zhehan and her crew cared for the ship almost as much as they cared for each other. That pride was instilled across her fleet, transforming the survivors of the ambush at Hawker's Gate into a focused weapon. Unfortunately, the size and prestige of *Revengence* made her the enemy's priority.

Flights of starfighters arrived, filling the space around the battered flagship with murderous intent. Air defense weapon systems flared to life, punishing the enemy craft the closer they made it. Dozens were struck. Some exploded. Others spiraled away, their pilots desperate to save their ships and their lives. Khe-Zhehan vowed to award every gunner on the ship if they survived. The fleet had been engaged for almost eight hours and, she feared, they hadn't gotten to the heaviest fighting yet.

One bright spot in this developing nightmare was the steady stream of ships fleeing Vau Prime. Countless refugees and loyal soldiers and politicians were being evacuated. Several ships were targeted and destroyed before she realized what was happening. After matters became clear, she redirected the bulk of her escort ships to protect the refugee trains. Every ship fleeing into the main shipping lines was a small victory. She struggled to imagine the terror filling those ships. Most were defenseless, relying on her fleet to protect and save them.

"Captain Avi, have we received any word from the planet on how many more evacuee ships we can expect?"

"No, ma'am," the stern-faced ship's captain replied. Her face belayed how exhausted she was. "We're tracking another two hundred in the battlespace. Three hundred and fifty have already departed the system. Estimating over ten thousand lives saved, but there is no way for us to know what remains planetside."

"Has the surviving command structure made it offworld?"

"Unknown."

The implication hollowed the veteran admiral. Not that she expected any different. Were their roles reversed she would either be on the last ship out or giving up her spot for someone more deserving. The true cost of leadership came from sacrifice, not reward.

Catching flickering images from one of the smaller screens tracking the escape ships, Khe-Zhehan watched five smaller civilian grade ships wink out of sight, enroute to star systems yet untouched by the civil war. She knew high value leaders were heading for Mannus Prime and, what she hoped, the forgings of a new universal order aligned with the founding principles of Conclave. Freedom, she learned, was the right of every sentient being, no matter how small. So long as she drew breath, she vowed to do her part to ensure it.

Those thoughts were thrown off by another warning siren and the roar of air defense guns barking back to life.

"Bring us within range of *Revengence*. Launch full salvos of anti-aircraft missiles. We can't afford to let the ship go down."

Captain Ryboth was new to command. Fresh faced and straight from the academy. After earning his position, he found himself in the unenviable position of having to choose a side. Either stay true to his uniform and oath of office or abandon central command in exchange for doing what was right. Ryboth thought himself a pragmatic man, making the choice easy. He remained with Vau Prime for two years.

It wasn't until a devastating engagement left his crew on life support praying for salvation, he learned the true depths of despair and the wrongness of his actions. He pleaded with Naval Headquarters for a rescue tow, but Krenz remained silent. His crew spent days struggling to survive. Almost out of food and water, many contemplated suicide lest they asphyxiated when the oxygen supply ran out. Then a miracle happened, and they were saved, but people he thought were the enemy came through when his own people refused to give him a second thought. The crew agreed to switch their loyalties to those who valued their lives. The rechristened *Forge of War* plunged into every battle Khe-Zhehan ordered them into. They racked up an impressive kill count many ship captains were envious of.

Seeing *Revengence* in dire straits, he led his stalwart crew into the fray once more. Standing in front of the command chair with hands clasped behind his back, Ryboth followed the flight of missiles screaming into the swarm of enemy fighters. Explosions rippled across the battlespace, flaring out as soon as they detonated. There was no mercy. No regard for enemy life. He flicked his gaze to the tactical screen to ensure no silent killers were lurking nearby to finish what was started almost a year ago.

"*Forge of War*, *Revengence*. Thank you for the assist," Khe-Zhehan's voice cackled through static.

Ryboth allowed a smile. Win or die, he knew he'd earned the praise of the woman responsible for giving them all a second chance. "Our pleasure, Admiral. Give us a moment and we'll have you a lane cleared to the heart of the enemy battlegroup." He cut the transmission and turned his attention back to his crew. "Tactical, open a channel to the rest of our battlegroup."

"Channel open, sir."

"All ships in Group Sigma, this is *Forge of War*. Collapse on me in assault pattern alpha. Blast everything out of our airspace. We're punching through for *Revengence* and the other capital ships. Weapons free. Engage at will. Godspeed and good hunting."

The deck lurched under his feet as his beloved ship raced into the next stage of the fight. A dozen other frigates and cruisers joined him.

"*Revengence*, follow us."

Admiral Degote studied the map of the current battle. Over five hundred ships were engaged throughout the system, with the wreckage of hundreds more already strewn across local space. He'd watched the universe tear itself apart as those unable to envision the Inquisitor General's future fled to foment further rebellion. The idea sickened him and all he stood for. A military man for almost five decades, Degote allowed his hatred for disunity to guide his hand. He promised both the Inquisitor General and Mobus Kale to keep the space over Vau Prime cleared of enemy influence or die trying.

This current insurrection pushed his tactical prowess to its limits, forcing him to abandon traditional Guard tactics in favor of more subversive, less honorable maneuvers.

Chicanery became the order of the day after the initial disasters when the enemy fleet burst out of the shipping lanes. He'd lost almost an entire battlegroup to the ambush but was provided both time and opportunity to strengthen his core defenses. Khe-Zhehan's assault fleet blunted their noses on the fresh hammer of his main fleets.

Minefields funneled the engagement zone into a two hundred kilometer wide swath as the tides of battle shifted back and forth at impossible rates. Degote suspected his opponent, a woman he knew well, would come for him, hoping to cut the heart of his fleet and break their defenses in one crushing blow. He counted on it and built his defense accordingly. Seeing his fighter screen decimated, whole squadrons disappearing, hurt but it was necessary to allow his foes to think they had the upper hand. Behind the massive bulk of *Liberator* awaited a hundred capital ships eager for their first kill in this war.

"First Officer, order all surviving fighters to clear out and give our friends a lane to advance. It is time we crushed this rebellion in one swift maneuver. No quarter and no prisoners. This ends here."

His fleet of killers warmed their engines and primed their guns. A half squadron of mixed cruisers and frigates plunged into the suddenly vacant space between fleets. Degote crossed his right leg over the left and sat back in his chair, eager to watch what came next.

Inquisition Headquarters, planet Vau Prime.

"The Inquisitor General plays a dangerous game with his resources," Sister Evangeline growled from within her hood.

"He wants to claim victory on his own merit. There is nothing wrong in that." Geres Auk lounged on an expensive couch in their freshly appointed quarters, eating and drinking to his heart's content for the first time since fleeing Crimeat after Baron Scura's death. Crumbs covered his tunic, lodging in the sparse beard he'd started growing recently. Two empty wine bottles lay on their sides on the table beside him. A viewscreen showed them up to the moment coverage of the battle raging just beyond the planet's gravity well.

"He wastes resources on petty posturing. This is pure folly."

"What difference does it make? We have food and drink and Lord Amongeratix will arrive within days. Enjoy this time while we can." He felt the heat from her glare and ignored it.

"We came here to prepare this planet for Amongeratix's arrival, not lounge before a vidscreen imbibing our way to drunken oblivion," Evangeline scolded. "Have you given thought to what happens if the enemy breaks through before his arrival? What happens to our mission?"

Geres paused, stopping his hand from shoving the roasted fowl leg into his mouth. "You worry too much, witch. This is the most powerful city in the universe. We have nothing to worry about. Not now."

Evangeline had had little contact with the outside world since attaining her full rank among the Order of Blood Witches. Men were anathema to them, as were the political games played by those in power. She stayed aboard the comet in the relative safety of the abbey for decades before Algiss Her turned her away from Ruma Zzein's mandates. Not that it took much. Evangeline always harbored the idea of inadequacies during her time in the sisterhood. She knew she had more to offer, more to accomplish. Joining the rebellion and serving in the Crimson Sisterhood offered her the opportunity to grow in ways Ruma Zzein never would. Drunk on her new power, she eyed replacing Algiss Her and twisting the new order in her own image. She just had to survive the final battle for Vau Prime first.

"This is where your brutish demeanor fails you, barbarian," she hissed. "Behemoth is mighty, but it is just one ship. What if Amongeratix's brothers have similar vessels? Armed with enemy fleets at their back, they could sweep in and destroy us all without pause … I must speak with the Inquisitor General before it is too late."

Geres tossed the leg down and wiped his palm on his tunic. "I shall come too. This is important enough for us both to investigate."

"Indeed." She rolled her eyes.

They stalked out into the side corridor and followed it into the main artery linking the housing quarters to the heart of the Inquisition command structure. Menials and low-ranking Inquisitors shied away or avoided them altogether for word had already spread of their arrival.

Geres found the experience amusing at best. He'd seen weakness before, having spent a lifetime in the service of those he deemed lesser men. To bear witness to such here, in the halls of power running over seven hundred worlds, twisted his stomach. His mind drifted to what he would do to correct their deficiencies were he in charge. The stylized visions of torment and violence put a smile on his face as he lumbered along beside the floating witch.

Reaching the turbolift, they soon found themselves standing before the heavily guarded outer doors to the Inquisitor General's suite of offices. None of the five Inquisitors, their faces concealed behind the mirrored visors of their shock helmets, flinched as Evangeline and Geres approached.

Noting their constricted stance, the witch surmised these were among the best Nye had, men and women sworn to defend him against the worst threats. Men and women who stood little chance of defeating her magic with their limited human capacities. "Stand aside. We will speak with the Inquisitor General now."

To their credit, none so much as flinched.

Geres stepped forward and cracked his knuckles. "The lady said move."

"You have no authority here, beast," the sergeant of the guard snarled in response. "We were not informed of your visit."

Geres rose to his full height and rolled his shoulders. "I'm not going to ask again."

The click-hum of a rifle charging filled the space between them. Magic danced in vermillion ribbons from Evangeline's robes. Geres crouched, ready to leap and wreak havoc. The doors hissed open to reveal Alain Nye standing with his hands clasped behind him, dressed in his finest white uniform and a scowl of disdain.

"You should not be here, Sister," Nye began, never taking his eyes from his people. "These men will die for me if I snap my fingers, though I did not expect to find violence readymade on my doorstep. Why have you come without summons?"

"We must speak with you. It is an urgent matter," she replied.

Feigning a glance at his wrist chrono, Nye stepped to the side. "Very well. You have five minutes. Sergeant, have your people stand down. No one fires unless I give the word."

"As you command, Inquisitor General," he said and clicked the safety on. His guards followed suit.

Nye smiled. "There, you see? There are times when diplomacy settles the moment."

Gesturing with an open hand, Nye allowed Evangeline and Geres to enter. Once passed, he gave the sergeant a nod and followed.

From the sounds behind him, as the door closed, Nye knew his people were shifting their stance to attack his guests should he call.

The Inquisitor General led them to his formal receiving office and made a show of taking his seat behind the antique desk dating back three hundred years. He watched as Geres sank down into the one couch against the far wall and folded his arms. Nye dismissed the man for the brute he was and lent his focus on the witch. Should any danger arise, it would come from her first.

"Perhaps you would care to tell me why you are interrupting me during the height of the current battle for our system?" he prompted.

"That battle is precisely the reason why we are here. You are losing too many ships and personnel to an inferior foe. I hope it is not from the false sense of security in knowing Lord Amongeratix is arriving soon. He has but one ship," Evangeline said.

Nye poured a glass of water from the crystal carafe on the corner of his desk and drank deep. "I was not led to believe you witches had tactical knowledge in human battles."

Evangeline lifted another few inches from the floor. "We are well versed in many aspects of what we deem human affairs. Do not make the mistake of thinking we are that far removed from you."

"I see. Why would I not rely on Amongeratix's massive battleship? He is coming to our aid, is he not? Or is there some other purpose to his visit? A diplomatic envoy perhaps?"

Evangeline explained her reasoning, accented by grunts and nods from her counterpart.

Nye listened with little passion, letting her speak while absorbing her fears, even the laten ones hiding behind her impassioned attempt to change his mind and adjust his field tactics. "I assure you, Sister Evangeline, my naval commander is exceptional at his job. While it may appear, our losses are crippling they are far from it. An additional three battle fleets are converging on the system as we speak. What little gains our misguided friends have will soon be dashed upon the hulls of broken ships. Amongeratix will have no need to risk his precious ship in the fray unless he chooses to make an example of the rebels." At her silence he added, "Now, if there is nothing else to discuss, I must ensure all his prepared for his arrival. There is yet much to be done. You may see yourselves out. I trust you know the way."

Evangeline resisted the urge to incinerate the man for his smugness alone. Instead, she offered a clipped bow and swirled about. "Come, Geres, let us go. There is little more to accomplished here."

Zevistya Spaceport, low continent.

The string of detonations trembled the ground for kilometers, funneling through the mountain passes to the open plains upon which the spaceport was built. The last vestiges of life on the low continent pressed together, their hopes clinging to a fevered dream that somehow salvation might still find them. Skyward, the once steady flood of shuttles had reduced to a trickle. Several wreckages could be seen from the control tower. What remained of the Prekhauten Guard were deploying forward in a last ditch effort to slow the enemy advance long enough to get the rest of the refugees airborne.

Colonel Apontee scanned the horizon for the telltale plumes of black smoke confirming vehicle kills. His scouts sent periodic reports detailing the near unstoppable tide of traitors surging toward the spaceport—Mobus Kale's last push to cleanse the planet of resistance. Apontee spied four spires of smoke but found no solace from them. Outmanned and outgunned, his meager forces couldn't hold for much longer.

He glanced to the unit kill board, waiting for those responsible to call it in. Their guerilla operations forced him to abandon traditional tactics. In the wake of Strannan's murder, the despondent Guards needed a boost. Apontee provided that in the form of incentives for the most effective units. Those recording the most kills received a day off or one of the last remaining bottles of alcohol in the supply building. His people took to it like sport, each competing to earn their due and, for a time, forget the enormity of their situation. The results went beyond his initial estimates. Close to a thousand enemy personnel and vehicles had been destroyed in the last week.

Behind him, Lieutenants Abernath and Mal watched in total silence. One stared at the radios, the other at the far mountain pass.

"Sir, scout vehicles are returning," Bryn Mal reported.

Apontee followed her pointing finger and felt his heart sink. “Returning hell, they’re in full retreat. How much longer until the last of the refugees are airborne?”

“We still need a few hours,” Jash Abernath replied. His voice shook as much as his slight frame. “We need more time.”

“We don’t have it.”

The blue-white flash of engines engaging caught his attention. The next flight of shuttles lifted off and gained altitude. Ground control crews herded the groups of refugees into position. Thus far, the evacuation resulted in the salvation of over twenty-thousand civilians and wounded Guards. Too many more waited their flight to freedom.

With heavy heart, Apontee knew what needed to be done. “Order the task force deployed to the forward trench. I want heavy weapons charged and ready within the hour. All infantry and light armor to the front immediately.”

“Yes, sir,” Mal replied and began relaying the orders.

For the men and women in those units, she knew it was a death sentence. Almost a thousand strong, the force comprised of volunteers; those willing to sacrifice their lives in the defense of others. Mal took inspiration from it and requested permission to join them—Apontee denied her. There was much yet to be done, he’d told her, and the future needed quality leaders if they were going to defeat Kale and break the civil war.

Now they watched as the remaining equipment confiscated from the raid on Tatarast Island deployed for the final time. Scout vehicles flowed through the lines. They’d done all they could and were little use in the coming battle. Each had orders to join the evacuation and, gods willing, live to fight again. Another flight of shuttles screamed down from the skies. One trailed smoke and veered away from the landing strip in a desperate attempt at saving the people on the ground as it gained velocity. Without slowing, it plowed into the ground, detonating on impact.

“I want the scout commander to report at once,” Apontee said after whispering a quiet prayer for the crew. “Keep this train moving, Lieutenants. Every civilian left on the ground is a stain on our honor.”

"Air defense batteries are coming online," Mal confirmed without being told. She knew, as did they all, that Kale's next move would be sending in assault craft to destroy the landing strips and cripple the spaceport.

The machine hum of automated air defense guns deploying across the rooftops as they cycled through their pre-combat processes vibrated the tower. Mal felt the raw power penetrate her armor and grew emboldened.

Apontee nodded. "Very good. Send a communique to Admiral Khe-Zhehan's flagship appraising them of our situation. With a little luck we'll break these bastards here and make them regret choosing the wrong side."

At her confirmation, he resumed his watch of the brave thousand as they took their positions, readied their weapons, and prepared for the enemy army to snake its way down through the mountains. Time was yet on their side, for Kale's forces wouldn't be able to meet them head on for some time. Not without being ground down piecemeal. No, the newly minted general may be a madman, but he was ever the sound tactician. His units would pour forth and deploy online, skirmishing to test Apontee's defenses before unleashing their full fury. Perhaps by then the last would have departed.

Perhaps.

"Damn it, Bryn, come on!"

Ears ringing and blood draining down the side of her face, Bryn Mal staggered to Abernath's position. Colonel Apontee was dead, as were most of the others. A flights of Raptor class assault craft darted in from their blind spot, avoiding the crossfire of the anti-air and took out the control tower with a barrage of missiles. That she and Abernath survived at all was a miracle. The delaying force was decimated. Only a handful managed to flee back to the safety of the escape shuttles before the line collapsed. Kale's forces allowed no quarter, slaughtering their foes to the last.

Jash Abernath dragged his counterpart up the ramp of the last shuttle, refusing to look back. Until now he'd never imagined what a full-blown battle between Guard forces would look like—he prayed to never see the like again.

Madness had descended on Vau Prime and the universe suffered for it. Yet despite the unchecked violence, Apontee's rescue operation was a success. Every civilian was offworld. Whether they made it their destination was no longer up to them.

The ramp closed and the shuttle launched without waiting to secure the passengers.

The defense of the low continent was at last concluded.

Krenz, planet Vau Prime.

Julian wept openly as he received word the spaceport had fallen, and all defenders were dead. True to Kale's promise, there were no prisoners. No survivors. His friends were gone. Slaughtered on the whims of madness.

"Let your tears loose, Julian," Aliz soothed, her arm wrapped around his shoulders. "Remember our friends. Honor their sacrifice and do not let despair grip you. I believe many were escorted to safety, away from Alain Nye's clutches. We may yet see them again."

"I wish I had your confidence."

She refused to let him see her face. Behind them came the last of his cell. Seven haggard survivors who didn't know how to die. They were broken, battered, and on the edge but each found a way to keep going in the face of the rampant hatred consuming the city. Aliz admired their tenacity, their perseverance. Each of those left, those precious few, embodied the best of humanity. She wished enough existed throughout the universe to set matters right and erase the nightmare of the past few years.

One thing she'd learned with her time amongst criminals and soldiers was few cried without being encouraged. Theirs was a hard life, filled with untold dangers and hardships the common population failed to understand. For Julian to break down after so many trials suffered, in her presence, spoke volumes. She vowed to do everything within her power to see him and the rest to safety. The beleaguered group struggled on, desperate to reach the hidden spaceport before time ran out.

Ahead, Gedrick Silk led them unerringly. His knowledge of the lower levels and the areas often deemed undesirable by those in power proved unparalleled. Armed with a rifle with half a charge left and naught but instinct, the shapeshifter proved a worthy foe for their hunters. Aliz marveled at the man, for his ability to transform into anyone he chose as well as his unwavering loyalty to those he'd sworn himself to.

"Wait here," Gedrick whispered and hurried ahead without pause.

Aliz held them up, taking up her rifle in defense as the Guards formed a loose circle and watched.

The wait wasn't long: Gedrick slunk back to them, his face a mask of dejection. "They have the port surrounded."

Not a sound ushered from the Guards. Professional to the last, even in the face of the end.

"How many?" Julian asked, his moment of weakness now passed.

"A full platoon," Gedrick replied. "Far too many for us to win through and reach the shuttle. I am afraid we must find another way offworld." He lacked the heart to tell that there was no other way. They were damned already.

A series of small explosions drove the Guards closer to the ground, eyes and rifles scanning for the source, but the narrow canyons of the city, even diminished by lower buildings and the open area just ahead, left them with a limited field of vision. Smoke and the stench of explosives wafted over them, heightening their confusion a moment before small arms fire erupted. Cries of pain followed. The hail of fire intensified.

The rush of boots drew Julian's immediate attention. He swiveled to meet their approach. Index finger curling over the well-worn metal of the trigger, he slowed his breathing as much as possible and took aim.

"Don't shoot! It's me," Edam Boone shouted over the roar of battle.

He and Thopos emerged from the growing haze. The criminals were filthy and Julian spied fresh blood stains on their clothing. "What in the name of the gods are you doing here?" he demanded, still not believing what he saw.

"Saving your asses," Thopos replied harsher than intended.

Edam gave the would-be torturer a stern glare before explaining. "Captain, you have been a constant source of irritation to my organization for far too long. So much so I had trouble with our last parting. This city might already be lost, and with it the last modicum of morality we will enjoy for many years barring a miracle, but my conscience weighed heavily. I don't care for this war. The fighting only destabilizes everything Zoraq sought to build. Alain Nye and his minions can be damned for it all. Easy at it would be to disappear underground and rebuild, I couldn't let good men and women die for no reason."

Aliz rushed forward to embrace the man. "Oh Edam!"

"Don't thank me yet, madame. We caught them by surprise, but they are regrouping," Edam said, forgoing the mention of potential reinforcements swarming the spaceport.

Unable to stand being relegated to obscurity while others fought for them, Sel stood beside Julian and said, "We can help."

"Please do," Thopos said. No soldier, he welcomed the chance to step aside and let the professionals take charge.

Julian gave silent consent and his squad hurried to join the fight. The Guard captain gave Edam's shoulder a thanking squeeze before he slipped around the corner.

With the last of the bodies dragged clear of the shuttle and the remnants of the insurrection cell aboard, Gedrick settled behind the controls to warm the engines. They'd picked up a transmission stating enemy reinforcements were enroute. Time was up. He glanced over his shoulder to the boarding ramp where Aliz and Julian stood with Edam Boone, reflecting on how odd this stage of his journey had been. He decided to give the humans time to part on their own.

Aliz stood with her hands clasped, wind whipping strands of her short, grey hair about. "You don't fool me, Edam Boone."

"How so?" His grin reminded her of a child caught in a lie.

"You're a good man. You and your people deserve better than what awaits. I knew befriending Zoraq would pay dividends, just not like this. Are you sure you won't come with us?"

Edam offered a sad look. "How can I? I have hundreds of lives looking to me to keep them safe. Should this war ever end, and people find it safe to return to Vau Prime once more you be sure to find me. The first round is on me, Aliz."

She gave the criminal one last hug goodbye and boarded the shuttle. Aliz doubted they'd ever meet again. Some words were just too hard to say aloud.

TWENTY-NINE

3215 A.G. (After Gods), Erdef City, planet Romalle.

Lady Emmest DeMauve smoothed the wrinkles from her blouse, carefully rubbing the soft of her palms so as not to ruin the fabric. Impeccably dressed, her hair fixed and pinned in place, she presented the image of a true lady and a respected, if purposefully misunderstood, member of society's upper tier. The brace of throwing knives cinched to her waist notwithstanding, no passerby would assume she posed a threat.

Reports streamed in from across the city. Thanks to her developed planning and the natural martial ability of her house chamberlain Mayn, the bulk of mercenary forces responsible for killing many of her peers and rivals was eliminated. Gando messaged to inform her of their capture of the vile priestess who'd set up Cardinal Breed to claim his place in the Conclave and Hargan and the Blood Witch were chasing down the one woman to blame for all of Romalle's problems. Loose ends were wrapping up, promising to allow Emmest the opportunity to return to the mundane triviality of her daily life. War, she was now assured, was not coming.

Yet a nagging feeling persisted as she waited. One she couldn't shake. Emmest became certain she was missing a key fact. The lynchpin to everything that had transpired these past few months. With the information broker's untimely demise, followed in close succession with Board Member Damal's purported suicide, those holding the answers were reduced to a handful. She'd been unable to uncover any other conspirators at the governmental level. So why then the worrying sensation in the pit of her stomach?

The room proved substandard but that was to be expected, all things considered. With but one entry point and a single, grim smeared window close to the ceiling, she found little to be enthused about in the apparent safehouse. Dust covered furniture sat scattered around the room, unused for years perhaps. Unwilling to sit, Emmest took to pacing to keep her mind prepared.

The wait proved shorter than expected. Hurried footsteps announced her visitor. Emmest moved to the murk of shadows along the back wall, away from any invading light upon the door opening. When the door did open, a frail woman slipped and pressed her back against it after it closed. Emmest repressed a grin, knowing the sensation of perceived safety was momentary. Instead of acting, she continued studying her prey.

Eiters had aged much these past few months. With her dreams of empire collapsing around her, she found grey hairs and lines where none had been. Constant fatigue, first from the vacancy left by adrenalin and then the fright of the walls closing in, left her in a cycle of stealing her strength and focus. The universe conspired to keep her down, proving no power was greater than the eternity of the cosmos.

Closing the door behind her, Eiters sagged against the battered metal and tilted her head back until she felt the hollow thump of flesh striking metal. She closed her eyes. Sleep beckoned, cruelly darting away when she reached for it. Growling her frustrations, Eiters slammed a fist back into the wall and cursed as pain lanced up her wrist into the bone.

"Shame, Eiters. A woman should know better," a voice commented from the shadows of the room. "Weren't you trained better throughout your upbringing? We are meant to be elegant. Respected. You look a mess."

"You!" Eiters' eyes narrowed as she hissed with recognition when DeMauve revealed herself. "This is all your fault!"

"It appears to me the majority of the recent chaos falls on your shoulders, not mine. I am merely here to correct our course of action and get Romalle back to where it is meant to be." She tsked. "The time for your poison is at an end."

"You are nothing, Emmest DeMauve. Naught but a hollow caricature of what a lady should be. Were it not for your late husband no one would know your name," Eiters spat. Fresh hatred flared in her eyes, her nostrils puffing out, cheeks reddening. "Why aren't you dead yet?"

DeMauve feigned a polite smile and took a step forward. "Not out of your lack of trying. Would it please you to know I have defeated everything you've thrown at me? All of your precious thugs and mercenaries are dead. Your allies, already thin from repeated betrayals, have been whittled down to nothing. As has your life. Are there any last words befitting a woman of your stature? Or shall I just kill you now and be done with it?"

Outraged, Eiters launched from the wall, fingers extended as she lunged for DeMauve's throat …

… The last thing she saw was DeMauve's boots marching past as warm liquid slid down her throat.

"Looks like you didn't have to use your magic after all," Hargan said without looking up from the body.

Sister Alessandra kept her opinions private, choosing to ruminate of the actions leading them to this point. The Order trained them from youth to ignore their emotions and focus on the moment. That being said, she wouldn't have minded having a chance to remind the now departed board member of the true power in the universe. "Is she the last of the conspirators?"

Hargan scratched the salt and pepper stubble on his cheek. "Near as I can tell. We've either arrested or rooted out her nest of villains. The priestess confirmed Eiters was responsible for having the Cardinal murdered. The only loose end needing verification is Kasop. He's the weakest of the three and not my pick to run the planet but he's the only one left."

"Singularity does not preclude him from corruption. We may yet find this Kasop complicit in many crimes," she cautioned.

Unwilling to accept the implications, Hargan gestured for the waiting investigators to collect Eiters' body. Enough blood had been shed this night. He prayed the storm of violence was at last at an end and the restoration of order could begin. The planet needed healing, perhaps a total restructuring to advance and become more than a target of opportunity. Hargan wondered if what Romalle needed was similar to what Eiters, Damal, and the others attempted. Was there any difference between method and implementation?

"No, but it doesn't imply it either." He got to his feet. "We should be going. The Inquisitors will have arrived at the board chambers by now."

They arrived at the official board meeting chambers where public policy, community hearings, and open trials were held. A small crowd was gathered outside, held back by the ring of armed guards brandishing rifles.

Hargan spied signs with angry proclamations in the back. A swarm of protestors shouting for the overhaul of current politics and the resignation of the board. Others showed their support, threatening to turn the gathering into a riot. Additional squads of Prekhauten Guards had been called in and he felt the opportunity to keep the moment peaceful slipping away. "This can get ugly."

Alessandra fixed the crowd with a baleful gaze.

The security perimeter broke for them to pass through. Hargan gave a reassuring pat to the young woman on his left and hurried inside. They found the trio of Inquisitors waiting in the corridor. Each looked tired beyond their years, as if the previous day's events drained from them a lifetime.

"You look like shit," Hargan told Gando as he extended his hand.

"I'm just trying to be like you," Gando returned with a grin as they clasped forearms. "How are you feeling?"

"I'm still alive. Can't say the same for Eiters. Whoever got to her first slit her throat from ear to ear." He snorted and shook his head. "She never stood a chance."

"Without her confession…"

"Doesn't matter. From what you told me the priestess we have the entire conspiracy exposed. Eiters would have been nice, but she's earned her fate." Hargan paused, sighing. "I need a vacation."

The meeting room doors opened and Emmest DeMauve appeared before Gando could retort. Dressed in a simple yet elegant gown of alabaster, she complimented the darker uniforms of the Inquisition. Hargan marveled at how not a single hair appeared out of place on her head.

Her gaze whispered predatory attention as they swept over the bedraggled group. Such alliances hadn't been forged in generations, prompting Emmest to reimagine how she might approach the future to achieve her desired results. The debacle with the Conclave and subsequent coup left a power vacuum on Romalle that, if not filled with strong, determined individuals, might result in the planet plunging into chaos and the darkness of war.

“Ah, good, you are all here,” she said after quieting the demons chattering from the corners of her mind. “You are expected.”

“Not all of us are here,” Tolde spoke. “Ragan has not yet returned.”

She regarded him with pursed lips. Their alliance was born of convenience. Both knew it but neither felt inclined to tip their hand. “He is safe. As are Riles and her young friend. The threat is no longer. They will join us after this.”

“I’d feel better if they were here now.”

“Inquisitor, you have my word on this. They are safe and well. They are also not required for what comes next.” At his glare, she added, “Now then, shall we go in? This delay serves little purpose.”

Tolde relented and gestured inside with an open palm. There would time enough to settle matters before his team departed for Wexanos. “As you say.”

“I insist,” Emmest stepped aside to give them access.

Gando took the lead, choosing to avoid confrontation. The others followed him, eager to be about their last task, leaving only Hargan who paused midstride and whispered so that only Emmest heard, “We could have used her alive. She had much to tell us still.”

He passed, leaving Emmest reevaluating her opinion of the man who should have died.

Tolde found the pomp of the moment ill timed. He had not come in official capacity. Indeed, their uniforms were borrowed out of the Inquisition supply section stationed on the far side of Erdef City. A small Prekhauten contingent stood off to the side, apart from the others, speaking amongst themselves. Since the onset of the war Tolde found the Guard more inclined to avoid the inevitable conversations of loyalty bound to arise when in mixed company. Not that he blamed them. He abandoned his Inquisition uniform as much as possible for that same reason.

Feeling out of place among the local officials and confused clergy, he scanned the room for quiet threats. Though he and the others stood weaponless, as per official requests, they radiated authority. He stiffened as conversation quieted upon their arrival.

"Relax, Tolde. There is little more to this than a change of authority. We've been through this before," Luma murmured from his right.

With Gando on his left, Tolde knew he overreacted. He let Luma's encouraging words soften his stance, enough to give him pause and reconsider his next steps. "True, there is little comparable to our usual audience with Tannus."

"Or the Blood Witches," she added.

Gando's head cocked as he listened, but he was wise enough to remain silent.

Tolde offered a quiet laugh. "We live interesting lives."

"I wish we didn't. I enjoyed my job before all this."

"What do you suppose comes next?" he mused to keep the conversation going.

Confused, she asked, "After this? We return to Tannus and try to end the war."

"No, I mean after the war. What happens to the warriors, embittered and shorn of their morality once the last shot is fired, and one side capitulates in surrender? Are we destined to remain victims of our vices? The sole proprietors of a vanquished legacy bereft of compassion or understanding."

Luma leaned closer. "Did you hit your head?"

"What? No. I'm serious, Luma. Once the ashes settle and society sees fit to rebuild there will no longer be a place for people like us. We are, and should be, anathema to any lasting peace. I have been dead once, but the memories of that past life continue haunting my every step. I feel, empty."

"You just need a break, Tolde. We all do. Tannus has driven us without pause for too long. He risks burning us all out before the final campaign."

"Will there be one? I wonder."

They fell silent as the crack of a gavel thundered through the room. Those gathered faced the podium at the center. A small, frail man stalked his way through the crowd and took his place behind the comforting crutch the podium offered. He coughed once, clearing his throat to garner additional attention.

"Ladies and gentlemen, Romalle has endured great challenge these past weeks. We have not only lost the guidance of Cardinal

Breed, but the wisdom and leadership of two-thirds of the City Board. I stand before you in humble resignation toward what must come next if we are to heal and advance as one society. Today I present, for the first time in official capacity, the Lady Emmest DeMauve. Her nomination for Board Member has been approved and seconded by myself, and Board Member Kasop."

Hushed murmurs rippled through the gathering. Old fears and debased rumors refusing to dissolve under the weight of fact and her recent actions to cull the growing insurrection haunting them all.

Unbent, Emmest flowed to the center of the room. Her head high and back straight, she presented the image of confidence, leaving Tolde questioning if this had been all her gambit from the start. Lesser crimes had been committed for greater gain. Spying then the defiance in her eyes, he knew Romalle was either in good hands or destined for a time of great turmoil.

"I stand before you with one mission, to renew this planet's grandeur. Not for the upper class or the rich, those weak-spined adherents to the old ways. No, I will usher forth a new age of prosperity and equality for us all. Whether you are the beneficiaries of birth or from the most distant of the tribes, there is room in our future for all. This I swear unto you all. The past is dead. Romalle belongs to the future."

A scattering of applause began, growing into a sweeping tide of enthusiasm once they realized she was done speaking.

Romalle had indeed been placed in good hands. A burden shifted, leaving Tolde deflated.

Luma caught him before his knees gave out. Slipping her arm around his waist, she guided him through the thin crowds, back into the hall. Few met their eyes in passing, for the Inquisition retained a measure of inherent mistrust among the population.

Soon sunlight filtered down on their faces, the casual reminder that there yet remained good in the universe.

"Are you all right?" she asked after helping him to a bench.

Placing his hands on his knees, his head bowed, Tolde took slow, deep breaths. Mind swirling, unable to contract to the point of singular thought, he saw the past and future collide. Only where the future should have been one of brightness, he found nothing. The icy fingers of fate recoiled, drawing away from the shell he inherited upon awakening on Rastarok.

"Tolde?"

"It's nothing. Just passing fancy." He waved off her concern. "Perhaps the knowledge my brother can at last know peace has settled in. And I did not expect to see Lady DeMauve instated in a leadership position so soon."

"It might be for the best. The previous board was corrupt, and the lone survivor might have ideations for filling their shoes as he expands his own bid for power." Luma eyed him with suspicion. "There are checks in place to ensure DeMauve doesn't overcome her station."

"Hargan and Gando."

"They are good men. Perhaps the best this planet has. I feel comfortable leaving knowing they are close to the board. With a little hard work and more than their share of good fortune they should keep Romalle from entering the war on the Inquisitor General's side."

The clipped ending to her sentence belayed her internal struggle with accepting the man she once looked to as the highest authority, filled with righteous intent and the wisdom wrought from a lifetime of experience to benefit humanity, was the architect of so much hatred. Once considered a rising promise among the Inquisition, Luma Kai approached her job with a zealot's fervor. The guilty were punished without mercy under the auspice of justice. Heresy was stamped out on a dozen worlds thanks to her efforts. She'd been paired with Tolde, she now understood, to keep him in line, to cause no waves as Nye made his opening moves. Lies. She knew that now, but it was far too late to return. Her lot was cast, fate decided by whims far beyond her ability to recognize. Left with little choice, Luma Kai accepted her future.

"Luma, I..."

"There is no need," she said. "We must all play our parts, though I fear for you. These are unnatural times, Tolde Breed, and the vagaries of fate swirl about you like a storm. I did not know this until now. Until seeing your reactions to your brother and when aboard

Behemoth. You are a lodestone, and I will stand by your side to the very end."

"Whatever that end might be?"

"Aye."

They were joined by the others shortly. Varying looks of contentment and consternation met them. Tolde met Gando's gaze with determination. "Inquisitor Gando, it has been an honor working beside you," he chose his words with care, gingerly feeling for a reaction. "I hope Romalle will remain free under your watch."

Gando folded his arms, his stance off putting. "I admit I have held grave concerns over my obligations to this uniform and to my planet. Your coming, unwelcome as it was, sparked the cataclysm of change, forcing me to at last take a stance."

Reaching up, he removed the rose label marking his allegiance to the Inquisition and handed it to Tolde. "Romalle shall remain neutral so long as I have a hand in matters. You have shown me much these past few weeks. For that, I can never repay you. You have my gratitude, and, if you will, friendship."

"That is one gift I gladly accept."

"One big happy family, eh?" Hargan joked.

"Born from necessity," Tolde confirmed. "I see you are healing well."

Hargan grunted. "Not sure I'd be out of bed if not for your witch. How soon before you depart back to wherever you came from?"

"Not soon enough," Sister Alessandra said. "Our focus is required elsewhere."

"There is one last matter needing my attention," Tolde replied. "I would like to give my brother a proper funeral. As a member of the Conclave he deserves that much at least."

"But not as your brother?"

"We were never close. He chose a pious life, expecting me to follow in his footsteps. Destiny had other designs on me. The Inquisition beckoned at the right moment, and I jumped, determined to be better than him in every regard. I wonder now what our parents would think. The better of us is dead while I linger on as the universe flames out."

"You serve your purpose, Tolde Breed," Alessandra injected. "There is little point in questioning how or why. These matters are beyond our control. All that matters is you continue pushing toward your destiny, whatever that may be."

"Your words offer comfort where none are to be found, Sister."

She drifted closer, until Tolde felt the subtle charge of her power wafting off her gossamer robes. "Tomorrow is never guaranteed. You know this. Come, let us see your brother and give him the gifts he needs in the afterlife. His journey may have ended, but we yet have far to travel before the final rest."

"Oh, cryptic. How dramatic!" Emmest DeMauve said from behind, announcing her arrival. She waited until they turned to face her before continuing. "For your parts in helping keep Romalle from plunging over the cliff I shall provide you with a proper escort, both to your brother's final resting place and to your shuttle."

Tolde bit back a retort and instead said, "Thank you, Lady DeMauve. I welcome it."

Her gaze pulled away, caught by the sudden movement coming down the hall. "Ah, there, you see? Young Ragan is safe and sound, though perhaps a little rattled from his experiences."

They watched the trio of youths, followed by the haggard figure of Lady Demauve's chamberlain, head for them. Each suffered from bruises and cuts. Clothes were torn. Hair singed. Riles Tenaru and her companion bore hollow stares and were littered with cuts and bruises, as if they'd witnessed more than sanity's decorum allowed. Tolde inwardly wept for them, for innocence was ever the first causality in war.

"Ragan, I trust you had an interesting night," Luma spoke first, eyeing his torn clothes and battered stance.

The youth blushed. "More than I cared for. Is there any world where we can just be happy?"

"You already know that answer," Luma replied. "It's good to see you in one piece."

"You nearly didn't. Tolde, your brother made some determined enemies," Ragan said. "Are we done yet?"

"Almost. Walk with me, Ragan," Tolde instructed. "There is a matter I wish to discuss."

Eager to at last be done with their ordeal, the rest of the group followed Emmest DeMauve and Mayn, and a small escort of ceremonial guard, to the waiting transportation.

Once alone, Tolde asked Ragan, "Have you resolved your conflict?"

"Conflict?"

"About whether you intend on staying here, with the girl. No one would blame you if you stayed. Our path is not one for the faint of heart."

Blushing, Ragan hung his head, locks of hair sweeping across his face. He hadn't thought anyone noticed. "She's better without me, I think. I don't belong here."

"Is this what you truly desire?" Tolde asked. Regardless of the reasons Ragan accompanied him in the first place, he knew having Ragan by his side meant something to the future. The boy possessed special qualities. Ones he didn't know he had. For that alone, Tolde found a spring of untapped hope.

Ragan stared at the backs of Riles and Nemineon. A heavy sigh served as his answer.

"Just say it," Riles demanded when the pressure became too much, threatening to drive her mad with unanswered questions.

Their relationship suffered from strain. Conflicting ideals and desired outcomes kept them apart. Riles learned, during those dark hours when life threatened to rip itself apart, how much those closest to her meant. She searched deep within her emotions and dreams for answers. The distraction Ragan provided awakened feelings she'd repressed for too long. Now if only Nemineon …

Nemineon, glum after the brief visit to Cardinal Breed's grave, refused to meet her gaze. The immediacy of departing for the tribes had faded, replaced by confusion as he succumbed to his mental demons. The thought of living without her crippled him, yet how could he see otherwise? Her infatuation with the offworlder sent a clear message.

"Nemineon, I mean it. Say what's on your mind." The unspoken or else made him shudder. "It's about Ragan, isn't it?"

He nodded, not trusting his voice or thoughts.

She grabbed his arm and pulled him closer to look him in the eyes. "Nemineon, it was nothing but passing fancy. Call it an attraction to something new. Something I've never seen."

"You admit to being attracted to him."

She blinked, taken off guard. "Yes. Ragan is a handsome man. What woman wouldn't be interested?" At his eye roll, she huffed. "You're missing the point. I might have thought he offered the pieces I am missing, but I was wrong. It turns out I've had everything in front of me this whole time."

"What do you mean?"

She punched his shoulder. "You, you lunk. I've had you in my life for as long as I can remember. You've stood beside me through my highest and lowest periods, even foolishly putting yourself in danger for me. Turns out I didn't need to look to the stars for love after all. I've had in you this whole time."

"I … I don't…"

Riles wrapped her hand behind his head and drew him in. "Shut up and kiss me."

Sister Alessandra stood in quiet reflection. The teachings of the Order clashed with the feeling spreading through her, for she had not been prepared for the human aspect of her assignment. She found herself changing. The knowledge of Tolde's inevitable passing fueled the immediacy of her task, yet for all her attempts at remaining distant, she found herself beginning to understand the raw passion with which her companions invested their actions in. Endeavors often deemed beneath the Order. It was, she decided, the human condition her sisters lacked.

She knew Tolde must die for the powers of darkness to be defeated. How and when remained obscured to her sight. The more she studied the reborn man the more she longed for the opportunity to set aside her robes, forgo her powers, and be a mortal woman. If only for a day. The brush with mortality threatened to undo all she'd striven for these long years and, instead of feeling natural fear, Alessandra thrilled at the prospect of the unprecedented.

She watched as the Inquisitors went about preflight checks and ensuring the shuttle had enough food and water for their return journey to Wexanos. There was diligence in their movements, rehearsed from countless times before. Ragan, much to bemusement, had fallen in somewhere along the way, doing his part for the crew like a seasoned deckhand. Change, she deduced, came for them all.

An arriving aircar drew her attention. Defensive magic coiled within, the automatic byproduct of intense training and superstition infused by a lifetime of impossibilities. Alessandra relaxed upon seeing Hargan and Gando emerge. Two veterans drawn together by fate and the desire to see their world remain free from the scourge devouring the rest of the universe. She drifted to them, intent on one final conversation.

"Investigator, I had not thought to see you again. We are prepared to depart Romalle."

"We just came to ensure nothing was amiss," Hargan replied. "There's been enough mischief for a lifetime already. Besides, I don't want to be the guy responsible for letting both Breed brothers die under his watch."

"You are, exceptionally human, Hargan."

"Not like I have a choice. I'll never profess to understanding your kind, but I have come to appreciate you, Alessandra. If the rest of your order shares your same qualities, the universe might be in good hands after all."

Folding her arms within her sleeves, Alessandra fought the urge to shed a tear. Her desire to embrace the grizzled man, to show him qualities she hadn't known she possessed until now filled her with renewed belief in the righteousness of her actions. Satisfied, the Blood Witch offered him a deep bow. "Investigator Hargan, it has been a pleasure working beside you. You have shown me much about myself and for that I will be in your debt. Thank you."

"All done back there?" Tolde asked when she boarded.

The shuttle ramp closed. Main engines fired. The shuttle vibrated as power built.

Gazing out the viewport, Alessandra took in the sights of Romalle one final time. "Yes. There is much I must report to the Grand Mistress."

"That's not going to happen. We've been ordered back to Wexanos. It seems Tannus has decided to launch his campaign to defeat his brother and end this war."

The shuttle shook as it lifted off and began the slow burn through the atmosphere on its course to the destiny awaiting.

THIRTY

3215 A.G. (After gods), exiting orbit, planet Vau Prime.

Space over the capital planet burned with the fires of war. Starships drifted, lifeless and hazardous as they were pulled down into the gravity well, their once majestic signatures reduced to broken dreams and inert metal. Frozen corpses drifted through the detritus, slamming off blast ruined hulls. Spread across the system a string of battles progressed with little reason. Those sworn to defend Vau Prime remained hard pressed to stall the enemy advance as the ever-hungry maw of war devoured all.

Watching it all, trapped aboard their shuttle, Aliz and Julian and the others clutched their harnesses locking them into their seats as Gedrick Silk deftly piloted them through a hail of energy weapons, flights of dogfighting starships, and exploding capital ships. Rubble danced from their hull, rocking the shuttle through its harried flight. Survivors of a once proud defense, they were the last to escape the ravages of Mobus Kale and Alain Nye. The sole owners of what once was and would never be. Distraught and pushed to their breaking, each struggled with accepting their status even as the promise of survival dimmed with each passing moment.

"I've located it," Gedrick announced.

Relief remained elusive however, for the distance between them and Admiral Khe-Zhehan's flagship proved almost insurmountable barring a miracle.

Grinding his teeth, Julian asked, "Does this tub have any weapons? We'll never make it defenseless like this." A trio of starfighters burst apart less than a hundred meters in front of them, emphasizing his point.

"The only weapons we have aren't strong enough to penetrate starships," Gedrick replied. "The only thing keeping us alive is my piloting skills which, I am sad to announce, are lacking in the midst of all this … Just stay strapped in. We will reach *Revengence*. I hope."

"That's not comforting."

Gedrick flipped a series of switches and said, "Revengence, this is shuttle 217. We are coming in hot. Request immediate support."

"Shuttle 217 standby. Assets are being diverted to you now."

They were rewarded with the sight of six dreadnaughts appearing on the edge of their field of vision. Julian's mouth dropped open as the ultimate weapons of warfare slashed through the battlespace with fury. Their rate of fire dwarfed every other craft in the immediate area. Enemy ships burst apart, gutted and dropping out of the fight under a punishing barrage of missile and laser fire.

For such a response to a random call for help spoke volumes to Julian on who Gedrick Silk truly was. Until this moment he failed to understand. Failed to recognize the value the shapeshifter brought to General Strannan. He wondered if they had lifted off without Silk would Khe-Zhehan's fleet be as motivated to rescue them.

A lane cleared and the shuttle burst forward.

Julian stared at the monstrous dreadnaughts flanking their passage as Gedrick sped the shuttle closer to *Revengence* and safety.

Captain Ryboth clutched the arms of his command chair. Clouds of thick smoke filled the *Forge of War's* bridge. A handful of his best lay dead at their stations. Those who survived struggled keeping their ship alive. Half his weapon systems were exhausted or inoperable. Engines were at minimal power. Warning alarms rang as life support systems throughout the ship failed. How many of his crew remained alive was unknown. Yet for all that, *Forge of War* continued meting out punishment on every ship drifting too close as she executed her final orders. With grim satisfaction he watched as the shuttle he'd been ordered to protect glided clear of the engagement area.

Dabbing the blood running from his right temple, Ryboth's face twisted in a mask of fury. "Weapons, target that cruiser! I want it out of my battlespace."

Remaining weapons unleashed a crippling salvo on the smaller ship threatening it. He was rewarded by watching the enemy bridge burst apart. He imagined the muted cries of shock and horror cutoff by the detonation and collapse of the hull. Like a missile, the enemy ship plunged down toward Vau Prime, trailing fumes and burning from within. In its wake stormed a squadron of hunter killers—space lit up with the power of a dying sun.

The *Forge of War* exploded.

"Admiral, we are down to thirty-five percent combat strength. Incoming enemy fleets now outnumber us five to one. We must retreat now while we are still able."

Pushing the loose hair away from her face, Khe-Zhehan saw her gambit flaming into ruin. Soldiers and civilians had been safely evacuated thanks to her bold maneuvers, yet more were slaughtered enroute to her fleet. She knew her hands were tied. Every action possible had been enacted and it still wasn't enough. Pride urged her to fight on. To throw her remaining resources into a hopeless battle despite the knowledge doing so would result in pointless deaths while delivering the system to her foes.

She was loathe to give the only command remaining. What choice did she have? "So be it. Give the orders. I want all surviving ships to disengage and head to the nearest jump points. Rendezvous at previous coordinates as soon as able. Pick up escape pods or smaller craft capable of fitting in their bays if able. This fight is finished."

"Aye, ma'am," her First Officer replied before relaying the orders to the fleet.

Tactical displays showed dozens of ships pulling away from the enemy fleets, desperate to escape before they were surrounded and ground to scrap metal.

Khe-Zhehan knew the sting of defeat. She'd felt it once before at the ambush of Hawker's Gate when Alain Nye's faction openly proclaimed war on the universe. This day she felt the bitter sting again, sinking into the fabric of her soul. She'd thrown everything into this gambit and, while those on Mannus Prime would hail her as victorious, Khe-Zhehan knew her actions were anything but vainglorious failures on a grand scale.

"Admiral! Urgent communique on channel one," Comms shouted.

Her head snapped about. "Put it through."

"…engence, this is shuttle 217…"

Silk! Davith Strannan's ace player's voice was coming through the coms. Hope surged within her. All was not lost. She knew ragtag units of Guards had been pulled from the low continent, among them several of the junior officers comprising the remaining command staff, but none were as high in the unofficial chain of command as Gedrick Silk.

"Captain, we do not depart this battlespace without that shuttle secured in our hold. Am I clear?"

"Yes, Admiral. Redirecting nearest assets to provide cover now. Estimated time to target seven minutes."

Seven long minutes of interminable worry over what could go wrong. To potentially sacrifice the largest, most powerful ship in the fleet for the sake of one man meant the difference between inspiration and arrogance. Khe-Zhehan watched with bated breath as the tiny shuttle beat impossible odds, burning closer to *Revengence* with each passing second. Her ruined nails drummed on the torn fabric of her chair.

"New signature has arrived. No class registration. Admiral, I've never seen anything like it," her helmsman shouted.

The bridge hushed into silence as the first images of *Behemoth* became available. Her stomach lurched. Nothing in her fleet was capable of defeating such monstrosity. Perhaps not in all the universe. Cold dread washed through her on a primal level. For how else could one reconcile the creation of such monstrosity with the advancement of a species?

"Admiral?" her First Officer asked with shaky voice.

Khe-Zhehan fumbled, struggling to put voice to her rising terror. "Captain, order all ships to disengage immediately. We cannot contend with this. Not today."

Additional orders were relayed through the fleet. She relaxed a bit upon seeing several signatures disappear from the tactical displays as her people fled. The shuttle, an insignificant insect on the backs of giants, raced closer, rocking as it passed through *Revengence's* gravity fields. Once the docking bays were secured, Khe-Zhehan ordered her ship's full retreat.

The battle for Vau Prime ended.

They lost.

Julian felt his strength fade as *Revengence* powered away from the engagement area to the unforgiving coldness of deep space.

Vau Prime shrank. All he knew and loved was gone, wiped away with the snap of fingers. Their failure marked much more than losing a battle. They'd lost their home. He shied away from his ragged band of survivors, content with letting his emotions devour him.

"This is not over, Julian," Aliz said, ever at his side.

For all of her projected confidence, he failed to see it. What could decent men do against such abject hate? Aloud he asked, "What was it all for?"

Aliz looked at him, instead of a strong soldier armed with convictions, she witnessed the first breaking that, if left unchecked, would devour his sanity. "Captain Julian, everything we did was for the greater good of the universe. Wars ebb and flow. This is but a minor setback. That a fleet of loyalists broke through enemy blockades to reach us, rescuing tens of thousands, speaks volumes to the determination of our allies. Evil may have earned a quiet reprieve for the moment, but against the full force of righteousness there can be but one final outcome. We must hold true to our convictions. Victory will come. I am certain."

He remained silent, watching until the last glimpse of Vau Prime disappeared.

The Great Library, planet Wexanos.

Matthias inhaled the pure air of this majestic planet, reminded of better times void of strife and conflict. Each time he returned to Wexanos, and the sanctuary Tannus dedicated his life to building, he found a greater part of himself eager to be done with the war. Here he found peace, tranquility, and a cleansing of thought and soul. This was a place he might at last call home, though a feeling tugged at the edges of his mind, mocking his simplicity as it reminded him the worst was yet to come.

"The others are returning, Master Matthias."

Golden sunlight caressing his face, Matthias was loath to turn away. Duty, however, was ever a cruel mistress. With a smile etched upon his face, he turned to meet the stern visage of the Chief Librarian. "Lead on, Fistel, though I daresay you can skip the master bit. I'm just a man, same as you."

Whether Fistel agreed or not remained unknown, for he swept up his yellow robes and scurried back to Tannus' private suite.

They found Fies and Annalilly waiting to whom Fistel bowed and handed Matthias off.

"How many others do you suppose are coming?" Fies asked his old mentor once Fistel left.

Matthias shrugged. "Who knows. We've been pulled our separate ways for too long. It's a wonder so many of us have survived."

"Plenty of us haven't," Annalilly growled. Her frustrations worn on her sleeve, she chafed under the fresh set of lieutenant bars Fies saw fit to commend her with. "I'm starting to think this war is never going to end."

"All wars end. It just depends on how."

They turned, surprised to see the reborn face of Tolde Breed entering. Beside him came Luma Kai, the Blood Witch, and the street thief from Rastarok.

Annalilly's scowl deepened as she considered their mismatched collection of rogues, castoffs, and heroes. None of it made sense. Only the cold steel of an ion rifle in her hands offered comfort, the ease of knowing what fate awaited her at the end of this journey.

Matthias reached out to clasp Tolde's hand. "It's been too long."

"Agreed," the Inquisitor replied. "How's your wound?"

"Healed up well enough and waiting for the next one."

Despite serving alongside them for as long as he could remember, Tolde never understood a Guard's humor. They had the uncanny ability of turning off their emotions when matters grew dire. He envied them that, though far too many veterans failed to learn how to turn those emotions back on once they were past their traumas.

Elisa and Ah'muf arrived a moment later. The knife at her belt, born in another dimension and alien to all they understood, sat heavily on her hip. "Looks like Tannus has gotten everyone back together." Elisa noted the absence of Paradise Tear, and her heart sank. "Well, almost."

Fistel returned, beckoning. "Lord Tannus shall receive you now. Please, follow me."

"We know the way, Librarian," Annalilly said with a frown.

Ignoring her barb, Fistel escorted them to a grand meeting chamber where Captain August was already sitting. A long, aged table of darkest natural redwood ran the length of the room. Plates and glasses of wine and ale were set out, the promise of a feast tickling their bellies as the group filed in and took their seats. Candles by the hundreds lit the room, providing the proper ambiance Tannus sought to convey as his chosen band was welcomed back into his embrace. One by one they sat, drank, and awaited both food and their host. They did not wait long.

Tannus entered and the conversation faded. He took his place at the head of the table in the only chair large enough to accommodate his massive frame. He held out a hand and gestured for them to remain seated, taking a moment to look at his champions, assembled from across the universe. There were fresh wounds among them, to mind and spirit. There was also renewed determination. He wept for them when none saw. It was the least he might offer for all their sacrifices.

"It does my heart good to see you all again. Though we are of different times, I have come to look upon you all as family, such that it may be. Would we have the luxury of meeting in simpler times."

"Tannus, where is Paradise? Is she still a prisoner of your brother?" Elisa asked.

Tolde flinched and Tannus felt for the man, this singular being who had already sacrificed so much for their cause and who had much left to give, wanting to tell him it wasn't his fault. That Paradise knew what she was about. He feared doing so in front of the others, knowing his words, while meant to comfort, would convey naught but weakness. "She is on her way here as we speak."

"Is that wise? There is every possibility of her being tracked," Tolde replied.

Tannus' eyes brightened. "True, but she has been given instructions. If all goes according to plan, my cousin will have changed ships repeatedly and stopped at several planets to throw my brother off her trail. Are there any other concerns I should be aware of?"

At their silence, he continued. "Tonight, we shall feast. Trade stories and rejoice in the fractured bonds of fellowship one last time. Paradise shall join us, along with the woman responsible for setting her free."

"What woman?" Tolde asked, stiffening.

"I believe she said her name was Presha Von."

August dropped her fork, face paling. "You cannot trust her! That woman is a snake."

"I appreciate your zeal, Captain, but I assure you, Presha Von has had her teeth pulled. She lacks the venom she once held."

Elisa shook her head, knowing each of them had encountered the fallen noble from Crimeat and found her villainous in every regard. "How can you say that? She has been at the heart of our troubles from the start. Even before our paths crossed in the wilds of Lethendweil."

A twinkle in his eye, Tannus replied, "The promise of redemption softens the hardest heart. This is a time to forgive old trespasses and forge new alliances. We stand at a critical moment. Each of you has executed my assignments with the brilliance I have come to expect. Yes, there have been setbacks, defeats, along the path, but you continue finding ways to succeed. You are to be commended for your actions."

Tolde opened his mouth to protest but thought better of it.

"My friends, we are now upon the crossroads of tomorrow. My brother has arrived on Vau Prime and, no doubt, is working to wrest control away from your Inquisitor General to reshape the world in his image. His armies gather, as do ours. We at last have the strength to meet him on the field of battle."

"Has the Grand Mistress been informed of your designs?" Sister Alessandra asked.

"She has. We are lockstep in this matter."

Matthias drained the last of his wine and settled back in his chair, fixing the giant with a stern gaze. "Where is this final battle to be had? With what forces?"

"It is my intent to lure my brother and his armies to Occanum and finish what was begun so long ago," Tannus replied. "You have already worked with our new army. They are training on Mannus Prime as we speak."

"They're not ready for the scale of combat you intone."

"They will be prepared. Once our affairs are settled here, we shall depart on my ship for Mannus. This is a moment I have long waited. I have failed too often throughout the centuries, ever allowing my brother to foment rebellion and chaos among your kind while I sit impotent upon this empty throne. No more. Today I stride forth, armed with the tools necessary to end his curse forever."

Elisa remained defiant as his gaze settled on her. Grimfurvor rested at her hip.

"But come, no more of this. We will leave for the final battle soon enough. Tonight, we feast and remember better times."

Despite the rising dread among them, they did as he instructed. Food and wine flowed until each had reached their fill. Tales of heroic deeds were met with gusto as each detailed their trials since their last gathering. Old friendships were renewed and, in doing so, the bonds of true brotherhood forged.

Tannus waited until the end to pull Elisa to the side. He had one final task for her before they departed. One he did not envy anyone.

"I can't get off this shuttle."

Paradise Tear studied her companion with concern. She'd learned much from the woman since their harried flight away from *Behemoth*. For all her vice and inherent weakness, Presha Von remained a strong woman. A figure capable of doing good for the universe despite her past crimes.

"No harm shall befall you here. I assure you," Paradise encouraged. "This is my cousin's refuge. His word commands."

"Do you not recall what I have done? I was instrumental in allowing Amongeratix to begin his war. I killed an entire planet, and for what? Base greed and the notion of becoming more than I ever was meant to be. My father lies dead at my feet for my sins, and I have abandoned all who once allied with me. I am a curse no one should be forced to bear, Paradise."

"You are guilty of all, yes, but we are not limited to the actions of our past. Without the promise of a better future what point is there to life?" she countered. "Presha Von, I give you my word, you shall not be accosted or mistreated while you are under my protection."

Eyes filling with tears, Presha relented. “Are you certain?”

“Yes.”

The power in that singular declaration imbued Presha with the faintest trickle of strength. She rose. “Very well. I trust you.”

“Good. Tannus is a fair man, but he was never one for exercising patience. Best we not keep him waiting.”

Eger City, planet Mannus Prime.

Tempest swept into the parlor, her face bright with joy. She clutched the datapad in her small fist, waving it above her head as she proclaimed, “The votes are in! You have been elected First Counselor. Congratulations, Governess.”

Adris Moscasco stared at her assistant as the news sunk in. She hadn’t doubted the outcome, though enough voices of dissent threatened to undo all at the last moment. The backing of the military helped convince enough dignitaries to vote in her favor, cementing the future. Behind Tempest came Cardinal Virom, General Torgast, and Admiral Falchi.

“Congratulations are in order.” Virom smiled and clasped his hands in victory.

“Thank you, Cardinal, but we haven’t accomplished anything yet,” she replied. “There is much yet to be done before any of us can consider this a success.”

“One step at a time.”

Word had reached them of the fate of Khe-Zhehan’s mission. The stalwart admiral suffered far too many casualties and losses for her liking, even with the influx of new arrivals choking Mannus airspace. Falchi and the military command had been forced to send new ships to nearby moons to accommodate them. Over a thousand ships now stood ready to take the fight to the enemy. It wasn’t just the fleet. The ground army now brimmed with almost a million soldiers. Combined with her intimate knowledge of the inner workings of the Conclave’s administration, Moscasco delivered new rifles, tanks, weapons, and more. The only factor missing was the one she both anticipated and dreaded in equal measure.

“Running a single planet proved challenging enough, but half the universe? During war? I wonder how many steps I have to take before it settles into a rhythm.”

"The war won't last forever, First Counselor," Torgast reassured.

"Perhaps, but the cost before it ends will be more than any of us can bear," she replied. "I wonder how much of our humanity has already been sacrificed in the name of outdated ideals rejected by a sizeable portion of the population? How much do we have left to give?"

"That is a question I'll ponder after the last round is fired. The last body laid to rest. Now we struggle to preserve our humanity. I have no qualms with such, for it has ever been the burden of those in uniform. We sacrifice so others don't have to," Falchi said in a measured voice.

Her stance softened as Moscasco let her thoughts drift back to Fies and his brave squad. Operating behind enemy lines, cutoff from supplies, weapons, and support, they plunged into the situation blind. She tried, and failed, to image having the constitution to do the same before realizing that was precisely what she'd done by arriving on Mannus Prime at the foundations of a counter government destined to shift the balance of power away from the crumbling detritus of the Conclave.

She smiled. "You would make a good politician, Admiral. Good words. Strong words. No wonder your soldiers follow you without question."

"If only others shared my same convictions this war might be ended by now."

Torgast grunted. "Or not. We tend to diminish the loyalty of those opposing us yet aren't they adhering to their own ideals and principles? It is easy to reduce our enemies, regardless of who they are, but once we strip away the uniforms and get to the heart we are all the same."

"I know, Torgast. That's what frightens me," Falchi admitted.

Absorbing their exchange, Moscasco found the debate compelling. Her political and religious opponents were no different, presenting a crisis of conscience at the most inopportune time. If they had any hope of forging a new destiny, she knew the greatest sacrifice had yet to occur.

Those seeking to elevate their status through the confusion and misfortunes plaguing a hundred worlds slithered through the cracks to foment new factions capable of shifting the balance of power. Moscasco had already seen more than her share of backstabbing, empty promises, and subtle threats during her short time on Mannus. Wolves ever lingered on the periphery, hungry for their opportunity to strike.

She found little connection to the old ways in this fledgling form of government. Religious adherence weakened, dragging the once cemented influence of the Inquisition with it. Left floundering, the remnants of the Prekhauten Guard were all standing between total chaos and the thin grasp of civility. The cyclical symbiosis of the three branches showed a weakness in human society now exposed and plundered in the name of the greater good. For those citizens liberated from tyranny a return to Conclave rule was rendered impossible. She prayed for the strength to ensure an orderly transition to a better form of government, one with the best interests of its subjects in mind, while fearing the worst.

"I find myself wondering what I've gotten myself into," Moscasco announced. "There are too many avenues that can go wrong. We are dancing on the edge and I fear what might happen."

"What of our special guest?" Virom asked, shifting the subject.

Moscasco scratched an idle finger down the side of her face. "He is a poison in our midst, but without proof of wrongdoing our hands are tied."

Falchi squinted as sunlight shifted into the chamber, temporarily blinding him. "You still mean to go through with the plan?"

She nodded. "What choice have I? Tinnus Har is a problem we must resolve before any positive steps can be taken to establish a new order for the universe. One I fear will cause immediate problems for the foreseeable future."

"Why not just take him to space and vent him?" Torgast brought up an old point.

"We have been through this, General," Moscasco chided. "Do we sacrifice our morality and risk becoming like our enemies or adhere to the principles of righteousness and retain a measure of dignity? I will not lead this body into the quagmire the Inquisitor General inspired." She shook her head. "Do not worry about Tinnus Har. Venomous as he may be, he lacks the teeth to cause harm. His greed and desire for power will expose him soon enough. Until then we maintain the course."

"I will have a platoon of Guards detailed to surveillance. Should he make a wrong move we will know," Torgast offered.

"I still don't like it, but like you said, what choice do we have?" Falchi replied.

"This matter must be settled before we proceed," Virom said.

"Good. It appears we are about to enter the next phase of this grand experiment, gentlemen. I wonder when historians look back on our deeds if they will judge us poorly?" Moscasco asked.

Neither had an answer.

Krenz, planet Vau Prime.

Behemoth loomed over the heart of Krenz, a cloud of gloom and corruption seething ancient hatreds. The monstrous ship blocked out the sun, cascading the central portion of the city in quasi-darkness. This darkness was a promise of an unavoidable future and the hunger of one being's desire to rule all. Thousands risked arrest or worse to slip outside, daring the breaking of curfew, to catch a glimpse of a ship that should not exist. Nothing in the Prekhauten Navy came close to matching the size of *Behemoth*. Detritus and space debris had begun to rain down, causing many to retreat to safety.

The awe continued as the belly of the beast opened and a score of dropships plunged downward. Drone fighters screamed in escort, weaving through the towering buildings in a display of force. Amidst the spectacle came a massive shuttle, black as midnight and oozing malevolence. Fumes curled around the fuselage as the pounding thrum of engines reverberated deep within the bodies of those assembled.

Alain Nye watched, breath caught in his throat, as the shuttle neared. This moment he longed for, both dreading and anticipating in equal measure, promised to mark the beginning of the next and final stage of his war against the universe. After years of plotting, manipulating both the Conclave and

Inquisition, and eliminating rivals and potential hindrances, he saw his goal at last within reach.

Rank upon rank of Inquisitors in dress uniform lined the square. Behind them stood battalions of Prekhauten Guards. They stood at rigid attention, weapons in salute as Amongeratix's shuttle touched Vau Prime for the first time. A scattering of red robed Cardinals clustered closer, each grappling with private demons and the possibility of advancing their positions through currying favor with the new lord of Vau Prime.

The shuttle's back ramp lowered, agonizingly slow to reveal the treasure within.

Nye found Mobus Kale clenching his mechanical fist over and over on his right. "Relax, General. This is but the next step in our evolution."

Stewing over the perceived defeat on the low continent, Kale managed to say, "My army is enough to crush our enemies. He should not be here. Not like this."

"Lord Amongeratix is the precise tool we require to see a fast end to the war," Nye explained. "You of all people should appreciate that. Now that he is here, you will be free to take the fight to our enemies across the stars."

"Words," Kale grumbled and fell silent as he got his first glimpse of the most infamous being in the universe.

Amongeratix stormed down the ramp, entering the heart of civilization for the first time. His coming sparked the changing of the tide for thanks to the greed and petty desires of the Inquisitor General, command of the universe was in his grasp. Towering over those assembled, he marched toward the command group, frowning at their meager displays.

For his part, Alain Nye cleared his throat, attempted and failed to calm his rising nerves, and stepped forward to meet the man responsible for igniting his passion to devour the universe. Horns sounded, ringing the unprecedented moment in. With the engines cut, silence settled over the gathering like an obscene blanket. Unease rippled through him, despite having already pledged himself to Amongeratix's cause. Decades of plans were at last coming to fruition and he suddenly felt very unprepared.

Amongeratix ground to a halt before humanity's current leadership. His perpetual sneer sent tremors through them. Raw power emanated off him, spreading through the crowds with miasmic fury. More than one Cardinal buckled. Guards stood taller. Inquisitors questioned their loyalty.

"My lord, welcome at last to Vau Prime," Nye began. "It is an honor to have you here. I have prepared the city for yo—"

Amongeratix moved in a blur. His hand reached out to catch Nye by the throat, crushing.

Kale jerked, eyes widening as Nye's face darkened, turning purple while he eyes bulged.

Struggling, Nye failed to pry Amongeratix's grip loose. He beat upon the steel cut forearms, kicked weakly. Darkness crept in, swallowing his vision until naught remained but an audible pop.

Alain Nye's neck toppled sideways, the last of his air leaving his lungs.

Amongeratix tossed the body aside and reared to his full height, daring any to challenge his ascendency. "Well?"

At the lack of response, Sister Evangeline swept forward, streams of red magic shooting skyward to explode overhead. "All hail, Lord Amongeratix!"

Mobus Kale stared down at the Inquisitor General's corpse, musing over the ease with which he was slain. He weighed his options. Perhaps enough combat power was assembled to slow Amongeratix, possibly even hurt him, though he doubted any human weapons capable of slaying one of the gods … He dropped to one knee and shouted, "Hail!"

As one, his Guards followed.

Amongeratix looked across the sea of humanity. He spread his arms, palms open, and tipped his head back to laugh.

His. It was all his.

EPILOGUE

3215 A.G. (After Gods), Abbey of the Order of Blood Witches, Acumensiis Comet.

Alone, Ruma Zzein watched the stars speed by. Her thoughts matched the cold darkness of space, spiraling through a host of futures and endings. Prophecies ran like unchecked tides, competing for their completion. She watched entire timelines evaporate; others arise. Generations unraveling through the prisms of her mind's eye. With heavy heart, she closed her eyes and shut out the noise threatening to drown her.

Forever Night, the ancient prophecy of the ending of the universe barreled toward them and, save but for a stalwart handful, humanity remained ignorant. She'd done all within her power to hedge her bets, building a coalition capable of defeating Amongeratix for the last time and restore order from the chaos of corruption consuming Vau Prime. All the pieces were in place. The final phase of the war ready to begin. Whether humanity stood prepared for the tide to crash upon the shore remained to be seen.

END

The Forgotten Gods Tales concludes with A GOOD DAY FOR CROWS

If you liked the Forgotten Gods Tales check out:

Stranded on a gunpowder age planet, a makeshift squad of space marines must do whatever it takes to survive long enough to be rescued.

They were supposed to be going home. Then the enemy found them. Sergeant Hohn managed to piece together ten fellow soldiers from their doomed ship. Not the best or brightest, the squad crashes on a forgotten world where gods and monsters rule.

Nestled in the heart of the great desert is the Heart Eternal. The city of Ghendis Ghadanaban has been the jewel of all peoples for millennia. But with its reputation comes danger. The city awakens to the murder of their god-king. A desperate crew is assembled to escort the fallen god's essence to the fabled mountain of Rhorrmere where he may be reborn and return to save the city from certain doom.

Time stands against all, for the powers of darkness have gathered. Can Hohn and his people survive long enough for their rescue? Will the god-king be reborn before its too late?

Find out in the first chapter of the Heart Eternal Saga, a sci-fi adventure combining the best of military science fiction and fantasy. Fans of Star Wars, Dune, David Weber, and Steven Erikson will love this one.

THE LAZARUS MEN

A LAZARUS MEN AGENDA

CHRISTIAN WARREN FREED

Welcome to the world of the Lazarus Men.

A thrilling sci-fi noir adventure combining the best mystery of the Maltese Falcon with the adventure of Total Recall and suspense of James Bond.

It is the 23rd century. Humankind has spread across the galaxy. The Earth Alliance rules weakly and is desperate for power. Hidden in the shadows are the Lazarus Men: a secret organization ruled with an iron fist by the enigmatic Mr. Shine. His agents are the worst humanity has to offer and they are everywhere.

Gerald LaPlant's life changes forever the day he accidentally witnesses a murder and discovers an alien artifact in his pocket. Forced to flee, he is chased across the stars by desperate men who want what he has and are willing to stop at nothing to get it. Along the way Gerald meets a host of villains and heroes, each with hidden agendas. If Gerald has any hope of surviving, he must rely on his wits and avoiding the one thing that could get him killed more than the rest: trust.

For he has the key to the galaxy's greatest treasure. Half want him dead. Half need him alive.

It's a race against time to see which wins.

THE CHILDREN OF NEVER

A War Priests of Andrak Saga

Christian Warren Freed

The war priests of Andrak have protected the world from the encroaching darkness for generations. Stewards of the Purifying Flame, the priests stand upon their castle walls each year for 100 days. Along with the best fighters, soldiers, and adventurers from across the lands, they repulse the Omegri invasions.

But their strength wanes and evil spreads.

Lizette awakens to a nightmare, for her daughter has been stolen during the night. When she goes to the Baron to petition aid, she learns that similar incidents are occurring across the duchy. Her daughter was just the beginning. Baron Einos of Fent is left with no choice but to summon the war priests.

Brother Quinlan is a haunted man. Last survivor of Castle Bendris, he now serves Andrak. Despite his flaws, the Lord General recognizes Quinlan as one of the best he has. Sending him to Fent is his best chance for finding the missing children and restoring order. Quinlan begins a quest that will tax his strength and threaten the foundations of his soul.

The Grey Wanderer stalks the lands, and where he goes, bad things follow. The dead rise and the Omegri launch a plan to stop time and overrun the world. The duchy of Fent is just the beginning.

The follow up to the L Ron Hubbard Writers of the Future award winning short: The Purifying Flame, the Children of Never is an all new novel set in a world of raw imagination.

BIO

Christian W. Freed was born in Buffalo, N.Y. more years ago than he would like to remember. After spending more than 20 years in the active-duty US Army he has turned his talents to writing. Since retiring, he has gone on to publish more than 20 science fiction and fantasy novels as well as his combat memoirs from his time in Iraq and Afghanistan. His first book, Hammers in the Wind, has been the #1 free book on Kindle 4 times and he holds a fancy certificate from the L Ron Hubbard Writers of the Future Contest.

Passionate about history, he combines his knowledge of the past with modern military tactics to create an engaging, quasi-realistic world for the readers. He graduated from Campbell University with a degree in history and a Masters of Arts degree in Digital Communications from the University of North Carolina at Chapel Hill. He currently lives outside of Raleigh, N.C. and devotes his time to writing, his family, and their two Bernese Mountain Dogs. If you drive by you might just find him on the porch with a cigar in one hand and a pen in the other.

www.ingramcontent.com/pod-product-compliance
Lightning Source LLC
Chambersburg PA
CBHW020355310726
48979CB00015B/2601/J

* 9 7 8 1 9 5 7 3 2 6 3 6 8 *